RAMONA BLUE

Also by Julie Murphy
Dumplin'
Side Effects May Vary

RAMONA BLUE

JULIE MURPHY

Balzer + Bray
An Imprint of HarperCollins*Publishers*

Balzer + Bray is an imprint of HarperCollins Publishers.

Ramona Blue
Copyright © 2017 by Julie Murphy
www.epicreads.com

Library of Congress Control Number: 2016950250
ISBN 978-0-06-241835-7

Typography by Aurora Parlagreco
17 18 19 20 21   PC/LSCH   10 9 8 7 6 5 4 3 2 1

First Edition

For my own holy trinity: Bethany, Natalie, and Tess—
this book would not exist and I would not have survived
writing it without you three

Well, I may be just a fool
But I know you're just as cool
And cool kids, they belong together
—*Yeah Yeah Yeahs, "Poor Song"*

AUGUST

ONE

This is a memory I want to keep forever: Grace standing at the stove of her parents' rental cottage in one of her dad's oversize T-shirts as she makes us a can of SpaghettiOs. Her mom already cleaned out the fridge and cabinets, throwing away anything with an expiration date.

"Almost ready," says Grace as she stirs the pasta around with a wooden spoon.

"I should probably leave soon," I tell her. I hate prolonged good-byes. They're as bad as tearing a Band-Aid off one arm hair at a time.

"Don't pretend like you have somewhere to be right now. Besides, you should eat before you go." Grace is like her mom in that way. Every time we've left the house over the last month, her mom has tried to unload some kind of food on us, like we were taking a long journey and would need rations. "Don't make me eat these SpaghettiOs by myself."

"Okay," I say. "The thought of that is actually pretty pitiful."

She takes the pot from the stove and drops an oven mitt on the kitchen table before setting it down in front of me. Scooting in close, she winds her legs between mine and hands me a wooden spoon. We're both white, but my legs are permanently tanned from life on the coast (though a little hairy, because shaving is the actual worst), while Grace's normally ivory skin is splotchy and irritated from all the overexposure to the sun. And then there are her feet.

I grin.

"What?" she asks, tilting her head. Her raven waves brush against her shoulders. She's obsessed with straightening her hair, but even the mention of humidity makes her ends curl. "Don't look at my feet." She kicks me in the shin. "You're looking at my feet."

I swallow a spoonful of pasta. "I like your feet." They're flat and wide and much too big for her body. And for some reason I find this totally adorable. "They're like hobbit feet."

"My feet are not hairy," she insists.

I almost come back at her with some dumb quip, but the clock behind her melts into focus, and I remember.

Grace is leaving me. I knew she would leave me from the first moment we met on the beach as I handed out happy-hour flyers for Boucher's. She lay spread out on a beach chair in a black swimsuit with the sides cut out and a towel over her feet. I remember wishing I knew her well enough to know why she was hiding her feet.

This is our last meal together. In less than an hour, her mom, dad, and brother will all wake up and pack whatever else remains from their summer in Eulogy into the back of their station wagon, and they'll head home to their normal lives, leaving a hole in mine.

"I'm gonna be miserable without you," says Grace between bites. We're both too realistic to make promises we can't keep. Or maybe I'm too scared to ask her to promise me anything. She tugs at my ponytail. "And your stupid blue hair."

"Not as much as I'm going to miss your hobbit feet."

She smiles and slurps the pasta off her spoon.

Grace loves this shit. It's the junk food she craves after growing up in a house where her mother fed her home-made meals like stuffed salmon and sautéed asparagus. SpaghettiOs or any other kind of prepackaged food marketed toward kids—that was the kind of stuff Hattie and I grew up on. With Dad working and Mom gone, we ate anything that could be microwaved.

I think I'm in love with Grace. But sometimes it's hard to tell if I'm in love with her or her life. Her adorable little brother, Max, who is still sweet, because he has no idea how good-looking he will be someday, and her mom and dad, always checking in and leaving out leftovers for us. And this house. It's only a vacation rental, but it still feels so permanent.

Grace tucks her black bob behind her ears. "Did you ever look up any of those schools I put on that list for you?"

I shrug. This is our sticking point—the one thing we can't get past. Grace says the only thing keeping me here after high school is me. And I can concede that, in a way, she is right, but Grace is the kind of girl who never has to look at a price tag or tell the clerk at the grocery store to put a few items back.

We sit here curled into each other as the clock on the microwave melts into morning.

"I should go," I finally say.

She nudges her forehead against mine.

If we lived in a world where only my rules applied, I would kiss her. Hard. And leave.

Instead we walk hand in hand to the porch, where my bike sits, and then we make our way down the gravel driveway to the mailbox still shrouded in darkness.

I rest my bike against the post.

"Text me when you get a chance," I tell her.

"Olive juice," she says. *I love you*, her lips read. Her mother used to mouth it to her when she was dropping Grace off at school so she didn't embarrass her in front of all her friends.

"I love you, too," I whisper back with my lips already pressed into hers. She tastes like SpaghettiOs and the cigar we stole from her dad's portable humidor. Her lips are chapped and her hair dirty with salt water from our midnight swim just a few short hours ago. I feel her dissolving into a memory already.

TWO

I leave Grace's house and ride past the trailer park, where my dad and Hattie are asleep. My days always start like this—before everyone else's, in the moments when the only thing lighting Eulogy is the casino on the waterfront. Today, I'm a little earlier than usual, so I take the time to ride straight down to the water. Carefully, I lay my bike down on the sidewalk and kick my flip-flops off before walking down the rickety wooden steps to the beach.

My Mississippi beach is very rarely love at first sight, but an endearing, prodding kind of affection. Despite her lack of natural beauty, there are many like me who love this place more than she deserves. It's the kind of place people on a budget choose for vacation. Thanks to the line of sandbars trimming the shore and our proximity to the Mississippi River, our water is brown and murky. Nothing like Florida's blue-green waves. But a family like Grace's can get a lot of vacation for their buck if they're willing to overlook the imperfections.

Sand kicks up around my ankles until I reach the water's edge. I press my toes deep into the sand as the cool water rinses over them briefly before pulling back. The moon hangs in the sky, chasing the horizon, as the sun whispers along the waterfront.

Water has always been my siren song. Any kind of water—oceans, lakes, pools. There's something about being weightless that makes me think anything is possible. My whole body exhales in a way that it can't when I'm standing on land.

The brightening horizon reminds me that I have somewhere to be. Shaking sand from my feet, I run back up to the sidewalk and slide my flip-flops back on.

A continuous stream of tears rushes down my cheeks as I direct my handlebars around the corner and down the hill to where Charlie waits in his truck. I hate crying. I mean, most everyone does. But some people, like Hattie, feel better after a good cry. When Hattie cries, it's like watching a snake shed its skin. Tears somehow let her regenerate, whereas crying only makes me angry I cared so much to begin with.

"You're late," Charlie calls. He wears his usual uniform of coffee-stained undershirt and twenty-year-old jeans. With his shaggy thinning hair, he looks like an old white guy who either traps little kids in his van or grows weed in his backyard. Thankfully it's the latter.

I squeeze the brake on my handlebars and push the tears back into my eyes with my other fist. "Overslept."

I don't have a history of being late, so Charlie shrugs it off. Maybe a five a.m. start time is earlier than most teenagers could commit to, but I treasure all my little jobs. My paper route, busing tables at Boucher's, and working whatever under-the-table cash gigs I can find. I guess, growing up, most kids wonder what they will do for a living. But for me, there was never any worry over what the job would be, just how soon I could start.

Charlie loads the basket on the front of my bike with papers for the second half of my route, while I fill my messenger bag. Charlie is the kind of man who will always look like a boy, and the uneven whiskers lining his upper lip don't do anything to help the matter.

"Going for the mustache look?" I ask.

He strokes what little facial hair he has. "Wanted a change. You like?"

"Change is good," I tell him as I swing my leg over my bike and wave good-bye.

I weave up and down the streets on my route, letting my memory guide me until almost every house has a paper waiting in its yard. The routine of it keeps the thought of Grace at bay, at least for a little while.

At the corner of John Street and Mayfield, I pass Eulogy Baptist, a bright-white building with perfectly manicured lawns and flower boxes under each windowsill. Dim light from the back office bleeds into the street, and I wonder if Reverend Don is getting in or leaving.

I turn the corner down Clayton Avenue, pedaling as I lean back in my seat and gently tap the brake while I career to the bottom of the hill. It's in this moment when I always feel like I'm flying. But then the bottom of the hill brings me back to reality.

Standing in front of my last house, which was recently added to my route, is a black woman in an unzipped terry-cloth cover-up with a bright-yellow bathing suit underneath, watering her flower bed. I always love morning people. They feel solid and reliable. Not like my mom, who sleeps past noon if no one wakes her up. Grace wasn't a morning person either. It was a small detail that always bothered me for some reason.

Grace. Grace, who I might not ever see again. I feel the tears begin to threaten.

"Mornin'," says the woman as the paper hits her lawn.

"Mornin'," I call back, pedaling past.

"Hey!" she shouts. Something hits me square in the shoulders, knocking the wind out of me.

"What the hell?" I mutter to myself as I loop back around to find I've been hit with one of my own papers.

As I reach down to pick it up, the woman's voice says, "Ramona Blue! Get back here!"

Her voice. I know it. And that nickname. Ramona Blue is what my dad called me when I was a little girl, because he could never get me out of the water. It's a name not many people know.

The woman walks to the edge of her yard and as she does, I see past the ten years of wrinkles. Dropping one foot to the ground, I stop my bike from rolling any farther as memories trickle back. "Agnes?"

"You get your heinie over here and gimme a hug!"

I drop my bike right there on the curb and fall into an embrace.

Agnes used to come down every summer from Baton Rouge with her husband and their grandson, Freddie, who they were raising. She was as much a part of my childhood memories as my own grandmother until the summer I turned nine and they just stopped coming. That was the first time I'd really understood that even if it feels like summer lasts forever here in Eulogy, Mississippi, it doesn't.

I can't think of many moments when I've looked in the mirror and taken an inventory of all the ways my body has changed. But here and now with Agnes squeezing me tight, her forehead barely brushing my chest, I feel like I'm some giant cradling a baby doll.

Agnes pulls away but holds my shoulders tight, examining me. She tugs on my long, wavy ponytail, and says, "Of course I'm not surprised. Your daddy always did let you get away with everything short of murder."

My cheeks burn, and even though the ache in my chest is as heavy as an anchor, I smile. She's referring to my hair. Ramona Blue with the blue hair.

Depending on when you catch me, my hair could be any shade ranging from royal blue to turquoise. I was thirteen the first time I dyed it with Kool-Aid mix and a little bit of water. To no one's surprise, I was sent home from school, but my dad came to the rescue despite how much he hated what I'd done to the blond locks I'd inherited from my mother. He fought with my principal until the whole ordeal had eaten up more time than it was worth. And my hair's been blue ever since, thanks to Hattie and her amateur understanding of cosmetology.

Today, though, I am in need of a dye job. The sun, salt water, and plain old time have left my hair a powdery shade of turquoise.

"You sprung up like a weed." She shakes her head, and I wonder what it is she's seeing in her memory of me. She points to my empty messenger bag. "Last house on your route then?"

I nod. "Yes, ma'am."

"You come hungry tomorrow morning." She pats my belly. "We're gonna have us a big ol' breakfast."

"I can do that," I say. "Okay."

Agnes's lips spread into a wide, knowing grin. "Freddie is going to die."

Freddie. All my memories of him are sun bleached and loud, but I try not to let myself be fooled by the past. Growing up can change you.

Hugging Agnes may have made me feel tall, but nothing makes me feel as large as home sweet trailer. Like always, I duck my head to pass through the front door of our trailer and walk down the narrow hallway leading to Hattie's bedroom and mine. They used to be one room, but with help from our uncle Dean, Dad blew out part of our hallway-facing wall, put a door in, and then added a plywood wall to divide our space on Hattie's twelfth birthday. After that, he bought her a wardrobe at the Salvation Army and all of a sudden our shared bedroom had become two.

I began to outgrow this place somewhere around the summer before ninth grade. I'd always been tall, but that last growth spurt tipped me over from tall to too tall. The ceilings of our trailer stretch as high as seven feet, which means my six-foot-three frame requires that I duck through doorways and contort my body to fit beneath the showerhead in the bathroom.

Inside my room, I rest my bike against my dresser, and just as I'm about to flip on the lights, I notice a lump lying in my bed.

"Scoot over," I whisper, tiptoeing across the floor.

Hattie, my older sister by two years, obliges, but barely. "Tyler is a furnace," she mumbles.

I slide into bed behind her. Always the little sister, but forever the big spoon.

We used to fit so perfectly into this twin bed, because like Dad always said: the Leroux sisters were in the business of growing north to south, and never east to west. But that's no longer the case. Hattie's belly is growing every day. I knew she was pregnant almost as soon as she did. So did Dad. We don't waste time with secrets in our house.

"Make him go home," I tell her.

"Your feet are so cold," she says as she presses her calves against my toes. "Tommy wants to know if you can come into work early."

"Grace left."

She turns to face me, her belly pressed to mine. It's not big. Not yet. In fact, to anyone else it's not even noticeable.

But I know every bit of her so well that I can feel the difference there in her abdomen. Or maybe I just think I can. Wrapping an arm around me, she pulls me close to her and whispers, "I'm so sorry, Ramona."

My lips tremble.

"Hey, now," she says. "I know you can't see this far ahead right now, but there will be other girls."

I shake my head, tears staining the pillow we share. "It's not like she died or something," I say. "And we're going to keep talking. Or at least she said she wanted to."

"Grace was great, okay? I'm not saying she wasn't." Hattie isn't Grace's biggest fan—she never has trusted outsiders—but I appreciate her pretending. "But you're gonna get out of here after graduation and meet tons of people and maybe figure out there are lots of great girls."

Maybe a few months ago, Hattie would've been right. Up until recently, the two of us had plans to get out of Eulogy together after graduation. Not big college plans. But small plans to wait tables or maybe even work retail and create a new life all our own in a place like New Orleans or maybe even Texas. A place without the tiny little trailer we've called home for too long now.

But then Hattie went and got pregnant, and even though neither of us have said so out loud, I know those plans have changed.

Tyler is here for now, but I can't imagine he's anything more than temporary. My plans were never extraordinary to begin with, and now that Hattie has my niece or my nephew incubating inside of her, they're even less important. Hattie's my sister. She's my sister forever.

"And I can't kick Tyler out, by the way," she adds.

I shake my head. "Yeah, you can. Just tell him to go home."

"This is sort of his home now."

I prop myself up on my elbow and open my mouth, waiting for the words to pour out. But I'm too shocked. And horrified.

She loops a loose piece of hair behind my ear, trying to act like this is no big deal. "Dad said he could move in," she whispers.

There are so many things I want to tell her in this moment. Our house is too small. Tyler is temporary. There will be even less room when the baby comes. I don't need another body in this house to tell me that it's too small and we've all outgrown this place. And yet I feel like I'm the only one of us who sees it. I'm the only one wondering where we go from here.

But with my legs dangling off the foot of my twin bed, I can't help but feel that the problem is me. And that, somehow, I have outstayed my welcome here.

Internally, I am screaming, but on the exterior the only sign of life is the tears beading at the corners of my eyes. "Is it dumb that I'm really upset about the Olympics being over, too?"

She laughs. "It depends. Is that why you're crying?"

"No . . . maybe a little bit."

Hattie wraps her arms around me and pulls me to her like Mrs. Pearlman's old Maine coon does with her kittens when they're done feeding. It's a momentary reminder that I'm the actual little sister. "I bet you could've been good enough for the Olympics if you'd ever even tried."

"Shut up," I tell her, fully aware that she's being so nice to me because I'm a mess of a human being right now. I've always loved the Olympics. Most kids were obsessed with SpongeBob or Transformers or One Direction, but something about Team USA and the swim team in particular always felt magical to me. It was like every person on that team was the star of their own Cinderella story and the whole country was rooting for them to get the prince—or princess. In fact, sitting on my dresser is an old Michael Phelps Wheaties box with Missy Franklin's face taped over his; she rules and he drools, obviously.

"You're the best swimmer I know, Ramona Blue."

I roll my eyes, but my lids feel heavier than they did a moment ago. "You don't even know any swimmers. You're the best amateur hairdresser I know and I don't see you styling the rich and famous anytime soon."

"I'm just saying." She yawns. "You don't have a tiny human in your body. You can still be whatever the hell you want."

I roll my eyes again and yawn back at her. I wish it were that simple. "I need to get some rest before our shift."

I close my eyes, waiting for her breathing to deepen. I will always love Hattie for her undying faith in me, but even from a very young age, I knew what it meant to be the kind of person with the time and resources to be something like a swimmer or a gymnast or a freaking speed walker. (Yes, race walking is totally an Olympic sport.) My sport—the special skill I've developed my whole life—is surviving, and that doesn't leave much room for following Cinderella dreams.

THREE

The oysters at Boucher's are the best reason to come to Eulogy. The decor at Boucher's is the second-best reason.

No, really. That's what all the travel website reviews say. Year-round this place is dressed for Christmas, with multicolor lights dripping from the ceiling and artificial trees in every corner. Unless it's pouring or unbearably hot, the patio doors roll up like the kind you see at an automotive shop. It's the type of place where you can find locals and tourists coexisting, because it's too hard to keep the food a secret.

I plop down at the bar in front of Saul, who slings his towel over his shoulder and chuckles. "Too young to serve, sweetheart."

I groan, letting my head fall down on the counter. Hattie and I slept for a few hours before coming in a little early for second shift.

"Hey, Saul," says Hattie as she walks in behind me. We both work here, mostly because it's in walking distance of our house and our forms of transportation are limited to our feet, my bike, and whatever rides we're offered from Saul or whoever Hattie is currently dating.

"What's her problem?" he asks my sister.

She hops up onto the stool beside me. "Grace and her family went home this morning."

"And Tyler is moving in," I whisper. And then mouth *Help me.*

He rolls his eyes—not at me, but at my sister—and shakes a hand through my hair. "I told you not to fall in love, didn't I? We're young. We're supposed to have sex with stupid people and get high at public parks or something."

I pick my head up enough to see him, and his ridiculous handlebar mustache is enough to make me smile again. Unlike Charlie's, Saul's mustache is thick and perfectly groomed. That, combined with his cutoff jorts and his Budweiser tank top, give him this dirty seventies porn-star look that would make anyone else seem like a pedophile, but not Saul. His look may age him a bit, but Saul is nineteen and fresh out of high school. The 'stache, shorts, and tank are all a part of what he calls his *beach trash aesthetic.* Saul treats his clothing like it's a costume—or armor even.

"Staff meeting in five!" Tommy, our manager and the owner's son, calls from the kitchen.

Saul pours me a glass of Diet Coke and, after checking to make sure no one is around, adds a splash of whiskey. He slides it over before leaning on the bar. "Sugar," he says, "you broke my rules."

Saul is the king of summer hookups. His rules are

law. And I broke all two of them. 1. Don't date a tourist. 2. Hook up in the closet all you want; just don't date in it.

Grace and I talked about her being in the closet a lot, but I never tried very hard to push her. It felt like a violation. And honestly I hated to imagine the contrast between her life here with me and the one she lived back home. I knew there was one boy her mom always mentioned, but Grace never brought him up except to say that she planned on breaking up with him at the end of the summer. It might seem silly now, but when I was with her, it was easy to believe that he didn't really exist. Or at least that he wasn't a threat.

"I bet your friends will be excited to see you," I said a few days before she left as we sat on a bench in front of the beach, with Highway 90 at our backs. Grace was one of those rare people in high school who was friends with all the different groups—nothing like me. She actually looked forward to the first day of school.

Her cheek was hot with summer as she leaned her head against my shoulder. I hoped that there was some piece of her that belonged only to me. A laugh or a smile or a look, even—some little corner of Grace that only I knew. Sometimes when I couldn't fall asleep, I wondered if she loved me as much as I loved her or if maybe she just loved the person she was realizing she'd been all along.

"Your parents love you," I said, and kissed the curve of her shoulder all the way to the base of her neck before our lips collided. "You should tell them."

She crossed her arms over her stomach. "I want to. And

I will. After I graduate, maybe. But I want to have all these good memories first, because . . . what if things change? Even in the smallest way?"

"Don't you wish you could be this person all the time?" I asked, trying not to sound pushy. "We could go on dates. Maybe even visit each other for dumb shit like homecoming and prom."

Knowing Grace's parents, they'd probably join some kind of club for parents of gay kids and march in pride parades. And if there weren't any pride parades to be found in Picayune, Mississippi, they'd probably start one.

Grace turned to me. "You don't get it." She sounded exasperated already. "You don't know my life back home. I can't just show up on the first day of school and tell people I'm gay or bi. It's not like a new haircut you get over the summer." She pressed her lips into a thin line, and I could see she was searching for words. "I get that we're supposed to hate high school, but I *like* my life. A lot. I like my friends and my classes, and I don't want to ruin that when I only have a year left."

I took a deep breath and concentrated on the tone of my voice. "I understand. I do. But doesn't it somehow cheapen the whole experience if you're hiding behind the person everyone else thinks you are?"

She looked away then, pulling her knees into her chest and picking at her chipped toenail polish. "There's a lot I could lose," she said. "A lot of people I could hurt."

Or a single person, I thought bitterly. Andrew. Her boyfriend. In moments like these I couldn't help but wonder if the temporary thing in Grace's life was me.

I shake my head, trying to somehow get rid of all thoughts of Grace. Saul was right about dating in the closet, and this is what I get for thinking I might somehow be different.

Ruth, Saul's younger sister, reaches over my shoulder and grabs my drink, knocking the rest of it back in a single gulp. She cringes immediately, coughing into the crook of her elbow. "Um, okay, that was way more than Coke."

"Ruthie! That was mine," I tell her. "I earned that little bit of whiskey."

She sits down next to me, tying her short waitress apron around her waist. "And how do you figure that?" she asks drily.

Ruth has the kind of outlook I would kill for. To her, this life here in Eulogy is temporary. A pit stop on her way to bigger and better things. And she's totally unapologetic about it.

"I paid for it in heartbreak," I tell her, eyeing the now empty glass.

"Hey, she might be back next summer," offers Ruth. "But probably not."

Saul swats her arm with a rag. The list of things Saul and Ruth have in common is short. Other than being related, they're both gay, Cajun, and white. That's pretty much it.

She shrugs. "I'm trying to be realistic."

And if Ruthie is anything, she is realistic.

I almost smile. Ruth and I have known each other almost our whole lives, because Eulogy is only so big, but we didn't become friends until the end of freshman year. Saul had just come out to his whole family, and no one took it well. And then Ruth came out, too. I remember not seeing either of them at school for a while, like they had something the rest of us could catch. Now I know they'd been sent to Florida for a few weeks to live with their grandparents and attend their church's revival.

It wasn't like that for me. When I came out, it was a blip. The type of news that flashes across the bottom ticker of the screen and then is quickly forgotten. Hattie shrugged and said, "Well, that explains a lot." And Dad thought about it for a few minutes before adding, "Nothing wrong with that." My mom, though . . . she still thinks this is a phase.

Eulogy isn't all potholes and trailer parks. There are chunks of this place that passersby drive through that make them think they could live here and that small-town life can be quaint and cozy. That's the part of town Saul and Ruth come from, and since Eulogy only has one high school, there are no walls to keep kids like them from kids like me, even though their mom would love that.

When Saul and Ruth came back from Florida, Hattie sought them out. Growing up, I was never invited to birthday parties or ever really had a best friend outside of Hattie or Freddie. Most of my social interactions were a result of being the little-sister tagalong. So it only makes sense that Ruth and Saul are in my life because Hattie put them there. Sometimes when she seems so thoughtless, I remind myself of all the times she made room for me in her life.

Tommy sticks his head out the kitchen door. He's a short black guy with a bald, shiny scalp. "Let's move it!"

Saul winks at me, and I follow him to the back.

After our staff meeting, we all go about our business for the afternoon and on into the evening. Ruthie and Hattie tend to their sections while Saul works the bar, which isn't entirely legal since he's not twenty-one, but that's never seemed to be an issue.

I bus table after table all night. I love the routine, and only wish it kept my mind busier. Between every trip to the kitchen I find myself checking my phone, hoping for a message from Grace. This morning, after falling asleep alongside Hattie, I woke to a picture from her. It was a dark, blurry photo of the *NOW LEAVING EULOGY! DON'T BE A STRANGER!* sign. I texted her back a frowning emoji but was unsure what else to say. I didn't want to look too needy, even though I very much felt that way.

She lives only an hour and a half away, but that's one and a half impossible hours for a pair of high school girls without cars.

"Ramona!" calls Tommy from the kitchen. "I need you on to-go pickup!"

I dump my tub of dirty dishes into the soaking sink and hustle to the to-go counter.

A light-skinned black boy with a near ubiquitous amount of freckles and short, curly hair sits perched on a bar stool beneath the takeout sign. I would know those freckles anywhere. "Freddie."

He's so intently focused on his phone that he doesn't even hear me.

"Freddie!" I shove his shoulder a little.

Finally he spins around on his toes, and his deep brown eyes widen with recognition. Without even taking a breath, he pulls me in for a hug. "Ramona Blue!"

My chest tightens a little, and I don't completely know why. This morning with Agnes, I felt like the giant, but now it's the other way around. Freddie, who was always a few inches behind, is still an inch or so shorter than me, but something about him makes me feel cozy. His arms and legs are gangly, but still lined with a thin layer of sinewy muscle. He almost reminds me of one of those plastic dolls with long, stretched-out limbs you can tie into multiple knots. His jawline is rough with stubble and acne scars. His dark-brown eyes are a little sadder than I remember.

"Are you guys here for a few weeks?" I ask.

He shakes his head. "For good."

My heart skips, and I push him a little too hard. "Seriously?"

"Grams retired, so she and Bart bought a place down here like she always wanted."

"Bart?" I ask.

His mouth turns into a frown. "Gramps passed away a few years back. She got married to Bart last February." He shrugs. "Good guy."

"Damn," I hiss. "I'm sorry to hear about your grandpa."

There's so much more I want to say. But there's some invisible barrier there between us created by the years we've spent apart.

He nods. "I think my gram called in an order?"

"Right. Let me track that down." I run around to the other side of the counter and pack his bag full of extra hot sauce, ketchup, and plasticware. "Y'all need plates?"

"Sure. Fewer dishes for me to do after dinner."

"Ramona!" snaps Hattie from the hostess stand. "I need table eight clear!"

I hand over the food and quickly make change for him. "Hey, I saw Agnes earlier today and she invited me over for breakfast, so I'll see you in the morning? Maybe we can catch up more then?"

He grins, and I notice he still has the same sliver of a gap between his two front teeth. "For sure."

We say good-bye, and I watch as he gets into a bright-white Cadillac turned orange by the setting sun.

FOUR

Hattie and I lie sprawled out on the couch. She woke me up in the middle of the night and asked me to come out here and watch TV with her because she had really bad indigestion from the crawfish étouffée we shared over our dinner break. I don't think pregnant people are supposed to eat fish, or maybe that's sushi? But Hattie said it was like wine and that a very little bit was okay.

Hattie's been having more and more trouble sleeping. When the Olympics were on, I didn't so much mind staying up with her, but now our late-night TV options are limited, and I can already tell it's going to be a total headache trying to get my body used to a school year schedule again.

I check the time on my watch—a hand-me-down of my dad's with an olive-green canvas strap and a black face. I have only an hour and a half until I have to be up for my paper route, and my body is already trying to fight off the idea of morning. Being a morning person is a lot more difficult when you don't get any actual sleep.

With Hattie fast asleep and her head in my lap, there's no going to bed now.

I scroll through my contacts until I land on Grace's number. Somehow the thought of texting her in the middle of the night is less daunting. Something about the moon makes us a little braver. Or a bit more foolish. I'm not sure. **Thinking of you,** I type. **Miss you.**

As soon as I've hit send, I immediately regret it. She could think I'm needy or clingy, sending her text messages this late at night.

But moments later, my phone vibrates.

GRACE: This is so much harder than I expected.

My lips spread into a wild grin. She misses me. And then an attachment comes through—a blurry, watery picture of her street in the midst of a downpour taken from what I assume is her bedroom window. The street is almost steaming with humidity.

I hold the phone to my chest and pretend that her view is my view and that instead of my sister's, it's Grace's head in my lap. I imagine different versions of us leading a life I can barely recognize.

"Ramona, Ramona." A rough hand grips my forearm. "Wake up, little *bebette*," says my dad, using old Cajun slang passed down from Grandma Cookie. Bebette, his little monster. "Gonna be late for your route."

I open my eyes to find the television turned off and my father hovering inches above my head. "I'm going back to bed before I gotta get back to the hotel," he says.

Dad looks exhausted, but that's nothing new. In the last few years the lines on his face have transformed from creases to wrinkles, revealing his every worry. Whenever I find myself bitter over how tall I am, I tell myself that it's a gift from my father. A constant reminder that I'm his girl. And my boxy jaw. That one is his fault, too.

He kisses my forehead before shuffling back to bed. "Take a banana with you."

Carefully, I lift Hattie's head and place a pillow beneath it as I get up.

"Don't forget Tyler's birthday party tomorrow," she says, her voice thick with sleep. "You ordered the cake like you said you would, right?"

Oh shit. Hattie wanted a cake from Stella's Bakery, and I completely forgot to call the order in yesterday. Stella requires forty-eight hours' notice and the woman doesn't budge for anything. My best bet is groveling in person after my route.

"It's all taken care of," I lie.

Quickly, I run to my room and pull on a pair of frayed denim shorts and the black combat boots Grace picked out for me at the Salvation Army. When I wore them the next night to show her how much I loved them, I paired them with a short sundress. *Nineties heroin chic*, Grace called it.

The dress didn't end up staying on for very long. I try pushing back the memory, but that doesn't stop the goose bumps on my legs.

I check my phone as I run out the door, wheeling my bike along. There was a time when the streets of our trailer park were paved, but now all that's left are cracked chunks of cement peppered with deep craters. Blame it on weather or horrible drivers or the shitty management company. Either way it's impossible to bike through, and the only way a car manages is by tiptoeing over each hole and crack. Most people have taken to parking on the street.

We had a house when I was a baby, back when my mom was still around. Hattie remembers it better than I do. But when Hurricane Katrina hit, the house flooded beyond repair and we lost everything below the waterline, including my dad's po'boy truck.

We were no different from anyone else, though. Everybody lost something or someone or a little bit of both. The three of us spent a few months surfing couches and holing up in motels, living off FEMA cards, waiting for the insurance money to come in while my mom went to stay with her sister in Arkansas. When she didn't come back, I asked my dad every night when she would come home to us, until eventually I stopped asking.

When the insurance check finally arrived, it wasn't nearly enough to replace all that we had lost, so Dad bought the FEMA trailer we'd called home for a few months by then and took a job as a cook/maintenance guy at Le Manoir, the oldest hotel in Eulogy and one of the few buildings that survived unscathed.

Mom never came home. Maybe it was the trailer. Maybe it was us. Sometimes catastrophes split you in half, and even if all the pieces are there, they might not ever fit back together.

When I was about nine or ten, we traded that trailer for a slightly larger one so that Dad wouldn't have to sleep on the couch forever, but this one is no more structurally sound than the last. The floors creak and in some places are deteriorating altogether. There's mold without a doubt, but it's easy to ignore anything we can't see. The roof sags with water damage, the walls are peeling from moisture, and I'd be lying if I said we haven't had a roach problem more than once. It's time for us all to move on, but none of us has any sense of where. Or how. And still, there's something comforting about this place.

As I coast through my route, I try to think of all the ways I can possibly convince Stella to make this cake. I concoct a handful of sob stories in my head, but Stella's as sympathetic as a gator.

If Grace were here, I'd ask her to make the cake. She may have craved things like SpaghettiOs and Pizza Pockets, but Grace loved to bake. One night we stayed up late making homemade doughnuts and ate every last one before her family woke up in the morning while we watched all the random Olympic games they play overnight, like handball and trampoline.

I wonder what she's doing today and if she does things like make late-night doughnuts even when she's not on vacation. It hits me that I don't know much about her life at home except that she quit soccer last year and has a best friend named Veronica who just moved to Texas.

When I finish my route, I find Freddie sitting in the grass beside a black trash bag full of weeds. He hasn't noticed me and is mid-yawn when a fat raindrop splashes him right on the tip of his nose.

"I didn't take you for the gardening type."

He eyes me over his shoulder. "Christ. It's early. I just had one of those moments where you're so exhausted you can't even tell if you're awake."

"Oh, these are my witching hours," I say proudly. "There's something about early mornings that makes me feel like I've got the whole damn planet to myself."

"Well, you can have it," he says.

The sky cracks with thunder, and the downpour is instantaneous.

"Y'all two get in here!" shouts Agnes from the front porch. She wears rubber sandals like they sell at the dollar store and a white terry-cloth zip-up robe.

Freddie grabs my bike by the crossbar and throws his trash bag full of weeds over his shoulder.

"Y'all can leave those both on the porch," says Agnes as she waves us inside.

It takes my eyes a moment to adjust to the interior light, but when they do, I find that the walls are lined with moving boxes, and the wood floors are so shiny that I take my boots off without having to be asked. I feel a little bit out of place in a nicer house like this, like by just standing inside of it I'm depreciating the value somehow.

Outside, the rain is already rushing down the street and pooling at the base of the hill. It wasn't even supposed to rain today, I don't think. But that's the way the weather is down here. It's almost like the pace of life is so slow that even Mother Nature is trying to rush us along and remind us we got places to be other than under the sun.

An older but sturdy white man with gray hair cropped into a military cut emerges from the hallway and kisses Agnes on the cheek.

She swats him away and says, "And this is my husband, Bart."

Bart waggles his eyebrows up and down. He wears jean shorts with a white undershirt tucked in and brown suspenders. The man is dressed for the sake of necessity and nothing else. I can already tell he's nothing like Freddie's grandpa, a short black man who always dressed for every occasion in a bow tie and matching handkerchief. But I like Bart instantly.

"Ramona," I say, introducing myself. "The newspaper delivery girl."

"And longtime family friend," adds Agnes.

Bart nods once, acknowledging that he's added this bit of information to the card catalog in his head. "Freddie," he says, "wanna throw some eggs on? I don't want nothing fancy. Sunny-side up and a slice of toast."

Freddie kicks his flip-flops off. "You're missing out, Bart. There's a whole world of breakfast food out there."

Agnes sighs, her soft body melting against her new husband. I guess because I've never seen my dad be affectionate like this toward anyone, I can't help but stare.

"I think I'll see if Freddie needs help," I say, and turn to follow him.

"Watch out!" says Bart. "The guy is particular about his kitchen."

I turn the corner to find Freddie tying an apron around his neck. "What can I do?" I ask.

For the first time, he looks nervous. "Um, actually I've got kind of a routine."

"Oh."

I perch on a stool and watch as Freddie spins on his heels, cracks and beats eggs, and crisps toast to perfection. It's like watching a wizard with an expertise in potions create his perfect blend of magic.

Sitting here, though, is a little awkward. I'm not quite sure how to talk to him or what to say now that we're not chasing each other across the beach or Hattie and I aren't forcing him to play pickle restaurant with us. I smile at the memory. We always wanted to play restaurant, but Agnes wouldn't let us cook anything, so instead she gave us a jar of pickles to use as our food. One time Freddie ate so many pickles that he puked them all over the driveway when we were riding our bikes later that afternoon. It was years before I could even get a whiff of pickles without feeling nauseous.

"All right," says Freddie. "Three servings of eggs Benedict and a Bart not-so-special special."

Agnes claps her hands with excitement as she sniffs her way to the kitchen. She fiddles with her tiny radio, which rests on the windowsill, before landing on the oldies station.

I wait for them all to sit, unsure which spot belongs to whom. But it's a round table and it seems that there's no hierarchy here. I slide into the empty chair across from Freddie as Bart digs in and Agnes says a quiet prayer to herself.

I like the way they include me without making a show of it. It has me feeling right at home and reminds me of the days when Agnes would take me and Hattie over to their rental house while my dad was at work instead of us wasting away with my grandmother in her sunroom while she forced us to untangle her collection of yarn. Agnes would make us all egg salad sandwiches with a splash of hot sauce and cut them into triangles. Afterward, the three of us would clean up while she watched her shows.

At Grace's rental house, her mom always made her little brother move so I could have the better seat or would remind Grace to offer me a water or a soda when I came in the door. I was very much a Guest with a capital G. A Guest who might have turned their daughter into a Lesbian with a capital L.

Agnes questions Freddie about high school registration while Bart is distracted with the wobbling kitchen table. He finishes his eggs and toast first, like he's being timed, and I get the feeling that he was in the military. "I need my Phillips-head," he murmurs.

No one presses me to talk, which is good, because this is the best breakfast I've ever had. My idea of a balanced first meal is two Pop-Tarts and a swig of Diet Dr Pepper. I was uncertain about the light-yellow sauce that Freddie poured over the top, but the combination of the eggs, the sauce, the Canadian bacon, and the English muffin is like

Thanksgiving dinner—meant to be mixed together for one specific flavor. "What is this called again?" I ask through a mouthful of food.

"Eggs Benedict," Freddie answers with a grin.

When we're through, Agnes piles up all our plates and eyes mine. "One step away from licking it clean, were ya?"

My neck feels like it's on fire, and I know it's bright red. It's always been where my blush gathers. "Yes, ma'am." I turn to Freddie. "That was so good. Where'd you learn to cook like that?"

He shrugs, and like every other normal person, his blush gathers in his cheeks.

"Certainly not from me," says Agnes. "But we've perfected the art of mornings, haven't we, Freddie? All those early practices and meets."

I wait for one of them to elaborate, but Freddie bites down on his bottom lip and takes the pile of plates from Agnes.

I hate to leave, but the clock only ticks in one direction, and whatever goodwill Stella might have stored away grows shorter with every minute that passes. "I guess I'd better get going home. Thanks, y'all, for the breakfast."

"You are not riding your bike home in that weather," says Agnes.

I glance outside. The rain hasn't let up, even a little bit. Stella's is a lot farther than home, but I don't have a choice. Hattie will give me the silent treatment until the baby comes if I fail to get a birthday cake for Tyler. "I'll be fine."

"Freddie, you take my car and get her home. My water aerobics class doesn't start until ten."

"Yes, ma'am," he says.

Agnes makes me wait on the porch while Freddie throws my bike into the trunk of her Cadillac. Once he's started the car and pulled it down the driveway alongside the walkway, I turn to Agnes. "Thanks again," I tell her.

She gives me a soft kiss on the cheek, and it spreads a bit of warmth through my chest, reminding me of all the ways she was a better mom to me during those summers than my mom ever was.

I dart though the pouring rain to the passenger-side door.

The interior of Agnes's car is beige and spotless with wooden beaded seat covers. I'm careful to keep my feet on the mat as Freddie reverses out of the driveway. The windshield wipers are working overtime to combat the relentless downpour.

"Which way?"

The clock on the dash says nine a.m. The bakery's been open for hours already. I feel like a jerk asking, but this would save me so much time. "Actually, I'm supposed to go by the bakery for Hattie. Would you mind dropping me there instead?"

He shrugs. "Tell me the way."

"You don't mind?"

He shakes his head. "Only thing waiting at home for me are more boxes."

Stella's Bakery is a little lemon drop of a building—a tiny yellow square made of bricks that Stella's grandsons repaint for her every summer. A least, it is when you can see it. Right now, it's a smudge of yellow behind a sheet of gray.

"I can't believe this place is still here," says Freddie as we dash through the rain.

I grip the door handle. "The only thing that really changes here are the people who pass through."

Inside, Stella herself sits on a creaking wooden stool with an old Regency romance novel held up to her nose. Stella may look like every other sweet, old white lady in town, but sweet she is not. The old guys who normally take their coffee and beignets outside are crowded around the little bar that lines the front window. They speak in sighs and grunts and whistles.

The floors are sticky with powdered sugar, and every inhalation is a rush of sweet dough. The glass cases are full of all kinds of pastries, ranging from beignets to plain old bagels. None of them look quite perfect, because Stella is of the mind that food is meant for tasting and not for looking.

"What'll it be?" asks Stella without looking up, her doughy fingers drumming the countertop.

If I don't get this cake, Hattie is going to chain me to a tree, pour honey on me, and leave me there until a bear comes along. Hattie came to me last week and said she bought Tyler a new gaming console and that didn't leave much for cake. I wanted to say no, but I keep telling myself that this is for her. Not him. Even though, actually, it is.

I inch my way toward the counter. I swear this woman can smell fear. "I know it's asking a lot, but I need a cake for tomorrow—"

"No can do." She looks up with a grin, and I am positive that Stella is one of those people who take deep pleasure in saying no. She taps her finger on a piece of paper taped to the counter that reads CUSTOM ORDERS REQUIRE 48 HR NOTICE. "And while we're at it, let me give you a little earful about you throwing my paper right in the path of my sprinkler. By the time I get home every morning, the damn thing is soaked through to the funnies section."

I sigh. "I'm sorry, ma'am. I'll do better in the future, I swear. But if you could—"

She taps her sign once more.

I nudge Freddie and turn to leave. "Let's go."

Freddie clears his throat and steps forward. "Miss Stella," he says, the twang in his voice dipping so far south it's borderline cartoonish. "My grandmama, Agnes Pearl Freemont, told me to tell you hello and that she'd like a dozen croissants."

She picks her head up again and grins, and this time it's the kind of grin that boys like Freddie are used to causing. Stella smacks the counter and digs her fists into her hips. "You tell that Agnes the only reason I forgive her for not coming around here herself is because she sent such a dashing young fella in her place. You must be as tall as your grandpapa."

He nods. "Taller, ma'am. And, uh, he passed away four years ago now."

Stella shakes her head as she piles her croissants and a few extra pigs in a blanket into one of her light-pink boxes. "Nothing fair 'bout that."

Freddie reaches for his wallet, and Stella automatically shakes him off. "On the house."

My mouth drops open. *Sorcery.*

With the box tucked under his arm, we both turn to leave. My shoulders slope downward as I try to imagine how I can fix this without Hattie crucifying me.

"Oh, Miss Stella?" asks Freddie as he doubles back. "No chance you could do that cake for tomorrow? A one-time favor?"

I hold my breath.

Her bushy brows furrow into a caterpillar. "Just this once," she says. "And don't y'all tell nobody I went back on my policy. Can't have rumors going around."

Freddie gives an all-knowing grin.

She shakes her finger right at his chest. "That charm might last ya," she says. "But your good looks won't be around forever." She turns to me. "Now what can I get y'all?"

I nod my head as fast as it will go. "Double chocolate, please."

"And I wasn't kidding 'bout my paper," she adds. "No point in paying for it if I can't read the damn thing."

"Yes, ma'am."

As soon as we're in the car, I turn to Freddie. "What was *that*?"

"Or thank you would be good, too."

I roll my eyes. "Yeah, okay, thanks."

"Where to now?"

I open my mouth to speak, but pause. I'm not ashamed of our little trailer. There's not much hiding down here, but I never brought Grace home. I didn't know how to, I guess. Grace knew I was poor and that I lived in a trailer, but there was always some kind of disconnect. Whenever I said the words *poor* or *broke*, she would give me a limp smile and tell me about one of the handful of times she went without in some way. So Grace never saw me in the yellow lights of my kitchen or on the brown carpet of my bedroom. But Freddie—he's the same Freddie who cried a little too often when we were kids and was always there when Hattie wanted to run off with her friends. Now he's a taller, more grown-up Freddie who doesn't always smell like egg sandwiches.

We tear apart a few croissants—they smell too good!— as I point him right and left until we're at the gates of my trailer park. "I'm good here," I tell him, unbuckling my seat belt.

"No way. It's still raining."

I lean back against the seat, resigned. "Watch out for the potholes."

And he does, but the uneven pavement still jolts us to my front door.

"This is me," I say. "And thanks again for your help with the cake."

He nods. "See you at school next week?"

"Yeah." I almost forgot that we're in the same grade.

Freddie and I are late summer babies, but a year apart, making him eighteen and me seventeen. Different school districts have different rules, I guess.

Next week feels so far away. And this random bit of hope I hadn't even realized I was housing in my chest begins to wilt. Freddie will go to school and he'll make friends. Of course he will. They'll tell him that I'm the white trash lesbian from the trailer park and that I'm so far down the social food chain that even the bottom-feeders are above me, which is why, unlike Ruth and Saul, no one really made a fuss when I came out. No one's really concerned with the sexual identity of a girl from a local trailer park.

He pops the trunk and I run around to get my bike.

My still-damp clothes are soaked again in an instant, but instead of racing inside, I knock on the driver's-side window. "Come to Hattie's party," I shout, talking as fast as I can so the interior of Agnes's car won't get too wet. "Well, it's her boyfriend's party, but she's planning it. Tomorrow night. Boucher's after hours." Maybe it's a desperate attempt to hold on to him and show him who I've become before anyone else at school can do that for me.

Freddie smiles. "Okay. Yeah." Rain splats harder against the leather interior, so he starts to roll the window up. "Should I bring anything?" he shouts through the cracked window.

"Just that panty-dropping charm," I call.

Even through his fogging window, I can see him blushing.

FIVE

That night as I'm falling asleep, my phone rings—loud and shrill. I never actually talk on the phone, so it catches me off guard.

Grace, the caller ID says. My heart presses against my ribs like it's a bird caught in a cage. My alarm clock reads 11:50. I clear my throat and pick up.

"Hey." My voice is too low, like I'm trying to sound sultry.

All that answers me are screams and laughter and music so loud it makes my speaker crackle.

"Grace?" I can barely hear my own voice. "Grace?"

I listen for a minute or two, trying to decipher voices. I recognize her laugh, but my heart immediately plummets.

I hang up and text her.

think you called me by accident. just making sure everything's okay.

I am trying hard in this moment not to feel like she's moved on from me so quickly. Grace is allowed to go to parties and laugh and have fun, but it still feels too soon.

Now I'm awake. It's too late to call Ruth or Saul, and Hattie's actually sleeping in her own bed, so waking her up would only mean sharing mine.

I reach under my bed for my Whitman's Sampler chocolate box.

If my house was on fire in the middle of the night, I know I could grab this box and everything would be okay. The box itself hasn't held chocolate in years, but instead the contents include the closest things I have to important documents and a life savings.

The top layer of the box is folded-up pieces of paper Hattie and I played MASH, our absolute favorite game, on when we were kids. Beneath that is a picture of the three of us one Christmas at Grandma Cookie's when she was still alive. She bought us green long-sleeved velvet dresses that our dad made us wear even though it was eighty degrees outside. Hattie's cheeks are flushed and she is visibly annoyed, while I'm sitting in my dad's lap, eyes ringed red from some tantrum I must have thrown just moments before. But my dad is grinning, wide and genuine.

Beneath that are a few magazine cutouts of Olympic swimmers. There's even a folded-up pamphlet from the swim camp the YMCA ran every summer when I was a kid. These, I guess, are my important documents.

Under all that is my disaster fund. Every penny I have to my name. Money my dad has always said I should spend on something foolish. I should probably open a bank account, but the idea of having a bank account makes me sad. It's not like I have a car or nice clothes that I can look at and be reminded of how hard I've worked over the last two years. So there's something therapeutic about laying out all my cash and being able to place an actual value on myself. It's like finally having an answer to a question you've wondered about your whole life.

I lay each bill out carefully and add in my tips from Boucher's and set aside enough money for Tyler's cake. When I add up what's left, I write it down on the scratch piece of paper where I keep a running tally of how much I've got in the box. It's a lot, but not really enough to start fresh somewhere or go on a summer backpacking trip.

I've definitely almost drained it a few times. Mainly to help Hattie out. Well, always to help Hattie out. Like that one time she egged her ex-boyfriend's house and ended up cracking both his bedroom windows. (She was arrested for that one.) Or the time she borrowed a friend's car and backed it up into a ditch. (The police were involved that time too.) Then there are the handful of times we've bought morning-after pills and the times she lost her phone in the ocean or dropped it in the toilet of a dingy club.

For a long time now, I've felt like my head was scraping the ceiling here in Eulogy and this little box of cash would somehow take me and Hattie both away. But here I am—thinking of how many diapers this will buy and how expensive cribs are. It would be so easy to leave and let Hattie figure this all out on her own, but my mom already left the both of us. I won't make my sister go through that again.

SIX

The next night, during my shift at Boucher's, my phone buzzes.

GRACE: butt dial!

That's it.

An ache tears through my stomach, and I think that maybe she meant more to me than I did to her. My fingers hover over the keyboard, but then my pride says to make her wait. I force myself to put my phone away.

As quitting time draws closer, everyone is quick to close out their tables. When the last customer leaves, Saul dims the lights (except for the string of twinkly lights strung above the bar) and sets out all the booze people have brought from home while Hattie makes a spread of all the leftovers from today that can't be saved for tomorrow. As I wipe down the tables, Ruth walks by every few minutes to knock her hips against mine.

I find Saul staring out the window behind the bar into the dark parking lot.

I give him a poke in the side. "Waiting on someone?"

His lips twitch before giving in to a grin. "No," he says. "No one at all."

I'm tempted to press him for more info, but behind us Tommy wearily backs out the side door and yells, "You break it, you buy it! Don't forget to set the alarm before you leave!"

The moment the door shuts behind him, Saul cranks up the brass band music that's been playing all day as much as the speakers will allow. A few nonemployees trickle in through the back door, and then the party starts without anyone having to say so. It's not that everyone at Boucher's much likes Tyler, but none of us can say no to a party—or rather, none of us can say no to Hattie, the real wizard behind the curtain of more than one Boucher's employee party.

Tyler wasn't even Hattie's boyfriend until she told him she was pregnant. To be honest, he'd been playing Russian roulette with almost every straight girl in town, and Hattie happened to be the one who lucked out. When his mom heard he'd gotten a girl knocked up, she kicked him to the curb. Now he's either being faithful to Hattie out of sincerity or because he needs a place to crash. It's hard to tell which.

Hattie doesn't see that. All she sees is a future with her baby girl (she's sure it's a girl) and Tyler, who is unemployed and sleeps more hours a day than Mrs. Pearlman's Maine coon.

But all I see in my future is Hattie and me taking care of the baby while Dad works himself to death, trying to make ends meet like he always has. Except with a baby, there will be more bills and more mouths to feed.

I shuffle back to the kitchen to hide Stella's cake and when I return, I find Hattie crouched behind the bar pouring red wine into a sippy cup she bought at the grocery store last week, which I had assumed would someday be for the baby.

"What are you doing?" I whisper-spit at her.

She tugs me by my wrist so I'm below the counter with her. "The internet says I can have two glasses of wine a week, okay?" She hands me the bottle of wine. "And don't look at me like that."

"You don't even like wine."

"Hey," she says. "I'll take it where I can get it. But don't tell Ruth. She's all over my ass about caffeine and deli meat and Caesar dressing and all kinds of crap."

She would be. Ruthie wants to be a doctor, and she's going to be a damn good one. "But what's the deal with the sippy cup?"

She flips the cup upside down. "Spill proof. A hack from my party-girl days." Her voice is reminiscent of a time that feels far away, but was as recent as early summer. Quickly, she kisses me on the cheek. "Thanks for the cake, sis."

"Yeah, yeah." Hattie hasn't offered to pay me back for the cake, which really wouldn't bother me much. I mean, the line between what's mine and hers is invisible if not nonexistent. But the fact that this is for Tyler—Tyler, of all people. Well, it rubs me the wrong way. Hattie's never been good with money anyway. She thinks money is only meant for spending.

Hattie shimmies her way over to Tyler, who I don't think even showered before his own party. His acid-washed skinny jeans are at least one size too small, but I think that's on purpose. His skin is so white it's almost blue, and I guess that makes sense if you consider all the time he spends in front of televisions.

Hattie pulls Tyler from the booth where he sits with his friends and several already empty beer bottles. Reluctantly he follows her to the makeshift dance floor, where Saul is thrusting his way between two rows of shrieking waitresses. When he's done, he whips around and beckons Tyler. At first Tyler shakes his head, but then, surprising me and, well, everyone else, he hands Hattie his beer and sprinklers his way down the dance line to Saul, who greets him by grinding on his hip. Whatever possessed Tyler to dance in the first place is short-lived, as his friends boo and he returns to his booth.

"Heteronormative bullshit," Ruth mumbles as she reaches behind the bar for an empty glass.

I shove the cork back into the wine bottle Hattie opened and grab an almost empty handle of Fireball whiskey.

I hope I'm wrong about Tyler. Because maybe if I'm wrong about him, my gut could be wrong about Grace. And maybe—just maybe—Tyler will stick around and be the guy Hattie deserves.

I head for the outdoor seating, past Hattie and Saul grinding on each other while Ruthie takes video that will someday serve as incriminating evidence of our youth.

Boucher's sits on the edge of a long dock, so I settle in with my bottle on the patio and decide I probably won't be getting much sleep before my paper route. Out here the music is faint, quieted by the wind and waves, like I'm hearing it through an old telephone. I take a swig of whiskey and let it burn all the way down my chest.

Grace never really mixed with my friends. I think she was sort of intimidated by Saul and Ruth. Somehow making out with a girl was okay, but hanging out with her gay friends? Well, that was taking things too far. And she and Hattie never clicked either. If I had to guess, it was because Grace always wanted us to spend time alone and Hattie isn't big on privacy.

"You mind sharing?"

I turn around to find Freddie framed in moonlight with a bag of chips in hand.

"Hey," I say as I drag a chair around next to me. "Sit."

He plops down and tears open the bag of chips. "Felt like I should bring something."

I reach in for a handful as I pass him the whiskey. "Good thinking."

"Sorry I'm late. I, uh, got stuck on the phone."

"Who even talks on the phone anymore?"

He snorts. "Plenty of people. You know, we used to be stuck writing letters to each other and waiting weeks or even months to hear back. The phone is a modern miracle, and now all of a sudden we're too cool for it?"

I laugh. "Okay, okay. Calm down, buddy. I didn't realize phones meant so much to you."

He smiles, but there's none of that easy charm I remember from yesterday morning. He's stiff and irritable. I know the signs all too well.

"Girl trouble?" I ask.

"Something like that." He sits down and glances around at the empty patio before taking the bottle from me. "Not much for parties?"

I shake my head. "Not tonight. Just enjoying the view, I guess."

"The view? Nothing to see out here."

He's right. All that lies in front of us is a curtain of pitch black with a few flashing lights off in the far distance.

"It's good, though," he says. "I like it. The rhythm is calming. I used to get really scared of the ocean when I was a kid. You remember that?"

I do, but barely. Way back when my parents were together and my mom worked at the beach-chair rental stand, Hattie and I would spend our mornings coloring and reading books while we sat under the fan in the rental hut. Agnes would come every afternoon with Freddie and take us off my mom's hands.

It started out with her renting a few chairs, but soon she noticed the two girls cooped up under the counter. It didn't take much convincing for my mother to let us play with Freddie on the beach during her shifts. Those few hours turned into afternoons at their rental, and soon enough it was a yearly thing. But at the beach Freddie was a wreck, especially when the water was murky. It didn't seem so weird, though. When I was a kid I was terrified of highways. I would call them "the road" and howl anytime we got near one.

"My gram," he says, "she'd make me close my eyes as we tiptoed into the water, and she'd say, 'Take it one step at a time.'"

I close my eyes now. I guess he's kind of right. Just the sound of the gulf. It's like I've broken the world down into little bite-size pieces. And maybe that's how I can survive without Grace. That's how I'll survive Hattie, and the baby, and Tyler. One day. One hour. One minute at a time.

I open my eyes again, forcing myself back into this moment here with Freddie.

"I can't believe you live here," I say. "And that you're . . . well, *you*."

"It's wild."

"One summer y'all just didn't come back." I was nine, and hanging out with boys was suddenly a big deal to everyone except me. But the summer Freddie didn't show up . . . that left a hole in my world. One that made me angry. I'd been left. Again.

"My gramps," he says. "His head started getting foggy."

"Alzheimer's?" I ask. Walter, our old next-door neighbor before Mrs. Pearlman, had Alzheimer's for the longest time before anyone knew it. He was always a serious man, but every once in a while he would start talking like his trailer was a submarine and that his kids were Russians. One day my dad caught him using the big Oriental planter pot he kept in his yard for cigarette butts as a toilet. It wasn't long before his kids moved him out and into a home.

"Yeah. Yeah, he would do things like take me to swim meets at my soccer field or call my grams my mom's name."

My brain pauses on the words *swim meets*, but I shake it off.

"But then it got worse. He got mean. We had to start hiding his keys and his wallet." He takes a swig of whiskey and laughs. "He bought an aboveground pool from an infomercial one night and had it installed in our front yard when my grams was at work."

I laugh, and then catch myself. "I'm sorry."

"S'okay. It was pretty hilarious." And then he adds, "He died of an aneurism the summer before ninth grade. In his sleep."

His hand sits on the armrest of his chair, and I place mine on top of his for a moment.

He flips his palm over so that we're holding hands.

I'm the one trying to comfort him, but this small bit of human contact feels like aloe on a sunburn. Maybe I miss Grace that much. I'm reminded of all the things Freddie doesn't know about me. I'm so used to everyone in my life knowing that I'm gay that it almost feels like I'm lying to Freddie by omission.

"I think my gram was relieved," he says. "Can't blame her."

We sit there for a minute, until I finally break the silence. "I don't mean to be an asshole by changing the subject, but you were on a swim team?"

He grins. "Yeah. Bet that's a surprise."

"I just—you hated the water."

"Gram always harped on me about turning my greatest weakness into my biggest strength, so she joined a club and got me signed up for the swim team. I even swam on my school's team freshman, sophomore, and junior years."

I'm awestruck and jealous at the same time. "Wow. You must be pretty good."

He shrugs, and turns his head away.

"Eulogy doesn't have a team, though," I tell him.

"I know," he answers flatly.

I think I've struck a sore spot. The heavy air around us is cut by my sister's voice. "Ramona, get your ass in here! And who's this—"

Freddie stands to greet her and he flips on that charm like a light switch. I can't believe the transformation. "Hey, Hattie." He grins.

She makes a show of squinting. "Well, shit," she says. "Little Freddie Floaties?"

He rolls his eyes. "Nice to see you, too, Hattie. And I can swim in the deep end now, just so you know."

She skips forward and gives him a wet kiss on the cheek. "Puberty was kind to you." Hattie turns to me. "I'm totally introducing him to Alma, that new waitress. How *cute* would they be?"

I shrug, but there's a warmth in my chest that I can't quite process. "Pretty cute, I guess?"

Freddie chuckles nervously. "I sort of—"

Heavy footsteps smack against the patio. "Babe!" Tyler slurs. "Where'd you go? Don't I get some birthday kisses?"

She smiles at us both, like it's so obvious how irresistible

Tyler is, as she grabs each of us by the hand. "Cake time!"

Inside, Freddie follows me to the kitchen while Hattie corrals everyone into a circle. I dig around for the birthday candles we use for customers, and Freddie helps me light each of the twenty candles until the cake is glowing. It's beautiful, and I only hate that it's for Tyler.

Freddie watches me from the other side of the cake through the tiny flames. "Let's blow them out," he says.

"What?"

"Do you like your sister's boyfriend?"

I wait too long to answer, which is more than I need to say.

"Steal his wish," Freddie says. "You deserve it."

A smile tugs at my lips. Freddie was always such a Robin Hood. He shared everything right down to the shells we'd spend all day collecting, and he expected others to do the same. "Okay." I close my eyes, and my head is filled with too many requests, like when you're a kid and you want to wish for infinite wishes. I think I want more from life than my cup can hold.

Inhaling deeply, I open my eyes and blow out each candle.

Freddie grins. "I feel good about it. Some good mojo in this room."

He relights the candles and we take the cake out to the dining room and no one suspects a thing. After everyone sings "Happy Birthday," Freddie turns to me. "You wanna go for a walk or something?"

We take what's left of the whiskey with us and walk

down to the other edge of the boardwalk past all the night-time fishermen and their coolers of bait and beer. Alongside the beach, overnight drivers pass us by on Highway 90. The streetlights are concentrated on the road, leaving the sand cool and dark between our toes.

"I don't know when I'm going to get used to you living here," I tell Freddie. "Doesn't it kind of suck that you're starting over for senior year?"

He shrugs and takes the bottle from where it dangles from my fingertips. "It really does. Or did at first, I guess. I fought with my gram, begging her to wait a year or let me stay with friends, but—" He stops abruptly.

"But what?"

He looks at me. "I decided it was finally her turn. She raised my mom and then me. I'll be gone in a year anyway. And I've got you, right? So I guess I'm not really starting over."

Ruth and I aren't like this with each other. Our friendship is much too utilitarian for that, so it's hard not to melt a little when he says things like that. "You'll make friends at school," I tell him. "You're just that kind of guy people want to be friends with."

In my pocket, my phone vibrates and I pull it out to check my messages. I don't even realize I'm holding my breath until I exhale, but it's only my sister.

HATTIE: heading home soon. your bike is still here. are you okay? ARE YOU DEAD? DID FREDDIE FLOATIES KILL YOU?

on the beach with Freddie, I type back. **see you at home.**

"Not who you expected?" asks Freddie.

I shake my head glumly.

Freddie kicks off his flip-flops. "Come on. I haven't been to the beach since I got here."

I step out of my sandals and push the glass bottle into the sand so that hopefully the wind won't carry it away, then follow Freddie past the shoreline. It's curious to think how well he knows me, but then again not at all. Eight years feels like a long time, but I can so easily remember us chasing each other on this exact beach. In the time Freddie and I have spent apart, we've changed in ways that have defined us. And yet there's something so familiar about this. About us.

"So you miss your swim team?" I ask.

He shoves a hand in each pocket. "I guess you could say that."

The tide splashes against our ankles and then pulls back in a rhythm that is steady as a beating heart.

"Have you ever tried so hard to be good at something . . . so perfect, but it just wasn't . . . enough?" Freddie asks.

I know what he means, but no matter how far back I try to think, I can't find an example. How is that possible?

All I can do is I offer him a sad smile and a nod.

He lets out a long sigh before squatting down and using both of his hands to splash me.

I shriek and splash him back, thankful to him for lightening the mood.

We skip around in the water, never going much farther than the hem of our shorts. I leave thoughts of Grace and the future on the beach for a little while.

We walk back to Boucher's, and I offer to give Freddie a ride on the back of my bike so he won't have to walk home. After I put my hair up so it won't slap him in the face, he stands on the seat stay and holds on to my shoulders. We both hoot as the wheels speed down his hill.

In front of his house, he hops off the back of my bike and pulls me to him for a hug. My chin fits snugly in the crook of his shoulder. Hugging at this height can be so awkward, but nothing about our embrace makes me feel like I'm bumbling.

In sophomore chemistry, Mr. Culver told us the most important thing to take away from his class was that the world isn't made up of isolated incidents. Knowing the elements was important, but even more relevant was knowing how they changed when combined with others. And that's what I'm most terrified of right now—how Freddie and I will change when combined with others.

I watch as he sneaks around the side of his house into the backyard.

I have some time to kill before my paper route, so I go home to change my clothes. Hattie is spread out in my bed with a limb touching each corner, and the bathroom smells like puke—from Tyler, I assume. Even though it might be nice to crash on the couch for a little bit, I can't get out of here fast enough. The whole process of being in my house feels like I'm creeping against the wall of a narrow, smelly hallway. Nothing about it says home right now.

As I'm walking my bike out of the trailer park, my phone buzzes.

GRACE: How can I be this lonely when I'm surrounded by people? I miss you.

Normally this sentiment would feel all too familiar, but tonight I didn't feel lonely. Not at all.

Some days are worse than others, I finally type. **I miss you, too.**

SEVEN

It's been three days since Tyler's birthday bash, and school starts tomorrow. I love this last day of summer almost more than the last day of school. Hattie and I have made a habit of clearing the day so that we can sleep in late and then get in one last sunburn at the beach before spending the rest of the day in a cool, dark movie theater.

Saul and Ruth have managed to get the day off too, which is some kind of miracle, since the four of us comprise a third of the waitstaff at Boucher's.

After my paper route, I come home to sleep for a few hours more, and I'm so stupid excited for today that I decide to sleep in my swimsuit, a mint-colored tankini that fits more like bikini bottoms and a crop top.

My eyes are closed for what feels like no more than twenty minutes when I hear heavy feet clomping down the narrow hallway outside my door.

I try to ignore the noise for as long as I can, but eventually I crack my door open to find Tyler and one of his greaseball friends piling up boxes of records and old gaming consoles and trash bags overflowing with clothes outside of Hattie's room.

"What are you doing?" I spit.

Tyler's friend shrugs and shoulders his way past me.

"Moving day," Tyler says. "Home sweet home, right, sis?"

A cringe rolls up my spine. I watch as the pile grows, edging me slowly back into my bedroom as the space around me continues to shrink.

Hattie finally emerges from her room. "Hey," she says, "so I don't think I can do the beach and the movies today."

I groan and slam the door behind me.

Moments later, Hattie's in my room. "Listen, you can go on without me."

I cross my arms over my chest. "It's my senior year, Hattie. We always do the beach and a movie."

She sinks down onto my bed beside me. "I know. And I'm sorry, Ro. But we have to get all that shit into my room, and it's just so much."

"He really does have a lot of stuff."

She sighs and rests her head against my shoulder.

"Like, can't we throw all that shit in a shopping cart and leave it out front for Mrs. Pearlman to pick through? We don't have room for all that stuff in here." Mrs. Pearlman is a connoisseur of junk and gossip.

"I'll tell you what," she says. "You help me get all that crap in my room and we can go to the movies."

I hold my hand out to her and we shake on it. "Deal," I say.

While Hattie gets started on Tyler's stuff and he begins to install his consoles in the living room, I text Saul and Ruthie and let them know we've got to bail on the beach. Saul sends a series of dramatically disappointed selfies and Ruthie simply responds with a **K**.

I decide that since we're already breaking tradition, I might as well invite Freddie to join us at the movies. I waver back and forth for a moment on whether I should call or text. Since I haven't officially waved my gay flag for Freddie, I don't want him to think this is anything more than us hanging out as friends. I opt for a text.

Tyler's crap is endless, and most of it is dirty laundry. And the fact that he took his dirty laundry from his mom's house to his girlfriend's house? Well, that pisses me off.

When Dad leaves for work, he calls to us from the other end of the hallway, because the floor is completely covered in Tyler's stuff. I can see my dad's neck and ears turning red—a sure sign of his rising blood pressure. I wish he would say something. Anything. Tell Tyler he can't expect to fit all this shit in our house or tell him he can't move in at all. But all Dad sees is Hattie. He couldn't make it work with Mom, so the best he can do is give Hattie and Tyler a fighting chance. "Y'all make sure to close the door when you're coming and going. Don't want that cold air to get out. Love you, girls."

Tyler doesn't say anything. Not even a weak thank-you.

"Love you, too," Hattie and I chirp back.

I glare at Tyler, but he's oblivious.

After the three of us spend a few hours weeding through boxes and trash bags, Saul picks Hattie and me up. I'm too lazy and sweaty to change out of my swimsuit, so I throw a dress on over and grab a flannel shirt for the movie.

As we're leaving, Hattie asks Tyler if he's sure he doesn't want to go. He says, "I'm gonna stay in and finish my game."

"And look at porn," I add the minute he closes her bedroom door.

Hattie shrugs as she locks the front door behind us. "He's not getting it here," she says. "I feel about as sexy as a watermelon."

"Well, I think you're a super-sexy watermelon!" Saul calls from his Jeep.

My sister takes the front and gives Saul a huge kiss on the cheek while Ruthie and I hop in the back, and the four of us leave to pick up Freddie.

"Sorry we missed the beach," I say on behalf of the both of us.

Ruth pulls her shoulder-length blond hair into a ponytail. She has that perfect, thick kind of hair that's only ever been dyed by the sun. "That's okay," she says. "Saul got into it with our parents this morning, so we didn't even go either."

He glances at me in the rearview mirror. "They're trying to institute some kind of curfew on me, like I'm not an adult."

"You didn't come in until four a.m.," Ruth reminds him.

"And you think Dad would've cared if a girl was dropping me off?"

She sighs and leans back into her seat, because he's right. The two of them have plenty of things that Hattie and I don't—a nice house, money for college (unless you're Saul and don't plan on going), and a guaranteed car as a high school graduation present. But something we have that they don't is our dad. He's not perfect, but he accepts the two of us in a way Saul and Ruth's parents have never been capable of. I'm not even allowed over at their house—as if I could somehow make Saul or Ruth gayer than they already are.

When we get to Agnes's, Freddie is sitting on the front porch waiting for us in shorts and a striped tank top.

"Is this the piece of meat you ran off with the other night?" asks Saul. "He's even cuter when I'm sober."

Ruthie rolls her eyes and nudges me to scoot over so that I'm sitting in the middle. "I hate uneven numbers."

"Get over it," I tell her. It's not so much uneven numbers but new people that Ruth isn't a fan of.

Freddie hoists himself up using the roll bar and slides in next to me. "Thanks for inviting me." His voice drops to a whisper when he asks, "You sure your friends don't mind?"

I laugh. "This is the most exciting thing to happen to them all summer." I pat his bare knee. "Guys, this is Freddie."

Saul whistles, and Ruth offers a short wave, which is probably the closest thing to cordial I can expect from her.

Ruth is all hips and thighs and makes no apologies about it, plus Freddie and I are definitely not small people, so it's a squeeze, but we fit. And to be honest, this is my ideal platonic people-sandwich.

"You know Hattie," I say. "And that's Saul and his little sister, Ruth. The three of us will be seniors together."

Saul speeds down the coastal highway to Gulfport, which is about a thirty-minute drive and has the closest movie theater.

"You got a girlfriend, pretty boy?" hollers Saul over the wind.

"I do," Freddie shouts. "Her name's Vivienne."

I turn to him with a raised eyebrow. A girlfriend?

He grins and shrugs.

I feel a little uncomfortable that he didn't tell me about her, and I'm not sure why. I almost say something or crack a dumb joke, but then I remember my own lie of omission. I promise myself to tell him about Grace as soon as I can.

"Long distance?" asks Hattie once we roll to a stop at the red light off the shipping docks.

"We're making it work," says Freddie. "When it's supposed to work, it does. But you gotta make it happen." He speaks with such conviction I almost believe him.

"Long distance is bullshit," Hattie tells him, but I know it's me she's talking to. "Just askin' for someone to get hurt."

Freddie grins. "That's how you know it was worth it. When it hurts."

Ruth and Saul both sigh for entirely different reasons.

The wind silences us for the rest of the drive and my

hair swirls above us, like a blue demon chasing us out of town.

When we arrive at Gulfport Galaxy 9, the storm clouds that hovered over the coast all morning have nearly caught us, so we help Saul put the vinyl top on his Jeep, which he's always lovingly referred to as the Heap (of shit) since it's broken-down more often than it's actually running. The Jeep is a yellowy cream color and before she was the Heap (of shit), he used her for mudding—which is part of the reason why she's in such tough shape now.

"All right, kiddies," says Saul as we stand below the marquee, studying the showtimes available to us.

"I want to see *Silent Bloodbath*," says Ruthie with determination.

Me, Hattie, and Saul all *oooooh* in unison.

"No can do," says Freddie.

"Is Freddie Floaties scared?" says Hattie in that horrible whiny voice she used to tease me with when we were kids.

He shrugs. "Promised Viv we'd see it together."

Saul rolls his eyes and mimes pointing a loaded gun to his head.

"It's cool," Freddie says. "Y'all guys see it and I'll chill in the arcade or see"—he scans the marquee for a moment—*"Kissing in French?"*

"Sounds good to me!" Saul steps up to the window to buy tickets for himself and Ruthie. "Two for *Silent Bloodbath*."

Before Hattie buys her ticket, she turns back to Freddie. "You could see it and pretend like you didn't."

Freddie grins but shakes his head.

It kills me—it really does—because we don't go to the movies often and I am *dying* to see *Silent Bloodbath*, but I turn to Freddie and say, "I'll go see *Kissing in French* with you."

He shakes his head at first but says, "Are you sure? You don't have to do that."

"At this point, I want to sit in a cold, dark theater and forget that school is about to start." It's a half-lie. Or a half-truth. I'm not sure. But I'm not going to let him see some lame rom-com by himself.

"Okay," he says. "But my treat, cool?"

I nod and follow everyone else inside to the concessions. Normally we pack our purses full of cheap gas-station candy and soda, but popcorn is half-price before two.

Saul swings back behind me as Freddie joins me with our tickets. "Blast from the past at three o'clock!"

"Huh?"

He kicks me in the shin. "Working behind the hot dog rollers. CarrieAnn Cho."

Behind the counter stands an Asian girl with deep-brown hair swept into a loose ponytail and a T-shirt advertising this summer's *Super! Big! Explosion! Aliens!* blockbuster tucked into her black pants.

She lifts her head and I feel the color drain from my face. "Oh shit." Instinctively, I take cover behind Freddie and crouch down a bit so that my height doesn't give me away.

"Uh, what's happening?" His voice is unsure, but he guards me like a wall.

Saul sighs. "The hauntings of first love."

"She was not my first love," I whisper. "More like my first kiss."

Freddie laughs stiffly.

"Ramona?" CarrieAnn's high-pitched, far-off-sounding voice finds me.

This wasn't exactly what I had in mind when I decided it was time to come out to Freddie.

I straighten my posture and take a few steps closer to the counter. She's petite and bouncy and reminds me of the fairy art from Hot Topic that Hattie was obsessed with in middle school.

"I thought that was Hattie." She points to my sister, who is loading an extra-large bucket of popcorn (which she has no intention of sharing, I'm sure) with layers of butter from the dispenser next to the condiments. She even goes so far as to take a cup meant for water and fill it with extra butter for the bottom of her bucket. "And I figured you couldn't be far," CarrieAnn finishes.

I smile. "You found me."

The thing with CarrieAnn is that she and I sloppily made out and fooled around a little at a party that Hattie dragged me to in Gulfport when I was in ninth grade and CarrieAnn was in tenth. Since she lived here in Gulfport, we never really saw each other. Different schools, different friends.

Based on all the voice mails and texts I received from CarrieAnn in the following days and weeks, she was having a personal revelation. And she was ready for something major—something I wasn't sure how to give her at the time. Listen, I was only fifteen and not really emotionally prepared to be her guide through the Gay Mountains.

Her texts started getting pretty intense, so I did what any normal person who is not really an asshole but is acting like an asshole would do: I ignored her. Since then, I've done everything in my power to avoid her until she went off to college in Atlanta last year. But I hadn't exactly factored in summer break.

"Wow," says CarrieAnn. "You look great."

I nod. "Thanks. You too. Nice uniform."

She smiles so wide I can see her gums. "Thanks. So I go back to school in a week, but maybe we could get together."

"Oh, wow. I go back to school tomorrow, so my week is pretty crazy."

"Maybe we could see a movie if you have time? I can get free tickets."

I open my mouth, but she doesn't even give me time to respond.

"I still have the same number I did in high school, so you can text me. Did your number change?"

I reach for my phone. "Uh—"

"Could I get two cherry slushes and a medium popcorn?" asks Freddie as he slides in beside me. "Ramona, you want any candy?"

CarrieAnn studies the two of us suspiciously.

I shake my head, relief marred with guilt sinking deep into my chest. As Freddie pays for his order, I slink back behind him and Saul.

"You two lovebirds set a wedding date yet?" Saul asks under his breath.

I punch him in the butt cheek.

"Ow!" he groans. "But kind of nice, too."

After we split ways with Saul, Ruthie, and Hattie, I turn to Freddie as we walk into the last theater at the end of the hallway. "Thanks for stepping in back there." I sip the slush he bought me.

"Yeah. Wasn't sure what that was about, but whatever it was, it was awkward."

We choose middle seats in the third row from the back, and we have the entire theater to ourselves.

"It's weird," I say. "She's kind of, like, obsessed with me."

He shakes his head, laughing a bit. "Don't tell me you've turned into one of those girls who thinks everyone is obsessed with them. *Uggggh*," he mimics, *"everyone's just, like, so obsessed with me."*

"No! Shut up. You know that's not me."

He smirks before shoving a fistful of popcorn into his mouth.

"But CarrieAnn really is obsessed with me," I say.

The screen in front of us plays the same trivia on a loop until the movie starts. The theater is dark and damp, so I take the flannel shirt I've got tied around my waist and put it on backward like some sort of blanket-shirt hybrid. We both stuff our faces with popcorn and shout trivia answers back and forth.

And then, out of nowhere, Freddie asks, "So, girls, huh?"

"Yep." I should say something more, but there's not much else to say.

"You've never dated any guys?"

I shrug. "Haven't even kissed one." And then I add, "Well, in recent years."

"Then how do you know you don't like guys?"

"I don't know, Freddie," I say, trying to hide my irritation. "How many boys did you kiss before you realized you were straight?"

He shakes his head. "That's not what I meant. You know it."

"So what did you mean?" The lights dim, and the previews start. Still, it's only us in the theater.

"I meant that, like, boy-girl is kind of the default that people go for even if it's not how they were born or whatever."

"It wasn't my default. Or whatever." My voice is sharp.

He doesn't say anything. Instead, all I hear is the crunching of popcorn.

The movie starts in a French-cooking class, and I immediately decide that the only thing that could make this movie interesting was if smell-o-vision was a real thing, which means not only are we feeling awkward, but we'll most likely be bored, too.

I don't get rom-coms. It's not that I don't believe in

romance or love stories, but for once—just for once!—why can't the girl sweep the girl off her feet? Or why can't the fat best friend get the guy? Why can't two guys get into a pillow fight in their underwear? It's the same old shit every time.

Freddie turns to me, interrupting the two star-crossed lovers on-screen in the midst of their picnic. "I didn't mean to sound like a jerk. I'm processing is all."

"Processing? It's not like someone died or something." And then I sort of feel like a jerk, too, for snapping at him. I take a deep breath and decide to give him the benefit of the doubt. After a few moments, I ask, "Am I your only gay friend?"

"I mean . . ." He pauses, and fidgets with his hands, like he would when we were kids and he was in trouble with Agnes for something like sneaking snack cakes before lunch. "I know gay people, but yeah. Basically."

I guess in most parts of the world, this might come as a shock, but down here, not so much. It's not that there aren't any gay people in the South; it's that our cliques and circles are a little tighter than they might be elsewhere. So it's not all that weird for a guy like Freddie to not have any gay friends.

I cross my legs toward him and practically turn my back to the movie, which has progressed into the rom-com's version of a training montage, where the beautiful couple traipse around town and rub their beautiful love in every-one's faces.

With a mouth full of popcorn, I say, "Tell me about

Viv." I want to prove to him that I am the same Ramona I was last night and the day before and all those years ago. It's not like I think he's some bigot. He's ignorant, and sometimes ignorance is as dangerous as bigotry.

He straightens up a little. "We met on swim team." He pulls out his phone and scrolls through his pictures to show me one of a black girl with muscular curves and hair cropped short against her angular face. Every inch of her looks deliberate.

"She looks intense," I say.

"She was. She is."

"So did you guys click or what?"

He shakes his head. "No way. She transferred to my school in the middle of ninth grade. She hated me at first." A slow smile spreads across his lips. He's probably reliving some memory in his head. "Kept calling me smug. I asked her out three times before she said yes, and when I asked her why she'd kept saying no, she said it was 'cause she didn't like quitters." He laughs to himself. "You know how some people are easy to be with? Viv was never like that. She made you work for it."

It was never like that with Grace. Maybe things would have been different if we'd met at school or while she was with friends.

"Me and Viv would always race after practice. I never stood a chance. She loves winning. More than anything. You know how people always tell little girls that if a boy is mean to you, that's how you know he likes you? Well, that's how Viv was. She was always name-calling and talking trash and kicking my ass in the pool." He laughs. "Her own horrible way of flirting."

"Were you guys on again and off again?"

"A few times. There were a few times." His gaze drifts for a moment. "So are you seeing someone now?" he asks hesitantly.

I sigh long and hard. "Grace." I shake my head. "Everybody down here has summer flings all the time, ya know? Including me. And then I met Grace back in June. So when you like someone, you've got the whole 'Do they like me back?' thing to contend with, but when you're gay, you sort of have to also feel out if other people are, too. It's like a double unknown. And with Grace it was hard to tell. I knew she liked me, but I didn't know if she *liked* me."

"Don't you have, like, gaydar?"

I laugh. "Well, I mean, sometimes I get vibes, but sometimes girls are just friendly. And I get that I stand out, but I think some people have this idea of what a lesbian looks like, and I don't always fit that image. But with Grace, God, it was painful for the first few days. We met while I was filling in for a few weeks at Palio's Bike Rental down on the beach. I'd already seen her around town a few times. I had a big line that day, and everyone was hot and annoyed. This guy got to the front of the line and started mouthing off at me for going too slow, but the paperwork for Palio's is intense, and they still use only hard copies. So anyway, Grace was standing there in this great swimsuit with the sides cut out and huge sunglasses painted like watermelons." I know I'm going into way too much detail, but I can't help myself. "She was taller than average for a girl, but not nearly as tall as me. Anyways, she tapped the guy on the shoulder and pointed over to his kid and was like, 'Um is that your son trying to eat a live hermit crab?'"

Freddie laughs. "She sounds pretty ballsy."

"Yeah. Yeah, she is." I'd never thought of Grace as ballsy, but I guess this whole summer was new territory for her, and sometimes it's easy to forget that it takes some amount of bravery to live your life one way and then suddenly diverge from that path.

I pull out my phone to take my turn and show him a few pictures. I linger for a moment on one of her and me in her room. Me sitting on the floor with her between my legs, resting against my chest like an armchair. She took the picture without me knowing. It was a reflection of us in the floor-length mirror on the back of her bedroom door. Her soft green gaze was directed at the camera, while my face was nuzzled into her shoulder. Her black hair against my blue waves looked like a day-old bruise.

I've always loved this picture, but now, looking back, it sort of makes me uneasy. Me looking at Grace; her looking at our reflection.

I'm being ridiculous, I tell myself. But the seed of a thought still buries itself in a recess of my brain.

"So how did you know she really liked you?" Freddie asks.

"Well, I hung out at her place a few times. Watching

TV and stuff. And then I spent the night. I couldn't fall asleep. I spent the whole night wide-awake as she kind of scooted in closer to me. I guess I started to get the hint. And if I hadn't by then, the extra-long hug when I left the next morning was a solid clue. I'm talking full-body hug."

"Man, I wish Gram would've let Viv spend the night."

I grin. On the screen in front of us, the heroine is sobbing into a bowl of popcorn. "There are some benefits," I admit. "But it can be pretty confusing, too. I don't get invited to slumber parties or girls' night outs or anything like that. Or maybe that's just because I don't have many friends."

"But you've got Ruth, right?"

I nod. "Well, that's true."

"Have you guys ever . . . ya know?"

I practically spit out my slush. "Oh God, no. Yeah, definitely not."

Freddie waggles his eyebrows. "Well, if you guys ever need my scientific opinion . . ."

"Oh, come on now. Seriously? Could you be any more of a bro?"

He looks sheepish. "Yeah, that was pretty bad, huh?"

"Worse than bad."

"I'm sorry. I'm sorry! That was gross. So, anyway, you and Ruth? Nothing there?"

I squint at him for a moment, trying to decide if I'm going to let him get away with that so easily, and decide to count it as strike one. "Right," I say. "Yeah, it would've been hard to not wonder, okay? The only two gay girls in one small town." I sigh. "But that would've been too convenient. Except we did decide that if we're single and really old, like fifty probably, then we'll get married and move to Vermont."

He shakes his head, laughing. "Why Vermont?"

I shrug. "I don't know. Ruth says she heard it was a really gay place, but for, like, gay old people."

"Like Florida? But gay?"

I choke on a piece of popcorn. "Oh my God! Yes!"

After we've both caught our breath, he asks, "So why don't you and Grace make plans to go to the same university?"

"Yeah right."

"What? Viv has partial swim scholarships at LSU and Florida State, but she's choosing LSU because that's where I'm going."

"You honestly think I'm going to college?" I'm glad it's too dark for him to really see me. I might never have had big plans of college, but I still feel like I'm mourning whatever the future might have held before Hattie got knocked up.

"Come on," he says. "Don't be another one of those small-town stereotypes."

I can't stop myself from rolling my eyes. "Speak for yourself, Mr. College Fund."

"Don't use money as an excuse, okay? There are grants. And loans even. People figure it out."

"Yeah, people who don't live in trailer parks. People who don't work two jobs through high school. All those people have *time* to figure it out." I should feel bad, but I don't. I've been getting the college lecture from random strangers for a long time now. It's almost as common as *You're so tall! You must play basketball!*

He's silent for a minute. "I'm sorry," he says, apologizing for, like, the fifteenth time today.

I shake my head. With all the differences between us, I almost can't believe that we were once inseparable for two months every summer. "No, I'm sorry. I have a lot on my mind." Like Grace and how she's kidnapped my heart and taken it north up the Mississippi River and Hattie and her belly carrying my niece. Or nephew. And how temporary Tyler is and how much space he's eating up in our already too small trailer and how Dad's going to work himself to death, which means at the end of the day, I'm the only hope she's got. So my escape fund? It will probably end up becoming a diapers and baby formula fund.

Despite all that, we talk for the rest of the movie, and I'm so thankful to have this empty theater to ourselves. I finish my slush and when Freddie doesn't want the rest of his, I finish that too. We stay until the credits are through. CarrieAnn hovers at the door, waiting for us to clear out so she can clean the theater. As we leave, I give her a quick hug and tell her good luck with school this year. I hope she finds her person.

Outside, the rain has passed, so we ride home with the top down on the Jeep. It's a day that feels like good-bye.

It's not high school that I'll miss. It's my summer breaks. The two months of freedom that almost make me feel like a tourist in my own town. Next summer won't be any kind of break at all. It'll be life, and the kind of life I've got ahead of me doesn't include vacation time.

SEPTEMBER

EIGHT

"You should come to the Y with me and Gram," says Freddie.

I shake my head. "For what?"

We sit on the curb of the alleyway behind Scrub-a-Dub Car Wash, sharing a half-cherry, half-lemon shaved ice while Freddie's on break. He landed a job spinning signs on the corner here. I don't think he really needs the job, but without Viv around, I think he has some time to fill. And his newfound friend, Adam Garza, whose family owns not one but two local Scrub-a-Dub locations and two more in Jackson, helped him land the gig.

Adam rolls back and forth in front of us on his electric-blue skateboard covered in band stickers, popping up and down from the curb every few moments. He's quiet, but also the kind of guy who says the funniest things under his breath during class. And he's cute, too. He's half Mexican and half Honduran and he has longish brown hair that is always falling into his eyes. I guess I imagined Freddie seamlessly fitting into the fold of jocks or something, but it makes sense he'd gravitate toward the kind of guy who has great hair and is too cool for this town, making him uncool in comparison.

Over the course of a few weeks, Freddie has slipped into my life like he was always meant to be there. We ride our bikes to and from school as far as we can until our roads diverge. Sometimes Adam joins us on his skateboard or Ruth hops on the back of my bike. But I always come over for breakfast a few times a week. We watch movies at each other's houses on the weekend and spend whatever free afternoons we have on the beach with Ruthie, Saul, and Hattie.

Freddie turns to me. "Gram's been giving me a hard time about how long it's been since I was last in the pool. I told her I'd go with her." He taps the toe of his sneaker against mine. "It'll be good. Help you clear your head. And pretty soon it'll be too cold for the beach."

I am sort of tempted, but the truth is: "I don't even have time."

"Last weekend you watched the entire second season of *Game of Thrones*. You have time."

"Shut up." I pass him the shaved ice.

"No spoilers!" shouts Adam.

I roll my eyes and discreetly pull out my phone to check messages.

"That show is way too old for the first two seasons to fall under the spoiler-free umbrella," Freddie tells Adam.

Adam shrugs. "I'll be sure to remember you said that, Mr. I've-Never-Seen-a-Single-Star-Wars-Movie."

I turn to Freddie as I slide my phone back into my pocket. "Wait. What?"

"My grandparents never really got into it, I guess? I mean, I know Vader is Luke's dad. That's pretty much the gist of it, right?"

I'm not a die-hard Star Wars fan, but Dad loves it. I can't imagine growing up without it. He even has a tattoo of the rebel symbol on his shoulder, and this is a guy who has zero pain tolerance.

Adam glances down at his phone. "My break is over." He groans dramatically and drops his board to the ground, rolling around the corner to the front of the car wash.

"I've still got a few minutes left," says Freddie.

My favorite part about visiting Freddie at the car wash is watching all the brightly colored soap drain in the alley. Between the smell and the rainbow suds, this might be the nicest alley in all of Eulogy.

"What's the deal with swimming?" I finally ask. "Why'd you stop?"

He groans and leans back on the sidewalk with his arms stretched out behind him, holding him up. "Every season, scouts show up to our meets, right? Like, college scouts."

I nod. "To recruit?"

"Yeah. Around the time you're a junior, you start to get a good idea of who's looking at you and who's not."

"Okay?"

"And well, no one was really looking at me."

"So you quit?" I ask. As soon as the words are out of my mouth, I regret them.

He prickles with irritation. "It's not that simple. Viv and all my friends were getting calls and offers from all sorts of places." He shakes his head. "Every time I got in that pool, I knew I was doing the best I could. I trained hard. I even broke it off with Viv for a while to concentrate on improving my times. And every day I felt like such a failure."

"But even if you don't get scholarship money or specific offers or whatever, you can still walk on at the beginning of the year and try out, right?"

He shakes his head. "You know how sports announcers are always talking about athletes quitting when they're at the top of their game?"

I nod. "Vaguely."

"Well, I get why they say that. Sucking at something you love to do really messes with you. The truth is I decided that I'd apply to all the schools where Viv got scholarship offers and that I'd go wherever she went."

"Are you serious?" I ask. I like Grace. I think I love her. But I can't imagine what it must be like to be in Freddie's position with limitless options and then to leave my fate to be decided by someone else.

When he looks at me, I can see all the heaviness that he's been carrying over the last few years. His grandfather's death. His on-again, off-again relationship with Vivienne. Uprooting his entire life so Agnes can live out her years here in Eulogy. Coming up short with swimming.

"Anyway," he says, "Gram thinks I should keep swimming even if it's just for the exercise, and she won't get off my back about it. She's got this theory that if I'm only competing against myself, I have nothing to lose."

I puff my cheeks and let the air hiss out slowly. "Well, I guess I can give it a go," I tell him. "But I'm pretty sure I'm going to be super slow and sucky."

"Well, at the very least, it'll be a short-lived ego boost for me."

I smile halfheartedly. "What about Viv?" I ask. "Have you guys talked since that fight?" A few days after school started, the two of them got into a fight because she hadn't called him back in three days.

He sighs. "We FaceTimed last night."

"Ooh, FaceTime sex?" I joke.

He doesn't say anything.

"What is it?"

Freddie shakes his head. "I need to go see her, ya know? She needs to *see* me." He finishes the rest of the shaved ice and sets the cup down on the gravel. "You call Grace?"

"Texting is easier. Talking on the phone requires privacy and, well, actually talking on the phone. Who even talks on the phone anymore?" I ask, trying to goad him.

"Excuses," he says. "And you know my feelings on that."

Freddie and I have different ideas of how to maintain a long-distance relationship. I'm scared to push too hard, and he's scared he's not pushing hard enough. I stand up and take the empty cup. "I'm supposed to go to my mom's with Hattie."

He reaches out a hand for me to pull him up. "Tomorrow. YMCA. Right after your route. Cool?"

I swing one leg over my bike and toss the cup in the Dumpster behind him. "What if my hair turns the water blue?" Hattie touched me up right before school started.

"Ramona Blue," he says. "Everything she touched turned a hue."

Tyler drops Hattie and me off at the Ocean Springs apartment complex in Biloxi. It's not a far drive from Eulogy, but our mom lives farther inland than we do. According to her, she's lived through too many hurricanes to plant herself right on the coast like the rest of us fools. But Harrah's, the casino where she works, is right there on the water.

"Do we have to do this?" I ask Hattie as Tyler pulls away. "And why doesn't he have to stay?"

She takes my hand. "You're here for *me*, remember?"

I nod. "Fine. But he's the one who got you into this situation in the first place. Don't forget that."

Hattie has yet to tell my mom she's pregnant. Her reaction shouldn't matter. We see the woman once or maybe twice a month. But it does to Hattie. She had more time than I did with Mom and Dad together as a unit, and I think she still holds on to the memory of it. The memory of what it felt like to have a mother. Especially now.

According to the court mandate from when we were kids, we're supposed to stay with Mom every other weekend, but once we got to middle school, the weekends sort of fizzled out, and now we're down to a dinner or two a month. Our weekends here were always miserable anyway.

Being this far from Eulogy, we were nowhere near any of our friends, and Mom has been working the noon-to-midnight Saturday shift since she took the job at Harrah's.

Hattie knocks on the door of the third-story apartment twice before my mom swings the door open. "Hey, girls. Come on in."

We're greeted by the faint scent of cat piss courtesy of Wilson, Mom's blind orange tabby.

Our mom wears the same clothes she wore twenty years ago, and seeing as she had Hattie at the age of fifteen, that can't mean anything good. She's too thin. Her hair is stringy. Short shorts show off her purple varicose veins and soft, lumpy thighs. She should wear a bra, but there's not much room for one beneath her tiny tank top.

She hugs Hattie first and then me. Neither of our limbs knows where to go, and it's like this every time. Two strangers embracing.

"Y'all kick off your shoes. I got the news on, but change it if you want. Making some cheesy noodles with hamburger meat."

My eyes meet Hattie's the second Mom turns her back. I nudge her on with my chin to get it over with, but she shakes me off.

"Have you talked to Aunt Peggy lately?" asks Hattie.

Mom responds from the kitchen. "Oh yeah. We talked the other day. She went on and on about that blood clot she had in her leg and her new compression socks."

The two of us sit on the couch, which also pulls out to be Mom's bed. The apartment is an efficiency, so it's all one room basically. When we were little girls, we'd all sleep on the foldout with Mom, but as we got older, she'd set up sleeping bags on the floor. That was around the time our weekend visits petered out.

Hattie and Mom trade small bits of information from each of their lives while I flip through channels on the TV.

As we sit down to eat, Mom turns her attention toward me. "Well, Ramona, it's your senior year. Soon enough you'll be on your own."

"Yep." Even though I basically already am on my own.

She spoons noodles into three separate bowls and pours us each a glass of milk.

"I don't drink milk with dinner anymore," I tell her. "Neither does Hattie. We haven't since we were kids."

Mom opens her mouth to respond.

"It's fine," says Hattie as she drinks down a giant gulp.

I can already tell that all that dairy is going to have her puking her guts out in the morning.

"You datin' anyone right now?"

I feel my sister's eyes on me. "Sort of," I say. "But she's not from here."

Mom chuckles. "This too shall pass." Without even pausing, she asks Hattie, "How's Tyler?"

I may not be a loud person, but I'm not timid. And yet something about my mom makes me feel so completely unheard, because no matter how many times I tell her that this—my life—is not a phase, she never listens to me.

Hattie wiggles in her chair a little. "He's good. We're . . ."

I wait for it. *Pregnant. Knocked up. Havin' a baby.*

"Good," she finishes.

"Well, I'm glad," Mom says. "You gotta find the good ones and nail 'em down quick, or else you'll get stuck with the discards."

I stifle a low groan.

We eat the rest of our dinner in near silence, talking back and forth about little things that mean nothing at all until Hattie breaks the quiet with a loud burp.

"Excuse—" Her face goes white as chalk. "Oh, I'm gonna be sick." She runs around to the other side of the table and into the bathroom, barely making it, before I hear vomit splatter against the inside of the toilet.

I'm right behind her, hovering like a protector. "Are you okay?" I whisper as I pull her hair wavy hair into a ponytail.

She nods as she throws up some more.

The smell wafts past me, and I have to duck my nose under the collar of my shirt to stop myself from puking right alongside her.

Mom stands in the doorway, like a clueless bystander watching a car accident.

Me taking care of Hattie. Her taking of care of me. I feel my future in Eulogy falling securely into place. "We're fine," I tell her.

And we are. We're going to be fine.

NINE

The next morning at the YMCA there's only one car in the parking lot. Forget butterflies. I feel like I've got a handful of bees buzzing around in my stomach.

When I showed up earlier with the paper in hand, Agnes was waiting in her yellow swimsuit and terry-cloth zip-up cover-up with an old shoulder bag with the logo of an airline that no longer exists.

An older gentleman in a velour tracksuit sits at the front counter. His filmy white skin is covered in age spots while his long hair is gathered into a thin white ponytail at the back of his neck, and the name tag pinned to his jacket reads *Carter*. We each hand him our cards—Agnes added me as a guest to their membership—and he files them into a small recipe box for us to pick up on our way out.

Agnes, Freddie, and I visit the locker rooms, where we leave our bags before heading out to the pool. I brought my comfiest swimsuit, a navy-blue two-piece with a sports-bra-style top. Being over six feet tall can make swimwear shopping—or just shopping in general—a challenge. I think the last time I wore a one-piece was around the time Hattie and I stopped bathing together. A one-piece on a girl as tall as me . . . well, that kind of camel toe might be a threat to national security.

Agnes fits a swimming cap over her hair and then places goggles around her head as she takes the steps into the pool. Freddie is quick to dive in with his goggles already on. After shaking the water out of his hair, he looks up to find me standing there in front of my lane.

I'm actually a decent swimmer, but I've never gone to a pool and just swum laps. I'm scared I might somehow do it wrong. I'm embarrassed that it never even occurred to me to bring goggles.

Freddie laughs at the sight of me and tosses me a pair of goggles. "Figured I should bring an extra pair for you."

"Thanks," I say. I take my time adjusting the goggles to fit my head, but really I'm stalling so that both of them will start swimming and I won't have an audience.

Freddie pulls himself up into a tight ball at the edge of the pool and springs backward into a backstroke. I take the elastic around my wrist and knot my hair into a quick braid before trying to mimic his dive off the block.

Mine feels more like a belly flop, but luckily, Agnes and Freddie are already in the zone, doing laps up and down the pool.

Halfway through my first lap, I'm already panting. I don't know if what I'm doing is freestyle or what, but it feels like I'm flailing around more than anything.

But I keep going. There's some kind of liberty in

knowing that each of us has our eyes on our own lanes. I swim from the deep end to the shallow end, and I have to admit: I'm sort of impressed with myself. Not because I'm good, but because I don't stop. The whole thing sort of feels like dancing. You don't know that you're doing it wrong until someone says so.

As I'm about to circle around for another lap, a hand grips my shoulder. I emerge, gasping for air, my heart humming in my chest.

Freddie hovers above me and holds out an arm to help hoist me up. "You got pretty into it, huh?"

I nod, because I haven't quite caught my breath enough to speak.

As I follow him to the locker rooms, a cranky-looking older white woman in a black Speedo swimsuit sitting on the bleachers says, "You ain't got technique, but ya got speed."

I swallow back a smile and shrug. I decide to take it as a compliment.

TEN

When I pull my cell phone from my backpack after school, I find two missed calls from Grace and one voice mail. My heart jumps into my throat. I listen to her voice mail as me, Ruthie, Adam, and Freddie walk out to the bike rack.

"Hey," she says. "It's me. Grace. I—I was calling to say hi. Just wanted to catch up is all." She's quiet for a moment. "I miss you." Her voice makes it sound like a question.

My body can't move fast enough. I need to talk to her. Or text her. Or go somewhere I can actually call her in private. My fingers and toes tingle like they've been asleep for days and are just now feeling a rush of blood.

I open up a new text message. **I got your voice mail. I should be home in about ten minutes. Call me whenever you want.** It takes all my self-restraint not to type in all caps littered with emojis and exclamation marks.

"Hey, this morning wasn't so bad, right?" Freddie asks.

"What'd you guys do?" asks Ruthie.

Still staring down at my phone, I say, "We, uh, went to

the Y. Swam a few laps."

Ruth turns to Freddie. "Wait, you actually got her to work out with you?" She whips her head back to me. "You never go running with me in the morning."

"Running is the worst," I tell her. "And it's so hot and sticky and gross. And where are you even running to?"

She shakes her head. "It's better than swimming into a wall."

"I gotta go," I tell them. "I'll see y'all in the morning."

"You don't want to ride home together?" asks Freddie.

"Can't," I say as I'm unlocking my bike.

He nods and waves as I swing my leg over the seat, and he and Adam veer off toward the car wash.

Ruth runs to catch up to me. "I've got the Jeep. I'll give you a ride."

I bite down on my lip, thinking. "Yeah, okay. Thanks."

My bike hangs out the back of the Jeep as Ruth pulls out slowly into the street at the pace of a snail.

I moan. "School zones."

Both of Ruth's hands are perfectly placed on the wheel and her eyes dart across the road, constantly surveying her surroundings. It must be exhausting to be so responsible. "What's the hurry anyway? Today's your off day, isn't it?"

"You're going, like, eight miles an hour. I can bike faster than that."

"You're avoiding the question."

"I want to get home so I can call Grace."

"Ahhhh," she says. "Still pining for summer love?"

"Come on. Don't give me shit about this."

She doesn't say anything.

"You've never even really been in a relationship," I tell her. "Someday you'll see how much love can suck, and you'll feel like crap for giving me a hard time."

She shakes her head. "Doubt it. And I've avoided getting involved with anyone for good reasons."

"Yeah, like what?" I ask.

We reach the end of the school zone, and she hits the gas so hard her tires squeal. I can see that this conversation is pushing Ruth to the edge of her comfort zone. She'll gladly talk about her future or Saul or their rocky relationship with their parents, but love? Not on her agenda. "Well, first off," she says, "my options here are limited."

"I'm hurt," I say.

She rolls her eyes. "Secondly, I have enough to worry about. I don't want anything to distract me from my goals. I'm not getting caught up with someone who might expect me to stay here."

Someone like me or Saul or even Hattie? We will probably live and die here. I tell myself not to take it personally, but the idea that life here—my life—isn't good enough for her still bruises.

We pull up to my house as my dad is unlocking the front door. Today was his early shift. His blue pants are covered in permanent stains, and his freckled arms are slick with sweat.

"Hey, Mr. Leroux!" calls Ruth.

Ruth has a little soft spot for my dad. Maybe because he's pretty much the opposite of her parents.

He turns. "Oh, hey there, girls. Ruth, I guess Saul trusts you quite a bit to let you drive that thing around?"

She smiles. "He's off with some new guy."

Dad nods knowingly. "No greater distraction than love."

"I don't know if I'd call it love," she comments drily.

Dad winks at her and ducks through the door.

"I'm sorry," I say. "I just—maybe it isn't the craziest thing to think Grace and I could figure it out." I shake my head. "I'm not stupid, though. I know she's not moving here or something, but *our options here are limited*," I say, mimicking her.

She scoffs at that. "That's not what I meant."

I sigh. "I know, I know. And hey, we always have Vermont."

A small laugh bubbles up from her chest. "There's always that." She reaches behind me and pulls a paper bag from the backseat. "Give these to Hattie. They're prenatal vitamins. Has she been going to regular doctor visits?"

I stuff the bag into my backpack. "I guess. I don't know?"

"You should know," she says.

"Okay, fine, I'll ask her about it."

"I don't want to be pushy or anything, but she, like, is growing a living thing in her body, and that requires medical attention."

"Aww," I say, "you care!" I reach across the Jeep and hug her tight with her arms pinned to her side.

She groans. "Stoooooop."

"You love it," I tell her.

She growls and bites my arm as a warning.

"Okay, okay," I say, hopping out of the Jeep to grab my bike. "I'll see you tomorrow."

Inside, Dad is sitting in his recliner reading a Clive Cussler paperback. "Hey, sugar," he says as he dog-ears his page and pushes his reading glasses on top of his forehead—a ridiculous pair with multicolored frames he picked up at the dollar store.

As I chug a glass of water, I check my cell to find no new messages from Grace. I sit down on the arm of his chair, and it's then that I realize my legs are a little achy from this morning. Working out is for rich people. I don't have time to feel this exhausted for no reason.

Dad immediately pulls me to him, and I curl into a ball in his lap while he hugs me tight. Being held by my dad is one of the few times when I still feel small. All six-five of him wrapped around my six-three frame reminds me who gave me my height and that maybe life up here isn't always so bad.

"I needed a good Ramona Blue hug," he says.

Sometimes when I don't know how to explain my relationship with my mom, I can only describe it as a void. Whatever she is to me is everything my dad is not, and vice versa.

He lets go, and I plop down on the couch across from him.

"I checked the medicine cabinet and noticed you were running low on your cholesterol meds and a few other things, too," I say. "Have you gone to the pharmacy to refill?"

"Waiting for payday," he answers.

"Well, is that gonna last you until then?" I ask. "I could float you the cash."

He shakes his head. "Who's the parent here, okay?" He smiles. "How was school?"

I shrug. "Went to the Y this morning with Freddie and Agnes."

He laughs a little too loud. "How'd you get conned into that?"

I roll my eyes. "Freddie."

"He's a good man. Glad you've got a real friend."

"I had friends before Freddie, Dad."

"Hattie's your sister," he says. "And Saul is, well, Saul."

Saul is Saul. He is the sun, and the rest of us are just orbiting around him. He doesn't have friends. He has an audience. "I have Ruth."

He laughs. "Ruth barely likes you."

I pelt him in the arm with the TV remote. "Ruthie barely likes anyone—except you."

"Jeez! That's gonna bruise." He grins. "Go do your homework or something like that."

I stand and pull my backpack up by the strap. "Don't read too many books. They turn your brain to mush."

I grab half a box of Triscuits for dinner and head to my room. We never really have family dinner. Since all of us work in the restaurant industry, preparing and serving other people's food, none of us is too quick to volunteer homemade meals.

I spread out my homework across my unmade bed like I might actually do something besides wait for Grace to call me back.

My phone vibrates and my whole body twists into a knot of tension. It's only a text from Freddie, asking where I ran off to so fast, but I'm too anxious to respond.

And then my phone really rings. It's Grace. I force myself to let the phone ring three times before I pick it up. I take a deep breath, and even though my door is shut, I whisper because nothing about our walls is soundproof. "Hello?"

She sighs into the receiver. "Hey, you."

It's melodramatic, I know, but I could cry. Instead, I try my best for nonchalance. "What's going on?"

"Nothing, really. Everyone's at my brother's soccer game."

"Why aren't you?"

"I stayed home from school, so now my mom won't let me leave the house for the rest of the day. 'On principle,' she says."

I nod, even though she can't see me. "Are you sick?" I ask with real concern.

For a moment, all I hear are her steady breaths. "Yes. No."

There's this wall between us that wasn't there before. I can feel it. And on the other side of the wall is some piece of her life that she doesn't know how to talk to me about. "Hey," I say. "You can talk to me. Even if it's about other people."

It'll hurt, I know, to hear about her life without me. Her friends. Her more than friends. But I'd rather her be transparent with me than to be left out of any corner of her world.

"It's Andrew," she says.

"So . . . I guess y'all are still together?"

She's quiet for a second. "Well, yeah. He's my boyfriend."

My mouth goes dry. I don't hate straight people, I swear. But the word *boyfriend*. I hate it. Especially coming out of Grace's mouth. It makes my toes curl. "I thought you were going to break up with him," I say, but it's more of an accusation.

"I was. I am."

I'm angry. At the both of us. Because somehow I had tricked myself into believing that he didn't mean anything to her. That what we were doing wasn't cheating.

"You don't get it," she says.

I don't respond, because she's probably right. I don't know what it's like to live a double life.

"I'm back here," she says. "And you're not, and now I can't remember why I was supposed to break up with him. I cheated on him. But I still like being around him."

I'm here. And you're not. It's all I can hear. Anxiety fills my lungs. And maybe she cheated on him this summer, but I feel like I've been cheated on, too. "Shouldn't you at least tell him about us?" It's hard not to feel like she's stomping through the memory of us with a giant eraser, removing any evidence of me.

She shrugs with her voice. It's this sound I can't explain. "We only have our senior year left. It feels silly to ruin it now. He's going to Iowa anyway. And—"

"I know how you feel about long-distance." I've felt lots of things about Grace. Sadness. Frustration. Confusion. But now I'm just pissed.

"Yeah."

I expect for the conversation to be over, but it's not. There's a moment or two of weighted silence before Grace says, "Oh my God. My mom started subbing at my school."

I'm both annoyed and relieved by the change in subject. I breathe in through my nose and out through my mouth a few times. I have to make a decision right now. I have to decide if I'm going to hold on to this anger, which could downright ruin my already fragile relationship with Grace, or if I'm going to stifle my emotions in favor of any future we might have.

"Awww," I finally say, "your mom's not so bad."

She laughs into the receiver. "No. This is bad."

I listen as she tells me all about how embarrassing her mom is and how she's only doing this because it's Grace's last year of high school and she's feeling sentimental. Her mom cries every time she sees her in the hallways and always checks in with all her teachers. I tell Grace about swimming at the Y and Freddie and how I knew him and Agnes when I was a kid. She asks lots of questions about

Freddie. She has no reason to be jealous, but the idea that she might be satisfies me a little too much.

We talk late into the night, taking breaks for dinner and for Grace to catch up with her family to get the play-by-play of the soccer game. When Hattie and Tyler finally come home, they head straight for Hattie's room. I narrate their actions and moans for Grace as we giggle back and forth, and I try not to gag. It's well past one in the morning when our conversation dissolves into heavy, sleepy breaths.

Hattie tiptoes into my room and looks at me with pleading eyes as she crawls into my bed, sighing into the cool sheets.

I flip my bedside lamp off and creep out to the kitchen for a glass of water as I whisper, "We should probably hang up."

Grace groans into the receiver. "What are you doing right this moment?"

I grin and sink into the couch. "Standing in my kitchen. Maybe turning on some TV."

"What would you even watch right now?" She yawns, and then adds, "All that's on is soft-core porn and infomercials."

"Hey, both of those things have the potential to be interesting." I reach for the remote and hit the power button. "And what do you know about soft-core porn?"

She laughs.

"Where are you?" I ask.

"In my house."

"Where in your house?"

"In my dad's den." Her voice sounds like a cat's purr. "Do you want to know what I'm wearing, too?"

Her words suck the air out of my lungs. "The answer to that is always yes, but you should go to bed."

She laughs. "I miss talking to you, but I miss other things, too."

My brain knows exactly what she means by other things. My lower abdomen aches like an unsatisfied itch. "Me too."

Grace wasn't the first girl I had sex with. That honor goes to Samantha Alice Jones, who I always called by her full name because it sounded so good all together. She was an incoming freshman volleyball player at Mississippi State and was down here at a camp training with her team. We met at Boucher's the summer before tenth grade. She was white with a port-wine stain on her shoulder, wore her curly hair in two braids, and snorted when she laughed. She was from Kansas and told me she was bi.

On the other line, Grace's breathing gets heavier, like she's fighting to stay awake. "Shit," she says. "I really should go to bed."

"You hang up first," I tell her.

"No, you," she says.

I sigh into the receiver and she giggles. "On the count of three," I say.

In bed, when I close my eyes, I see Grace. I see her in the moonlight of her bedroom at the vacation rental. The shadows drape across her bare skin like a robe.

Every inch of my body is on fire just thinking about it.

My eyes spring open as Hattie flips over on her back beside me. I try to remember what it felt like to have privacy.

Quietly, I tiptoe to the bathroom, which is the only place in my entire house where I can be alone with my memories of nights spent with Grace.

ELEVEN

In the morning, I go with Freddie and Agnes to the Y to swim laps again.

I feel like I'm starting to get the hang of this, and I sort of love the idea of having my own lane for this slice of time a couple of days a week. It's my own private world, and I don't have to worry about how good Freddie is or if Agnes is watching or if Hattie is doing something stupid or if I can pick up any extra hours at work. All I have to do is stay in my own lane.

As I'm hoisting myself out of the pool, Freddie says, "Hey, wait up. Let's race just once. Whatever stroke you want there and back."

"I thought you were only supposed to be racing against yourself," I tease.

"Humor me."

I shake my head and say, "Fine, but there's not going to be much of a competition."

The two of us position ourselves on the blocks while Agnes heads to the locker rooms.

Freddie counts us off. "On your marks, get set, GO!"

Again, my dive is a belly flop. This time I try the butterfly stroke, letting my upper body propel me forward while my legs work in unison like a mermaid's fin. Or at least that's what I'm going for. I probably look like I'm drowning and break-dancing at the same time.

After the second lap, my body slams into the wall like when you're roller-skating and you don't know how to stop. Freddie is waiting for me in the neighboring lane.

"I was wondering when you'd make it back," he says.

"Shut up," I spit, wanting to say much more, but unable to because my lungs are on fire.

Freddie pulls himself out of the pool. "Someone's a sore loser."

Between breaths, I say, "Someone's a shitty winner."

He holds an arm out for me, and I begrudgingly take it. "Come on," he says. "Let me have this. Besides, after all those wasted years of training, you gotta admit it'd be pretty embarrassing if you kicked my ass."

I ignore his hand and get out of the water on my own, just barely, though. I've got to admit: even I'm surprised by the adrenaline that's coursing through my veins. "Go on," I tell him. "I need to catch my breath."

As he leaves for the locker rooms, I sit down on the block and pull my goggles off my head. I cringe as the elastic pulls at my wet hair. I suck at this. Freddie beat me fair and square and by a lot. I think that's supposed to make me miserable, but it doesn't and I'm trying to figure out what exactly that means.

Finally I stand up to leave the pool. The woman in the black Speedo I saw last time is sitting in the same spot on the bleachers. Her short, spiky hair seems to match her prickly persona.

As I pass her, she doesn't even bother turning to me when she says, "Gotta learn pacing. You burn out too fast. Anyone can sprint. Stamina is something you have to earn."

I stop. "I'm not trying to be, like, a swimmer or anything."

She turns to me. "Oh, you're a swimmer. You either are or you aren't. And you are. You're just not any good yet."

I shake my head and jog down the hallway to the locker rooms. I can swim. Of course I can. The ocean is my backyard. But I'm no stranger to adults telling me how I should use my body. With my height, it's nonstop questions about basketball or volleyball or whatever other sports where my stature might serve as a benefit. But sports, and any other extracurricular, have always felt like a waste of time. If it's not something I'm going to be paid for, I don't really have the time to waste. Or the energy to invest.

Back at Agnes's place, Freddie whips together a frittata with cheese, mushrooms, spinach, and sun-dried tomatoes. The last three ingredients are the type of things I would never eat individually, but somehow Freddie has the ability to make them taste good. And of course, a plain sunny-side-up egg for Bart.

"Hey, Gram?" he says once we're all seated. "This week's Viv's birthday, and I was thinking I could drive back on Friday after school for her party."

Agnes doesn't look up from her plate. "And what about your shift at the car wash?"

Freddie looks to Bart, who shakes his head and concentrates on his eggs. "I thought maybe I could call in this one time. Or maybe Adam will cover for me."

Agnes makes a *tsk* noise with her tongue. "You know how I feel about commitments."

"Come on, Gram," says Freddie, resorting to that boyish tone I recognize from when we were kids. It's the same charm he used to help me get Tyler's cake—and he clearly knows how to wield it to get what he wants. "You know leaving Viv wasn't easy."

Agnes's shoulders sink, and I see the weight of responsibility she carries and how well she understands the sacrifice that moving here was for Freddie. "Okay," she relents. "But only if this one"—she motions to me—"agrees to go with you. I don't like the idea of you making that trip by yourself."

Freddie turns to me.

I take a moment too long to swallow my mouthful of frittata. "I'll—uh, have to see if I can get someone to cover my route on Saturday morning."

Agnes doesn't look up. "My kind of girl."

I shrug in Freddie's direction, but his attention is in a far-off place outside this house. His legs bounce so aggressively that Agnes reaches under the table and pats his knee until he stops.

We ride our bikes to school, the humidity so thick my

hair doesn't even begin to dry until third period, which is the only class Freddie and I share. I'm dozing in and out of Ms. Pak's economics lesson when Adam, who sits behind me, taps my shoulder. He reaches down low and shoves a note into my dangling hand. I glance back to get a read on him, but it's Freddie, who sits two desks behind him, who I find winking at me.

In my lap, hands positioned underneath my desk, I unfold the full piece of notebook paper that's been folded into a sad piece of origami.

In surprisingly beautiful handwriting, the top of the page reads:

REASONS TO GO WITH ME TO BATON ROUGE

1. BEEF JERKY, AND NOT THE SHITTY KIND. I KNOW THE BEST GAS STATION IN LOUISIANA, WHERE THEY MAKE THEIR OWN JERKY. IT'S A SPIRITUAL EXPERIENCE.
2. YOU GET TO LEAVE THE COAST.
3. HAVE YOU EVER EVEN LEFT THE COAST?
4. I'LL LET YOU DRIVE THE CADDY.
5. YOU CAN MEET VIV. YOU GUYS WILL LOVE EACH OTHER!
6. AND THE REST OF MY SWIM TEAM FROM BACK HOME.
7. HOT GIRLS. I KNOW LOTS OF THEM.
8. I WILL PAY FOR ALL YOUR MEALS.
9. YOU'RE A GOOD FRIEND.

I grin and try to fold the paper back the same way it was given to me, but give up and stuff it in my pocket. Under the cover of my desk, I text Charlie about my paper route this weekend to see if anyone can cover.

A few seconds later, he responds. **I'll check with my little bro**, he says.

When the bell rings, Freddie follows close on my heels with Adam behind. "Well?"

"I'm working on it," I say.

He nods and bounces on his toes a little.

"Working on what?" asks Adam. "Your strokes?"

"Ugh." Freddie shoves him.

Adam turns to him innocently. "What? I know you've been getting up early to stroke it."

"Swim strokes," Freddie says. "Swim strokes, you perv."

I turn to Adam, grinning. "Nope. He got a membership at the YMCA to practice his strokes. The *M* stands for masturbation, obviously."

"You're both filthy human beings," says Freddie. "Oh, wait. Adam, you think you could cover my shift this Saturday?"

Adam groans, his head rolling to the side.

Freddie grips his shoulder. "Come on, man."

"My mom's gonna make me cover your shift either way." Adam turns to head to his next class. "You owe me!"

Still following me, Freddie asks, "So did my list sway you?"

I stop and turn to him. "Your next class is on the other side of the building. And I will let you know as soon as I know. Chill out, okay?"

He stomps off like a toddler, but in a half-joking way.

"What was that all about?" asks Ruth as she emerges

from a neighboring hallway.

I turn to follow her, still laughing at Freddie. "Cute boy not getting his way."

"He knows you're not exactly his target audience, right?"

I shrug. "Cute is cute."

Her upper lip curls. "Yeah. Nope."

After school Freddie is waiting for me at the bike rack. I hand him my phone with my text message exchange with Charlie open for him to read.

"Enjoy your weekend?" It takes him a moment. "Enjoy your weekend! YES!"

He jumps up and down and yanks me off my feet as he spins me around in a circle. "I swear to Christ, Ramona, you're my best friend." When he sets me back down, he pulls my fist into the air as he hums "We Are the Champions."

I know he's probably exaggerating, but the idea that I'm someone's best friend fills my rib cage with summer.

TWELVE

If you head straight west, Baton Rouge is technically a two-hour drive from Eulogy, but we're making a little bit of a detour.

See, I told Freddie I could go with him out of town before I gave him my one and only condition: that we take Grace with us.

Freddie agreed without much hesitation—maybe because he was too high on the idea of seeing Viv or maybe it was he didn't think Grace would actually say yes.

But she did.

That night when I got home and checked my phone, there was a partially clothed picture of Grace waiting for me, with a follow-up text asking me to delete the message after I opened it.

Now, listen, everyone who pretends they don't send nudes or partial nudes are either celibate, still use flip phones, or lying. But it was the first time Grace had ever sent me anything like this. After all, we were together all summer, so there was really no need then.

I took a minute to devour the picture. She stood in front of her mirror with one arm covering her chest and the other holding her cell phone. Tiny gray shorts were slung low on her hips. Her black bob has grown out since I last saw her, and mostly conceals her face. To anyone else, she might be unrecognizable. It was sort of innocent, but just the sight of her made me think I could walk to her house all the way up in Picayune if I had to.

I'm not this sex-crazed maniac or anything, but I'm a human being. I think about sex. Girls think about sex. Sometimes a lot. I hate this idea that boys are thinking about sex nonstop and girls are thinking about—what? Stationery and garden gnomes? No.

The second I'd memorized every detail of the picture, I called Grace. I heard her pick up the phone, and before she even said hello, I said, "Are you trying to kill me?"

She laughed. "I told you I miss you."

"What if I said you could see me sooner than you think?"

"What do you mean?"

"I'm going to be driving through Picayune on my way to Baton Rouge. Maybe you could join me? Like, a weekend getaway?"

"I don't know," she said, too quickly. "My parents probably wouldn't be okay with that, and I have things going on. . . . I have stuff I probably shouldn't miss."

"Can't we at least try asking your parents?" I hated that I sounded desperate.

She was quiet for so long I almost checked to see if we'd

lost the connection. "Can't hurt, I guess," she finally said.

It took some convincing, and me talking to Grace's parents on the phone, and then my dad talking to Grace's parents on the phone, but she said yes.

And that is why I am sitting in the front seat of Agnes's Cadillac, begging Freddie to drive faster.

Freddie is in charge of the music, and his preferences are rap and folksy white guys with acoustic guitars. Two polarizing options, if you ask me. The stereo is so loud; I have to keep my window down to drown it out a little bit.

The road winds through swampy forest that crawls right up to the edge of the pavement on either side. It's a scene I'm so accustomed to, but I wonder what it must be like to see something like mountains or giant redwoods every day. At what point does another's person's extraordinary become your ordinary?

Grace's house isn't as grand as I'd decided it would be. It's nice, though. The grass is cut so evenly it looks like someone trimmed it with scissors. She lives on one of those cookie-cutter streets where there are only two or three types of homes, but they all stand apart in a slight way with different colors of paint and bricks.

Freddie stands a few feet behind me as I ring the bell.

Grace's mom answers almost immediately. She rubs her soapy hands down the front of her apron. "Oh, sweet Ramona! Your hair is almost brighter than I remember. We just finished up dinner. I wanted to wait for y'all, but Grace said you wouldn't have time."

I smile. "Good to see you, Mrs. Scott. This is my friend

Freddie." I motion him forward. "We've known each other since we were kids."

"Oh, how nice!" she says.

Grace jogs down the stairs behind Mrs. Scott, and I try not to stare at how shiny and smooth her legs are. Her raven-colored hair bounces around her shoulders, and it feels like that moment when you're seeing a movie in 3D and you put your glasses on for the first time, and the screen jumps right out at you. That's what's happening in this exact moment. Life is jumping right out at me.

She runs past her mom and throws her arms around my neck. "I missed you!"

"Me too," I say, hugging her back and trying so hard to look normal. Like two girls who are friends and nothing more.

She turns back to her mom and gives her a kiss on the cheek.

"You've got that cash I left for you? And all the emergency numbers?"

Grace nods. "Yes, ma'am."

As I introduce her and Freddie, I can hear words coming out of my mouth, but my whole body feels like it's lit up in bright neon and buzzing with electricity like one of those beer signs.

We walk down to where the Cadillac is parked on the curb. "Take the front seat," I tell her.

"No, no. All yours," she says as she slides into the back.

"Or you guys could both sit in the back," says Freddie. "I'll play chauffeur."

I can't tell if he's kidding, but his offer is tempting.

Grace laughs. "No, that's ridiculous."

As we drive past the *THANKS FOR VISITING* sign of her perfect little town, she leans forward and begins to braid random pieces of my hair. My eyes catch hers in the rearview mirror, and she kisses my shoulder blade.

This is too good to be true. This is my extraordinary and I can't ever imagine it being ordinary.

Freddie side-eyes me, but I can't stop smiling. I can feel the nerves vibrating off him as we drive closer and closer to Viv's.

We cross the state line into Louisiana, and there's no real change in scenery. Louisiana's roads are as shitty as Mississippi's.

Freddie's playlist cycles through twice, and I have to turn around every few minutes to smile at Grace, because I can't believe she's right here behind me. I reach back in the crevice between my seat and the door and hold my hand out. It takes a minute, but she reaches forward and squeezes my fingers.

As we veer off the highway and into the suburbs, I quickly realize that Vivienne's house is much more like what I expected Grace's to be. It's a two-story house that looks more like a three-story. The tall windows stretch from the ground floor all the way to the ceiling of the second floor, with a huge chandelier sending shards of glittering light out into the street. I swallow back any doubt about my clothes or my shoes or not belonging in a neighborhood this nice.

By the looks of things, Vivienne's parents are either out of town or in a coma, because the place is dripping with teens under the influence of the substance of their choice. But since her house is tucked far into a cul-de-sac, the noise isn't nearly as bad as you'd expect. Still, it's a noise complaint waiting to happen.

Freddie parks the car down at the bottom of the hill and turns to me. "I look okay, right?" He wears tight jeans that are shredded along the knee and rolled at the bottom, with a fitted blue-and-white-striped T-shirt and high-tops. He looks like a boy who can dress himself, which is a lot more than most boys I know can say for themselves.

"You look great," I say. "You remembered her present, right?"

He nods. Freddie spent what was probably three weeks' worth of sign spinning on expensive noise-canceling head-phones for Viv when she travels on the bus to swim meets.

Grace and I follow two steps behind him. As we enter the house, it's clear that Viv and Freddie have bonded over music.

Freddie turns to us. "I'm gonna go find her," he yells over the speakers.

"Well, we should say hi, too," I say. "At least wish her happy birthday?"

Grace nods. "Yeah, then we'll let you guys catch up."

He gives us a sharp nod. A few people stop him, giving him drunken hugs. Standing in the foyer is a light-skinned brown girl in a flowing coral-colored maxi dress with a matching hijab loosely wrapped around her hair.

"Hey! Lydia!" Freddie calls to her.

Her face lights up with surprise. "Oh my God! I—"

He interrupts her. "You look great. And I heard about Ohio State! That's huge. Congrats!"

"Thanks, dude. Yeah, I don't know. The scholarship's pretty small, so I'm hoping for an academic scholarship and maybe some grant money."

"You gotta take it," he says. "Too good of an opportunity."

"We'll see." She shrugs and peers past him at Grace and me.

"Oh!" Freddie smacks his head. "I'm sorry. This is my really good friend Ramona, and her girlfriend, Grace."

Well, not officially my girlfriend. Yet. I reach for Grace's hand, but she's taken a step back with her arms crossed over her chest. She smiles tightly and offers a short wave.

Don't overthink this, I tell myself. *Don't overthink this.*

Lydia nods. "Awesome. I like the hair," she says to me.

"Thanks."

"So you've been staying in shape?" Lydia asks Freddie.

"Um, well, yeah, I've been doing some—"

"Freddie?" calls a voice from above. "What are you doing here?"

A tall dark-skinned black girl in a short aqua dress rushes down the stairs wearing three-inch heels. She somehow manages to not trip *and* look graceful.

"Viv," says Freddie, turning his back to the rest of us. "Happy birthday."

I watch Vivienne's expression as she tries to piece something together. "I thought you weren't coming. I told you not to come."

Oh God. My stomach plummets.

Grace reaches for my hand and squeezes tight.

The moment feels so uncomfortable I can hardly look at Freddie. But at the same time I'm annoyed that he didn't prepare me for this.

He grins, but I can see his expression faltering. "I wanted to surprise you," says Freddie. "I couldn't miss your eighteenth birthday. Come on, babe." A nervous laugh comes out.

His back is still to us, so I can't read his expression, but I don't think this is how he expected the night to go. Why is it so much more painful to watch other people embarrass themselves?

"Hey, Freddie," I say, gently touching his shoulder. "I think we're going to grab a drink."

Something on Vivienne's face snaps, like she's realized there are other people here. "Hi," she says with a forced smile.

Freddie sputters for a moment before awkwardly introducing Grace and me.

"Happy birthday," Grace offers.

"I guess we'll let y'all catch up," I say.

"I think that might be good," says Vivienne, her gaze

trained on Freddie.

I squeeze Freddie's shoulder before leaving him there with her. If there were a birthday cake at this party, I'd steal all of Vivienne's wishes and give them to Freddie. I think he's going to need them.

THIRTEEN

We weave in and out of rooms, searching for a corner to claim. Everyone in the living room is grinding their baby-makers together, while the dining room is reserved for drinking games, and all the people on the patio are either passing around blunts or gathering around tall bongs.

I reach for Grace's hand as we head into the kitchen, but her fingers slip straight through mine. Ever since we moved past the foyer, I've felt her pulling away from me. I know she's shy and isn't one for crowds. But no one knows us here. We're strangers. So I can only assume this has nothing to do with her being shy.

The counters are lined with coolers of beer and bottles of liquor. I grab us each a beer and we head out past the patio to the pool, where couples are gathering on lawn chairs. It seems to be the most chill place to hang out, with some people making out and others just talking.

We sit together on the edge of the pool, and Grace opens her purse to show me tons of mini bottles of horrible-flavored liquors. "My dad used to travel for work," she says. "And he always saved the mini liquor bottles from the hotels."

"Whoa." I didn't see Grace drink at all over the summer. Not even once.

She shrugs. "A little liquid courage, I guess."

"I think I'll stick to beer," I tell her.

"More for me." She opens one of her mini bottles and downs it in two shots.

The moonlight highlights her cheekbones and the tip of her narrow nose. In another world, this could be our life. Both of us in the same town, being together whenever we want.

She reaches for another mini bottle. "Freddie seems nice."

I let my hand fall to her thigh, running my fingers up her leg as I trace constellations onto her skin. "He's a good guy."

She finishes off her second bottle in two gulps.

"Maybe take it easy on the booze, ya know?"

She faces me, clearly annoyed. "It's a party, isn't it?"

"You're right," I say. I don't want to argue about something stupid, so instead I lean into her and push the hair off her neck before gently kissing the soft spot behind her ear. She turns to me and laces her fingers through my hair.

"I missed your hair." She closes her eyes and lets it tickle her nose. "You're impossible to forget. Do you know that? I almost hate you for it."

And then I kiss her before she can say another word.

"I'm still with him," she says, her lips moving against mine.

"I don't care," I lie.

She responds, parting my lips with hers and not being at all shy with her tongue.

She is here. She's here with me. In my arms. Not his.

Each of our hands roams, pressing hard against the other's skin, as if the clothing separating us might somehow dissolve with every—

Grace pulls back, out of breath.

"Andrew," she breathes. "I can't keep hurting him. I can't lie to him like this."

"What about me?" I ask. I don't mean to say it out loud, but I do. "Have you ever thought that you're hurting me as much as you're hurting him? And did you ever think that maybe it's yourself you're lying to?"

But she doesn't hear me. She shakes her head vigorously and stands up, pulling her feet out of the pool. "I knew I shouldn't have come here this weekend." She walks off, leaving wet footprints on the concrete.

"Grace! Wait!"

A pothead in a Hawaiian shirt mimics me. "Grace! Wait!"

"Fuck off!" I shout.

I take my feet out of the water and grab her purse, flip-flops, and my boots. Dodging in and out of the crowd, I follow her path to the side of the house and through the back gate.

And there she is. Grace sits on the curb by the mailbox. I guess she realized she could only get so far without shoes and a phone.

She stands, steadying herself on the mailbox. "You can't kiss me like that," she says. "In front of people."

I drop our shoes and her purse in the grass. "Grace, no one even knows you here. And it's not like I have anything to hide," I spit out. "What's the big deal?"

"I don't know how to make this any more obvious for you!" Her voice grows louder with each syllable.

There are two sides to every story and two versions of every person. The version of Grace speaking now is the doubter. She's the same person who wouldn't come out to her parents and would only hold my hand if no one was looking.

She shakes her head back and forth, and her lower lip trembles. "Sometimes I feel like you're trying to make me into this person—this person that I'm not. You keep talking about me being in the closet like it's some sin to not know who I am yet! I'm just as confused about Andrew as I am about you." She pauses. "I'm going through something here, Ramona, and that doesn't mean I'm hiding. It means I'm learning, and I get to do that, don't I?"

I take a step back instinctively. I've always known that whatever we were, it wasn't perfect and it could never quite be defined. But I feel . . . led on. Her phone calls. Her texts. All she had to do was cut me off. Let our physical distance fade into emotional distance.

Red, searing anger settles in my chest. "Listen," I say

finally, my words clipped. "I'm not making you do any-thing or be anyone. It's not like I forced you to make out with me back there."

She plucks her purse up off the grass and clumsily puts her flip-flops back on. I can see the two mini bottles of liquor taking an effect now. "It's all black and white for you. I'm gay or I'm not. I'm with you or I'm not. That's not real, Ramona. Real life is messy and complicated. I have a whole world—an entire existence—that you're not a part of."

I cross my arms over my chest. "Well, I'm sorry if I've complicated things for you."

"I can't give you what you want." Her voice is firm and completely sober for a moment.

I shake my head furiously. "Maybe I tried to make us something more, okay?" My voice is desperate in a way I barely recognize. "I'll admit that. But it wasn't just me in this, okay, Grace?" There are only so many more words I can get out without breaking down. "Every . . . every time I kissed you, you kissed me back."

"I liked kissing you!" she shouts, reminding me that she's had too much to drink, too quickly. "It was fun. But Christ, Ramona, the summer is over. Maybe in your world summer lasts forever, but not for me. You know, it's like you get to live in that little town and work your little jobs and never really grow up. You don't have to face the future in the same way I do." She turns and stomps down to the bottom of the hill.

"My *little* town? My *little* jobs?" I shout at her, but she doesn't turn around. She leaves me up here to bleed out.

I lie down in the soft grass of a yard belonging to a girl I've just met as my whole body fluctuates between rage and despair, skipping up and down like a heart monitor.

After a few moments, I hear steps in the grass and Freddie plops down next to me.

"Hey, where's Viv?"

"Inside," he says as he rips up little fistfuls of grass.

"How'd she like her present?"

"She liked it." He sighs. "But she didn't want to keep it."

"That sucks."

He lies down next to me. "She thinks we should just be friends. And according to her, friends don't give each other outrageously expensive headphones."

"Oh." I loop my arm through his. "I'm so sorry, Freddie."

"Everyone else saw it coming. In fact, I saw everyone watch it coming. Even Gram said that maybe we should take a break. See where things are after graduation. And it's not like Viv didn't give me plenty of hints. I didn't want to see it, so I ignored it."

"I think I know how you feel," I tell him.

"Can I tell you something?" he asks. "Something I didn't tell anyone else. Well, not any of my friends."

"Of course."

"Gram gave me the option of us waiting to move until after I graduated."

"Wait." I try not to sound as shocked as I am, but based

on everything I know about Freddie, I just can't fathom this. "Why wouldn't you just tell her you wanted to wait?"

"For selfish, stupid reasons," he says. "I was tired of watching everyone succeed without me. Blame it on ego. I thought whatever I had with Viv was strong enough to survive a year spent a few hours apart. We could pick up right where we left off in college. Maybe I'd find something new to be good at. Something that could make me extraordinary like swimming does for her and our other friends."

"Wow." I don't even know what to say.

"What about you?" he asks. "Where's Grace?"

"It's over." The words fall out of my mouth like two drops in a bucket. "Is it bad that I was hoping it'd work out for you and Viv, because if it worked out for y'all it might work out for me and Grace?"

"If it is, I'm guilty of the same." He shakes his head. "The universe is such an asshole. Or maybe we just have really shitty luck." After a minute, he says, "I'm sorry. I'm sorry if bringing you both here triggered it in some way."

"Was bound to happen," I tell him. "I guess it was good to get it over with at least."

"Freddie?"

We both sit up and turn around.

Viv hovers behind us, a few feet away. "You can still stay here tonight if you want." She looks at me and smiles. "And your friends, too."

He looks to me briefly. "Nah. We better not."

"Um." I shouldn't interject myself, but if we don't stay

here, where are we going to go?

She nods quietly. "Be careful."

As she walks back inside, and only loud enough for me to hear, Freddie mumbles, "Happy birthday."

We walk to the car in silence. I glance at the time on my phone. It's past one in the morning and Freddie and I are both exhausted. Driving home tonight is not in the cards—not to mention that Agnes would kill Freddie for driving home so late. I'm trying to map out in my head what we'll do for the night. Maybe we can find a cheap hotel or hang out in a diner.

Grace is waiting for us.

Freddie sees her sitting on the curb beside the car with half the contents of her purse spilled out on the pavement, including ChapStick, tampons, her phone, loose dollar bills, and a handful of emptied mini liquor bottles. He turns to me. "I guess neither of our nights went as planned."

I walk around to the front seat and slam the door shut behind me.

"Grace, we gotta get you in the car," I hear Freddie say.

I watch in the side mirror as she puts her purse back together one piece at a time. He reaches down to help her up. The minute he closes the back door behind her, she's snoring.

Freddie sighs and leans his head against the steering wheel after pulling his door shut.

"Thanks for that," I whisper.

"Yup."

"Um, I hate to bring this up, but if we're not staying with Viv, where are we staying?"

"Well, I hadn't really gotten that far." He sits up and reaches for his wallet in his back pocket. After flipping through his cash, he says, "I've got sixty bucks and Gram's emergency credit card. Which I'd rather not use."

I open the center console, where I'd stowed away my wallet, which is actually just a Lisa Frank pencil bag. "I've got eighty." Eighty dollars that I didn't intend to spend and only brought for serious emergencies. I don't think Freddie understands what a sacrifice it is for me to fork over this wad of cash, but I don't think I have much of a choice at this point. Between hotel, food, and gas, what we have won't get us far.

Vacancies aren't easy to come by on a Friday night. We end up at a motel in a room with two double beds and a broken hot-pink Jacuzzi. Like, it's just sitting there in the middle of the room next to the television, which might be older than me and Freddie combined.

Freddie helps Grace into the room and forces her to drink an entire bottle of water before going to bed, while I bring our bags in.

She plops back on the bed. "You're cute," she says to Freddie, in between sips. "Can I tell you something?"

"Do what you gotta do," Freddie says as he helps her pull the blankets back.

"I've never dated a black guy. Does that make me racist?"

Freddie looks at me, and I shrug and shake my head. He laughs, because I think it's all he can do, but I can see the clear discomfort in the way his posture goes rigid. "Not last I checked."

It's a gross thing to say, and I would tell her so if I thought she would even remember it in the morning, but instead I roll my eyes in Freddie's direction.

His lips spread into a thin smile.

"It's not that I wouldn't," Grace says. "Just that the opportunity never presented itself."

"Okay," he says. "Bedtime."

Grace spreads out like a starfish and gets as far as unbuttoning her shorts before passing out again. Freddie turns her on her side, and when he sees my questioning look, he explains, "Don't want her to choke on her own puke or something."

"Sure, don't want that," I murmur sarcastically as I lock the door—three deadbolts and a chain.

"I can sleep in the Jacuzzi," he volunteers.

"That thing looks like a giant bowl of herpes." I shake my head. "Besides, if I'm getting bedbugs, so are you."

He cracks a smile, but just for a second.

I take the bathroom first, but the grimy floors and rusting sink have me moving quicker than normal. I hover above the toilet to pee and am careful not to swallow any water when I brush my teeth. I bet people might walk into my trailer and be as grossed out as I am by this hotel room, but I guess at home at least I know whose butt has been where. If anything, this gross room is a distraction from the elephant in the room. The very drunk elephant.

While Freddie takes his turn in the bathroom, I slip into a pair of old boxer shorts and one of Dad's old undershirts. I take one last look at Grace and pull the blanket at the foot of her bed up to her chest.

This is not how I expected tonight to go. Every time I close my eyes, all I see is Grace leaving me there at that pool. Her voice rings in my ears, telling me I'm just a phase. I try to block it all out, but even when I force my head to bite back the memories of tonight, I can hear her breathing. Right here. Less than three feet away from me. I force myself to breathe through the tears.

By the time Freddie comes out, I've turned off all the lights and have decided to play Russian roulette with the bedbugs by sleeping underneath the covers.

"Fuck," whispers Freddie as he stubs his toe on the corner of the bed.

"Are you okay?" I whisper back. "Sorry, I should have waited to turn the lights off."

"It's fine."

"Follow my voice."

His silhouette shuffles along the side of the bed, careful of his other nine toes. "I can sleep on top of the blankets if you want."

"Scared you're gonna get me pregnant or something? Come on. Get in."

He does, and I immediately realize how small a double

bed actually is. And how weird it is to sleep next to some-one with hairy legs.

"I have to tell you something," I say.

"Okay." His voice is slow with hesitation.

"I've never dated a black guy either."

"Har, har," he says.

"I'm sorry about tonight," I tell him.

His breath is warm and minty. "Yeah, I guess we both had high hopes."

I feel tears rolling down my face and onto the pillow. But it's so dark that I don't care, and I hope that Freddie feels like he can cry, too. I can feel the pain we both share like a cloud hovering over us.

I wonder, for a moment, what it would be like if we could take these feelings we have for other people and pour them into each other, like that could in some way fill the empty space eating the both of us up. It's not that easy, though.

It's in that moment, in that moldy, decrepit motel room, that I realize how much we have in common. We are both so much in love . . . or lust or infatuation—whatever you want to call it. And it doesn't matter how much either of us wants to make it work. We have to be wanted back, because this shit is a two-way street.

Sleeping in the same room with Grace but not in the same bed is a stark realization. It's like hearing some-one has passed away, but not being able to believe it until you see their body for yourself. This is the moment when I know once and for all that I'm searching for something—something I can't even articulate. The only thing I can say without a doubt is that whatever I need, it's nothing Grace Scott can give me.

I fall asleep with my knees tucked into my chest and Freddie only inches away.

FOURTEEN

In the morning it's not an alarm that wakes me, but the sound of Grace puking.

Freddie and I both stay there in bed for a moment before he says, "You think she's okay?"

I groan. "I'll check on her." I get out of bed and knock on the bathroom door. "Grace, you okay?"

"I need to go home." I hear her cough and spit into the toilet. "Please just get me home."

I nod. My mouth is too dry to talk and my eyes are swollen from crying. For a moment, I have to force myself through the horrible ritual of remembering what happened last night.

We get ready quickly and in silence. Without me asking, Freddie turns around so that I can slip my shorts on. When Grace comes out, she's wearing her huge sunglasses, but they can't hide her stringy hair or chalk-like complexion.

The drive back to Picayune, Mississippi, is only an hour and a half, but the stale silence in the car makes me feel like our travel time has been doubled. When we finally do drop Grace off, I get out to help with her bag in the trunk.

"Thanks," she says as I hand it to her.

I don't look up to meet her gaze. "Yeah."

Her mom swings the front door open. "Morning, girls! Ramona, would you and your friend like to come in for breakfast?"

I clear my throat and put on a smile so painful it makes my jaw ache. "No, ma'am. We oughta head home!"

"Next time!" she calls. "Y'all have a safe drive home."

I wave as she steps back inside, leaving the door open for Grace.

I don't know what to say to her. *Bye? See you never? Thanks for breaking my heart?* But Grace speaks first.

"I know we . . . I was drunk last night." She takes a deep breath and then exhales harshly. "But sometimes the truth comes out, even if it's not the right time. I'm sorry. I wish it hadn't ended this way. Take care of yourself, Ramona."

Any lingering hope I'd had of last night being a drunken mistake evaporates.

I watch her walk to the front door, her purse in one hand and her flip-flops in the other, and I wonder if this is the last time I'll ever see her.

"You want me to wait until she gets in?" Freddie asks gently.

I shake my head. I don't want to start crying again.

On the way home, we share war stories. I tell Freddie about my explosive fight with Grace in the yard, and Freddie tells me about Viv wanting to date other people and about how she wants to be able to go to dances and parties and not worry that he'll be upset or jealous. He blames himself over and over again for ever choosing to leave, but I have to trust that everything happens for a reason. I have to.

"I'm done with this," he says.

"With Viv?" I ask. "For good?"

He shakes his head. "Not just her. All girls."

I laugh. "You're not alone, my friend."

His speed slows as we enter a construction area. "I'm serious. No more girls. At least not until after graduation. You in?"

I shrug and roll down the window so I can drag my fingers through the thick morning humidity. "Why the hell not?"

OCTOBER

FIFTEEN

I keep thinking it will take a lot to keep my pact with Freddie, but it doesn't.

Grace disappears from my life like the most careful burglar, leaving not even the whisper of a fingerprint behind and stealing only parts of me I can feel and not see. I feel the impact of her absence during every lull in conversation and in the quiet morning hours when I ride my paper route. It's only been a week since the party, but already it feels like months.

As Hattie and I hike up the stairs to our mom's apartment, she stops on the landing, a little out of breath.

"Shit," she says. "My feet are killing me."

I glance down and can see that her ankles are chubbier than normal, straining against her strappy sandals. "Too many hours on your feet."

She inhales before exhaling through her nose and starting back up the stairs.

"You're telling her tonight, right?"

"Get off my dick about it." And then a second later, she

adds, "And yes. I'm telling her. As if it's any of your business."

In the last few weeks, Hattie's body has really begun to show the evidence of her pregnancy. Last Tuesday I found her crying in the bathroom. She stood in front of the mirror in a neon-green bra and her favorite denim shorts, her hair dripping wet. Her little stomach had popped out recently, making it impossible for her to button her shorts.

"At least you don't have to deal with your period right now," I said, trying to comfort her.

That just made her cry harder, which made no sense to me because our periods were always one step below a crime scene. (Thanks, Mom.)

Unsure what else to do, I snuck into her room, where Tyler was still sleeping, and retrieved a pair of gym shorts for her to change into.

Hattie would never say so out loud, but when things like that happen, I wonder if she wishes she could go back and make this decision over again. I would have understood, and no matter what Dad believes, he would have left the choice to Hattie. He said as much when she told him she was pregnant. But Hattie was insistent that she was keeping this baby. Even if she had wanted an abortion, we only have one clinic in the whole state and it's all the way up in Jackson. Plus it's a lot of money up-front. So I guess the logistics of that decision wouldn't have been all that simple either.

Upstairs, our mom's door is cracked open, smoke curling out the top.

"Mom?" Hattie calls as we let ourselves in.

"I burned the casserole," she yells from behind a wall of smoke. "Don't worry! I already ordered Chinese!"

Hattie coughs into the crook of her arm as I run around opening every window that isn't broken.

"Y'all wanna eat down by the pool?" Mom asks.

I turn to Hattie, who I know is annoyed that she just walked all the way up here for nothing.

I shrug. "Yeah. Okay."

Mom grabs a twenty from her purse and tucks her scraggly old cat, Wilson, under her arm. The three of us sit on the steps, waiting for the delivery guy.

When he finally arrives, we stake out one of the rusting patio tables. The pool is a cloudy, unusual shade of blue and the tiles trimming the edge are cracked and faded, like the rest of the property. Wilson sniffs around but stays within a few feet of our voices.

"Oh shoot," Mom says. "I forgot plates. Y'all mind eating out of cartons?"

Neither of us answers, but just reach for the plastic silverware in the bottom of the bag. Wilson lies out on the concrete beside us, catching any bugs that dare buzz too close to his paws.

It's business as usual as Mom drones on about the casino and all her friends there as if we know them. Hattie and I pass the orange chicken and beef and broccoli back and forth between mouthfuls of fried rice. At least the food is better than usual.

"Ramona's been swimming at the Y a few times a

week," says Hattie, practically sacrificing me on the conversational altar. "She's getting real good."

I fidget in my seat. "It's something to do." But I'm scared it might be more than that. I can feel my body getting stronger with each workout, and though I still can't beat Freddie, he beats me by a little less every time.

"Well, girl, if you're just looking for something to do, I can think of a million better ways to spend your time." She smacks at my arms. "You don't want to get too muscular either. Ladies weren't built for that type of look."

"I wouldn't call Ramona a lady." Hattie snickers.

I shrug off both of their comments and opt to keep the peace. "I go with my friend Freddie. He used to come round here every summer when we were little with his grandma, Agnes. They live in Eulogy now. A few blocks north of the train tracks."

Mom slaps her knee. "I remember those two. I swear you and Freddie were the cutest little pair I'd ever seen."

I purposely shovel too many pieces of orange chicken into my mouth, leaving myself unable to respond.

My mom puts her carton of shrimp lo mein down on the table. "So are you two . . . ya know, seeing each other?"

I swallow a bite. "Mom," I say, my voice low.

"What?" she asks. "He was a fine young boy. And I'm not one of those people who thinks people shouldn't mix. Like, racially speaking."

I shake my head. I can't find one bit of sympathy in my heart for her. "Do you even know how racist you sound?

And it's not like I'm kissing girls just because the right boy hasn't come along to turn me straight."

"That's politically correct nonsense. Anyway, you can't blame me," Mom says as she lights a cigarette. "I want to see you get married. I need *grandbabies*."

Of course she does, because taking care of her own babies was such a breeze. "Well, I'm pretty sure Hattie's got you covered there," I say under my breath.

The air goes still for a moment before Hattie throws the rest of the beef and broccoli in my lap. "I can't believe you!"

Okay. I deserved that.

"What's she trying to say, Hattie Leroux?" demands Mom. "You tell me right this instant."

Hattie reaches over and takes the cigarette from between Mom's fingers and tosses it in the pool. "I'm fuck-ing knocked up, okay?"

Mom claps her hands over her mouth. "Well, this is a little earlier than I expected! My baby's gonna be a mama!"

And once this baby comes into the world, Hattie will always be a mom first and not my sister. I stand up, shaking the food out of my lap. Wilson is quick to collect the scraps.

Mom scoots in closer to Hattie. "Baby. I've been there. I understand what you're going though. Is Tyler the daddy? I was wondering what he was sticking around for."

And this, I think, is why Hattie really didn't want to tell Mom. Not because Mom would be angry, but because it would make her just another girl who was too stupid and too young. Just like Mom.

"You *are* keeping it, right?" Mom asks.

"Yes, ma'am." Hattie nods, not looking away from Mom's hand on her wrist.

The way she answers makes me feel guilty for the decision I know I would've made.

We spend the rest of the evening lying on plastic lawn chairs while Mom relives each of our births and tells us all about how temperamental we were as babies. I have the baby pictures to prove that she was there when we were in diapers, but I can't imagine her doing anything but leaving. Whenever I try to imagine Mom when we were kids, all that's there in my head is a shutting door.

After Tyler comes to pick us up, Hattie gives me dagger eyes the whole way home in the rearview mirror.

She tells him about the big reveal, and he shrugs. "She would have found out eventually, right? Doesn't really matter who told her or how."

Tyler glances up to me in the rearview mirror, and I realize that if he's taking my side, I might be even more in the wrong than I'd imagined.

"I wish you would've been there," Hattie tells him.

"Wouldn't want to interfere with lady time."

When I can't sleep that night, I settle in on the couch to watch TV, but all that's on is paid programming.

The woman on the screen is trying to explain how horrible it is to cut a tomato with a regular knife. She tries all these different knives and sighs dramatically, but only makes a bloody disaster on her cutting board.

"I'm still mad at you," says Hattie from behind me. "But I am sweating my ass off back there in that room. Scoot over."

I do as she says. "I'm so sorry," I tell her.

She pulls my head into her lap. "That chlorine is turning your hair green."

"I thought it looked different."

"We'll dye it this weekend." She scratches my scalp with her acrylic nail and splays out each section of my hair so that it looks like I've been electrocuted. "It's okay. If it had been up to me, I would have told her on my way to the hospital."

"She didn't seem upset or disappointed at all really."

"I knew she wouldn't be," says Hattie.

"Hey." I turn my head to face her. "How did you know you wanted to . . ."

"Keep it?"

"Yeah." I nod. "I mean, you're going to be responsible for a whole other human being."

She laughs. "I don't know. I guess I thought that maybe this baby could be the start of something new. For so long, our family has been built around Mom and Dad and their past and a storm we can barely remember. But I just figured that maybe this baby could be about our future and what we want our family to look like. I mean, it sucks that we don't have family dinners or birthday parties. And I kind of want that for me and this baby and Tyler. Don't you want something like that for yourself too?"

I smile with my lips pressed together.

Tyler is about as permanent as an afternoon thunder-storm. Hattie will see that soon enough. And maybe it's going to take Hattie a while to figure out that this baby is about more than playing house, but if there's one thing I don't doubt, it's my sister's ability to love. Love isn't all you need, but it's a start, I guess.

SIXTEEN

It is stupid hot outside. It's like Mississippi didn't get the memo that it's mid-October, and we've been left to melt.

On Saturday night, two weeks after my and Hattie's dinner with Mom, Freddie comes to hang out for the last bit of my shift, and once Tommy leaves, he even helps me bus a few tables.

"Where's Adam tonight?" I ask.

"His little sister's birthday party," he says. "He tried to sneak out, but when his mom caught him, she made him wear the prince costume his cousin was supposed to wear and dance with all his sister's friends."

I try not to laugh. "Well, that sounds fair."

"Yeah. Try telling Adam that."

After the last customer finally leaves, Saul slams the door and locks it all in one motion. "We're going swimming, y'all. And not in that dirty-ass ocean."

"No one has a pool," I remind him.

He shrugs. "Plenty of people have pools."

I shake my head at him skeptically.

"I know people, okay?"

"Straight boy," he says, pointing to Freddie, "you're invited, too."

After running through our Saturday closing duties, which are a little more extensive than other nights since it's the end of the week, we all meet in the parking lot. Agnes dropped Freddie off, so we're all left to squeeze into Saul's Jeep.

"I need to run home for my swimsuit," I say.

"Me too," says Ruth.

Saul clicks his tongue at me. "Y'all can swim in the suit the good Lord gave you."

Ruth shrugs. "Whatever. I'm wearing a sports bra anyway."

I feel myself shrinking a little. I'm not modest really at all, but somehow there's a difference between swimming in your underwear and swimming in a swimsuit that looks like underwear.

I turn to Freddie. "Agnes won't mind that you're out this late?"

"I turn into a pumpkin at midnight," he says. "I told her I'm crashing at Adam's anyway."

"I make a mean pumpkin pie," says Hattie as she locks the door behind us.

We all pile into Saul's Jeep, and he drives us down dark, twisting residential roads.

The thick evening heat has my mind wandering back to this summer and the first time Grace and I kissed. It was a Movie on the Green night downtown, where they show a movie on a projector outside city hall. Grace's family was going, and I told her I'd meet her there after work.

When I showed up, she was waiting for me at the fountain that sits in the center of Eulogy's only roundabout. Across the street, families were spread out on picnic blankets, watching *The Goonies*.

We'd held hands the night before, but I couldn't decide if it was supposed to mean anything. I'd been racking my brain all day, to the point where Hattie could barely tolerate how distracted Grace had me.

"Let's go for a walk," she said as she popped up from the edge of the fountain.

She wore a short white dress and mint-green sandals, and she smelled like a perfume of salt water, sunscreen, and bug spray.

As we headed in the opposite direction of the movie, she looped her arm through mine. We walked by darkened shop windows and rows of trees strung with twinkly lights.

She made the first move when she pulled me down a dark alley and kissed my bare shoulder. My eyes searched for hers in the dark. My hand slipped down her arm to intertwine with her fingers, and I kissed her on the lips. She kissed me back in the most ferocious way. For a moment, I was too shocked to even move, but soon our bodies were pressed up against the back door of one of the shops.

"I think Adam's family lives out this way," Freddie says, pulling me back into the present.

Saul parks in front of a huge white house with a tall wrought-iron fence lining the perimeter of the property.

"What is this place?" asks Ruth.

"A friend of a friend's place," says Saul. "They let me come here and swim whenever I want."

Hattie's lips twist into a pout. "Well, then why is this the first time the rest of us have been here?"

"A boy's gotta keep a secret or two up his sleeve, okay?" Saul says.

We follow him up the driveway, and he squeezes through a gap in the fence, and I follow behind him. "You're sure we can be here?" I whisper to Saul.

He winks at me once and presses a finger to his lips. I should stop him. I should stop all of us, but my shirt is drenched with sweat, and there's obviously no one home. It's not like we're breaking into the actual house or anything.

"Yeah," says Hattie, pointing to her belly while she eyes the fence. "Not gonna happen."

Saul and I share a look, and I know what he's about to suggest is completely moronic, but I don't have any other ideas. "What can't go through," he says, "must go over."

Hattie shrugs and turns to Freddie and Ruthie. "Y'all gotta hoist me up."

Ruthie holds her hands out for Hattie's foot but shakes her head. "This is the picture of maturity. Helping our pregnant friend jump a fence. Maybe I should put this on my med school applications."

"Hey," says Hattie. "If I fall, at least you can be the first responder."

"Is that supposed to be comforting?" Ruth asks.

Freddie grunts a little as he pushes Hattie over the other side, and thankfully Saul and I are both tall enough that she doesn't have a long way to go without a safety net below her.

Once she's safely over, Ruthie squeezes through the fence.

"You're sure we're allowed to be here?" asks Freddie with one foot still on the other side of the fence.

"Positive," calls Saul as he skips up the driveway and around the corner with Ruth and Hattie close behind. Normally Ruth wouldn't be down for something like this, but if there's anyone she trusts, it's Saul. Even if deep down sometimes her intuition says she shouldn't.

Saul always knows someone who knows someone, so it's no surprise that he knew about this pool. He's resourceful, and I don't know if he was always that way or if it developed out of necessity.

Freddie hesitates, and I hold out my hand. "Come on," I tell him, swallowing my guilt. "Trust me."

In the backyard, Saul rustles around in the bushes for a minute, looking for the pool lights.

While it's still dark, I shimmy out of my shorts and Boucher's T-shirt and jump into the pool in my pineapple underwear and purple-and-pink-polka-dot bra.

"Found 'em!" Saul calls, illuminating the backyard.

The pool is beautiful and is so much more luxurious than what we normally swim in at the Y. Rocks cluster together to create a fountain that drips into the deep end of the pool.

Saul tears his tank top and shorts off before kicking off his flip-flops and cannonballing into the deep end. He's not at all shy about his tiny neon-green brief underwear.

Ruthie and Hattie undress without ceremony. Ruthie wears black boy-shorts underwear and a pink sports bra while my sister struts her stuff all the way to the pool in a pink lacy thong and a turquoise push-up bra.

"She's still got it, y'all!" calls Saul.

If she weren't pregnant, I might wonder what Freddie thought of her. Hattie's always been the hot and sexy one, and she would be the first one to say so.

Freddie turns his back to all of us as he pulls off his shorts and T-shirt to reveal a pair of blue boxer briefs. He's got nothing to be shy about, but I like that he is anyway.

The water is colder than I expected, but my body is quickly adjusting. Hattie floats on her back into the deep end, where she sits behind the waterfall with Saul while Ruthie does handstands in the shallow end.

I lean up against the side of the pool with Freddie, and everything from our chins down is under water, but I still catch him peeking down at my bra and underwear. I write it off as plain old curiosity.

There's something about the air around us that is absolutely electric. Maybe it's because I know we're not supposed to be here.

"Up for an impromptu race?" I ask.

Freddie shakes his head. "I don't think so. I don't think my ego can handle the possibility of losing in my underwear."

I blow a few bubbles in the water. "Hey, it's a lot more coverage than what you swim in during the week."

"Yeah," he admits, "but at least then everything is . . . secure."

I nod vigorously. "I think I've heard enough."

He grins wickedly. "I'd be up for a cannonball off the waterfall, though."

I nod. "Let's do it."

We run along the side of the pool and up the back side of the rocky waterfall, which I don't think is meant for climbing. As we stand there a few feet from the edge, Freddie takes my hand. "You ready?"

I squeeze his fingers, and we run, flying into the air before crashing into the deep end.

I let myself sink down to the bottom and open my eyes, even though it burns. Freddy's blurry figure swims toward me, and his hand brushes my waist as he reaches for my arm, pulling me to the surface with him.

As we emerge, my hair fans out around us like blue lava. "That was fun."

"You've got a mean cannonball." He grins, displaying the gap in his front teeth. "If only your dive off the blocks was as good."

I splash him in the face with his mouth wide open and swim away as Ruthie, Saul, and Hattie climb up the rocks.

Freddie chases me to the shallow end and walks through the waterfall to where I'm sitting on a little underwater bench. "Truce?"

I grin from the shadows. "For now."

He sits down beside me. "Do you ever miss Grace?"

"I do. But it's not as constant as it used to be. Now I just remember her every once in a while. And it's weird things that remind me of her. Like, certain canned soups and doughnuts with sprinkles and vampire movies. But it feels manageable all of a sudden. It wasn't always like that."

Freddie leans his head back on the rocks. "I just feel stupid all the time. Like, when I remember Viv, I miss her. But I feel sort of embarrassed, too, like I should have known better. Everyone saw this coming except me. Even Viv. I wouldn't listen, though."

"I don't know. I think that's part of it. Sometimes you've got to live through it yourself." Because the mood has grown so somber so quickly, I splash him.

"I thought we called truce!" he shouts.

"It was temporary, sucker!"

He's quick to splash me back, and it's not long before our water war has spread and we're out from behind the waterfall, using Ruthie, Hattie, and Saul as human shields.

The lights inside the house suddenly flip on and a voice is shouting, growing louder and louder until we can finally make out that it's a man and he's angry. "Who's out there?"

We all freeze, looking to Saul for our cue.

"Uh," he says. "Run."

I practically jump out of the pool, forgetting any embarrassment I might have about running around in my underwear, and grab all the clothes and flip-flops I see, constantly checking behind me for Hattie and Freddie.

I hear the back door slide open. "I've called the police," the deep southern voice says. "And this is private property! I could shoot y'all just for steppin' a toe past that gate."

"Fuck," I whisper the moment we get to the gate. I shove Freddie through.

"What's this guy even talking about?" Freddie's voice is frantic. "I thought we had permission to be here."

My face gives me away.

"Are you serious?" Freddie shouts. "You let me trespass without even telling me?"

"I'm sorry," I squeak.

Saul is already down at the Jeep, pulling it up the driveway for the rest of us.

I feel horrible, but my guilt will have to wait. "Y'all help Hattie out on the other side," I tell Freddie and Ruthie.

I squat down, letting her use my thigh as a step stool. "We gotta move, Hattie."

"I'm trying," she says. "You try doing this with a beach ball in your shirt."

"Hey!" the man's voice calls. And this time he's much closer. "Y'all ain't going anywhere. I'm done with you kids sneaking in here when no one's renting the place. And if you have any doubt, you should know I'm carrying a pistol, so don't you try nothing funny!"

Hattie topples over the other side of the gate, but Freddie catches her.

The four of us pile into the Jeep, and I'm not even fully in the car before Saul is reversing down the driveway, going much faster than any backward-facing car should.

We're quiet for a few minutes as Saul weaves in and out of streets, going exactly the speed limit. I sort through all our clothes and try to give everyone their stuff, but I can't find Ruth's shorts or Freddie's sandals.

It's not until we've made it out to the coastal highway that Saul breaks out into hysterical laughter.

And maybe it's the tension, but so does everyone else.

Except Freddie. And me.

I nudge him with my elbow to try to get a read on him, but he rolls his eyes and shakes his head, turning away.

"Whose house was that anyway?" asks Hattie.

"Just a summer rental house that Todd used to clean. He used to do deliveries for Boucher's, remember? We hooked up there a few times and would sneak into the pool when no one was renting it. I guess that must've been the property manager, though."

"Yeah, well, that was a little too close," says Ruth over the wind. "I'm applying to colleges right now, Saul! I can't really afford to get in trouble."

"What?" He looks to her in the rearview mirror. "You don't trust your big bro?"

"It's not that," she mumbles.

Saul shakes his head. "Whatever. You think that asshole would've actually killed a couple of kids on a rental property? I doubt it."

Freddie sits in the middle with his arms crossed. "Really? You doubt that. Don't know what world you're living in."

It's quiet for a minute before he adds, "I need you to take

me to my friend's house."

"Sure," says Saul, his eyes drifting to me in the rearview mirror.

I shake my head discreetly, hoping that he doesn't press the issue any more.

Freddie dictates directions, and as we pull up to Adam's house, I'm surprised by how beautiful it is. Adam lives in a large robin's-egg-blue plantation-style home with a wraparound porch. The house, though, is second to the sprawling live oak with branches so low they crawl across the yard. Deflated balloons dangle from the porch railing, and Adam sits waiting on the steps in black slacks and a blue jacket with a gold epaulet on each shoulder.

I hop out of the back of the Jeep behind Freddie and follow him up the driveway.

"You guys are soaked," says Adam.

"Yeah, I'm gonna need to borrow some clothes," says Freddie. "And some shoes if I can."

"Sure thing." Adam still hovers between us.

Freddie gives him a tight-lipped smile. "Give us a minute, okay?"

"Oh, right!" he says. "Privacy. Sure. Yeah. I'll be inside. But hey, don't ring the bell. My parents are asleep."

As Adam walks inside, the clouds above shift, so that the moonlight creeping through the branches is reflecting off Freddie's face now. "You don't get it, do you?"

To be honest, I don't. Yeah, the whole thing was irresponsible, but we had a good time and no one got hurt. But more than anything, I hate the feeling of him being mad at me. "I'm sorry," I tell him. "I really, really am."

He takes a few deep breaths. "We click," he says. "And it's almost easy to forget all the things that set us apart. Maybe sneaking onto private property is just some kind of stupid antic for you, but from where I stand, that's how black kids get shot."

I open my mouth to argue but am silenced when I remember the moment I told him to trust me, even though I knew, I knew, I knew that we had no business at that house. "I'm sorry," I say again.

Freddie massages his forehead, grimacing as he does. "You can't pretend to be color-blind or some shit when it's convenient for you, okay? I'm black. This is the skin I wear every damn day. You're my best friend. You can't tell me that you don't see that my black life is not the same as your white life." He closes his eyes for a moment and shakes his head, like he's answering his own silent question. "Maybe you haven't thought about things like this before, because you don't have to. I get that. But when I tell you I'm uncomfortable, I need you to listen, okay? I know there's stuff I don't understand about the gay thing. But you need to understand that my life in this skin is different from yours."

The guilt I felt earlier is nothing compared to the ignorance I feel now. How could I not know? How could I be so selfish as not to realize that he was hesitant for a reason? My skin crawls with shame. "I understand. God. I can't believe I was so stupid. I feel awful. I know that doesn't make it better. I don't have any excuse."

All his words ring true. Sure, Freddie has more money and lives in a nicer house, but when someone with a gun catches the two of us on their property, one of us is more likely to be carried out on a stretcher, and it's not me.

I step toward him and hug him tightly. "I won't ever put you in a position like that again."

"Okay." He hugs me back and whispers, "Good night, Ramona Blue."

As Saul drives the rest of us home, I let my head fall back and watch the stars drifting by from the open top of the Jeep. I've spent a lot of time thinking about what it means to be gay, especially in the South, but if I'm being honest, I haven't spent much time thinking about what being black in the South might mean. Or anywhere else for that matter.

Anger and shame weigh heavy on my chest, but this isn't about how I feel. It's about Freddie. I hate that this is a reality he has to live with every day, and I wish I had some kind of answer to the bigger problem, but I don't.

SEVENTEEN

Halloween falls on a Friday, and everyone looking for a real good time has made the hour drive to New Orleans, while everyone else is going to Melinda Harold's masquerade party. That actually makes it sound much classier than it is. Really, it's a huge party Melinda's parents have been having for at least a decade now, and the perk is that the adults are too drunk to care how drunk all their kids are.

I sit on the bathroom counter watching Hattie carefully apply fake white, feathery eyelashes. She's dressed as an angel, I think, in a short lacy nightgown that isn't the kind of thing you actually sleep in and cascades over her bump.

"You sure you don't want to come with us?"

I think back to the last huge party I went to and how well that went for me. "Positive." Originally, we were supposed to hang out with Ruth and Saul, but Saul pulled out at the last minute. Whatever reason he ditched us for, Ruth wasn't happy about it, so she opted to stay home. Left with the choice between Hattie and Tyler or my couch, I will always choose my couch.

"Babe!" Tyler yells from the living room.

"Babe!" I mimic.

Hattie rolls her eyes. "Y'all gotta learn to like each other." She steps back and takes one final look at herself before applying a coat of icy-pink lip gloss. Turning to the side, she examines her hem. "Do I look too pregnant in this?"

"You are pregnant."

She groans. "Let's go! Put on your costume, Tyler!"

Tyler shuffles down the hallway. He wears his usual uniform—slightly too tight skinny jeans and a heavy metal band T-shirt.

Hattie hands him the red cape hanging from the bathroom door and the headband with devil's horns.

"Do I have to wear the headband?" he asks.

"Babe, it's a couple's costume. Without the horns, you look like some weirdo in a cape."

Tyler huffs as he pushes the headband into his purposely greasy hair. "Let's roll, Mama."

Him calling my sister Mama makes my stomach turn.

I shoo them both out the door and hand Hattie her jean jacket, because I am cold just looking at her. The weather down here is sporadic at best, but tonight actually feels like Halloween, with wind rustling through the trees.

The minute the door shuts behind them, I do a little victory dance.

I never have the place to myself. Or at least I feel like I don't. Maybe it's because our place is less than seven hundred square feet with four grown adults and one baby on the way, but some days it feels like my little smidgen of a bedroom is disappearing. Especially with Hattie always sleeping in my bed.

In the kitchen, I dump the bags of candy my dad picked up into one giant mixing bowl and then hunt down the cat ears I've worn every year since seventh grade. After slipping on my favorite flannel shirt and coating my legs with bug spray, I sit out on our front steps and wait for the trick-or-treaters.

As I pull out all the Tootsie Rolls for myself, it's a pretty steady parade of neighborhood kids. Some actually have good costumes, but most wear hand-me-downs or a mash-up of found objects. I know a lot of families go to nicer, bigger neighborhoods to trick-or-treat, but a lot of people who live here don't really have a way of getting around other than their feet.

Around nine, and as the stream of trick-or-treaters is thinning, I get a text from Freddie saying he just got out of work and that he's coming over with pizza.

I hand out candy to a few ninth graders before calling it a night and heading inside with my bowl of mostly Tootsie Rolls.

Walking through my front door, I realize that Freddie's never seen the inside of our trailer, and for a moment I look around and see our place for what feels like the first time. One plaid couch and a puke-brown recliner complement the puke-beige carpet. Peeling linoleum in the kitchen. Dingy white cabinets. A low-hanging ceiling that bows in the center. Discarded hotel artwork from Dad's job.

I'm not embarrassed, or at least I tell myself I'm not. There are times when my life feels like a shrinking box that only money can expand, but most days it is a simple life that we've worked hard to maintain.

Before Freddie shows up, I decide to do the dishes to hopefully reduce some of the clutter.

Freddie arrives, balancing a large pepperoni-and-mushroom pizza in one hand and two DVDs in the other and wearing a T-shirt that says *This Is My Halloween Costume.*

"Gimme, gimme, gimme!" I say, taking the pizza from him.

"Nice cat ears." He kicks his shoes off and plops down on the couch like he's been here a thousand times, not even blinking at the fact that we don't have a kitchen table. "Okay," he says, holding up each DVD case. "We've got possessed dolls or murderous hillbillies."

"I'll take murderous hillbillies. Do you think we need plates?"

"Nah," he says. "Just eat out of the box."

"Sounds good." I grab a half-full liter of Dr Pepper from the fridge for us to share and put in the DVD.

We sit hip to hip on the couch with the pizza box balancing on our knees as we pass the soda back and forth. Freddie's body is warm, and he still smells like chlorine from this morning. We've been swimming almost every Monday, Wednesday, and Friday. I'm trying not to get too used to the routine, because I know that when Freddie leaves for school, I'll be going back to my usual life, which doesn't include a pool membership.

With the only light coming from the TV, we sit in a shadow of blue and stuff ourselves full of pizza. The movie is unnecessarily gory and kills everyone who is not blond and big-boobed in rapid succession.

"The black guy always gets it first," says Freddie. "I just want to see a movie that does, like, the ultimate fake-out and brings the black guy back to life."

"Or what if he was alive the whole time and crawled back to where his friends were and saved their asses at the very last minute?"

He chuckles. "The black guy saves the day."

What I think, but don't say, is that Freddie has saved almost all my days since he reappeared in my life a few months ago.

We push the pizza box to the side and move on to my bowl of Tootsie Rolls. We watch the rest of the movie, taking bets on who will be next to die.

When my dad comes home from his shift at the hotel, he waves hello. "You get any trick-or-treaters?"

"Yeah, a bunch of neighborhood kids." I motion to the pizza. "We got some leftovers if you want them." He's so bad at remembering to take lunch breaks, and none of the management at the hotel is in any hurry to remind him.

"Can't say I've ever turned down pizza." He gladly takes our leftovers before stumbling to bed. I'll never figure out how it is that some people can work so hard and get paid so little, while so many people who are paid the most hardly work at all.

We put in the next movie, and before long our shoulders slump and our heads sink into our chests, and we're both asleep.

I wake briefly when my sister and Tyler come in. Tyler is drunk. I can tell by the sound of his shuffling feet. I keep my eyes barely closed as Hattie turns off the TV and throws a blanket over the two of us.

And that's when, in his sleep, Freddie pulls me close to him like a rag doll. Sleep is this fuzzy cloud hanging low around my head. I could force myself to wake up all the way and scoot to the other end of the couch. Or even tell Freddie he should go home. But I don't. Because just the feeling of being touched—being held—is the release of a pent-up sigh.

A few hours later, I wake to the sound of sizzling. With the blanket wrapped tightly around my shoulders like someone's tucked me in, I peek over the back of the couch to find Freddie in my shitty little kitchen with its peeling linoleum, making eggs in an old frying pan, one that's not nearly as nice as his at home. He's the first person, I think, who I've not been related to, who has found a way to fit into my world—my world that has always felt so much smaller and less important than everyone else's.

NOVEMBER

EIGHTEEN

Every day I think of Grace a little less until she is an itch of a memory, like when you know you're forgetting something, but you don't know exactly what it is.

With Freddie around and Hattie's stomach growing every day, life is faster and more all-consuming than I ever remember it being before. I look forward to the mornings when I go swimming with Freddie and Agnes. I'm getting faster and I feel stronger. My legs barely even burn after my paper route anymore.

One day after school, I go with Hattie and Tyler to BabyCakes to look at, well, baby stuff. "So are we registering or what?" I ask. Hattie isn't even due until April. I can't imagine what she could possibly need so early.

She shakes her head as she fingers through the bottle nipples in the first aisle. "Not today. I just want to get a feel for this stuff." Her brow furrows as she checks over her shoulder. "Where's Tyler?"

"No clue."

"Tyler!" she calls.

"Coming!" he yells back as he rounds the corner on one of those motorized scooters.

Hattie crosses her arms over her belly. "What the hell? Those are for, like, people who need them."

Tyler speeds down the aisle toward us and then hits the brakes hard, forcing the wheels to squeak. "Who's to say I don't need it? I had a long day at work yesterday, okay?"

"It was your first day," Hattie reminds him. "You only filled out paperwork."

"That's why it was so long."

Tyler finally has a job, and it's thanks to Dad, actually. He got Tyler in with the maintenance guys at the hotel. Dad went out on a limb, but it was for Hattie, not Tyler.

We zigzag up and down the aisles, the motor on Tyler's scooter humming behind us.

"All this shit is so expensive," says Hattie. "How do normal people even have babies?"

"We'll figure it out," I say, but the truth is I don't know. This stuff really is expensive. You need strollers and cribs and bottle warmers and diapers and ointments and diaper bags, and it never seems to end. For such a little person, it seems like an awful lot.

The three of us stop below an aisle of hanging mobiles. Fish, trucks, angels, ballet slippers, rabbits, construction hats, princess crowns, clouds, trees. Every type of thing you could think of dangles above our heads, and the three of us, even Tyler, are mesmerized. The ceilings here aren't too terribly tall, so with my height, my head is nearly in the same space as the mobiles.

"I like the stars and the clouds," says Hattie, pointing to a light wooden mobile with hand-painted white puffy clouds and gold shooting stars. "I wish we could paint clouds on her ceiling."

"Maybe we can," I say. Even though there are no extra rooms in the trailer and all the ceilings are already dark with water stains.

"Her?" laughs Tyler. "It's a boy. I'm a straight shooter."

"Gross," I mumble.

"And I like the fish," he says. "He's gonna be a fisher."

While Tyler plugs the scooter back in, Hattie buys a pair of lavender booties.

"You don't really care if it's a boy or a girl, do you?" I ask as she hands the cashier a ten-dollar bill.

She smiles with her lips sealed and absentmindedly rubs her belly. "No," she says. "Not even a little bit."

On Thursday morning I wake to a text from Saul.

If you are receiving this text, you are invited to my house-warming party on Saturday eve. Yes, I, Saul Pitre, have left my mother's bosom in favor of the bachelor life. Food, beverage, and good times provided. Price of admission: your body. HELP ME MOVE.

And then moments later I receive another text directed specifically at me.

Ramona dear, bring the straight one.

It doesn't take us long to move Saul. He has mostly clothing and a large DVD collection of B horror movies.

The trickiest thing is the mattress and box spring, but with a little effort, we maneuver it in.

Afterward, we all lie spread out on Saul's floor, because he doesn't actually have any furniture.

Hattie corralled Tyler into helping with the promise of free food. The two of them sit with Tyler's back against the wall and Hattie's back against Tyler. He traces lines on her stomach absentmindedly while she closes her eyes. To be honest, I'm surprised Tyler even agreed to show up.

Ruth is lying facedown in the kitchen, pressing her body hard into the cold tile floor while Freddie is sitting beside me beneath the fan as we both beg it to spin faster. Today was another unseasonably humid day and maybe not the best day for Saul to move.

"Oh my God," I moan. "Feed us."

Saul pops down onto the floor like his legs are made of springs, with both his arms full of Styrofoam to-go containers. "Po'boys from Risky's."

Ruth crawls over and snatches a box for herself. "Mine."

A few moments later, with my mouth full of food, I turn to Saul. "So this was sort of spur of the moment, don't you think?" Now that I am not in need of food in a primal way, I can ask what I've been wondering all day. "Were you saving up for this place or something?" Every time I think I know everything there is to know about Saul, he nonchalantly strolls out a new piece of information about himself, like his life is some kind of clown car. So it's not all that odd that he sprung this on us.

Behind Saul, Ruth raises her eyebrows and makes a face

that says there's more to this story.

"It was time," Saul says.

"Really?" Hattie scoffs. "That's all you're giving us?"

"Yeah," says Ruthie. "And don't you wonder how he's affording this place all by himself?"

"That's a good point, Ruthie!" I say. "You wanna be bad cop?" I ask her.

"Y'all are so nosy." He takes another bite of his sandwich and takes his time chewing and swallowing before setting it on the container. He pushes down on his knees and takes a deep breath. "I met someone, okay? And it's pretty serious."

"What!" I shout. I expected that Saul had been maybe dipping his toes into something illegal to afford this place or that his parents asked him to move out after catching him mid-hookup. But a serious relationship? That might have been the last thing I expected.

It's silent for a moment, before Hattie asks, "So where is he?"

"On a boat."

Ruth puts her sandwich down, and the words spill from her. "He met a roughneck over the summer and has had this huge secret relationship with him and now they've got their secret love bungalow or whatever and our mama is fuh-reaking out."

Oil. Offshore drilling. It's the fastest way to make money around here without going to college. A few weeks on the rig and then a few weeks off. It's a sweet deal for as long as you can maintain going back and forth like that.

Does a number on your social life and your body, that's for sure. "Wait," I say. "You're tellin' me this guy isn't out or it's some kind of secret thing y'all got going on?"

"He's out to me?" His voice is tiny.

"Saul!" I gasp. "You're breaking your own rules!"

"Rules?" asks Freddie. "What rules?"

The natural light in the apartment shifts as the sun begins to set, and for the first time I notice how nice this place is. It's only a block off the coast. All the appliances are new. All the flooring is real hardwood and new tile. It's better than any place I've ever called home.

I sigh. "No dating in the closet. And no long distance."

Saul's eyes meet mine, and there's something in them that I recognize. He's got this desperate yet thrilled look to him. Saul is in love. Part of me wants to hug him and tell him that some things are worth breaking the rules for. But I can't.

I think back to Grace and how all I wanted was for someone to tell me we could make it work. Some kind of reassurance that I wasn't setting myself up for heartbreak. I look to Saul and give the most encouraging smile I can muster. "I can't wait to meet him."

His face lifts. "Let me grab my phone and show y'all a picture."

As he runs to the bedroom, Hattie turns to Ruth and says, "There's no chance of this ending well."

Instead of saying she's right or wrong, I pull my knees into my chest and chew on the french fries in my to-go box. Freddie scoots close to me and touches my thigh. "You okay?" he whispers.

I nod. I want this to work for Saul. He deserves to be happy, and if he does, maybe I do too.

NINETEEN

Me, Freddie, Hattie, Dad, Saul, Agnes, and Bart are all huddled around the kitchen table and the extra card table Agnes set up to accommodate all of us in her kitchen. In true Agnes form, each table is dressed in matching table-cloths with homemade centerpieces.

Agnes clinks her knife against her wineglass. "Before Bobby"—she motions to my dad—"carves this bird, let's go around and say what we're each thankful for this year."

A few weeks ago, Agnes asked me what my family did for Thanksgiving, and I told her the truth: we order pizza. Agnes, of course, was outraged and demanded we all come over for a late dinner after Dad finished up at work. So here we all are in the closest things we have to church clothes. We look like a gang of sinners at an Easter service—especially Saul in his red polyester pants and denim button-up shirt. Tonight he's an honorary Leroux since he couldn't get the time off work to go with Ruthie and their parents to visit the rest of their family in Florida. Or at least that's the story he told. Really, I think his loverboy is about to have some time off the rig and he doesn't want to miss a second of it.

It sounds bad, I know, to brush off such a major holiday with some greasy takeout. But Dad always works on Thanksgiving, and Hattie and I aren't the type of people who are willing to cook for hours in the name of a holiday we don't really care about. With the casino open 365 days a year, my mom's place isn't really an option either.

One year, though, when we were both in elementary school, and we were still making an effort to spend half our holidays and birthdays with Mom, it was her turn to have us on Thanksgiving, so she took us with her to work and left us in a corner booth at the buffet. Hattie and I ate crab legs and green Jell-O and played MASH for hours.

MASH, if you've never played it, is a silly game we used to play as kids. All it requires is a piece of notebook paper and a pencil. The game told us all the things we thought made an adult life. What kind of house we'd live in, how many kids we'd have, who we'd marry, and what kind of car we'd drive.

Back then it never occurred to us that those factors might be minor details when we were grown up.

But right now, all Agnes wants to know is what we are thankful for in this exact moment.

She reaches for Bart's hand to her right. "I'll go first. I'm thankful for this man and the adventure he's embarked on with me. Just when I thought my journey had come to an end . . ." Her voice trails off for a moment, and her eyes are glassy and wet. "I'm just grateful for this. All of it."

179

Bart's response is as direct as his wardrobe. "My girl," he says. "And her Freddie."

And then it's my turn.

I take a sip of my sparkling apple cider. I'm thankful for Hattie, even though she drives me nuts and even though her life is ballooning so quickly it's practically edging me out of my own home. I'm thankful for my dad, even though he's always busy and tired and working, because he's there. Always. And I'm thankful for Freddie. His friendship has saved me bit by bit every day. It's like I was drowning, and Freddie has slowly pulled me to the surface.

"Family, friends, and good food," I say. It's a generic answer that I immediately regret, but I don't always know how to say the things I can so clearly see in my head and feel in my heart. Freddie catches my eye from across the table, where he sits between Saul and Hattie, and gives me a wink.

My dad stands. He clasps his hands together, but then shoves them in his pockets, like he's not sure what to do with them. "Right. I'm thankful for my girls and for this goddamn delicious deep-fried bird."

He's right. The turkey smells amazing.

Down South we don't cook turkeys for hours until they're dry and the only way to salvage them is with gallons of gravy. Most every household slathers their bird in Cajun spices and dunks it in a deep fryer in the backyard for thirty minutes. Granted, the tradition has been known to cause a house fire every now and again, but the aroma is intoxicating enough to drive you mad. I don't even have to touch this turkey to know the meat is going to fall right off the bone.

Next is Saul. He's thankful for many things. "Oh my word," he says. "The list is long, but I'll just say reality TV, discount liquor stores, spray tans, and tourists. And boys in good jeans."

Everyone laughs except for Bart, who nervously stares down at his empty plate like he might make food magically appear there by the sheer power of his will.

Freddie licks his bottom lip and then chews on it for a moment, like he's thinking and doesn't mind that everyone else is drooling for this turkey. "I've got lots to be grateful for," he says. "But right now, I'd have to say Ramona."

I can feel the heat crawling up my neck, turning my skin red. I don't know if it's because everyone's looking at me or because Freddie is looking at me, but I can't bear to make eye contact with anyone or anything except the fried turkey at the center of the table. I feel like I've swallowed a magic seed, causing flowers to sprout up in my belly, and now they're swelling against my rib cage.

"I guess when we moved here—and you know this, Gram—I thought my senior year would be something I just had to get through. To survive." I glance up long enough to see him shaking his head. "But now I'm trying to hold on to each day."

Hattie—perfect, obnoxious Hattie—breaks the silence and says, "Freddie! You sweet son of a bitch!" And plants a fat kiss on his cheek. There are few times when I think so, but why can't I be more like Hattie? Because I would very much like to crawl under this table and squeeze Freddie's neck.

Hattie grins, and it's an expression I know. She rubs her belly like a crystal ball that's full of secrets. "I should wait until Tyler gets here from his mom's," she says. "But, oh, hell! I'm thankful that we're having a baby girl!"

And in that second every last bit of attention is diverted to Hattie. I sigh as quietly as I can, the weight of being the center of attention easing from my chest. I am so thankful for her never-failing ability to steal the spotlight.

Everyone erupts into coos and squeals—even Bart grunts his approval. Dad circles the table and kisses Hattie's forehead. His eyes are full of tears that he never allows himself to shed. "My girls," he says. But he's not talking about Hattie and me. This time his girls are Hattie and his future granddaughter. I'm happy for my sister. I am. But for a moment, I want to freeze us all in time and stop the world from changing.

After lots of hugs and kisses and a few tears, my dad uses Agnes's electric knife to cut the turkey, and we all pass around an endless supply of side dishes and fixings. There's none of that awkward politeness. And I guess it's because we're family. This odd little group of people—my favorite people in the world—makes up my family.

After dinner, Freddie and I volunteer to do the dishes, and we hear no protest from Saul or Hattie. As I'm tying Agnes's apron around my waist, I notice that Freddie's khaki pants are a smidge too short, but his butt still looks great. And I tell him so.

"Hey," I say, and smack my hand against his backside loudly. "Those pants and your ass." I whistle, channeling Hattie.

I love asses. Everyone's got their thing, and mine is butts. I wish I could be classy and say I love hands or eyes or lips. But it's asses, and for as much as I love a nice lady ass, I can appreciate a good guy ass, too.

"Well, you don't look so rough yourself," he says.

"Thank you," I say, and give a twirl in my thrifted sunflower baby-doll dress. It actually looks like the kind of thing my mom might have worn when we were little.

Freddie scrubs while I load the dishwasher.

"What's that noise?" He tilts his head and pauses.

I don't have to check to know. "Hattie. She's started snoring." Which has made sleeping in my own room even more difficult than it was before. Her chain-saw-like snores drown out the football game on TV.

After we finish the dishes, we sit at the kitchen table, still in our aprons, sharing a hot toddy we convinced Bart to make for us. All around us are pies and cookies and a bowl of leftover Halloween candy that Agnes put out with the desserts in the hope of getting rid of it before Christmas.

I steal a notebook from Agnes's junk drawer and write out *MASH* at the top of the page.

"MASH?" asks Freddie.

"You've never played MASH?"

He shakes his head.

"Well, I'm about to pop your cherry."

"What does MASH stand for?"

"Mansion, apartment, shack, house. Okay, now give me two girls' names."

"People I know?"

"Doesn't matter. People you know. Celebrities. Whatever."

"Ruth," he says. "And you."

"And now I add two," I explain. "Viv."

"Shit. Come on, Ramona. Push the knife in a little deeper."

"Hey," I say, "we gotta have some real-life options. I'll throw in Beyoncé to balance it all out."

"Okay, I guess that's fair."

"Dream big, right?" I grin and write down each name. "Okay, pick two cars."

"Easy. A Jeep Wrangler like Saul's. Makes me feel like I'm in Jurassic Park," he explains. "And a 1948 Chevy pickup. Like Bart's."

I nod as I write them down. "And I choose a Winnebago and a Mary Kay pink Lincoln town car."

"Touché."

"And how many kids do you want?"

"Zero or two," he says without hesitation.

I glance up as he loosens the tie around his neck—one that I can so perfectly picture Agnes buying for him. It's navy blue with yellow-and-white stripes.

He shrugs. "What? I guess I'm kind of an all-in or not-at-all kind of guy."

"Okay," I say. "And I'll go with twelve and forty-three."

He balks at that.

"If anything, it'd prove that you're in . . . uh, good health."

"Okay," he says. "Now what?"

I swivel the notebook around and hand him the pencil. "Close your eyes and draw a spiral down there at the bottom of the page."

He does as I say, his lips splitting into a slow grin.

"Now stop."

I count the lines in his spiral like Hattie and I would when we were kids. When we'd play MASH, I'd think of the results as this distinctly adult life that we would someday have.

But that's not the case, because I feel like an adult now. I live at home with my dad. I'm not married. I don't have kids, or a car even, and I won't be eighteen until next summer, but childhood ended long ago. It seems to me that childhood ends and adult life begins the moment you stop believing your parents can rescue you. As much as I love my dad, I stopped thinking that a long time ago.

"Twenty-two," I say.

I count to eleven starting with *M* for mansion and go through each category until I've got answers for every category. "Well," I tell him, "you're going to live in a mansion with zero children. You will drive a Winnebago. And you'll be married to . . . me." My neck does that thing again where it fills with heat.

"Let me see that." He takes the paper from me and studies it very carefully. "Well," he finally says, "you can't argue with science." He takes a spider ring from the bowl of old Halloween candy, reaches across the table, and takes my hand. "Ramona Blue Leroux—wait, I don't know your middle name."

I pull my hand back a little, but he doesn't let go. "I don't have one."

He shakes his head in disbelief. "I think that makes you soulless in some cultures. Just FYI. But whatever. Ramona Blue Leroux, will you spend the rest of your life with me in a mansion with our zero children? Till death do us part?"

"Fine, but I'm only doing it for the ring."

He pushes the black spider ring down my finger right next to my mood ring, which is a pinky-mauve color at the moment, and finally lets go of my hand. He cradles my hand in his for one . . . two . . . three . . . four . . . five . . .

I pull back and take a sip of the hot toddy we've been passing back and forth. "I need some air." I never feel awkward around Freddie, but right now I'm hyperaware of every little thing right down to my breathing.

"Yeah. Let's go out back."

I lead the way and plop down on the porch swing in the backyard.

Freddie sits down next to me without turning on the patio lights, and we swing together in the dark for a few minutes. I fidget with the spider ring on my finger, and even think about taking it off, but that's dumb. Freddie was just joking, and so was I.

"You ever been flounder fishing?" I ask, searching for anything that doesn't have to do with the future.

"No," he says. "I've actually never been fishing at all."

"What? You gotta be kidding me."

"I guess it wasn't really Gramps's thing."

"My dad used to take us before he got promoted at the hotel. Back when he had more time." I let my toes skid along the cement as we keep swinging back and forth. "Or maybe it was that we were younger and wanted to be with him more. You know all those people you see on the beach at night in galoshes with big old flashlights and buckets? They're fishing for flounder."

He smiles, his teeth sparkling beneath the moonlight. "I used to think those were pixies or giant fireflies or something."

"Ro!" calls my dad from inside the house. "We're leaving in a minute. I gotta get Hattie off the couch."

"Okay!" I call back, and pop up from the swing. "It was nice of Agnes to have us over tonight." I'm one step away from babbling to fill the silence.

Freddie stands. He's only an inch or two shorter than me. My eyes have adjusted to the darkness out here so that now when I look at him, he's more than a silhouette. I can see all the little details, like the dusting of orange freckles across the bridge of his nose and the scar above his right eyebrow. The gap in his teeth. All the things that make him Freddie.

"And thanks for what you said. At dinner," I add. "I feel the same, just so you know." The unlit porch makes it a little easier to say what I've been feeling out loud. The dark has a way of doing that. "A lot of the good I've got going on right now is because of you."

Again, he's quiet. Freddie, who always has something to say, says nothing as he takes a step toward me. We're so close that as we exhale in unison, our bodies press together.

Freddie tilts his head to the side and kisses me lightly. On the lips.

I gasp at first and he pulls back an inch. My heart feels like a fire alarm in my chest. *Freddie*. Freddie kissed me, and I don't think it was an act of friendship.

Maybe it's that I've missed touch—any touch—so much that I can't stop myself, but I loop an arm around his waist, pulling him even closer to me. This time, I kiss him.

And to my surprise, my first thought isn't that I'm gay or that Freddie is a boy or that he's one of my best friends. His lips are lips. They're soft and they taste like pumpkin pie and whiskey.

He deepens the kiss. Or maybe I do. But either way our bodies curl together like vines.

I lose myself in the kiss for only a moment before I remember who these lips are attached to. *Freddie*. I pull away, panting into the space between us. "You're supposed to be swearing off girls," I remind him. "And I'm supposed to be . . . well, you know . . . doing that, too."

He wipes his thumb across his lips. I wonder what I tasted like to him. "I'm sorry," he says. He's breathing as heavy as I am. "I mean, if that's something you want me to be sorry for."

My heart is beating in my ears, and I don't respond, because I'm freaked out. I'm confused. I don't know what's happening at all. I'd just found some sort of balance in my world, and now the entire universe has shifted.

"I'm sorry," he says again. "I really am."

"Ro!" calls my dad. "Time to motor!"

Freddie looks to me, and I can see the slightest fear in his eyes, like he's realized what this kiss might cost us. "I won't do it again. Not unless you tell me to."

"I'll call you later."

I run around the side of the house and meet my dad on the front porch. The three of us pile into his truck, with me in the middle as usual. Saul waves, stifling a yawn, as he gets into his Jeep beside us.

On the way home Hattie falls asleep on my shoulder, and the possibility of waking her up is the only thing stopping me from pulling every blue hair out of my head. I want to scream into the jacket I've balled up in my lap. I want to cut this one moment out of my life and put it in my chocolate box to store under my bed, because all I can see is the domino effect this is bound to have on our friendship.

And yet, I didn't pull away from him. Instead, I kissed him. This is as much my fault as it is his.

When we get home, Tyler is asleep on the couch, watching free HBO. It's a holiday weekend, so all the premium channels are free, meaning we can actually watch our favorite shows on TV instead of on sketchy websites.

"What are you doing?" spits Hattie. "You were supposed to come to our Thanksgiving dinner when you were done."

Tyler stands and rubs the heels of his palms in his eyes.

"I'm wiped, babe. Did you know they put, like, a serum in turkey to make you sleepy?"

"Is that some kind of conspiracy theory?" I ask.

"You know, we never actually landed on the moon either," he says.

"I can't believe you bailed on Thanksgiving dinner," Hattie tells him.

Hattie and I look to my dad, like he should somehow referee this conversation.

Dad shakes his head. "Off to bed, girls." He turns to Tyler and gives him one firm nod.

"We're supposed to be a family, you know?" my sister says. "We're supposed to be that for this baby."

"I can't do this tonight." Tyler walks back to his and Hattie's room and closes the door.

She turns to me. "Can you believe him? The father of my daughter, ladies and gentlemen." And then she walks into my room and slams the door behind her.

I groan and shuffle my feet all the way to my room before knocking on the door.

Hattie swings the door open as she trips out of her clothes. "Can I borrow a T-shirt?"

I dig through my dresser until I come across a soft one. "Here."

She pulls her dress off over her head and takes the shirt, but it barely stretches over her belly. Hattie looks down at herself. There's at least a five-inch gap between the hem and her underwear. "Shut up," she preemptively tells me.

We climb into bed, and I listen as she tells me all the

reasons why Tyler is going to be a horrible dad. Her voice is tiny when she admits the one reason why she can't let him go. "I can't help but wonder what would have been different if we'd had Mom *and* Dad."

Me too, I think.

We're both quiet for a minute. I want to say it: Freddie kissed me and I kissed him back.

My life is balancing on a scale. On one side is everything I hold dear that makes me feel normal. Hattie and Dad, knowing where I fit and that I'm a lesbian, Ruth and Saul, and even my friendship with Freddie. On the other side is the kiss we shared tonight. But all I can think is: *I kissed him back.*

I wish my life was a game of MASH and that I could close my eyes and draw a spiral to tell me which way to go.

After Hattie falls asleep, I reach down under my bed and grab my chocolate box. I slide the spider ring off my finger and tuck it between a roll of cash and a few folded-up games of MASH for safekeeping.

TWENTY

For the first time since August, I haven't talked to Freddie in days.

I keep thinking he'll call me, but then I remember I promised to call him and that the blame here is shared.

This morning, I did my route as fast as I could and sped past Freddie's house without even looking to see if Agnes was outside in the flower bed.

"Hey," Ruthie calls while I'm chaining up my bike in front of the main entrance at school, her mom's car pulling away behind her. She hasn't said so, but I'm sure she misses having Saul around for rides.

I wave and wait for her to catch up to me. "How was Florida?"

"Boring without Saul. But my grandma did ask my mom if her and my dad were still 'boinking.' But then she tried to set me up with her thirty-two-year-old handyman, so that basically ruined any goodwill I had toward her."

I laugh. "Aw, that's great."

She rolls her eyes. "Do you even realize how much more

my house sucks without Saul? My mom keeps buying me all this stuff for my dorm next year, and it's all pink. Jesus."

I laugh.

"So what about you? How was Thanksgiving?"

Oh good, Freddie kissed me. I kissed him back. "Good. Uneventful." And for the first time, I get this twisting knot of guilt in my stomach. As if by kissing Freddie I've somehow betrayed Ruth. Ruthie! Of all people. It makes no sense.

As we walk into the main hallway, she points over to the locker bank. "Hey, there's Freddie and Adam." She raises her arm to wave at them. "You know, Adam isn't so bad. I kind of feel like a jerk for never talking to him before he became friends with Freddie. Hey!" she calls to them.

I swat her arm down. "Don't."

"What?"

I shake my head. "It's nothing. We just—I gotta get to class."

She yanks me away by the wrist. "Not until you tell me what's going on."

I trip along behind her as she pulls me into the library and all the way back to the biography section.

Mrs. Treviño, the new librarian, whose wardrobe is way cooler than I've ever seen in stores around here, circles behind us, careful to make sure we don't mess up her perfectly shelved stacks. "I can you help you girls with the catalog if you're looking for something."

"We're good!" Ruth calls sweetly. She lowers her voice. "Okay, what happened?"

I run my fingertips across the tops of the dusty books. The only time anyone checks these out is when a teacher requires that one of your sources be an actual book. I've never been a big reader, but I wonder what it would be like to live in a house where you had room and money for bookshelves full of books you don't have time to read.

"It was nothing. . . ." I see the determination in Ruth's eyes. She's the smartest person I know, and if anyone has an answer to this, it's her. I hesitate for a second, recalling the quick tinge of guilt I felt a moment ago. But I shake it off. I have no reason to feel that way. "Okay, I have a hypothetical question."

She crosses her arm over her chest and leans against the shelving unit. "Let me hear it."

"What if someone, like say Saul, who is definitely gay, kissed someone of the opposite sex?"

The tension in her forehead eases. "Everyone experiments. I mean, even straight people are a little bit gay. I think Saul went to freshman homecoming with a girl. I dated Matt Hankins in ninth grade for four months. Four months of kissing a Dorito-flavored mouth with unchecked facial stubble irritating my skin."

"Right. I get that. But what if said person wasn't feeling very confused about it?"

She raises an eyebrow. "What are you saying?"

"I don't really know." Every bit of hesitation and uncertainty reveals itself in my voice.

Ruth gives me a thin but sympathetic smile. "I guess

if you really get down to it, I identify as a homoromantic demisexual."

My forehead wrinkles into a knot. "A what?"

"Exactly," she says. "But if I say that to people like my parents, their heads would explode. So I call myself a lesbian, and I'm okay with that."

She gives me a hard look. "Listen, I don't know exactly what it is you're trying to figure out, but I would be careful about leading on other people before *you* know what you want. Freddie isn't—"

"This is hypothetical," I remind her.

"Right. Of course. Well, this *guy* isn't just some guy, and this hypothetical person might wanna be careful that they don't mess up a good thing for no reason. Especially if this hypothetical kiss was just some hypothetical fluke, because this hypothetical person is definitely only attracted to girls."

I nod my head, slowly at first and then firmer. "Yeah. You're right."

"But, really," she says, "it couldn't have meant anything, right?"

"Oh yeah," I say. "Totally."

"And maybe these two hypothetical people should do everything they can to get back to normal and just be friends."

I don't know why, but I can't look her in the eyes right now, so I pick at the spine of the J-K-L encyclopedia and nod.

Ruth softens a little. "Listen, I'm not a really . . . I don't know . . . a mushy kind of person, but you know who you are. I remember hearing you came out in ninth grade, and thinking, 'Wow. Not only does she know who she is, she's being who she is.' You don't have to let this one hypothetical thing change you if you don't want it to."

I try not to let her see, because I think Ruth would hate that more than anything, but her words make me tear up. I don't know how to respond, so I say, "I guess we should get to class."

At lunch, Freddie is quick to find me in the courtyard outside the cafeteria.

"Hey," he says. "Can I sit down?"

"Yeah," I tell him. *Act normal. I kissed him back. Don't be awkward. I kissed him back.*

"I know I was supposed to wait for you to call me—"

"Yeah, listen, I wasn't feeling super great this weekend, and then Hattie and Tyler were arguing, so things were sort of crazy." All I hear is the conversation I had with Ruth this morning. I've got to do whatever I can to get us back to normal.

"Right." He nods, and I can see that I could give him any excuse and it would all mean the same thing: something has changed. "You up for an extra swim in the morning? We can make up for today."

Relief floods my chest. "Yeah! For sure!"

"You're Ramona?" asks a white guy wearing a T-shirt that says *What the frak?* tucked into cargo shorts. "You're

Ramona," he says, confirming it for himself. "They said to look for blue hair."

"Um, yeah?"

Freddie looks at me like *you know this guy?*

"Right, so I'm Allyster. We've gone to school together since eighth grade."

"Okay?" He waits for me to say something else. "You look familiar." Just like everyone else. Eulogy may not be so small that I know everyone by name, but I remember faces.

"Well, I should," he says.

"Can we help you with something?" asks Freddie.

"No, not you. Your grandma already sent in a check."

Allyster sits down next to me, forcing me to scoot in. I should be annoyed, but I think I'm more amused than anything. "A check for what?"

He opens the binder he's been clutching against his chest to a printout of a spreadsheet. "You're the only person in our senior class who hasn't purchased ad space in the yearbook for a senior page."

"I'm the *only* person?"

"Well, the only person who isn't incarcerated or on maternity leave."

"So what if I don't want a senior page?" I ask.

He pulls a loose paper from his binder with all the necessary information, and it looks like the type of thing that's probably been pushed to the bottom of my locker. "Your call," he says. "But we're striving for a hundred percent participation here. Don't want anybody to be forgotten when they open our class time capsule."

Allyster walks off, leaving Freddie and me.

I hold the flyer up. "How freaking dumb is this? I can't believe people are actually paying money for this."

He scratches the tip of his nose with his index finger. "It's not that dumb, really. I mean, I'm doing it."

"Well, Agnes did it for you."

"Only 'cause I asked her to."

I glance over the paper. "So what? You just send in some pictures and, like, a final shout-out? I guess it seems weird to me to put these pictures and memories in this book that no one's gonna ever look at after graduation. And then to charge for it."

"Or maybe it's a chance to say thank you to the people you love and put a cheesy senior picture to use."

The first bell for next period buzzes. I shove the flyer in the front pocket of my backpack. "I'm not asking my dad to pay for that. He's got enough to worry about. And I'm for sure not forking over any cash for it." I stand up and sling my backpack over my shoulder. "And it's not like my time in high school has been all that memorable."

He holds a hand to his chest dramatically. "I'm insulted."

I swat his bicep, but he reaches for my hand and holds it inside of his.

"Hey, maybe we should talk about what happened?"

My heart thumps against my chest. "I don't think there's anything to talk about."

His lips twitch. I recognize the hesitation in his expression, because I feel it, too. He's torn between accepting my answer and pushing for more. "Nothing?" he asks.

I shake my head and pull my hand back. "Nope."

"Oh," he says. "I almost forgot. Adam wants to know if you and Ruth want to come over while he takes my"—Freddie holds his fingers up in air quotes—"'sweet, sweet Star Wars virginity.'"

Just then Adam pops out of the crossing hallway, as if he'd been summoned. His board is strapped to his backpack, and judging by the whiskers above his lip, he's experimenting with facial hair. "Oh," he says. "You won't want to miss this. I predict tears. Like, full-on man tears."

Freddie snorts and turns to Adam. "What's the capital of Thailand?" Adam has barely any time to react and block himself before Freddie shouts, "Bangkok!" and punches him in the nuts. Well, almost. It appears that Adam has adequately defended himself.

"Okay, you almost got me that time," Adam says.

"All right, boys," I say. "Ironically, I've got to go to geography."

Freddie grins. "At least you know the capital of Thailand."

I roll my eyes but can't hold back a laugh as I head in the opposite direction. I don't think anything says *just friends* like watching Freddie punch another guy in the nuts. Everything is going to be fine.

"Hey!" Adam shouts. "What about Freddie's Star Wars deflowering?"

A few heads turn. I grin. "I'm in."

TWENTY-ONE

That night Freddie picks Ruth and me up in Agnes's Cadillac to take us over to Adam's house for the Star Wars deflowering.

Adam's house is still as breathtaking as I remember it being.

"Adam's parents know we're coming over, right?" asks Ruth.

"This place is so big they might not even notice we're there," I tell her.

It blows my mind that the person who lives in this house isn't an asshole. I know not all rich people are jerks, but you would look at this house and think that the most popular kid in school lives here.

Adam swings the front door open as the three of us file up the steps. He hands us each a plastic toy lightsaber upon entrance.

"Did you go out and buy these just for tonight?" asks Ruth.

"Oh, no," a woman's voice says from the neighboring

room. "That's from his personal collection."

We all peer around the corner to see a woman with bouncing chestnut curls and a perfectly round face sorting through piles of receipts as she sits behind a polished, commanding desk. When I imagined Adam's mom barking orders at the car wash, this is not the woman I had in mind. The wall behind her is a floor-to-ceiling bookshelf, with a set of French doors leading into the foyer and another into the kitchen. On the other wall is a large picture window that fills the room with natural light from the setting sun.

Something about this house makes me feel like I can breathe. It's different from the McMansion where Viv's birthday party was. I'm not intimidated by this house. I just never want to leave it.

"Way to rat me out, Mom," says Adam.

Ruth side-eyes me from where she stands on the other side of Freddie. Ruth and Saul's parents are southern and formal. Well, I guess you could call them stiff. I can see she doesn't quite know how to react.

The French doors leading into what I'm guessing is the kitchen open and a petite woman with glossy black hair swept into a loose ponytail enters with a beer in each hand. "For my queen," she says, and hands Adam's mother one.

She takes it but eyes her suspiciously. "Don't think this makes up for the mess of receipts you threw on my desk this afternoon."

She holds one arm up innocently. "I am but a simple woman who needs her wise and patient wife to sort through the graveyard of her finances every quarter."

I gasp. Audibly. I don't mean to. But oh my God. Adam has two moms and never told us. I look to Ruth and find that her eyes are just as wide as mine. Freddie grins, and I can't tell if he knew too or if he's just making an effort to be polite, unlike Ruth and I. But of course he knew. He must have.

Ms. Garza, the first one, with chestnut curls, turns to Ruth and me. "Children, a lesson to you: never marry down."

Ms. Garza, the second one, assaults her wife's cheek with kisses. "Or," she says, "marry your accountant. Especially if she's pretty. Looks and brains, I tell ya."

"By the way," the first Ms. Garza says, "you can call me Pam, and my wife here goes by Cindy. Having two Ms. Garzas under one roof can be a little confusing."

Cindy laughs. "Or when Adam would call for Mommy when he was scared to go to the bathroom by himself in the middle of the night."

"When was that?" asks Freddie. "Last week?"

Pam and Cindy both laugh, their heads knocking together.

Adam rolls his eyes, but I feel so taken aback. I look to Ruth again, the shock on her face finally dissolving. The Garzas really do keep to themselves, and they live on the outskirts of town, so I guess this isn't so huge of a surprise, but I feel weirdly cheated to just now find out that two women married to each other live right here in my tiny town and I never even knew.

I glance at Adam again and back to his moms, who are

whispering to each other, and then back to Adam. Adam—perfectly good, nice, respectful Adam—has no idea how good he has it. Sure, having gay parents in Mississippi isn't a total breeze, but his parents love each other and they've built this whole incredible life for him and his sister.

"Adam, son," Pam finally says, "are you going to introduce us to your friends?"

"Oh, yeah." He nods to Freddie. "Y'all know Freddie from the car wash." He turns to Pam. "Mom, he spent the night after Julia's party, remember?"

His little sister's birthday party. The night we snuck into that pool. I cringe at the memory.

"Ah," Pam says, "yes, but he was in too much of a hurry to stick around for my French toast."

Freddie laughs nervously. "Yes, ma'am. My gram needed me home early that day. Not only will I make it up to you in the future, but I'll make you the egg dish of your choosing."

I ignore the way my body sings with affection for him.

Pam smiles, and I see that it's her smile that Cindy probably fell in love with. She has the kind of smile that's wide and dazzling and defines her entire face when she aims it in your direction.

"And this is Ramona," Adam continues, "and Ruth."

Cindy's eyebrows pop up. "Well, this is the first time Adam's ever brought ladies home."

Adam's cheeks turn beet red. "We're watching *Star Wars*," he says.

"Well, you'd better leave the door open to that movie

room, mister," Pam tells him.

A movie room? An entire *room* dedicated to watching movies?

"Mom," he says, "they're lesbians. And not even with each other."

Cindy's lips twitch for a moment, like there's something she wants to say to us. For a moment, I wonder if she has some weird yet wonderful bit of middle-aged-lesbian advice to impart to us. But instead she just treats us like we're totally normal, which is somehow even better. "Leave the door open like your mother asked."

Beside me, Ruth smiles.

Freddie steps forward in his usual charming way. "Thank you," he says, "for having us over on a school night."

"Manners, eggs, and girls who don't even want to sleep with our son," says Cindy. "Y'all are welcome here anytime."

"Anytime," Pam echoes, her smile warm and genuine.

I nod. Some part of me feels tender and exposed, but not in a bad way. It's a small gesture, but it has big meaning.

The three of us follow Adam up the stairs as he and Freddie take turns swatting each other with lightsabers.

The movie room is a dark, windowless space with three deep-brown leather love seats. Ruth and Adam each claim their own love seat, so Freddie and I are left to share the one in the middle.

Before sitting, I hesitate for a moment as I realize how close together we'll be. But it doesn't matter, because we're friends. Just friends. And besides! We're in a room with

Adam and Ruth. How much more unromantic could it get?

"Hey," says Ruth in a voice that's a cross between a whisper and a shout. "When exactly were you going to tell us that you have two moms?"

Adam shrugs. "They're my parents. When were you going to tell me you have a mom and a dad?"

Ruth shakes her head. "No, that is not the same thing."

I swallow back a laugh. "I mean, Adam, we're lesbians. You having two moms would've given you major gay street cred with us."

He throws up his arms. "I don't know! They're my moms. I didn't really know how to be like, hey, P.S. my moms are super gay for each other. It's not like I'm ashamed of them. But they're my parents. I don't know."

"And you didn't tell us either!" Ruth says to Freddie.

Freddie shrugs. "It's not a big deal."

Except that it is. But maybe Adam is protective of his moms or maybe he felt awkward just throwing it out there. I don't know, but knowing they're here . . . well, it's a nice feeling.

Adam doubles back to the door and cracks it open before starting the movie, which plays from a projector overhead. The room is so dark that it's easy to believe we've been transported to a long time ago, in a galaxy far, far away.

I've sat, curled up with my dad in our little trailer, watching every Star Wars movie in almost every order imaginable. Dad prefers to start with Episode I. He says that trilogy is the worst, so it's best to get it out of the way anyhow, but Adam starts with Episode IV: *A New Hope*, the first movie ever released in the series.

Freddie quietly hums along to the music, and when he catches me smiling at him, he whispers, "What? It's not like I've never heard the theme song."

On one side of us, Adam mouths every single line, and on our other side Ruth is asleep before Luke accidentally plays R2-D2's message meant for Obi-Wan Kenobi.

"Why do Leia's buns make me so hungry?" asks Freddie. "Like, they just make me want cinnamon rolls."

"Oh my God, shut up," says Adam.

"And there are literally zero black people in this movie."

"Bro," says Adam, "the whiteness is blinding, I get it, but this movie is super old. And at least you end up getting Lando Calrissian."

"Lando who?" asks Freddie while R2-D2 dukes it out with a gang of Jawas.

"Lando Calrissian," I say. "And he ends up being a traitor."

"Who ends up being a good guy," argues Adam.

"Who still starts out as a traitor," I say.

"It's not perfect, okay? Can we just watch the movie?"

Freddie cracks a few jokes about how old everything looks. But still, it doesn't take long before he is simultaneously riveted by Luke and Leia and laughing at Han Solo's cockiness.

Because I've seen this movie so many times, it's easy to get caught up in watching Freddie.

He sits with his hand between us, palm facing up. I tell

myself it's just the way he's sitting, but it feels too much like an invitation to ignore.

I rest my hand next to his so that all that's touching is our pinkies. I think I do it to prove to myself that we can be friends. We can touch and it can mean nothing—or well, as much as it means when my hand brushes up against Ruth's or Adam's or Saul's.

But instead what I find is that my heart, my whole heart, has made its way to my pinkie along with all the blood that runs through my veins. My heart pounds in that one little finger as it barely brushes against his.

The light from the screen cascades over Freddie, creating a silhouette, and I watch his Adam's apple bob as he swallows, and his pinkie crosses over mine, like we're making some kind of promise. A silent pinkie-swear in this great big house as we watch a movie about a fatherless boy who's searching for his one true home in a great big galaxy.

We sit like that until Adam turns the lights back on as the credits roll. Then the two of us quickly pull our hands away. Ruth slowly wakes up, yawning and stretching. Freddie and I sit with our arms crossed over our chests, trying to put as much distance between us as possible. As my eyes adjust, I realize that Freddie and I are much braver in the dark than in the light.

DECEMBER

TWENTY-TWO

The next morning I'm sluggish as my legs pump the pedals of my bike. Sharing a twin bed with Hattie has turned into a regular occurrence. She's stopped even bothering to try sleeping in her full-size bed with Tyler. *He gets too sweaty*, she says, *and your room is the first one off the AC vent.* It's true that my room is cooler than my dad's and Hattie's, but I keep thinking that's not the only reason she's taken up residence in my room.

Having Tyler in our house feels like a stranger's begun occupying the room next to mine. The thought of him living in our house and eating our food—all free of charge—grates on me more and more every day. I know Dad feels it, too. He's just too nice to say so.

And truthfully, my head was too full of questions last night for me to ever shut down and fall asleep. The only conclusion I came to was that Freddie and I must do everything we can to stay friends. And friends don't make a big deal of holding hands—or pinkies?—during movies.

As I fly down the hill to Freddie's, I kick my legs out

and let the pedals spin on their own. The drive home last night was only slightly awkward, and I totally chickened out and asked Freddie to drop me off before Ruth.

When I drop my bike in Freddie's driveway, Agnes is sitting on the porch, drinking her morning coffee. "Brought your swimsuit?" she asks.

"Yes, ma'am."

The front door swings open as Freddie comes walking out with his gym bag hanging from his shoulder.

"All right, kiddies," says Agnes. "Let's motor."

"Shotgun," I call, trying my best to act normal.

Freddie walks himself to the backseat.

"Not gonna fight me for it?" I ask.

"I think that'd be a losing battle." He half smiles, but his voice is flat.

A little twinge of disappointment settles in my belly.

We drive with the windows down as Agnes listens to her talk radio show.

At the YMCA, the only car in the parking lot belongs to Carter, the old man who works the front desk in the mornings.

The three of us drop our bags in the locker rooms and change into our suits before heading out to the pool. Agnes takes her usual end lane and Freddie beside her and me beside him. We all dive in and begin to swim our laps, each hitting our rhythm.

I love the way my body reacts to water. I know that I'll pay for pushing myself as hard as I am this morning, but in this moment I can't feel my muscles burn. I am weightless, and my brain is on autopilot as my body does exactly what it is supposed to do. I can hardly remember that I'm exhausted and frustrated and confused. I barely let myself blink, though, because every time I do, I see Freddie's freckles.

I swim back and forth and back and forth. The only thing that stops me is Freddie as I'm about to do a flip-turn to make another lap.

"It's gettin' late," he shouts, his voice muffled as I shake the water out of my ears. "We better hit the showers."

I nod into my heaving chest. "Right."

Freddie pulls himself out of the pool and then turns to offer me a hand, but I pull myself up. It takes me a minute to find my balance after swimming so furiously for almost an hour, and he timidly steadies me by my elbow.

"Thanks," I tell him.

The woman in the black Speedo, who is always coming as we're going, sits on the bleachers, stretching her arms over her head. "You didn't look like a mess out there," she says.

Freddie turns to me, a question in his expression, but I motion for him to go ahead without me and he obliges.

After weeks of unsolicited comments, the woman finally extends a hand to me and says, "Prudence Whitmire."

I shake her hand. "Ramona."

"You ever swim on a team?"

"No, ma'am."

She nods. "Figured as much."

A dead quiet sinks between us as I realize that's all she

was going to say. "Well, it was nice to meet you." My voice is too perky, but it's the best I can do to hide my disappointment at her criticizing my swimming skills.

But she hasn't dismissed me yet. She stands and walks the two steps down the bleachers to me. Standing on level ground, I can see that she's quite petite and barely even comes as high as my chest. "Listen," she says. "I'm not saying you're some kind of prodigy or anything, but I just retired as head swim coach over at Delgado Community College in Slidell. If you ever decide you want to swim for more than fun, and maybe learn a thing or two while you're at it, maybe I could help you get a foot in the door there." She shrugs and walks off toward the diving blocks.

"Thanks?" But she doesn't hear me over the music from the early-morning water aerobics class.

As I walk to the locker room, I file her offer away in my permanent memory bank. It's a nice gesture that unfortunately doesn't mean much to me. I can't imagine there's much scholarship money for community college swim teams. Still, there's a little hiccup in my rib cage from being flattered, even if it was in the most bizarre way.

Steam billows out from the stall where Agnes is already showering.

Thankful for the privacy, I strip out of my swimsuit and hang the towel from my bag on the hook outside my shower stall.

The water heats up quickly and opens my chest, forcing me to breathe clearly. I use the shampoo and conditioner in the dispensers, even though I know Hattie would kill me for not using the color-safe stuff she buys at the beauty shop.

The faucet in Agnes's stall stops, and a few minutes later she says, "I'll be waiting in the car, dear."

After she leaves, I rinse the conditioner from my hair. I turn off the water and dry off for a moment before wrapping my towel around my chest. I get as far as putting on my underwear when I hear a loud crack and then the power goes out. It's not until this moment that I realize that I am in a windowless interior room. I hold my hand up in front of my face but see nothing. Total darkness. Panic bubbles up from my chest and into my throat. I reach out frantically and find the lockers to my left.

"Ramona?" a voice calls.

It's Freddie. In the women's locker room.

"I'm in here," I say. "But I can't see anything."

"Carter's looking for flashlights out front, but he's not having much luck."

"Okay, so what does that mean for me?"

"I guess they were working on some lines and a generator blew."

I turn to grab my T-shirt, but instead trip over the corner of a bench.

"Are you okay?" calls Freddie.

"Just kind of disoriented."

"Do you want me to come in? I can try to use my cell phone for light."

I pull my towel tighter around my chest. "Um, yeah. Go ahead."

"Marco?" His voice is playful, and it eases my anxiety. Logically, I know that there's no one in this locker room except for Freddie and me. But the dark makes me feel claustrophobic.

"Polo," I answer. We would play Marco Polo on the beach with Hattie all the time when we were kids. Freddie always wanted to play on dry land, and Hattie and I would sneak off into the ocean, because we knew he'd never try to find us there.

"Marco?"

"Polo."

We go back and forth a few times as he follows my voice to the far corner of the expansive room. And then I see the light from his phone as he rounds the corner.

"Here," I say. "I'm right here."

He lifts his phone so that it's shining on me.

I squint and block my eyes with my hand.

"Oh, sorry," he says. "I didn't realize you weren't dressed." His words are clipped, and I don't have to see him to know he's blushing.

"I couldn't see," I tell him.

He holds his phone out to me. "Here. Take this. I'll turn around and wait for you down there."

"Thanks."

Quickly, I tug my jeans up my still damp legs and put my bra and T-shirt on. After shoving my wet swimsuit into my duffel, I turn to see Freddie still standing with his back to me a few lockers down. His shoulders rise up and down evenly, like he's taking meditative breaths.

It makes me want to comfort him. To give him the same calm he gives me.

I step forward lightly and put his phone down on the bench with the light still shining upward and gently trace the line of his shoulder with the tips of my fingers. Because just like out in Agnes's backyard and in Adam's movie room, the world is dark and it's hard to remember that we exist outside of this moment.

He goes still.

"Ramona." There's no question in his voice.

He turns to me and my fingers rake across his shoulder blade around to the broad expanse of his chest.

When I was in fifth grade, Rebekah Paulson sat in front of me. She had waist-length jet-black hair that moved like a beaded curtain concealing her face. I would have to sit on my hands just to stop myself from my running my fingers through her hair.

And that's how I feel now, here with Freddie. I've never wanted to touch a boy in the way I want to touch him. It makes me feel uncomfortable, but I'm starting to think that maybe the gist of life is learning how to be comfortable with being uncomfortable.

"Ramona." He says my name again, but this time it sounds like a plea. "I want to kiss you."

I bite down hard on my lip. "I want that, too."

If our first kiss was a polite introduction, this one is a shouting match.

With his head tilted upward and one hand cupped behind my neck, he uses his free hand to pull me flush against him. Our feet twist together until I'm pressed against the lockers with a handle digging into my back, but I don't care.

My hands run across his upper body and over the top of his scalp, begging my fingerprints to leave their mark and to memorize every bit of him.

Kissing him is different, yes. But it's not. Kissing Freddie doesn't feel different because he's a boy, it feels different because he's Freddie. Kissing him varies in the same way that kissing Grace was different from kissing CarrieAnn or any other girl.

Freddie presses his hips tighter against mine, and then I feel the real difference. I gasp.

"I'm sorry," he blurts. He pulls himself back and almost falls over the bench behind him, but I catch him by his arm.

"I wanted you to kiss me," I say without hesitation. "I wanted it on Thanksgiving, too."

He inhales and exhales deeply as if to get his own body back under control.

"We better get going," I tell him, because if we don't, I feel like my clothes might not stay on much longer. Adrenaline pumps through my body, and I either have to move or touch him.

Freddie nods quickly, his eyes still wide. He takes my bag from where it sits on the bench and holds a hand out for me. Barefoot, I follow him as he uses his cell phone to guide us back out to the hallway.

The corridor is lit only with faint natural light, making

it easier on our eyes as we emerge from the dark locker room.

We hold hands for a moment longer until we reach the end of the empty, partially lit hallway.

In the car, Agnes is shaking her head. "Bet you got a little scare in there, huh?"

I settle into the front seat. "So dark I couldn't see my own hand in front of me."

She glances up at her rearview mirror. "Well, Freddie, what'd you think of your first venture into a women's locker room?"

"Enlightening," he says. "Very enlightening."

TWENTY-THREE

Over the next few days, nothing and everything changes. We're still Freddie and Ramona, but we're versions of ourselves who share secret kisses and under-the-table hand holding. When we eat lunch with Ruth or Adam and see Hattie and Saul after school, I marvel at the fact that they don't see the difference between us. That feeling I get when I'm riding my bike down the steep hill of Freddie's street is the only way I know how to explain it. The world around me is a blur except for him.

I feel like every moment not spent alone is a race to find some bit of privacy. It's not that we're hiding anything, but it seems so odd to announce something to our friends that we can't even name ourselves.

There is this unexpected guilt every time I kiss Freddie. Like I'm doing him some kind of disservice by not being straight or that I'm somehow betraying Saul and Ruth by kissing a member of the opposite sex. But it's fleeting, because holding his hand and touching his lips feel like home.

On Thursday afternoon, before last period, I find a note in my locker. I unfold it with care and find *MASH* written across the top of the page in long, skinny penmanship I immediately recognize. I have to bite my lips to hide my smile as I slide the note into my binder and sit in the back row of last period.

After checking to make sure no one is paying attention, I close my eyes and draw a spiral with my pencil at the bottom of the page, counting each line so I know which options to circle.

M	A	S	H
(MEAL)	(ART MUSEUM)	(SURPRISE)	(HARRISON COUNTY CHRISTMAS MARKET)
BUS	AGNES'S CADILLAC	BIKES	BART'S TRUCK
CASUAL	FORMAL	MATCHING	80'S

I raise my hand for a bathroom pass so that I can drop my completed game of MASH in Freddie's locker. After school, I duck out as quickly as I can. Not because I don't want to see him, but because for once, it's nice to be the one being chased.

TWENTY-FOUR

On Friday morning, Freddie and I have locked ourselves in the single-stall restroom at school reserved for handicapped students. No one really uses this bathroom much, though, except to hook up. I used to roll my eyes at couples stumbling out, but oh, how the tables have turned.

I'm sitting on the lip of the sink with my legs spread and Freddie kissing petals down my neck. "I've got our matching outfits under control, by the way," he says, referring to our game of MASH.

"Do you?" My voice is uneven, clearly affected by his lips on my throat. But then I laugh at a memory so old I wonder if I made it up. "Do you remember that year on the Fourth of July when Agnes made us dress up like presidents for the parade?"

He pulls back for a minute, bracing his hands on my thighs. "Oh my God, yes. I was Roosevelt. You were Truman—"

"And Hattie was Lincoln, and she cried because her beard was itchy."

He smiles. "Those suits were so hot. It was July. What was she thinking?"

It's so hard for me to comprehend sometimes that we're still the same people we were then. There's just a lot more kissing, and Freddie's not scared of the ocean anymore. "Hey, should I plan to be out all night on Saturday? I can get Hattie to cover for me. Not that my dad really cares if I'm out late."

"That's up to you," he says coyly.

"Well, actually, that's more than likely up to Agnes."

He kisses my nose quickly like a pecking bird. "Curfews are made to be tested, right?"

On Saturday morning after my paper route, I work the breakfast and lunch shift at Boucher's, so by the time I get home, it's already two o'clock in the afternoon.

In my bedroom, waiting for me is Hattie, of course. She's sprawled out on my bed, reading a paperback romance in a pair of cheer shorts and a sports bra. Her growing belly looks like a melting sun on the horizon of my bed. "Tyler's at work," she announces, as if I am at all concerned by the cretin's whereabouts.

For a moment, I start to wonder how much time she spends in my room when I'm not here, but before I can get worked up, I remember that I've got to shower and change.

I don't have time to bother with washing my hair, so I twist it in a knot and hop in the shower. The head on our shower is so low that I've actually got to go out of my way to get my hair wet if I want to. I scrub and rinse the smell of dirty dishes and sweat from my skin. As I'm getting out, the door swings wide open and then slams shut.

It was quick, but not so quick that I didn't recognize Tyler in the doorway.

"You don't knock?" I scream as I wrap the towel around my chest. Anger boils under my skin.

"It was unlocked," he says from the other side of the door. No sorry. No excuse me. But of course he doesn't say those things.

I swing the door open. "Well, you wouldn't know it was unlocked if you hadn't tried the handle, and besides, the lock doesn't even work."

"Damn," he says. "I didn't see anything. It's almost like looking at a guy anyway."

"How are you so ignorant?" All I can register is red-hot anger. I can't believe the stupid dribbling out of his mouth, and just being in the same place as him makes me feel completely unreasonable. It's one of those moments where I wonder how I can truly love Hattie if she honestly thinks *this* is a good decision.

He's silent.

"What? Because I'm a lesbian? A *dyke*?"

"What's going on out there?" calls Hattie.

"Your little sister's overreacting."

Hattie sticks her head out my bedroom door, the yellowing paperback dangling from her fingers. "Are you being an asshole to my sister?" She looks to me. "Is he?"

I glance between the two of them. "It's fine. Just a mis-understanding."

She gives him a pointed look and shuts my door behind her.

I check the towel to make sure it's tight around my chest before I point my finger right in his face and say low enough that Hattie can't hear, "Don't forget whose house this really is, you piece of shit."

Back in my bedroom, Hattie is sitting on my bed with her book.

"Where are you off to?" she asks.

"Hanging out with Freddie." I turn my back to her and put my bra and underwear on, before opening my tiny closet. Most of my clothes reside on the floor or in the never-ending cycle that is my laundry basket, but the good stuff—and there's not much of it—stays hanging because I don't get around to wearing it much.

I pull out a yellow-and-black-striped trapeze dress and a peach shirtdress with little white cats all over it. I know Freddie's taking care of our outfits (whatever that means), but I still want to look different when he first sees me.

"Whoa there," says Hattie. "Are you getting dressed up?" She stands up and leaves her book facedown on the bedspread.

"If by dressed up you mean I'm wearing a dress that doesn't have pizza grease stains on it, then yes."

"You wanna tell me what's going on?"

"I'm hanging out with Freddie."

She glances to me and then to the two dresses in my hands.

"We're going out and I don't know where, so I don't want to look stupid."

"It's not like it's a date or something," she says.

And when I don't respond, she takes the dresses from my hand and hangs them on the doorknob before forcing me to sit on the bed.

"When you say you two are going out . . ."

I take a deep breath.

"Ramona Blue, you know this house is too small for secrets."

And that's the truth, isn't it? Maybe that's why I haven't told anyone about what's happened between us, because for once I'd like to have a secret to myself. But Hattie is my sister, and hiding from her is as easy as fitting a car through a keyhole.

"Freddie's taking me on a date. I think."

Her face looks like I've smacked her with a frying pan. "What does that even mean?" she finally asks.

"For me?" It hits me like a brain freeze. Part of me thinks I've been avoiding this question all week and part of me thinks the only reason I feel the need to answer it is because someone asked. But regardless, I don't know the answer.

"Listen," she says, "I get that your options here are limited, but you don't want to mess stuff up with Freddie just because you're bored."

"I'm not bored," I tell her. "You don't even know what you're talking about."

"Well, I'm here if you want to talk." She tucks her paperback under her arm. "Wear the cat dress."

After she leaves, I slip the cat dress over my head and glance in the mirror. She's right.

TWENTY-FIVE

After styling my hair into two braids that crisscross over my head like a messy headband and putting on my boots, I wait for Freddie out front.

I watch as Bart's truck, his beloved 1948 Chevy pickup, rocks over the potholes toward my trailer. I wonder how much talking Agnes had to do in order for Freddie to borrow it.

He hops out of the driver's side and pauses for a moment as his eyes drink me in. "Well, you look lovely, but as promised . . ." He holds out a black tuxedo T-shirt for me that perfectly matches the one he's wearing with his dark-wash jeans shredded on one knee and high-top sneakers.

His cheeks flush, making his orangey freckles stand out even more than usual.

"You look pretty," he says. "You are pretty, I mean."

I slip the T-shirt over my head, mussing up my already messy hair. "Thanks." But my voice is too low for him to hear.

He opens the passenger door for me before jogging

around the front of the truck to his side.

He flips through radio stations restlessly as we drive out of town.

"Where are we going?"

"Not far. I don't think."

"But it's a secret?"

"New Orleans," he says. He never was good with secrets. "I love it at Christmastime, especially."

My rib cage tickles with excitement. "NOLA is my favorite." And I'm a little relieved we're venturing out and away from Eulogy. I'm still not sure how we exist in public.

"I know," he says. "Me too." His shoulders bounce. There's electricity in the air. I can feel it. "Favorite city. Favorite person."

I grin as he turns the music up. We take the scenic way there, making our drive about an hour and a half long, and soon after we cross the state line, we're driving down narrow strips of land with rows of newly constructed houses on stilts sitting at the edge of Lake Pontchartrain.

According to my dad, all of this was wiped out by Katrina, too. Anytime he talks about Katrina in regard to Louisiana, there's a bitterness in his voice. When the world thinks of Hurricane Katrina, they imagine the overflowing Superdome and the Ninth Ward and the flooded historic streets of the lower Quarter. No one thinks of our Mississippi and the incredible damage that forever changed the coast. No one talks about the industries and livelihoods that were lost.

I often wonder what my life would look like if I had lived in a world where Katrina didn't happen. In that universe, my parents are still together and we're not rich, but we're not scraping by like we have for as long as I can remember. And all the deserted concrete slabs that line the coast are occupied with buildings that have stood against the same hurricanes my dad witnessed as a boy. It's a different world, but not one I'll ever have the privilege of existing in.

In our little trailer park, not even a mile from the coast, we're sitting ducks. Folks in Eulogy don't use years to measure time. They use storms, and I guess I'm just waiting for the next big one.

I get a little fidgety as we cross a huge steel bridge into New Orleans that can be raised up and down for larger boats to pass through. I remember, as a kid, being so mesmerized by the idea that an entire structure could adjust for one boat—one single boat that happened to be too tall. As I got older and the inches kept adding up and the growing pains became almost unbearable, I remember wishing that the doorways of our trailer could raise up and down just for me.

I'm impressed with Freddie's ability to maneuver the traffic, but I'm in the habit of staying quiet, because when we were kids my dad would get anxious with all the added cars and pedestrians. We pull into a skinny parking lot that runs the length of the Moonwalk, which edges up against the Mississippi River. The walk is lined with tourists and

men with towels thrown over their shoulders and shoe polish in their hands as they try to talk anyone who will make
eye contact with them into a shoe shine.

"Are you hungry?" Freddie asks.

"Starving."

"Good."

We walk out of the parking lot and down the steps
to Decatur Street. Sprawled out in front of us is Jackson
Square, a beautiful green space in the middle of the French
Quarter. Behind us, overlooking the Mississippi River,
is a ginormous Christmas tree with huge gold and red
ornaments and an equally huge star on top. Oversize red
bows hang from every lamppost in sight. The Quarter has
this smell—and I don't particularly hate it, even though I
should. It's a combination of once-exquisite day-old food,
puke, and the sticky-sweet scent of frozen daiquiris.

Freddie points to St. Louis Cathedral. "I used to think
it was the castle from Disney World."

And I see it, too. There aren't as many turrets, but it's
bright and white, like a beacon.

That's when he chooses to take my hand, when I'm
distracted and not ready, but so ready. Our hands clasped
together makes my breath catch, which seems silly since
we've been pressing our bodies together in whatever quiet
corners we could find for the last week. But this is outside,
in the middle of the day, and it somehow feels even more
intimate than a kiss.

We're not a secret. I tell myself this over and over again.

I know what it's like to be a secret, and this is not it. But there's a freedom—almost the same kind I felt so briefly with Grace at Viv's party—that comes with being strangers in a big city.

As I let Freddie lead the way to wherever he's decided to take me, I am only the Ramona who exists in this moment. I'm on a date. With a person who happens to be a boy. And we're holding hands. I am Ramona and he is Freddie and that's it.

We walk a few blocks toward Canal Street, and every time someone points and laughs at us, I have to remind myself that we're wearing matching tuxedo T-shirts. Freddie stops at the corner of Chartres and Toulouse behind a line of people.

"They, uh, don't take reservations," he says.

The sign hanging above our heads is white with a pink fleur-de-lis and simply reads *The Grill*.

"This was my favorite place growing up," Freddie tells me.

"I've never even heard of it," I say with bemusement. I think that's one of the many wonders of this city: you can come here your whole life and always find something new to discover. "But I'm excited to see what's so special about it."

"I don't know if it's all that special, but I thought so when I was little." He squeezes my hand once and pulls me closer to the building so that his body is protecting me from the sudden gust of wind. It's almost a wasted effort because of my height, but I appreciate the thought.

I press my nose to the glass and see that the inside is an overcrowded light-pink-and-white diner with a bustling waitstaff in black pants, white chef jackets, and bow ties. I can see little Freddie being fascinated by this place. There are no tables or chairs, but instead one big bar that lines the kitchen with dark green bar stools. Twinkly lights hang from the ceiling and a small aluminum Christmas tree sits next to the jukebox. Based on the line of people, I'm assuming it's good, but I know what it feels like to revisit something from your childhood and find that the mysterious magic it once held has evaporated.

The line moves fast and we are quickly ushered inside to two bar seats at the end of the row. Despite the place being loud and packed, our little corner feels quiet.

A tall black man whose name tag reads *Hugo* takes our drink order and tells us the catfish sandwich is his favorite. "So what'll we have for food?"

Freddie doesn't even glance at the menu before saying, "Grilled cheese with eggs. Sunny-side up."

I sputter for a moment and choose the first thing I see. "Pancakes?"

"You got it," says Hugo.

Freddie turns to me. "Sorry. I guess they try to get people in and out pretty fast, but it's great diner food."

"It's okay." It's not what I expected for a date, but I guess nothing about this is what I expected. And I don't even know if I've really been on a date. Do people even go on dates anymore? With Grace it was more like hang out, make out, watch TV, hang out, eat food, make out.

(Which, if I'm being honest, is nothing to complain about.)

"So, I never asked. How did you like *Star Wars*?"

He latches his pinkie with mine. "It was good."

"Yeah?"

His lips fall into a faint frown. "Got me thinking about my dad."

I squeeze his pinkie with mine.

"I had such a big crush on you when we were kids," Freddie blurts, changing the subject abruptly.

My cheeks grow warm, but it might just be the rising temperature in the packed diner. I go along with the subject change, not wanting to make him talk about anything he doesn't want to. "Did you really?"

"Yeah. You were like this wild summer child who was always in a swimsuit, with hair full of sand. I didn't even realize until, like, fourth grade that your real name wasn't Ramona Blue. You were as much a character in my life as Santa Claus was."

Hugo returns with our drinks and whips two straws out like a set of swords. "Food'll be out in a minute."

"You were like my own Peter Pan," says Freddie. "I thought you would never grow up and that you'd always be this constant fixture on the beach, challenging other kids to races in the sand and swimming-noodle duels."

His words suck the breath right out of my lungs. No one has ever summed me up in such a succinct way. I feel like Peter Pan, and it's like Eulogy is my Neverland. "I guess that makes you my Wendy Darling."

He grins. "I like that."

I laugh. "I thought you guys were so rich. I thought everyone who visited the coast was rich. I knew *we* weren't rich, but we got to live in the place where everyone else vacationed, so it seemed like a fair trade-off."

"Did you like me?" he asks. "Even a little bit?"

"I remember feeling a faint curiosity," I admit. "But I think I was too busy worrying about why I wanted to kiss girls."

"How did you know?" he asks. His brow furrows, and I can see he's trying to make sense of us with what he knows to be true about me in mind. Frankly, I'm trying to do the same. "Were you ever scared that you were supposed to be a boy or something?"

"I was never confused about my gender," I tell him. "I've definitely always felt like a girl. The confusing part was *liking* other girls. Not feeling like I wasn't one." I know I should be disappointed that his understanding of my sexuality is so elementary, but at least he's eager to learn. Growing up in the deep, deep South, I might have found it easy to assume that my feelings for girls made me less of one.

He takes a sip from his drink. "Will you think I'm some gross dude if I admit that I was kind of disappointed when I found out you were into girls?"

"Yes, but no," I say. "I guess it's like when someone you like is already with somebody else."

He nods. "Yeah. Sort of. But I thought we—this!—was impossible."

"But you had Viv!"

235

"I did," he says. His shoulders fall into a downward slope. "I guess maybe that's why I tried so hard to make it work with her even when I knew it was over."

On one hand, this revelation elates me, but on the other, I feel so much more pressure not to mess this up.

"Grilled cheese for the man in the tux," says Hugo. "And pancakes for the lady in the tux." Then he drops our bill on the table.

Freddie pulls a twenty from his pocket. "No change."

"My two favorite words," says Hugo.

I don't know if I'm starving or if the pancakes are really that good, but I finish every last syrup-doused crumb.

After we're both done, we take a stroll back toward Jackson Square, and this time it's me who finds Freddie's hand first. "So Viv," I say.

"It was over long before that party." His voice is sad but firm.

I feel for him, but not in a commiserating way like I did at first. Now I'm more upset that anyone would dare hurt him.

We sit down on the steps of St. Louis Cathedral and watch as artists lining the fence of the square sit camped out on the ground creating more art, scratching their dogs' bellies, and chatting back and forth about tourists and upcoming local events. To our left is an impromptu street brass band playing "Go Tell It on the Mountain." And beside them are a few psychics with folding chairs sitting behind card tables as they wait for night to fall and for the inhabitants of the Quarter to turn curious.

"Was she your first girlfriend?" I ask.

"Does that make me pathetic?"

"No," I tell him emphatically. I want to ask. I shouldn't. It's none of my business. But maybe it is. "Is she the only girl you've ever been with?"

"Been with?" He smirks. "If you're going to ask it, you have to say it."

I try to swallow, but my mouth is too dry. "Is she the only girl you've ever had sex with?"

He nods. "Yep. For a while, I even thought she might be the last."

"Are you serious?"

He turns to me. "Ridiculous, isn't it?"

"Unrealistic? Yes. Ridiculous? No."

"I thought I'd found it. I don't even know if we were in love, but we were happy, and . . . and happy is more than my parents ever had, if what they had was anything at all. It's sad that sometimes we let ourselves believe that if it's not bad, it must be good."

I carve out a corner of my memory for his words, because it's a sentiment I don't want to forget. It's an idea that feels dangerous, because it makes me want more, and suddenly I'm reminded of Prudence Whitmire, the old lady at the pool, and her offer to put in a good word for me at Delgado Community College. But I push her from my head, because the last thing I want to think about when I'm on a date is that woman and her inability to keep her opinions to herself.

"You don't talk about them much," I say, referring to

his parents and trying to pull myself away from thoughts of the future. "Do you know where they are now?"

He shakes his head. "I think my dad's out in California somewhere. My gram said she heard he's got a wife and kid out there now. I might have a sibling that I don't even know. Isn't that nuts? I can't think about it for too long, because it'll eat me up." He drums his fingers on his knee. "I guess good on him for having a life. He just forgot to let me know about it. And my mom—there's no telling." He laughs drily. "She's like bad cell reception. Never there when you need her most. Last time I saw her was the day after my gramps's funeral. She was late. A whole day late."

Having Agnes must make up for a lot, I'm sure, but hearing about his parents still makes me feel like shit for even complaining about my mom. She's a flake, sure. But she's a semi-responsible flake.

"Come on," says Freddie. "You gotta dance with me." He stands up and pulls me with him.

"I don't dance."

That doesn't faze him. "Me neither." He takes my arms and drapes them over his shoulders as he gently holds my hips. "This seems like a good place to start."

My hips sway like they're attached to marionette strings controlled by the music. It's a song I know so well from my childhood, a brass band cover of "Sexual Healing." Maybe that's weird, but it was always one of my dad's favorite brass band covers.

"Look at you go!" says Freddie over the music.

Our bodies inch closer together as the crowd claps along

to the beat. And then his hips are pressed against mine and his hand is on the small of my back. Our upper bodies are loose as we let the trumpets possess us. There are whistles and hoots.

For a second, I let myself look around, and a crowd has formed around us, the band, and a few other couples. Passersby toss cash into hats and open instrument cases. We're just as much a part of the performance as the band. The trombone kicks in and our feet stomp along to the music.

"People are staring," I say.

"Let them," he says, and kisses my hand before spinning me out and twirling me back in so that his chest is pressed against my back.

I'm scared that this might be the happiest moment of my life. I'm scared, because I don't want it to end, and because this can't be it. I need more. I need more moments like this. Everyone should dance in the middle of a beautiful square with a freckled person they love.

Love, I think suddenly. It's just a thought, I tell myself. It might not be true. But I do love Freddie. In what way, I don't know. But I do.

The song ends and the crowd gives a loud cheer before quickly dispersing. The two of us are out of breath, chests heaving, and I'm smiling so wide my cheeks ache.

The band comes by and shakes our hands. I search my pockets for a few bucks to drop in the trombone case. (It is my personal philosophy that dresses without pockets are useless.) They transition into "O Holy Night," and a whole new crowd has already gathered.

The sun has dipped far below the horizon of buildings, and all that's left is a faint early-twilight glow.

Freddie takes my hand. "Let's walk."

And we do. We walk all over in our matching T-shirts. We wander into stores full of beautiful things we can't afford. We take pictures in souvenir shops, wearing feather boas and ridiculous hats. We slide into a photo booth and Freddie says to make serious faces and then tickles my armpits, making me laugh so hard I can't breathe until the last frame, when he kisses me and I kiss him back.

I pull him into a store on Decatur Street called Hex. The windows glow with candles, and in a small corner of the store a woman sits behind a partially closed curtain, telling fortunes. I can see that the store makes Freddie a little nervous—or maybe it's the girl behind the counter with the shaved head. He hovers close behind me as I look very carefully at all the spell kits. You can buy a kit for love, money, happiness, justice. Anything you can think of.

Freddie drifts from me as I study the bowls of crystals and stones. It's incredible to me to think that all these objects can hold so much meaning, but at the end of the day they're objects and only we can give them meaning.

Freddie kisses my temple. "I'll be outside."

The curtain at the back of the shop opens, and a man comes out with a worried expression. Behind him, the fortune-teller gently touches his shoulder and he nods a thank-you. She's not the person I expected to see behind the curtain, that's for sure. She wears mom jeans with a floral oxford tucked in. Her bangs are teased, and she looks like she should be chasing kids around an outlet mall.

Her eyes are warm when she says, "Aren't you the tall one?"

It's something I hear all the time from strangers, but it still takes me by surprise. Sometimes—and especially on days like today—it's easy to forget yourself.

"Blue hair, too." She squeezes past me to the office behind the register. "Blue is for stability, if I recall, but sometimes it's good to shake things up. Isn't that right, Sam?" she asks the girl at the register.

"Yep," she says, her voice dripping with indifference. "Shake things up."

I twirl a loose tendril around my finger and nod. After looking around for a minute or two longer, I buy a few prosperity crystals for the chocolate box under my bed and meet Freddie outside.

The woman's words stick with me, though. On most days, I would shrug it off, but today is different. Today is not an average day in the life and times of Ramona.

He looks down at his phone. "Quarter to midnight," he says.

"Oh, wow." I yawn. "I guess we should start heading back."

We walk hand in hand back toward the car and stop at the Café du Monde to-go window for two café au laits and a bag of beignets for the ride home.

The drive is quiet as we sip our coffee and try not to get

powdered sugar all over Bart's truck. After a while, I feel myself slipping in and out of sleep for the next hour and a half.

Freddie wakes me up, and I expect to be home, but instead we're at the base of a dark, empty bridge.

"Do you trust me?" he asks.

I stretch my arms out, forcing myself to be alert. "Nothing good ever follows that question."

He checks the rearview mirror and turns his headlights off. There are no streetlights. All that's left is the hazy glow of the moon above. In complete darkness, he begins to drive over the bridge.

"Roll your window down."

I do as he says.

It's a little bit terrifying and it's a little bit peaceful.

"We're floating," he says.

And I see it. I feel it. We're in a truck coasting through the stars, hovering high above Eulogy. I am Peter Pan and he is Wendy, and this moment will last forever. We are flying.

TWENTY-SIX

I sit with my legs stretched out and propped up on a chair on the patio of Boucher's with Ruth as she finishes her lunch. Beside her is a small stack of letters with letterheads from her top-choice universities. Three acceptances and one wait list.

"I can't believe I got wait-listed at University of Texas," she says.

I tilt my head back to fully soak in the winter sun rays. "Was it your number one choice?" I ask.

"Well, no."

"Okay, so why does it matter then?"

"It's the principle of the whole thing," she says. "I met all their requirements and then some. I was the perfect candidate."

"It's not like they said no," I tell her, slightly annoyed.

"It's not like they said yes." She takes a few bites of her chicken strips. "So that thing we talked about in the library the other week? The hypothetical friends hypothetically kissing?"

I keep my head tilted back and am grateful for my sunglasses. I haven't been avoiding Ruth, but I haven't really gone out of my way to hang out with her lately in the week and half since my date with Freddie. I firmly believe that a lie by omission is still a lie, and well, Ruth is really hard to lie to. "What about it?" I ask.

"Well, how did that go? Hypothetically."

I shrug, squeezing my eyes shut behind my glasses. My voice is too high when I say, "Good. Fine."

She nods. "Just wondering. Anyway, what about you next year? You still have time to figure something out."

I sit up and glance around. "You're looking at it."

She rolls her eyes and runs her fingers through her dusty blond hair. "I don't get it, Ramona."

"I'm happy here." I know it's a lie the minute I say it. It's not that I hate Eulogy or my Mississippi roots, but it's that feeling of ducking down when I walk into a too-short doorway or hunching over when I'm in the shower. Like I've outgrown my life somehow. And now, after my trip to New Orleans with Freddie, I feel it everywhere.

Ruth puts her chicken strips to the side and pulls her backpack into her lap. "So you and Freddie went to New Orleans on Saturday?"

"Who told you that?" All I can hear is the conversation we had in the library after that first kiss.

"Hattie," she says. "We all watched movies together at Saul's."

"Do you still miss him? At home?" I ask, referring to Saul. Partly because I'm curious and partly because I need to change the subject.

"It's hard," she says. "I'm trying not to feel like he's abandoned me. I gotta remember that I was going to abandon him soon enough anyway. He has his own life now, which makes me feel better about having my own."

My chest aches at the thought of all of us creating our own lives separate from one another. Except that Hattie needs me in her life on constant standby. So while Saul is off with his boyfriend and Ruth is busy with all her premed stuff and Freddie is at LSU, I'll most likely be here in a holding pattern.

From the inside of her backpack, Ruth pulls out a stack of folders and booklets. "I picked these up for you at the college fair a few weeks ago. Do whatever you want with them," she says. "But at least look at them first, okay?"

I take the stack from her, and each thing has a seal or a logo from a different community college within a few hours' driving distance of here. "What are these?" I ask.

She shrugs. "Options."

"Ruth, you gotta quit with this stuff." I shove the stack back across the table.

But she pushes it back. "There's no reason you should be stuck here forever. I know you're over this place. It's so obvious."

"No reason? Are you serious?" I ask, trying not to raise my voice. "I have plenty of reasons. I have no money, no car, a knocked-up sister, mediocre grades . . . I can keep going," I tell her.

"Those aren't reasons," she says. "They're excuses." She

takes her plate and walks it back to the kitchen, leaving the stack of brochures and catalogs there.

I wait until she's out of sight before thumbing through the stack. I spy Delgado Community College and flip through the pamphlet before putting all of them in my backpack.

TWENTY-SEVEN

We were never good about splitting up our time equally between Mom and Dad like the court had mandated, but Christmas Eve has always been Mom's. Meaning it was the final hurdle to jump before I could relax and enjoy my winter vacation from school.

This year Christmas Eve falls on one of Mom's workdays, so me, Hattie, Tyler, and Freddie all make the drive down the coast to the row of casinos, where the lights never stop twinkling.

There's something beautiful about the casinos from the outside, but when we walk inside we're hit with that familiar haze of smoke that, for me, will always smell like Christmas Eve. Once you're inside, there's something so disorienting about the lack of windows, which makes you forget whether it's day or night.

Mom is waiting for us at the entrance to the buffet. She wears her uniform of black cigarette pants, a white tuxedo shirt, and a black vest with a red-and-green-plaid bow tie for the holidays. Her hair is done up in a high ponytail that makes her look too young, and dangling from her ears are Christmas tree earrings made of little pom-poms. She waves us over, past the security guard.

Mom goes for Hattie's belly first, petting and cooing at it. "Baby," she says. "Look at you and that tummy. You look almost as big as I was when I was full term with you."

Hattie sighs. "Merry Christmas, Mama."

"And this must be the proud papa!" says my mom as she makes her way to Tyler. "You ready to have your life flipped on its ear?"

Tyler, who has so perfectly crafted the I-don't-give-a-shit face, is as white as a sheet. "Uh, yes, ma'am."

There's not a lot I admire about my mother, but her newfound ability to turn Tyler into a nervous little boy might be her most redeeming quality.

And then there's me. "Hi, Mom."

She takes my hand and then takes the hand of an unsuspecting Freddie. "And who is this?"

"Freddie Floaties," Hattie pipes up.

My mom squints. "Well, I haven't seen you since you were a little tyke hiding behind your grandmama's legs."

"It's nice to see you again, Ms. Leroux."

My mom winks at him. "Let's get some grub."

Mom loves when we visit her at the casino. This is her in her natural element—in a place where she is more than the woman who lives in a one-room apartment and got pregnant too young and left her family when they needed her the most. And even better, we brought more people for her to show off her kingdom to.

She leads us to a U-shaped booth at the buffet before we all split up to fill our plates.

Freddie stays close to me, and we both opt for fried chicken and mac and cheese. Tyler piles his plate high with crab legs, and Hattie goes for the mashed potato bar and shrimp cocktail. Mom waits in line at the carving station for ham and all the traditional fixings.

We reconvene in our giant booth, where Tyler has started in on his plate before anyone else could even sit down. I'm not saying there's a good way to eat crab legs, but I am saying there is a bad way, and Tyler seems to have mastered it. He cracks and slurps and cracks and slurps and cracks and slurps, and it is turning into the most annoying song I'll never be able to get out of my head.

"So have y'all thought about what's happening once the baby comes this spring?"

Tyler freezes mid-chew with a fresh crab leg in his hand.

Hattie reaches under the table for his hand. "Yep, we've been making a few plans, right, babe?"

Tyler nods and swallows. "Sure."

"Have you really?" I ask. Foot in mouth. I can taste it.

Hattie narrows her eyes at me. "As a matter of fact, we have."

"So where's the baby going?" asks my mom. "Y'all know your dad's trailer is only so big. It's not some clown car that you can keep squeezing more people into."

Well, she has a point there.

Freddie clears his throat, and I try to tell him sorry with a side-eye glance.

"Not that it's any of y'all's business," Hattie says as she dunks a shrimp in cocktail sauce. "But the baby is going wherever it is that we're going."

"And where is that?" I ask. I should really shut up. But the frustration I've felt since the moment Tyler moved into our house has begun to boil, and there's no going back now.

Beneath the table, Freddie touches my thigh, and I pull away in annoyance at his attempt to reel me in.

"We don't have to have it all figured out right now," Hattie bites back.

Tyler is quiet. And so is everyone else. Even my mom. None of them see what I see. They can't possibly understand that at the end of the day, it's me and Hattie. Just the two of us. I would jump into the Grand Canyon for my sister, but there's something unfair about the fact that by being born her sister, my destiny is predetermined. I will always be a few steps behind her, picking up the pieces and putting them back together again, waiting for my own life to start.

"This baby is coming whether you're ready or not," I say. "And *he* hasn't done jack shit since he moved in except beat the highest score on his lame video game."

Tyler takes the napkin out of his lap and throws it on the table. I can see his ego swelling. "I don't know where you get off disrespecting me and the mother of my child—"

"The mother of your child? She was my sister long before she was the mother of your child, and—"

"Okay, okay," Mom says, trying to settle us down.

"Everyone, chill out for a minute."

We eat in silence until Mom turns her attention toward Freddie and me. "You've never brought a friend to Christmas dinner before," she says. "Not that I'm complaining."

"That's because they're not friends," Hattie blurts.

Well, I guess I deserved that.

An elated squeal comes out of my mom. "Ramona, do you have a boyfriend?"

Freddie looks to me, waiting for my answer.

There is a battle inside of me between my feelings for Freddie and my indignation toward my mother. The idea of hurting Freddie makes me sick. I know what it's like to be hidden. But I cannot stomach the thought of my mother thinking some boy just came along and turned me straight.

"We . . . are good friends."

I try to explain myself to him with my eyes, but he looks away and studies his plate.

I wait for Hattie to call me out, but she doesn't. She's a good sister. I'm not.

Merry Christmas to me.

We take the coastal highway back to Eulogy, and Tyler drives to Freddie's house first to drop him off.

When we pull into the driveway, I get out as soon as Freddie does. "Give me a minute," I tell Tyler and Hattie as I slam the door behind me.

"Freddie," I say. "Freddie, wait. Hear me out."

He turns around but says nothing. His shoulders rise up and down, and the veins in his neck bulge with irritation.

I hold my hands out in caution. "You're not a secret," I say. But this all seems so familiar, except that it's not me on the receiving end this time. "We are not a secret. But coming out to my mom was the hardest thing I have ever done. Every time I see her it's almost like I'm having to come out all over again, because she just won't get it through her head that this is more than a phase."

"So I guess I'm the phase then?" He takes a step toward me and into the stream of light radiating from inside his house. And now I can see all the pain and all the hurt right there written into his freckles. "This is just a phase."

Carefully, I place a hand on each of his biceps. "Nothing about this is a phase." I don't know how true it is, but my feelings for him are too intense to be so temporary. "For my mom, the world is black and white. If she knows I'm . . . dating a boy, she'll think I'm 'cured.' And that you're to thank." I shake my head. "But there's nothing wrong with me."

"Does it matter what your mom thinks?"

I shake my head. "Of course not." But she's still my mom. My horrible mom.

I see the confusion on his face. "So does this mean you're bisexual?"

I wish I could just say yes. I wish I could put myself in that box for my sake and his, but I don't know. For a moment, I think of Grace and how I so desperately wanted answers from her. To know who she was so that I could know what that made us. I feel a brief twinge of guilt, because now I think I might better understand how

Grace felt all those months ago.

I don't know if I'll ever want to be with another boy again. But what I'm not confused about is this: I want to be with Freddie, and that is the only thing I know in this moment. So I tell him, "I don't know. I haven't decided what this means except that I like you. I like kissing you and holding your hand and being with you, but I don't know that means yet. And that is all I can give you right now."

The tension in his jaw eases slightly. "Okay," he says. "That's okay. But you should know that this isn't some casual thing for me. I feel . . . very strongly about you. About us. Viv had me on the back burner for a long time." He takes a deep breath. "I can't do that again. Especially not with you."

His words weigh heavy on me. I've seen Freddie have his heart broken. If it happens again, I don't want it to be my fault.

Behind us, Tyler honks the horn.

I shoot my arm into the air, my middle finger raised. It's not like I can make things any worse at this point.

Freddie reaches deep into his pocket and hands me a paper lunch bag that's been flattened and folded several times with a blue ribbon tied around it. "Open it at home," he tells me, and gives me a quick kiss on the lips. "Merry Christmas, Ramona Blue."

"Merry Christmas, Freddie Floaties."

The whole way home I sit with his present in my lap.

In the front seat, Tyler and Hattie bicker back and forth,

but tonight I am tuning them out.

At home, Tyler and Hattie both go to Hattie's room, which is a surprise, but I guess right now Tyler is in better graces with my sister than I am.

I untie the electric-blue ribbon and lay it flat on my bed to put in my chocolate box. Inside the brown bag is a leather cord bracelet with a light-blue evil eye in the middle. Attached to the cord is a tag from Hex, the store we visited in New Orleans. The tag reads *LIGHT-BLUE EVIL EYE. Meaning: communication and willpower.*

I slip it onto my wrist and hold my hand to my chest. I didn't get Freddie anything. We don't really do Christmas presents at home, so it didn't occur to me. Getting him a present now would be too obvious.

But I'm going to make it up to him. I will make it up to him when he least expects it.

TWENTY-EIGHT

Saul swings his door open and shouts, "Happy New Year!"

"Could you ask them to leave their shoes outside the door?" asks a voice from inside his apartment.

Saul rolls his eyes, but can't stop himself from grinning. "You heard him." He's trimmed his facial hair and has traded his porn-star chic uniform of cutoff jorts and a tank top for fitted charcoal pants and a soft blue button-down shirt. He almost looks . . . like an adult. A hot adult with a job that doesn't involve a margarita machine.

Freddie, Hattie, Tyler, Adam, and I all kick our shoes off and leave them on the mat to the side of the door, where Ruth's sneakers already sit. As we file inside, Saul hands us New Year's hats—feathered headbands for Hattie and me and plastic top hats for Freddie, Adam, and Tyler.

Saul reaches into the kitchen and yanks a short Latino boy with caramel eyes and a buzz cut away from the sink by his wrist. "Y'all, this is Reggie."

Reggie nods at us once. "Rogelio, but I go by Reggie."

He has a faint accent and rolls his *R* when he says Rogelio. He shakes each of our hands. His fingers are callused like my dad's, and he wears khaki pants and a black polo shirt. The two of them standing together look like a pair of gay dads.

"Reggie," Saul says, "this is . . . y'all. Though I've never met you." He points a finger in Adam's direction.

Ruth steps out from the hallway with a feathered headband gathered in her fist. "Saul, this is Adam. The guy I was telling you about with the two moms. Be nice. Adam, this is my brother. If he makes you uncomfortable, he's doing it on purpose."

Saul winks at Adam.

"The guy with the two moms?" Adam asks. "Is that all I am to you now? No wonder I didn't tell you sooner."

Ruthie rolls her eyes but laughs, and I think I can feel a bond forming between them.

"I've heard a lot about each of you," says Reggie.

Saul laughs. "And none of it was good."

Hattie shoves him.

Reggie and Saul are the perfects hosts. They've set out plates of finger foods and cookies with little paper appetizer plates that say *Happy New Year* in gold. It's almost easy to ignore Ruth scowling in the corner.

Saul has everyone gathered around their brand-new TV as he links it to the internet and shows videos of one of his former classmates, who has not so secretly posted videos of himself doing covers of pop songs.

"Isn't this the guy who tried out for *America's Next Superstar*?" asks Adam.

"Oh yeah," says Ruth. "They put him through to Hollywood."

"As a joke," Saul adds. "I would honestly feel bad if the guy weren't such a jerk."

Ruth clicks her tongue. "No, you wouldn't."

"Okay, you're right."

"We should do shots every time he touches his ear like he's got one of those earpieces in it," says Adam.

"I'm out," says Ruth, plopping down on the couch.

Saul yanks a bottle of whiskey off the bar. "Oh, it's on."

While they pour themselves shots, I peruse the snack table with a beer dangling between my fingers.

"The legendary Ramona Blue."

I turn to find Reggie. "Can't say I don't live up to the name," I say, stroking my tousled locks.

Reggie leans up against the counter behind him and spreads his arms out on either side to brace himself.

I take a swig of beer. I've been sipping it for too long now; it's warm and flat. "We were all a little nervous about you," I admit.

Reggie looks up to me. His eyes have a shine to them that makes it hard to look away. It's easy to understand what Saul sees. "I like that."

"How so?" I ask.

"I love Saul." He says it so simply. "And y'all do, too. If you're suspicious of me, it's probably because you're protective of him. I'm in favor of anyone who's in favor of his best interest."

"I'll buy that."

He points to Ruth, sitting on the arm of the couch with her arms crossed. "Now, she flat-out doesn't like me."

I twist my lips together as I search for the right words. "I wouldn't say that. Ruthie doesn't like change."

Reggie says nothing but nods along.

"You gotta understand," I tell Reggie. "Saul challenges Ruth in a way that only he can get away with. He makes her braver and funnier. The two of them in that house together were like two pillars holding each other up. She keeps him accountable. She's the reason he puts gas in his tank and pays his car insurance instead of investing in something ridiculous like a Dolly Parton pinball machine." I sigh. It's hard not to think of Hattie. "She's not sure how to exist without him." I'm not sure I'm even talking about Saul and Ruth anymore.

"She resents me then."

I half smile. "You took her sunshine. Can you blame her?"

His shoulders slope.

I hear Freddie's deep laugh behind us. "Don't worry," I tell him. "She'll find her own soon enough."

I watch Ruth for a moment as she tries not to laugh at some story Adam is telling her. For so long I believed I was the only person who truly knew what it felt like to be left. But maybe it's not just standing still that gets you left behind. You can be going places and still find yourself abandoned in some way.

The rest of the night is spent playing games and telling horrible jokes. Freddie and I don't even hang out much, but I can feel my body rotating around him like we're two magnets. Saul is the DJ and plays all his favorite obnoxious dance music.

I can taste the excitement in the air as we draw closer to midnight, despite Hattie dozing off on the couch. With a minute to go, Saul runs around making sure we each have noisemakers.

We all turn to the TV for the last of the countdown. "Five!" we shout as the Times Square ball on the television begins to drop.

"Two hundred and nine!" shouts Adam with a near-empty bottle of whiskey in his fist.

Freddie pelts him in the head with a throw pillow, but he doesn't relent.

"Two hundred and ten!"

The rest of us shout over him to finish the countdown. "Four, three, two, one!"

"Happy New Year!" I yell, and blow into my noise-maker.

Tyler pulls Hattie in for a kiss, and Saul gives Ruth a kiss on the cheek before Reggie twirls him away and dips him, planting a kiss right on the lips. Adam looks to Ruth and the two high-five.

I turn to Freddie and I can't help but see Christmas Eve play out all over again, when I told my mom we were just friends. Running my fingers over my wrist, I fiddle with the evil-eye bracelet he gave me.

Then I step forward and slide my hands up both his arms. I can feel goose bumps forming as I do. Freddie's eyes are wide but steady on my every movement.

I take another small step forward and I kiss him. I kiss Freddie in a room full of all the people I love most. It's my way of telling him he's not a secret. He is not a phase.

Freddie kisses me back, one hand sinking into my hair and the other wrapping around my waist and up my spine as his lips softly melt into mine. For a moment, my body melts against his, and it's easy to ignore the deafening silence around us.

JANUARY

TWENTY-NINE

"Well, add that to the list of shit I thought I'd never see," Saul says.

A door slams shut behind us, and we both pull apart at the same time.

I glance around to find an array of responses staring back at us. Tyler: blank. Hattie: smug. Adam and Reggie: delighted confusion. And Saul: total surprise.

"Ruth," I breathe.

Freddie tells me with his eyes to go find her, and I nod.

I don't have to go far. She's sitting there on the steps a few feet from Saul's front door.

She eyes me over her shoulder. "Just needed some air."

"Can I join you?" I ask.

She shrugs.

But I take it; knowing her it's the closest thing to an invitation I'll get. "Saul and Reggie seem good together," I say. "Really happy."

She cuts to the chase. "So you and Freddie?"

I nod. "Yeah."

She exhales. "I guess that turned out to be more than a one-time hypothetical thing."

I pull my knees to my chest. "You think I'm making a mistake."

"No. Yes. I don't know."

I laugh. "Well, that's encouraging."

She shakes her head. "Friendship turned romance is like the breeding ground of mistakes. But not because he's a boy. I don't think so at least. I mean, it's not like he magically turned you straight or something."

I practically snort. "Yeah. No shot of that happening."

Ruth groans. "I feel so stupid."

She blinks and a tear rolls down her cheek. After wiping it away, she rips the headband Saul finally forced upon her off her head.

I get it. I understand why Ruthie is upset. Saul just left home. I'm . . . making out with a boy. It's a lot of unforeseen change all at once.

"I don't even like you." She laughs. "In any other town we would have never been friends."

"But this isn't any other town."

"You don't have your shit together. You don't care about your future. You have the most ridiculous hair." She pauses. "But you make me feel normal."

I reach for her hand, but she only lets me hold it for a second before pulling back.

"First Saul, and now you." She pauses for a moment. "I know that doesn't really make any sense. I know that liking guys in addition to girls only changes what you decide to call yourself. You're allowed to have the realization that sexuality is fluid or whatever. But in this weird way I feel like I'm losing you. And Saul, too. I'm losing both of you at once," she says. "And if you and I don't have this thing in common anymore, why are we even friends? Ya know?"

"Ruthie, nothing between us is changing. You know that. Our lives are . . . evolving, sure, but whatever it is that exists between us will always be there. Maybe liking girls was the common thread that drew us together, but it's not all that's kept us together and you know it. And I still like girls. A lot. Kissing Freddie doesn't suddenly erase that part of me."

She sighs. "I know."

We sit quietly, but the world around us is anything but silent. Music and shouts of "Happy New Year" echo from the apartments above and below.

"It makes me sad," she says. "To see you kiss him." And then she quickly adds, "I'm not jealous."

"I know," I tell her.

"It's never been like that between us. But I feel like part of you is dying. And it's the part I most recognize." She shakes her head, like she's trying to shake some thought in place and make it stick. "Feelings are gross. Did you know that? They're the actual worst."

I smile. Feelings are gross. If I'm being honest with myself, there's a small part of me that is sad every time I kiss Freddie, because I feel like little by little the person I thought I was is disappearing. Almost like I've lost what makes me special. But there has to be more. I'm made up of tiny pieces; scattered, they're nothing more than sharp edges. But all those pieces combined are what make me Ramona.

"I wish I had answers," I tell her. "I wish I could tell you I'm gay or straight or bi or a homoromantic demisexual." I laugh. I can't help myself. "Do you know how much easier that would feel? But I don't know what all this means. Maybe I won't for a while or maybe I'll know next week."

"It doesn't make sense to me," she admits, "how you can *not* know." She shrugs. "But I guess I don't have to get it, do I? I just gotta be here for you." She turns to me. "And I am. Just so you know."

I smile warmly and nudge her in the ribs with my elbow. "We'll always have Vermont, though, right?"

She nods. "We'll always have Vermont."

We talk for a while longer about what it's like at home without Saul and how her parents have responded to Reggie. I don't know if we're okay, but I feel like maybe we're redefining what okay means for us.

We all stay the night at Saul and Reggie's. Hattie and Tyler take the guest room. (It still blows my mind that Saul even has a guest room and how adult that makes him.) Ruth takes the couch and Adam spreads out on an air mattress in the kitchen, leaving Freddie and me with an unzipped sleeping bag as our blanket on the floor. But I don't mind it. Reggie lays a few thick blankets and throw pillows beneath us, forming some sort of pallet.

It's not long before Ruth is lightly snoring a few feet away. Adam took a little too much advantage of the no-parents situation and drank himself to sleep an hour ago. Fireworks still shoot off all along the beach as Freddie and I whisper back and forth in the dark. We each lie on our sides, turned toward each other.

"Does Ruth hate me?" he asks.

I smile. "No more than she hates everyone else."

"That's good, I guess?"

"That's good," I tell him.

He traces my hairline with his index finger as I take his other hand and kiss each one of his knuckles.

"What are you doing tomorrow?" he asks.

"You mean what am I doing today?"

"What are you doing today?"

"Nothing," I say. "Everything."

"I want to do that with you. Nothing and everything."

I nod. "I want that, too." We stay like that for a while, studying each other with the tips of our fingers, like we're reading braille. He drags his fingers along my side, pulling my shirt up as he does, and every inch of my skin begs for him as he connects the dots all over my upper body. It's such an innocent touch that feels much more wicked than it looks.

"Can I ask you something?" His voice is gravelly. "Something personal?"

I press my face to his neck. "Of course."

"So you're not a virgin, right?" he asks.

"Right."

With Freddie, it's not a matter of if we will have sex. It's a matter of when. It terrifies me and it excites me and it's not because he's a guy and I'm a girl. It's because he's Freddie and I'm Ramona. The way my body reacts to his . . . it's something I have no shame in saying I want.

Freddie wraps his arm around my waist and pulls me back to him. I press my hand against his chest, and he runs a finger over the evil-eye bracelet. "I've only been with Viv," he says. "But you know that."

"Do you . . . are you ready to be with someone else?" I ask.

"Are you?" he asks.

"I think I've found the right person."

His fingers begin to roam again, and it's not long before my skirt is rucked up around my waist and his hand is discovering places it's never been.

Later, we talk for a little longer about tiny things, like how we both want to see the Olympic Games in person one day, and mysteries, like how there are tons of undiscovered species in the ocean. The gaps between his responses grow further and further apart as he sinks into the first sleep of the New Year.

In the window, behind him, the sky glows with the smoky haze of fireworks.

THIRTY

"You're not swaddling tight enough," I tell Hattie.

Nurse Pearce, a round black woman with ringlet curls, pops her head over Hattie's shoulder. The deep circles beneath her eyes scream overworked, but her chipper voice sings, "She's right!"

Hattie growls and narrows her eyes at me.

"You're the one who asked me to be here," I remind her.

She shakes the baby doll free of the blanket and it makes a *clunk* sound when it lands on the changing table.

"Tyler is the one who should have come," I say. We're only a few days into the new year and he's already proved that he's the same shitty baby daddy he was last year. "I mean, if we suck at this, imagine how bad he'll be." But it's not just that. This creeping anxiety spreads through my veins, reminding me of my impending fate. If Tyler can't be here for Hattie now, what else won't he be here for? It's like being at school and doing a fire drill and seeing how horribly unorganized the teachers actually are and how little your peers are paying attention. Sure, it's only a drill, but someday the real thing will happen. For Hattie, that day is coming sooner rather than later.

"At least he's working." Her voice is tired, which makes me think maybe she's not as clueless about all this as she's been letting on. Part of me wants to see her get it over with and call it off with Tyler. But then I'm holding out hope that he isn't the person my heart and head say he is.

I take the blanket from her and smooth it on the counter in front of us. "Okay, let's do this shit."

The pregnant woman behind Hattie glares at me as her husband in his slacks, dress shirt, and tie checks the time on his chunky silver watch.

"The baby can't actually hear you," I say under my breath.

Before we can finish reswaddling the doll, Nurse Pearce says, "Let's talk labor relief positions, people. Take a seat on the mat with your partner."

Hattie tosses the half-swaddled baby doll on the table. "My feet are killing me."

She sits down slowly on the blue gym mats at the center of the room, balancing on one knee at a time. A few months ago, I would have described my sister's body as a spring. You could press her down for a moment, but the minute she felt the pressure ease, she would bounce back to life.

I sit down behind her like Nurse Pearce instructs the class to do.

"Ladies," she says, "relax. Ease into your partner. Trust

them to support you."

I remember sitting like this with Grace in her bedroom, behind closed doors. She would never quite rest the full weight of her body against mine, like she was scared I couldn't hold the two of us up at once. But Hattie's body sinks against me and she doesn't hold back. I brace my hands on the ground on either side of my hips so that I can more easily support us both.

Hattie drops her head against my chest. "Oh God," she says. "You wanna know what would feel good right now? A bath."

The stopper on our bathtub drain has been broken since we were too old to take baths together anymore. Or maybe we stopped taking baths together because the stopper was broken. Either way, it wasn't anything I ever really missed.

"Baths are kind of gross if you think about it," I say. "You're just sitting in water full of dirt and dead skin."

"Well, thanks for ruining that for me."

"Now," says Nurse Pearce. "Repeat after me: five-one-one."

The entire class does as she says.

She holds up five fingers. "Contractions five minutes apart lasting one minute long for at least one hour. That's when it's time to call the doctor."

I commit it to memory. Five-one-one.

As Nurse Pearce circles the room, discussing breathing techniques with individual couples, Hattie says, "I think I want a Mardi Gras–themed shower."

"Okay?"

"That was a hint."

"Right." I nod. Oh God. I don't even know where to begin. "Well, I mean I was already working on your shower," I lie. "But, ya know, it's supposed to be a secret and all."

She laughs dryly. "Liar."

"Yeah, you're right."

"Maybe Mom will help you."

"Yeah," I say. "Not gonna happen."

"You know all that anger takes a lot of energy."

"You don't like her either," I remind her.

"No," she says, "but I love her." She rubs her belly. "Ruthie and Saul will help you."

"This is going to be the gayest baby shower of all time," I tell her.

"Perfect."

Later that afternoon, Freddie picks me up in Agnes's Cadillac. He gets one free car wash at work every week, so Agnes has taken advantage of that.

"Thanks for coming with me," Freddie says as the car rolls over the rocky terrain of the trailer park.

"Well, it was either this or homework," I tell him.

As he turns onto the street, he holds out a hand for me to take. I realize I've never held someone's hand in the car like this. A small, minuscule thing that somehow makes me feel like we're an actual couple.

As we pull up to Scrub-a-Dub, Adam points us to the entrance like he's directing an airplane on a runway.

Freddie rolls down the window. "Son, I need to speak to your manager."

"I run this bitch!" shouts Adam.

Cindy, Adam's mom, swings open the door to the office and gives Adam a Look with a capital *L*.

"I have an itch," he shouts.

"Nice cover!" I call.

He nods and gives us the thumbs-up.

The car wash is the kind where you don't get out of your vehicle, so Freddie directs the car onto the tracks as an attendant sprays down the grille and the windshield.

As we roll into the garage, water sprays at us from both sides and multicolored soap spits out onto the windows, shielding us from any natural light.

"Whoa," I say. "Got pretty dark."

"I actually love it," says Freddie. "I wish my job was to drive the cars through the wash instead of dancing outside with a giant sign. You know Adam's mom is ordering a rubber ducky costume?"

"Oh man, I gotta see that."

"Well, it's on back order. I'm hoping it doesn't arrive until after graduation."

I feel my lips slipping into a frown at the mention of graduation. Our days are numbered.

"I decided I'm still going to LSU," he says. "It's where I've always wanted to go. And I heard Viv changed her plans and decided on Florida. So no chance of running into her at least." He notices then that this is not a subject I have much to add to. "But forget that. I have a question."

I swallow. "Okay."

"I don't want you to get freaked out."

"Well, that freaks me out a little." I laugh nervously.

He takes both my hands in his. "I know you may not be ready to label yourself, and . . . that's been hard for me to understand, but I'm okay with it."

"Okay . . ."

"But I was wondering if you would be interested in labeling us?"

I inhale sharply. "What do you mean?" Even though I know exactly what he means.

"Will you be my girlfriend?"

Another round of rainbow soap splashes across the windows. "I—do we . . ." I've played the role of girlfriend before. That's nothing new for me. My brow furrows for a moment as I turn this over in my head. I know I'm ready to take this relationship further . . . in a physical way. And it doesn't make sense for me not to make this commitment too. It's not a label that means much to me. If fact, thinking back to Grace and Andrew, it's a label I once loathed. But it means something to Freddie, and for that reason, I say, "Yes."

His face lights up with a stupid grin as he leans over the center console and kisses me in the dark car under a kaleidoscope of soap and bubbles, and I think everyone should make out in a car wash at least once. The car rocks gently against the brushes and the dryer until the employee guarding the end of the wash is whistling at us and waving us on to the exit.

THIRTY-ONE

It's been a slow night at Boucher's. January always crawls by, and we're only two weeks in. Ruth and I start our closing duties early in the hope that Tommy will send us home before our shifts are up, and as we're refilling ketchup and hot sauce, Freddie texts me.

FREDDIE: let's play house tomorrow.

ME: what does that entail?

FREDDIE: do you work tomorrow?

ME: It's my Saturday off.

FREDDIE: my gram and Bart are going to the swap meet tomorrow morning.

It's the first time Freddie and I will have a chance to truly be alone for an extended amount of time without sneaking around in empty classrooms or stolen moments when we can duck away from our respective obligations.

ME: I just have my route.

FREDDIE: Which ends at my house.

ME: True.

FREDDIE: All roads lead to me.

I fidget with the evil-eye bracelet tied around my wrist before responding. Ruth hums "Silent Night" to herself, even though Christmas is long gone. While she moves on to her next table, I slide into a booth and study my phone.

ME: So just me and you?

FREDDIE: Me. You. No pressure.

I suck a deep breath in through my teeth.

ME: I'll see you in the morning.

Freddie sits on the steps of his porch in joggers and a tank top. Agnes's car is parked in the driveway, but Bart's truck is gone. Like Freddie promised, they've gone to Biloxi for the biannual Southern Mississippi Swap Meet. I went a few times with my grandparents when I was younger. No cash is exchanged—only junk. It's the only time of year when all the crap littering people's front yards and garages is given actual value.

I park my bike against the porch railing, careful to avoid Agnes's flower bed. I pull Freddie up with both my hands from where he sits on the stoop, and he kisses my nose.

"Good morning," he says. The chill in the air covers his bare arms with goose bumps, but my body is still warm from the bike ride here.

Last night I stayed up for hours, playing out different scenarios of what might happen today in my head. But every time, I made the same decision.

As Freddie leads me inside, a huge yawn escapes me. "You wanna have breakfast?" he asks. "Or maybe lie down? Watch some TV?" I can see he's nervous too, and that somehow eases my own nerves.

I've only seen Freddie's bedroom in glimpses, which seems like a silly thing to get anxious about. But I am. "Let's go to your room," I tell him.

He swallows. "Is this you coming on to me?"

I grin. "Oh yeah."

The dinosaur wallpaper border trimming the ceiling of Freddie's room is definitely a leftover from the previous owners, but it's easy to imagine little Freddie growing up in this room, too. He has a few rap posters up and an old calendar still set to September of last year, like he'd decided to stop keeping track of time.

His queen-size bed is a four-poster with green plaid sheets and beat-up Spider-Man pillowcases, which have undoubtedly known Freddie at least as long as I have.

The bed is rumpled but made, and it reminds me of the night we shared a bed in that disgusting hotel room. It feels like so long ago. The heartbreak I felt that night is a memory so distant I can hardly remember it being real.

I wait for him to close the door behind us, but then I realize: he doesn't have to.

I take a quick step toward him, and then another. Him with bare feet and me with my boots on makes me even taller than usual. I dip my forehead down and let it rest against his shoulder. His fingers knead against my waist, like a cat's paws.

My lungs shudder as I sling my arms around his neck. I respond with an openmouthed kiss and slide my tongue past his lips.

I want this. I've wanted it since that day we kissed in the locker room, but that doesn't make this moment any less nerve-racking for me. Freddie's . . . equipment is different from what I'm used to working with. What if I'm terrible at it?

He groans, deeply. "This isn't why I invited you over. I mean, it is, but it's not. It doesn't have to be."

He wraps his arms around me and presses me so hard against him that I can feel our ribs crash together.

"This is why I came over," I say between rasping breaths.

I pull back and sit down on the edge of the bed, crossing my foot over my knee. I am suddenly dizzy. This is the moment when Freddie and I change our relationship forever. When we are more than childhood friends or Peter Pan and Wendy Darling. My fingers shake as I pull at the tight knots on my combat boots.

Freddie kneels down in front of me and places his hand on top of mine, stilling my nerves. He takes over the action of untying my shoes, and does so gently. Once he yanks off my first boot, he takes my other foot and places it on his thigh like how Hattie would before I knew how to tie my own shoes. After removing my boots, he removes my socks one at a time, and I swallow a giggle because I know my feet reek after the bike ride here.

But he doesn't seem to care. He sucks the air right out of my chest when he kisses my knees through the holes in my jeans one at a time.

I take off my T-shirt and unhook my bra with one hand, and something about undressing myself evaporates a sliver of my anxiety and reminds me that maybe having sex with Freddie won't be so different from my past experiences. As sweet as it was for him to help me with my boots, there's something powerful about taking off my own clothing and choosing to reveal myself to someone as dear to me as he is.

Freddie, still on his knees in front of me, looks up. "If you're not ready," he says, "we don't—"

I pull him up by his biceps and he's on top of me. "I'm ready," I tell him.

And so is he. Or at least his body tells me that he is.

I slip my hands under the elastic waist of his sweatpants and run my fingers down along his thighs. He sits up a little and takes off his tank top, revealing the acne scars on his shoulders. We both look down to the point where our bodies meet, and I place his hands on the button of my jeans and nod. Carefully, he undresses my lower half. I slide backward toward the head of the bed to help him pull my jeans off, and soon we're both sitting there on his bed, completely naked.

Freddie stands, and I watch his hazy silhouette move in the early morning shadows. He opens his closet door and reaches for a shoe box on the top shelf. When he returns, he sits on the edge of the bed right next to me. I watch as he puts on a condom in front of me with expert precision, and I guess if I had one of those things, I'd want to make sure I knew how to properly protect it, too.

"They don't really show that part in the movies," I tell him. I guess it's a moment that should be awkward, but it's not.

He turns to me. "You're sure? You can change your mind whenever you want."

"I know I can." My heart doesn't pound with nerves. My fingers have stopped shaking. I am sure.

Freddie lies back with his head toward the foot of the bed, and I curl my body against his. He kisses me gently, and even here with the two of us completely naked, his kisses make my stomach feel like it's full of feathers.

When he braces himself above me and asks me to say yes once more, it's not a nod or a grin, but a firm confirmation. "Yes," I tell him. "I'm sure."

Afterward I slip on my underwear and borrow a T-shirt from Freddie. He yanks his sweatpants back on, and the two of us stand in front of his window overlooking the backyard with January sunlight streaming in. He kisses my forehead. My cheeks. My nose. My earlobes. My eyelids. My legs feel weak, but not in the same way they do after a morning of swimming laps.

We are the same people who chased each other across my sandy Mississippi beaches summer after summer and that we're the same people who were so heartbroken just months ago.

I was so scared that by having sex with Freddie, I would lose part of myself—part of my identity. Instead, I've embraced another facet of myself. Life isn't always written in the stars. Fate is mine to pen. I choose guys. I choose girls. I choose people. But most of all: I choose.

After a moment, we pull the curtains shut tight and

crawl into his bed with the sheets wrapped around our shoulders.

Freddie falls asleep with his arms coiled around my waist and his forehead buried in the crook of my neck.

THIRTY-TWO

We sleep in late. Later than I ever have before. And when we wake, even though the world outside is cold—well, cold for Mississippi—Freddie's room is hot with sunlight waiting to be let in.

Freddie makes us omelets with all kinds of ingredients I would never try on my own, like smoked salmon, cream cheese spread, capers, and fresh dill. I set the table and turn on Agnes's radio and fill our glasses with fresh-squeezed juice. It might be lunchtime, but it's still breakfast. It's still our morning.

My heart is elastic. I realize it for the first time. For so long I thought there was a limit to how much love I could hold and who I could give it to. But life is so much more dynamic than that. Love doesn't disappear when you give it away, and new love doesn't make old love any less legitimate.

And that's it. That's what I've found with Freddie.

"What?" he asks, and turns to face me with the spatula in one hand.

I sink into a kitchen chair and press the tips of my fingers to my lips. I don't even realize I've said it out loud. "I love you," I tell him again.

He holds on to it for a minute. I can see him collecting my words and tucking them away. His brow furrows.

My heart pounds in my chest so violently that I wonder if he can hear it, too. But I force-feed myself Ruth-style logic. I didn't say I love you to hear it back. It's fine. I say it over and over again in my head.

"I think I love you, too, Peter Pan." And then he just turns around and finishes our omelets, like he's said the most normal thing either of us could imagine. It's casual, and normal and perfect.

I slowly let out the breath I was holding. I want this to be my normal—to be my every day. A world where I don't have to worry about my dad or Hattie or our rotting trailer or my dim future stuck here in this Neverland.

Maybe I can't have that. At least not all of it. So I take his words and I save them for the chocolate box beneath my bed.

We spend the rest of the day curled up on the couch. I put my pants back on, but I've already gotten too used to walking around pantless, which is a liberty I don't have in my own home.

When Agnes and Bart finally make it back home, they're both a little too busy to notice us. But I can feel the difference even in the way we sit, and I can't believe there's not some glowing sign above our heads that reads: *XXX JUST HAD SEX XXX*. It was like that with Grace, too.

Something about having sex with someone for the first time makes me feel like the whole world knows exactly what we've done.

Freddie clears his throat too often and spends more time staring at the ceiling than any sane person should.

Agnes sneaks up behind us and tickles each of our necks. We both jump a little. *Oh God. She knows.*

"I like having y'all two around the house," she says.

I laugh in a short burst. "Thanks for, uh, letting us watch your TV and eat your food." *And have sex in your grandson's bedroom.*

"Ya know," she says, sauntering back into the kitchen, "Vivienne was a sweet girl, but she never came around the house. That girl was always in a hurry to be somewhere."

"That's because you always asked her too many questions," calls Freddie over his shoulder.

I turn my head away from Freddie and cover my smile with my fist. I swell with pride a little too much at the fact that Agnes prefers me over Viv. And I'm thankful to her, too, for noticing the change between Freddie and me without making some big deal of it.

"What do you have to do tomorrow?" asks Freddie.

I turn back to him and rest my head on his shoulder, suddenly feeling much more comfortable with Agnes in the house. I've almost forgotten that my weekend is only halfway over. "I'm supposed to plan a baby shower for Hattie," I say.

He laughs. "Yeah, I don't even know where to start there."

"Did someone say baby shower?" shouts Agnes from the kitchen, where she's washing some of the china she swapped for in Biloxi.

"Yes, ma'am," I call back to her.

She appears in the living room again, drying her soapy hands on her apron. "Oh, Ramona darling, if it's not overstepping and if your mama doesn't have any other plans, I'd love to help host a shower for Hattie here."

I turn around in my seat and pop up on my knees. "Wait. Are you serious?" I shake my head. "And trust me. My mama doesn't have any plans at all."

She shrugs. "I don't have any granddaughters—at least not ones I know of—and I've known you and Hattie since you were both just little bits."

"That would mean so much," I say. "To both of us! And it'd be a major help."

"Well, good. It's decided then." She crosses her arms over her chest like she's ready to get down to business. "Now, I think we can do some pink, but I really like the idea of doing different kinds of pastels."

"I know Hattie likes lots of the baby stuff with stars and clouds on it. Oh! Or she said we could do a Mardi Gras–themed shower."

"I like that idea quite a bit." She nods. "Well, I think we're gonna have to plan us a shopping trip."

It's not that I'm suddenly excited for Hattie's shower, but I'm no longer dreading it, which is more than I thought was possible. After Agnes checks her calendar, we settle on a date.

I stay for dinner and Agnes makes too much spaghetti with Cajun sausage meatballs. After dinner, when I decide to head home, Agnes insists that Freddie take the truck and drive me home with my bike in the back and that I take home enough leftovers for everyone.

As we pull into the trailer park and the road turns into a path of rubble, I can hear a shouting match happening, which is nothing new, except the closer we get to my front door, the louder the shouting grows. We turn the corner in time to see Hattie throwing a potted plant on the hood of Tyler's car just as he's getting in the driver's side. The ceramic pot shatters, leaving a dent.

"Oh, Christ." I jump out of the passenger-side door and set the leftovers and my bag on the roof of the truck. "Whoa, whoa, whoa! What's going on here?"

"Mind your own business, little sis," says Hattie. Her face is splotchy with anger and her finger is pointed right at Tyler. "How am I supposed to expect anything from you? How are we supposed to count on you?" she asks him. And the *we* she speaks of does not include me. These are the questions I've been waiting for Hattie to ask for months, but now that she finally is, it's strangely unsatisfying.

"I don't want to be a maintenance guy for the rest of my life," yells Tyler, his head sticking out the car window.

The door across the street creaks as Mrs. Pearlman joins the audience.

"And what else do you think you're gonna do with your life? Huh, Tyler? You think you're gonna go to some fancy college or become a famous bass player? You think

286

someone's going to pay you to test video games all day or some bullshit? I don't even think that's a real job!"

She picks up another plant and hurls it at his windshield. I hear a crack but can't tell if it's the pot or the glass.

"Should we call the police?" Freddie whispers.

I shake my head. For a moment, I'd actually forgotten he was even here.

Maybe in other neighborhoods, people call the cops for stuff like this, but not here. In my neighborhood, this is just another night.

"You think I want to wait tables for the rest of my life?" asks Hattie.

"No one made you keep it," Tyler retorts. "You chose this. And now you're no better than your whore mom."

I hear a low *ohhhh* among the slowly growing crowd of onlookers.

"Don't talk to my sister like that," I shout.

For the first time, Tyler truly realizes I'm here. "Oh great," he says. "The whole committee is here now. I know how you can't make decisions without your carpet-munching sister. I can't even believe you'd let *that* near our kid."

A wave of disgust and hostility washes over me. I want so badly to make him feel as small and as dumb as he is.

"Hey!" Hattie shouts. She snaps her fingers at him and then slaps her hands on the hood of his car. "You don't talk about my sister like that. This is about me and you." I feel Freddie step forward behind me, but I push him back.

Hattie turns to me. "Ramona, go inside."

"No," I tell her. "For as long as he lives in this house with us and is part of your life, this asshole is my problem, too."

"Well, lucky for you, because I'm out of here," says Tyler. "One Leroux sister on my ass is bad enough."

Hattie's shoulders melt into a slouch, and I can see she's losing her will. "Baby, don't go. We can find you another job."

I can't understand why she would ever want him to stay, but I almost get why she might be torn between putting up with his bullshit and losing the father of her kid.

Tyler isn't having it. "I'm done with this shit, Hattie. Call me when the baby's born."

The tears start rolling down her cheeks, melting her heavy clumps of mascara immediately into charcoal rivers. "Baby, I need you. We need you. You're gonna be such a good daddy."

I grit my teeth and try so hard to feel for her in this moment, but I can't. I won't. "Good riddance," I say a little too loudly.

Tyler cranks the music up so loud his speakers crackle. He reverses out and what's left of my dad's potted plants on his windshield falls to the ground.

Hattie goes inside and slams the door, locking herself inside.

Freddie touches my arm. "Let me take you back to my place."

"You should go." I shake my head and pound on the door. "Let me in, Hattie!"

"I need to be alone!" she yells back.

"Come on, Ramona," he says. "I can't leave you here."

"Please, Freddie. Just go." I turn to him. "I gotta deal with this on my own."

He pulls me close to him and whispers, "Call me if you need anything. Seriously, anything."

We share a quick kiss in the shadows of the porch light.

I keep knocking on the door as he walks down the steps and leaves my bike there against the side of the trailer along with my bag and the leftovers before getting in Bart's truck and driving away.

After a few minutes, the lock finally clicks and the door swings open. Hattie stands there, mascara running down her cheeks.

She stumbles into my arms and I hold her. Her belly presses against me, reminding me that I will always choose her even when she doesn't choose me. The Leroux sisters. It will always be the two of us in the end.

THIRTY-THREE

The house is quiet until my dad gets home later that evening.

I sit on the couch with my world lit homework spread out on the coffee table.

He sits down in his chair. "Your sister home?"

I nod. "She's in my room."

He takes off his baseball cap and drops his keys inside before placing it on the table next to my papers. He chews away the cuticle on his thumb. Dad's fingers get so dry they chap sometimes from washing his hands in the kitchen so often. He's no good at putting on lotion and leaving them be. "She, uh, talk to Tyler at all?"

"Oh yeah." I balance my pencil between my fingers, tapping it on the table.

Behind us my door creaks as Hattie tiptoes out to the living room with her arms crossed over her chest. Her face is red and she's all puffy around the eyes. She rocks back and forth on her heels, and I know her every behavior so well when she's upset like this. I can see that she's psyching herself up to talk without crying all over again. "Tyler left," she finally says. "He's not coming back."

My dad first glances to me for a moment, and I can see the fleeting relief in his eyes before he turns to Hattie and says, "I'm so sorry to hear that, baby."

I bite my tongue and say nothing at all.

She goes back to my room and when the door shuts behind her, the two of us exchange illicit half smiles.

And yet part of me is a little sad. If Tyler won't be here to take care of her, then who will?

Hattie stays home from work on Sunday and Monday. I can't tell if she's using the baby as an excuse or if she's actually sick, but either way, she's in no rush to make up her shifts like she normally does.

When I see Freddie at school on Monday, my entire body buzzes, and every time I close my eyes it's memories of Saturday morning that I see.

We walk our bikes home and after school he kisses me behind the Phillips 66 on the corner of Lancaster and Bell. It's as exciting as always, but comforting in a way I never expected. We don't say we love each other, and it's something I appreciate. It's not a phrase I want to wear out.

On Tuesday, after my paper route, I go to the Y with Agnes and Freddie. It's been only a few days since we last swam laps and it's not one of our usual pool days, but my body is hungry for it. Most of all, though, my head needs the space to digest the last few days.

After changing, I shove my bag into my locker and take my goggles and swim cap with me to the pool.

I dive in—an exercise that is finally becoming more dive and less belly flop—and find my rhythm even quicker than normal. For a while I swim butterfly, which is the stroke I've had the hardest time mastering.

At the pool, after Agnes and Freddie are done, I've been hanging back to watch the other swimmers and see if I can pick up any techniques to try on my own. The workouts are starting to feel too short, like by the time we're done, I'm only getting started.

There's something about propelling myself through the water that makes me feel limitless, like maybe Prudence Whitmire and her offer to get me on the Delgado Community College swim team aren't so ridiculous. I'd have to get a job almost immediately, but I think after helping Hattie get set up with a crib and some emergency cash, I'd have enough to pay for rent and food for a month. And I could always take out loans for tuition, even though that kind of financial investment in myself makes me want to puke from anxiety.

As we're finishing up, Freddie and I race the last few laps. We start on the blocks, gliding through the air, and maybe it's my height, but I'm pretty sure I have the better start this time. I go for freestyle. My arms slice through the water like knives. My whole body feels unstoppable. We go for four laps, and when I'm done, I grab onto the edge of the pool. As I come up for air, I look to Freddie's lane. Suddenly he breaks the surface, and the first thing he sees is me.

For a split second his expression jumps from confusion

to disbelief, before he turns on that charm and that glowing grin. "Hey! Congratulations!"

Agnes is hooting and hollering from the bleachers. "I've been waiting for that for weeks!"

I almost feel bad at first. Despite the smile, I can see his ego deflating. But then I remember: I beat him. I swam my ass off and I beat Freddie. That's amazing. I can't stop smiling. "Thanks."

On our way to the locker rooms, Prudence Whitmire shouts, "You thought about my offer any?" She sits on the ground in a deep stretch. Purple veins twist around her legs like vines.

Agnes and Freddie look around like they can't figure out who this crazy lady is even talking to.

I'm still glowing from my win, and it takes everything in me not to shout YES. "Um, still thinking," I tell her. But reality crashes down almost as soon as the words have left my mouth. I was crazy to think it could actually work. Who will watch the baby when Hattie goes back to work, and how will we pay for doctors' visits or day care? Or what if the baby is born with some condition that requires expensive medication?

On our way home, Agnes and Freddie grill me.

"Who was your friend?" asks Agnes.

"Her name's Prudence Whitmire. Y'all have seen her before, surely," I say, trying to brush it off.

Freddie watches me in the rearview mirror. Agnes let him drive today.

"She says hi sometimes. Talks to me about swimming."

"Come on now," says Agnes. "I'm too old for that coy act."

So I tell them about Prudence or Coach Whitmire or Mrs. Whitmire. I don't even know what I should call her. I explain that she offered to help me get on the team at the community college and that she thought I'd been improving.

"Oh," says Freddie. "Wow."

"You really have been getting a whole lot better," says Agnes. "And that's such a wonderful opportunity."

"Well, she's right. You're getting pretty good," says Freddie. "You beat me today."

"Only 'cause you let me," I say, trying to suss out whether or not he actually did. It's so silly, but it's a small nagging doubt in the back of my mind.

"Ha!" Agnes shakes her head. "You think this boy lets anyone win when it comes to the pool?"

"She's right," says Freddie.

"Well, Ramona Blue," says Agnes, "looks like you've got some things to consider."

"What's to consider?" asks Freddie. "If you've got your high school transcripts, you don't even have to take the SAT to get in since it's a community college. And I bet there might be some scholarship money if you can make the swim team."

"Or even federal grant money if you get on it soon," says Agnes.

I shake my head. "Okay, let's not get ahead of ourselves here." But my cheeks glow, and I can't believe I actually told someone else about Coach Whitmire's offer. I decide I should call her Coach. It feels wrong to call a woman her age by her first name.

I tell myself if Agnes and Freddie didn't even bring up me staying here and taking care of Hattie and the baby, then maybe my future isn't so obvious after all. Maybe the future is still unwritten.

When we pull into the driveway, Bart is pacing across the porch. It's odd, but somehow very much like him. As we open the car doors, he rushes to us. No, to *me*.

"We gotta get you to the hospital," he says, clasping me by my shoulders. It's the most words I've ever heard him string together at once. "None of you's been picking up your phones."

The color drains from my face, and my mouth goes completely dry of words.

Freddie checks his cell. "Mine was on silent."

Agnes opens the glove box. "Shoot, I forgot it was in here."

I pat down my pockets, but I know I left it at home. I always answer my phone.

Bart's pushing Freddie and me into the backseat, and my body doesn't even have time to respond to what's happening.

I think I'm crying. My whole body feels frantic and everything is moving too slow and too fast all at once. My immediate thought is Hattie, and then I think, *Oh God, no.* My dad. He was in a wreck. He's hurt. One of them is hurt. But I can't even cobble together the words to ask what the hell is happening. And worst of all, I can't breathe.

"Bart," says Agnes as we're backing out of the driveway. "Bart, what's going on?"

"It's the baby. It's your sister, Ramona. Some kind of lady problems. Your dad said to get you to the hospital pronto." He takes the keys from Agnes and hops behind the wheel. "You three get in."

Eulogy has a few urgent-care clinics, but the closest hospital is about fifteen minutes away in Gulfport. And now I really am crying. Tears and snot drip down my face, and my wet hair has soaked through the back of my T-shirt. I didn't let Hattie trim it a few weeks back before Christmas. I was annoyed with her about something stupid. She's supposed to touch up my blue, too. And I don't know why, but all I can think about is my damn hair and how if she's not around, I'll have to cut all of it off, because I can't manage it on my own.

My sister and my unborn niece are in the hospital. Their lives could be in danger and all I can think of is my hair. It's such a tiny, meaningless thing, but it feels catastrophic. And somehow I think my brain is protecting me by forcing me to concentrate on this inconsequential thing.

I duck my head down between my knees and breathe. Just breathe. Freddie rubs his hand up and down my back the whole way there. His touch is a temporary relief.

All I can think about is that I was so silly. I was so silly for just moments ago imagining I could ever leave this place.

★ ★ ★

There is lots of waiting before anyone will let us see her. Dad is sitting near the nurses' station, and Agnes and Bart have left to get coffee and whatever other stuff they can find in the hospital cafeteria.

I sit next to my dad on a tiny bench, curled into a ball, snug against his side. Freddie sits across from us, and I know that, if at all possible, he feels even more useless than I do.

Hattie woke up in a pool of blood. No one was home. She was alone. That's all we know. I wasn't there for her. The doctor promised us she'd let us see Hattie as soon as her condition had stabilized. The bleeding hadn't stopped.

This horrible little part of me keeps thinking that maybe if she loses the baby it won't be such a bad thing. I'm disgusted with myself for even entertaining the thought. I try to scrub it from my brain, but the guilt has already sunk down deep into my belly.

Briefly, my eyes meet Freddie's, and he tries to offer me so much in that one glance, but it's like I live in this tiny little bubble, and the only other people I have the capacity for are Dad and Hattie. In this moment, Freddie is a stranger. He's an outsider, who will never understand what it means to be a Leroux.

Suddenly the extreme contrasts between our worlds are so apparent. For a brief time in history, we overlapped. His life didn't seem so different from mine. But here, in this waiting room, I am reminded of my priorities. Before I belong to anyone, I belong to Hattie. I belong to my sister. I belong to our life in this little town.

The doctor comes in just like I've seen in so many

movies. Dad and I stand up right away. I can count on one hand how many times I have been to a doctor, and the gist of it is that if a bone wasn't broken or if a fever didn't break a hundred, medical attention was nothing more than a luxury.

The doctor is a younger white woman with unruly red hair and a thick Yankee accent, one I've never actually heard anywhere other than TV. "Mr. Leroux?" she asks.

"Yes, yes. And this is my other daughter, Ramona."

She nods twice, once at Dad and once at me. "I'm Dr. Donahue. I see your daughter Hattie has been receiving care at the free pregnancy clinic in Eulogy."

My dad's face is a puzzle. He has no clue. I love our dad, but he sort of dropped out of the parenting game once Hattie started using tampons. As far as he's concerned, babies miraculously appear, especially when they come out of his own daughter's vagina.

"Yes," I interject. "She's been going for regular checkups. She and the baby are perfectly healthy. That's what they said at the last visit."

"Well, it seems they missed a few things. Actually, this happens quite a lot with these clinics. You can't blame them, though. They don't always catch some of the more advanced complications, and—"

"Is she okay?" I interrupt. "Is my sister okay?"

"Yes. For now, she and the baby are stable. She's still bleeding, but it's beginning to taper off. Mr. Leroux, your daughter has a condition called placenta previa. Basically, what this means is that the placenta is covering the opening of Hattie's cervix."

I can see my dad's eyes glaze over a little.

Dr. Donahue goes on to explain how this can cause extreme bleeding, and that Hattie will have to have a C-section when the time comes to deliver the baby, because she's so high risk, and that she'll be on bed rest for the remainder of the pregnancy.

We leave Freddie in the waiting room and follow Dr. Donahue to my sister's room. Hattie sits up in bed, propped up by pillows. She's hooked up to an IV, and the minute I see her there, the tears start again.

I push past Dad and Dr. Donahue and pull her into my arms. "Are you okay?"

I can feel her trying not to cry, but it doesn't work.

"I'll leave you three alone," says the doctor.

My dad sits down on the bed lightly, like he's scared he might somehow break Hattie. He squeezes her foot. "Baby, baby, baby. You're gonna be fine."

"I can't work anymore," Hattie says through sobs. "They said I can't work until after the baby's born. It's only January. The baby isn't due until April. How am I supposed to buy diapers or—or baby clothes and formula? Tyler isn't answering my calls, and—"

"Hey," I say. "Hey, we've got you." Hattie's life is a tightrope, and I'm the net underneath. Sometimes she forgets I'm even there. But I am.

My dad scoots farther down the bed and touches his

hand to Hattie's belly. "It'll all work out," he says. "Always does."

He says that, but sometimes it doesn't work out. Sometimes you've gotta make it work out, and I think that's what my dad never quite got. That's why we're still living in the same deteriorating trailer that was only ever meant to be a temporary fix.

Hattie nods into my shoulder. "It was like a freaking horror movie this morning," she says. "Blood everywhere. And I couldn't get ahold of either of you." She shakes her head. "I called you both before I even called nine-one-one."

"You're crazy," I tell her.

She looks up at me, and I'm reminded of how much smaller than me she is. Despite our ages, she will always be the little sister. "You're my nine-one-one," she tells me.

I pull her knotted hair back away from her face. She looks so unlike herself in this moment. No makeup. Greasy hair. It's almost as if the makeup and the hair—it's all an armor. The protection she wears to survive it all. Here, in this hospital bed, flanked by me and Dad, Hattie can be the mousy version of herself who is scared and doesn't have the ability to trust that it will all magically work out. Because it might not.

"I'm sorry," I tell her. "I am so sorry I didn't have my phone on me." I kiss her forehead. "I am always here for you. Always."

THIRTY-FOUR

I sit with Freddie, Adam, and Ruthie in the courtyard at school. The three of them are busy working on their senior pages for the yearbook.

"How can I say 'Eat a dick, EHS,' but in a more eloquent way?" asks Ruthie.

"Uh, yeah," says Freddie. "I think that's as eloquent as it gets."

"Say it in French," Adam says. "No one will ever know what it actually says, and it'll look classy."

Ruth points to Adam. "Okay, that's actually a good idea."

Adam pulls out his phone to translate. "*Mangez un pénis, EHS*. At least according to Google."

Normally, I would laugh, but honestly all I care about right now is graduating and snagging a full-time gig at Boucher's. I don't have time for senior pages or prom or whatever else people are buzzing about.

I flip through Ruth's Spanish notes, ignoring the two of them and just trying to absorb enough information to pass. In the week and a half since Hattie's trip to the hospital, I've started picking up her shifts at Boucher's, which means I've been working until about eleven p.m. every night. Tommy let me start waiting tables, too, whenever he needs an extra body, so that means I've been getting a few tips here and there.

I haven't quite figured out how much I need to earn to make up for Hattie being on bed rest, but what I do know is that I can barely keep my eyes open during class and whatever social life I had is becoming slowly nonexistent. I've even had to cut back on swimming in the mornings. I've been too exhausted.

"I'm gonna grab a Coke," says Ruth. "Y'all want anything?"

I shake my head, and so does Freddie. Adam is too consumed by the blank page before him to care.

Freddie reaches across the table for my hand. "Hey, how you been holding up? How's Hattie feeling?"

I shrug. "I'm good. Just picking up extra hours to help her out. And she's okay." I laugh a little to myself. "I think she's taking bed rest a little too literally. Just freaked out about this Spanish test right now," I say, returning to Ruth's notes.

He clears his throat. "Hey, I didn't want to make a big deal of this—and it's not a big deal. But I bought you a senior page in the yearbook."

I drop the notes I'm holding. "What?" My voice is thick with annoyance.

Freddie pulls back some, letting go of my hand. It's not the type of response he was expecting. "I wanted to do something nice for you."

"You shouldn't have wasted your money."

"It wasn't a waste of money," he says. "And it's not for you to decide how I *waste* my money. I thought I'd let you know, since the deadline for rough drafts is coming up."

"It was nice of you to think of me, but I don't need you to buy me stuff like that. I'm not a charity case. If I wanted a senior page, I would have bought one for myself."

"Or a thank-you would work," he mutters.

Behind him, I can see Ruth slipping through the crowd toward us.

"I'm gonna get Ruth to quiz me outside the Spanish room." I grab my backpack and hers and walk off without another word.

"Whoa," says Ruth. "We're going somewhere?"

"Yeah." I pass off her backpack. "Let's study some. Away from here."

The truth is, what Freddie did was incredibly sweet and kind and so *him*. If I could just take that stupid senior page and write a letter to him, I would. Because he deserves that. He deserves the kind of person who can be present and live in the moment with him. Someone who can be excited about what colleges he gets accepted to even if he's already decided on LSU. And someone who will encourage him to swallow his pride and go to open-call tryouts for the swim team.

But those aren't my concerns. My concerns are utilities and diapers and ER bills and whether or not the trailer is even safe enough to raise a baby in.

And this stupid baby shower.

FEBRUARY

THIRTY-FIVE

I have slaved over Hattie's shower. At least I think I have until I show up at Agnes's the Saturday morning of and see all the food and decorations she's contributed. Suddenly the king cake I picked up at Stella's Bakery and the invitations I dropped off at the post office feel trivial.

Every inch of Agnes's house is covered in purple, green, and gold confetti, streamers, and balloons. There's even a giant tower of diapers, which have been individually wrapped with glittering ribbon to match the rest of the decor. The mailbox out front is decorated with balloons to signify to guests that they have arrived.

Every detail is so thoughtful, it makes my eyes water. And this isn't even my shower! I don't know what kind of luck was on my side the day Agnes invited us to play with Freddie on the beach, but I'll always be thankful for her.

"The decorations are amazing!" I call to Agnes in the kitchen. "Hattie is going to die. You did way too much."

"It was nothing!" she says. "And I figure I'll leave most of them up until Ash Wednesday anyhow."

Mardi Gras isn't for another week or so, but the minute the clock strikes midnight and the New Year begins, the decorations start going up. I guess people not from around here assume that Mardi Gras is all about Bourbon Street and flashing your boobs for beads, but we've celebrated ever since I was a little kid. We even have huge local parades with floats that shut down our streets for days. King cake, which is basically shaped like a giant doughnut and sort of tastes like coffee cake, was as common throughout my childhood as birthday cake.

As I'm balancing my gift in one hand and the cake in the other, Bart squeezes past me through the doorway, nodding a silent hello.

"He's going fishing," says Agnes as she relieves me of the cake. "Can't get out of here fast enough." She tsks.

I glance around, searching for the face I know I'm bound to see.

Freddie and I have really only seen each other at school over the last few weeks. I've only been by for breakfast and swimming a few times lately. My weekends have been consumed with work and helping Hattie out around the house, and to be honest, my body is too wiped for much else.

It's easier this way. I know the end of the school year is fast approaching and that soon Freddie will leave. Everything that's happened over the last few weeks has only served to remind me how different we are. I am so thankful to fate or God or whatever it is that's pulling the strings on this puppet show and that our lives have run parallel to each other for the last few months. But life is about to take us in two totally different directions.

Still, the thought of seeing him outside school has my stomach twisted into a ball of knots. "And Freddie?" I ask Agnes. "Is he around?"

"Oh yeah," she says. "Said he wouldn't miss it. I think he's in the shower at the moment. He's gonna help us in the kitchen. Keep people fed."

Agnes takes my gift for Hattie and the baby and glances down at my bright-purple dress and my green polka-dot tights. "You look absolutely adorable, my dear." She hands me a stack of throws and dish towels. "Now, do me a favor and put these in the hallway linen closet for me before anyone gets here."

"Yes, ma'am." The hallway is warm with steam and immediately reminds me of the last time I was this deep into Agnes's house. As I'm shoving the pile of blankets and towels into the closet, the bathroom door swings open, and all the pent-up steam curls right out into the hallway.

Freddie sticks his head out the door and grins when he sees me. He wears a towel slung low around his hips and holds it tight with one hand as he pulls me into the bathroom with the other.

The cramped quarters of the hallway bathroom don't leave much room for either of us to situate ourselves, so when Freddie shuts the door behind me, I slide up onto the counter and am practically sitting in the sink. It's the most privacy we've had in weeks.

"I feel like I've barely had you to myself lately," he says. "You haven't even been by for breakfast lately. Or swimming. You're not gonna beat me again if you don't stay in practice."

I inhale deeply and let myself memorize the smell of warm soap and fogging mirrors. "You know it's been crazy with Hattie and work." My legs spread a little as he comes to stand closer to me and presses his palms to my knees. He kisses me lightly on the lips and then down my neck before pulling back at the sound of Agnes slamming a cabinet door in the kitchen.

He groans. "I wish we had more time."

"And a little more privacy," I add. I know he's referring to immediate time, but it's hard not to think about the thing neither of us has talked about—the elephant in the room. Graduation. Not to mention both of our great track records with long-distance relationships.

Still, I don't realize how much I've missed him until I'm right here with him. I force every doubt about the future out of my head.

My hair curls around my face from the humidity, but I don't care. Gently I tip my head forward and let my forehead rest there against his bare chest. My breathing is a little shallow from the damp air, but if I just don't move, I'm fine.

And that's what I wish, that after all these weeks of nonstop motion with double duties at Boucher's and my early-morning paper route, I can stand still for a moment. Here with Freddie seems like a good place to rest. To just breathe.

"You okay?" he asks. "I know it hasn't been easy these last few weeks."

I nod. "I will be or I am. I'm okay. Hattie's okay."

He spreads little kisses down the part in my blue hair. "That lady at the Y. Prudence, right? She's been asking for you."

"Yeah." I sigh. "I need to let her know I appreciate the offer."

He leans back, forcing me to pick my head up. "And that you're going to take her up on it, right?"

I shake my head. Not today. "I can't have this conversation with you right now."

"Ramona, come on."

I shake my head again. Quick anger boils up in my chest. "I don't know how it is that you can't see how different our lives are. I can't leave. I have responsibilities."

"Hattie can take care of herself. She has your dad, too."

I pull back from him. "Really? You think my pregnant sister who's on bed rest can take care of herself? And you think my dad who's scraping by as it is will magically be in the position to help her? Wow. You must know something about my life that I don't."

"All right," he says, in his calm voice. "Chill out. I didn't mean it like that. I know things are hard for you."

I nod sarcastically. "Do what you always do. Defuse the situation. Make me feel ridiculous for even being upset."

He says nothing, but I can see the shock on his face.

I don't know why, but I want Freddie to fight with me.

I want to argue and shout and for him to show me that everything is not okay. But it doesn't matter.

"I have to help your grandma set up." I slide off the counter and let myself out.

After I shut the door behind me, I take a moment to gather myself and pull all my frizzing hair into a sloppy bun. I can feel how red my cheeks and chest are, but there's nothing to be done about that.

I help Agnes set out tiny finger foods like mini quiches and triangle sandwiches. I want to ask her how much this whole thing cost her, but the truth is I don't think I can afford to reimburse her for much. It makes me anxious, but all I can do is remind myself that this is for Hattie and not me.

Little by little, people start to trickle in. It's mostly girls Hattie graduated with, a few people from work, and some of Agnes's friends. I invited our mom, too, who only called to say that she would have hosted a shower for Hattie if I'd just asked. I didn't know if I should count that as an RSVP or not.

Freddie stays in the kitchen mostly and only briefly ventures out to refill the veggies and dip and other finger foods. I try to catch his eye so that he can somehow see that I'm sorry for losing it this morning, but he's too busy. Agnes mixes her signature punch into a crystal bowl with scoops of rainbow sherbet, which make it frothy and fluffy—and almost otherworldly.

I am left to small talk, which I'm learning is an actual skill. No, I don't have any plans for college. Yes, I work a few part-time jobs. School is good, but I'm anxious to be done. No, I haven't thought about what I want to be when I grow up. Because I've already grown up, which is what I don't say out loud. More of Hattie's friends from high school show up. I use the word *friends* loosely, because truthfully these girls don't give two shits about Hattie. They're just here to spy on the first girl to get knocked up out of wedlock from their graduating class.

And then the girl of the hour arrives in her chariot. Saul and Ruth are more careful than normal with my sister as they help her down from the Jeep.

Hattie wears a white sundress that probably fit her boobs at some point in time, but not today. The empire waist of the dress flares out and a large pink ribbon is secured tightly above her belly and tied into a big bow. Really, the only thing missing is a gift tag.

Her hair is curled and teased into a pouf at the top of her head, and her makeup looks like she could press her whole face to a mirror and leave a full imprint from brows to lips. And I guess to anyone else, she might look ridiculous, but to me, she looks like herself, and after her horrible scare in the hospital, nothing could make me happier.

"Well, shit, Ramona," says Saul. "You're a mother-freaking Martha Stewart." He reaches over me for the little paper cups with a few inches of dip on the bottom and stems of carrots and celery and peppers sticking up.

"That," I tell him, "is all Agnes and Freddie." I say his name a little too loudly, hoping he'll hear me and somehow appear.

Saul crunches down loudly on a piece of celery. "Quite efficient. So how do these baby shower things work?" he asks.

I clip three clothespins to his shirt. "Okay, this is supposed to be, like, a mixer game is what Agnes calls it. If someone catches you saying 'mommy,' 'daddy,' or 'baby,' they can steal a clothespin from you. Whoever has the most clothespins wins."

"Like an actual prize?"

I nod.

He glances around. "These bitches won't even see me coming." And then he's off, squeezing into conversations with his veggies and dip in one hand and sherbet punch in the other. I marvel for a moment at how he fits into this place so easily. Saul was meant to live his life here in Eulogy. He's like a goldfish, content with the size of his bowl and not too concerned with what might exist elsewhere, because he is the king of this domain.

I seek Hattie out and find her sitting in Bart's recliner, sipping punch. She nods along as a few girls from high school trade gossip. After they migrate to the refreshments table, I sit down on the armrest.

"How do you like it?" I ask.

For the first time I can ever remember seeing, my sister's eyes are filled with stars. "Ramona, it's perfect. It's like some kind of magazine or something." She's already wearing some of the Mardi Gras beads we'd used as table decorations.

"Well, most of that was Agnes."

"You helped," she says. "I knew you wouldn't let me down." She leans her head against my shoulder. "Did you remember to invite Tyler's mom? I want her to feel involved . . . if she wants to be."

I nod. "I did."

"Is she coming?"

"She couldn't make it, but she had a gift sent over."

Hattie looks up to me. "Well, that's gotta count for something, right?"

"I think so," I tell her.

Behind us one of Hattie's old friends from high school says, "Did you see that boy in the kitchen? Black guys aren't my thing, but he's cute."

I turn to Hattie, and she shakes her head. *Dumb bitches,* she mouths.

"Hands off," another girl whispers. "He's dating Hattie's sister. First girls. Now black boys. She must be really trying to give their poor daddy a heart attack."

Okay. That's it. I stand, whirling around, and open my mouth to say something, but Hattie beats me to it. "Gretchen," she says. "MaryLou, I know y'all are just here to check out the class slut. I get it. Someone had to get knocked up first, but y'all can just leave your presents on the gift table and take your backwards attitudes out of here. Don't let the door hit ya where the good Lord split ya."

The girls stand there in their pastel dresses, shock registering on their spray-tanned faces.

"And those party favors at the door are for *actual* guests," I say, slinging my arm over Hattie's shoulder.

We both watch as they leave with their purses and plates of finger food in hand.

"You're good people," I tell Hattie, feeling an extra rush of warmth for my sister.

"I know we are," she says as we sit back down.

"Okay, people!" Agnes claps her hands together. "Let's dig into these presents!" While everyone gets situated, she pulls an ottoman up next to Hattie and hands me a pen and a notebook. "You write down who gave what for thank-you cards," she whispers.

"Yes, ma'am."

Hattie opens each present with care, like she's trying to savor every single moment, and I'm diligent in writing down every name and gift. I don't think either of us have ever opened this many presents at once in our entire lives. I underestimated how much people lose their shit for babies.

Dad's boss's wife even brought one of those special trash cans for diapers. And Agnes's present was a baby swing that can sit on a table. Saul and Ruth's gift is an array of things both practical and nonsensical, but my favorite is a neon-green onesie that says *Pizza Rolls, Not Gender Roles*. And Freddie very thoughtfully gifts a little pink-and-green swimsuit with a matching hat and an inflatable float with a canopy over it. There are also lots of diapers and pink frilly onesies and handmade blankets and burp cloths and a few gift cards too.

Freddie hovers in the kitchen, and I can feel his gaze on

me while I watch Ruth and Saul polish off the rest of the mimosas on the drinks table. It would be so easy to turn and give him a quick grin to let him know we're fine and that everything's okay, but as the day progresses, even a gesture that small feels like a promise I can't keep.

When Hattie gets to my present—a big teal bag with pink-and-white-striped tissue paper—I hold my breath. I hadn't realized how nervous I was for her to actually open it.

"There's no card," she says, and then again a little louder, "There's no card in this one."

"It's from me," I say.

She bounces her shoulders with excitement. "Better be good, Ramona Blue."

Hattie pulls the paper from the bag a little too roughly, and I have to stop myself from telling her to be more careful.

When she looks down into the bag, her expression is puzzled, but she pulls the gift out by a string.

Finally, I reach in and help her adjust it so that the whole thing hangs properly. "The mobile," I say. "The one with clouds and stars that you saw at the baby store."

"Oh, Ro," she says. "It's so thoughtful." Her cheeks burn pink and she smiles so hard her eyes squint.

I shrug. "There's more."

On the bottom of the bag, folded in fours, is a piece of paper. The room grows quiet as she unfolds it and reads to herself.

She looks to me, her jaw slack, and then back to the paper.

"Well," says Saul, "you gonna tell us what it is or what?"

She blinks and a fat tear rolls down her cheek. "It's a crib. Ramona got us a crib."

My sister yanks me by the arm and pulls me into the recliner with her. "How did you even afford this?" she whispers.

I hug her back but am careful not to squish her belly. "I've been saving, I guess."

I got the crib on sale, and still, it was a nice chunk of change. But the saleswoman says it converts into a bed and that the baby can use it until they're five or six. If I'm being honest, I don't even know where there is room in the trailer for it, but we'll deal with that when the baby comes. I don't know. But a baby needs a crib. My niece needs a crib.

The doorbell buzzes for a long moment, like someone's holding their finger down on it.

"I got it," calls Freddie.

"Well, y'all got the party started without me," says my mother's voice the moment the door swings open.

Hattie clears her throat. "Hey, Mama. We weren't sure if you were coming."

"Well, of course I'm here. Why wouldn't I be at my only grandchild's baby shower?" Her words are slurred and exaggerated. Our mother doesn't necessarily have a drinking problem, but she's never shied away from a bar. And right now, in the middle of the afternoon, she's drunk. The woman is toasted.

I stand up and hand the notepad to Ruth. "Y'all keep

doing presents." I turn to my mother and grab hold of her elbow. "Mama, let's get you a plate of food."

My mother trips beside me and past Freddie. I can hear Saul and Ruth go into distraction mode as I force my mom into a seat at the kitchen table.

"How'd you get here?" I ask, and hand her a plate of tiny sandwiches.

For the first time I take note of the denim miniskirt she's wearing. Her legs are smeared with self-tanner, and the white fur trim on her camel-colored boots is dingy and discolored. Her hair is a little greasy, and I almost feel bad that she felt so left out of Hattie's shower that the only way she knew how to show up was drunk.

But then I don't care. I shut my feelings for her off like a faucet. My mother crosses her veiny legs and points at Freddie. "I see you stuck around." She turns to me. "They never do, ya know."

I shake my head. "You're one to talk." I don't want her bringing him into this.

"Excuse me?"

I shove a glass of water into her hands. "How'd you get here?" I ask again.

She rolls her eyes. "I drove, of course."

My mother is a grown woman who showed up drunk to her oldest daughter's baby shower. I couldn't feel guilty for not including her in this even if I tried. I reach into the pocket of my dress and start to call my dad, but then remember he's at work. I need someone else to be the adult in this situation.

Freddie is smart to say nothing as my mom sloppily picks at the plate of finger foods.

"Okay," I finally say. "Once everyone clears out, we need to get her home."

"I can help," offers Freddie.

I hate for him to have to deal with this, especially after this morning, but I think my options are limited. I glance to him and then to my mom's car, which is parked half in the front yard and half on the street. She's lucky she didn't hit the mailbox, or even worse: a human being.

"If you can drive her home, we'll take care of her car later."

He nods hesitantly. I can tell the idea of being alone with my mom makes him nervous, and I can't really blame him.

After presents, Agnes asks everyone to count their clothespins. Saul steps forward with pins clipped up and down the front of his shirt and crows, "Nineteen!"

A few older ladies sigh as Agnes hands him the candle and gas station gift card she'd bought as the prize.

"Awww, yeah!" says Saul. "I owned this shower."

After a thank-you from Hattie to Agnes and me, everyone is pretty quick to leave. The tension brought on by my mother's presence is palpable, and I can't fault anyone for averting their eyes.

Once everyone's gone, I give Agnes a quick hug, and she whispers, "Your mama's not driving home, is she?"

I shake my head. "I think Freddie was going to help me get her home."

She nods. "That'd be best. Y'all take the Cadillac and we'll get her car sorted when Bart comes home."

I reach for Agnes's hands. I wish she were my family. I wish it so badly. I wonder if God runs some kind of lottery up in heaven and that's how he decides who's going where and with whom. I love Hattie and my dad. And shit, even my mom, too. But I can't help but wonder how much of life is predestined simply by the house you were born into. "You made today perfect," I tell her. "I'll never forget it, and I know Hattie won't either."

She squeezes my hands tight. "Y'all girls deserve it." She hesitates before letting go, and I wonder about all the unsaid things between us.

"Didn't even give me the chance to host the damn thing," my mom slurs from the kitchen.

Agnes looks to me. "You pay her no mind while she's in this state."

Hattie, Ruthie, and Saul all pile into the Jeep. Agnes agrees to store most of the presents in her garage until Hattie has had a chance to sort through her bedroom. I lead my mom toward Agnes's Cadillac, and she starts to put up a fight about leaving her car, but Agnes is quick behind me to whisper something to my mom. And whatever it is she says, it's enough to keep my mom from making a scene.

With her in the backseat, we drive in silence to her apartment. She rides with the window down the whole way, so anything Freddie and I might even say would be drowned out regardless. We hold hands, though, and that seems to speak more than any words might.

When we arrive, Freddie offers to help me get her up the three flights of stairs, but I decline. She's reached that sluggish stage of drunkenness where her legs are as useless as limp spaghetti. But she's also bound to say absolutely anything, and I've put Freddie through enough over the last few months as it is.

I sling her arm over my shoulder and pull her along with me one slow step at a time. She helps slightly by steadying her hand on the railing.

We're halfway up the first flight when she says, "You're my baby. My beautiful baby. Your daddy and me, we always loved Hattie. But you were the one we planned for." She laughs to herself. "Not that planning ever does much good anyway."

I never knew that, but it makes no difference, really. I try to make it feel meaningful—that she really wanted me—but she doesn't want me now, so I can't find it in me to care. "Come on," I say. "Keep moving."

We make it up to the first landing, and she stops, bracing both hands on the railing. I stand there for a moment, letting her take a break. "I thought I was ready," she says. "We had your sister and then we decided she couldn't just be an only child." She turns to me, her eyes squinting beneath the harsh security lights. "I thought that if we planned you, we must've been ready. I must've been ready."

I pull her arm back over my shoulder. I don't want to hear all the drunken excuses for why she couldn't be there.

There's only one reason she wasn't there for us: because she chose not to be.

Wearily, we start up the next flight. "But then that storm came and it wiped everything away. It was like Noah's flood. Everyone had to start from scratch. And so did I."

This is unfair for so many reasons. And I don't even believe in fairness, but if anything were ever wholly unfair, it would be this. My mother in this state, spewing her confessions, like she somehow deserves to feel better. To feel the release of pressure that comes from sharing a horrible truth, but her not sober enough to feel the raw hurt that occurs when you finally admit out loud how wretched you truly are. Instead, I'm left with all the feelings and the memories of this moment, because she will wake up tomorrow and vaguely remember the outline of today.

She shakes her head. "You were always the responsible one. Sometimes I think you just chose being gay, because you had to figure out some kind of way to disappoint us."

"Wow, Mom. Charming as ever," I say through gritted teeth.

But she doesn't even hear me. "I don't worry about Hattie, though. Not one bit. You know why?"

"Why?" My voice comes out like a scratch against my throat. I don't even mean to respond to her, but it's like I can't resist.

"Because she's got you. You won't ever let her fall.

That's true family," she says. "That's the kind of family I never was to you girls."

Hot tears spill down my cheeks, and I yank her the rest of the way up the stairs. I don't even bother unfolding her couch, but instead let her pass out with a pillow and a blanket on the floor.

I lock her door behind me, and I don't look back.

THIRTY-SIX

"You okay?" Freddie asks as he clicks on his blinker to turn out of the parking lot.

I nod. "Take me home, please." I'm exhausted by all the emotional highs and lows today.

"Sure," he says.

I roll the window down and force myself to feel the harsh chill of this February evening. Pulling my hair loose, I let it tangle into knots that only Hattie will be able to brush out.

As we pull up in front of my house, I turn to Freddie. I force myself to say the words I've been forming for weeks now. "I can't do this anymore."

He takes my hand and squeezes, and it's then that I realize he thinks I'm talking about my mother and life in general, which somehow makes this worse.

I wiggle my fingers out of his tight grip. "Freddie, we can't do this anymore."

He slides the car into park and turns to me as he throws

an arm over my seat. "What do you mean? What are you talking about?" His voice is raspy and full of ache.

"I can't be your girlfriend." I wipe a tear away, and I don't know if it's a new one or an old one. Inside, the car is dark and my now rolled-up window is cold to the touch. Light from my front porch floods the dashboard, but we remain in shadows. "I love you."

"Ramona, I love you, too. I wasn't kidding when I said so."

I take his hand, and his grip squeezes so tight. "It's not enough. Sometimes it's just not. Not right now."

"You're not making any sense." He gets louder with every word. "You're wrong. I know you can't see what I see right now, but we can survive this. You . . . you can't just cut people out of your life when things get tough."

It's so hard not to agree with him. I don't have to end this tonight. Freddie will hold on tight enough for the both of us. At least for now. But soon he'll leave. He'll leave like everyone else, and I'll be here. Forever Peter Pan.

I take my hand back and wipe away my tears. I wish he could see the landscape of our lives from my point of view. "I don't regret it," I tell him. "Not a single moment. But there's nothing about us that's made to last."

His expression is dark and unreadable. "You don't have to do this. You don't have to give in to the idea that your life is supposed to turn out a certain way." He threads his fingers through my hair, but they get stuck in the tangles. "I get a say in this, too. And I'm not letting you go so easily." He pulls me gently toward him.

I kiss him lightly on the lips and reach for the handle of the car door. "I need to go."

Maybe Freddie doesn't understand today, but I'm doing us both a favor in the long run. "Good night," I tell him.

THIRTY-SEVEN

Inside, Hattie is sitting on the couch, telling Dad all about the shower, and I can tell that Mom showing up drunk is barely even a memory for her. That small thing gives me great satisfaction.

"There she is!" says Dad. He stands and gives me a tight hug and a kiss on the cheek. "I'm so lucky you two have each other."

Hattie watches me carefully. I shake my head discreetly at her to let her know I don't want to talk about it right now.

She pats the ground in front of her, and I sit down with my legs crossed. She pulls the hairbrush from her purse and gently loosens each one of my tangles. I close my eyes and listen as she rehashes the whole day for Dad.

Outside rain begins to splatter against the tin roof and the wind rattles the windows, but here in this little trailer of ours with my sister and my dad, I'm okay. We're going to be okay.

The next morning, I call in sick for my paper route.

Partly because I feel awful and partly because my bike is still at Freddie's house. But it's nice to finally have a day off from work, so missing one paper route is something I'm willing to pull a double for later in the week. Later that afternoon, Freddie drops my bike off and I force Hattie to answer the door while I hide inside.

I watch him through the blinds as he talks to Hattie. He makes a move to come inside, but Hattie says something and shakes her head. The bags under his eyes tell me he slept about as much as I did last night. Just twenty-four hours ago he held me in his arms in Agnes's bathroom, and now this. I could run out there and make all of this go away, but it would only be a temporary fix.

After he's gone, Hattie asks, "What's the deal with you two?"

"We—it didn't work out. I don't really want to talk about it."

She could say she told me so or that there will be others, but instead she only says, "Hey, let me touch up your hair today, okay?"

"Yeah," I tell her. "That'd be good."

On Monday, Ruth is waiting for me at the bike racks. "Hattie told us," she says almost immediately.

I am simultaneously annoyed by how big of a gossip my sister is and grateful that she already broke the news so I don't have to.

I nod. "There's not much to talk about."

Ruthie shrugs. "I don't even like talking."

And then I hug her. She hugs me back. Ruth is at least six or seven inches shorter than me, but she always feels bigger than me somehow. In this moment it's easy to feel protected and safe, like I might actually survive the rest of the school year. In this moment I'm so grateful for her and how little effort is required for us to be friends.

The next night, Tommy cuts me loose a few hours early because work is so slow. At home I find Hattie sitting in my bed with piles of makeup in between her legs as she uses the mirror of an empty compact of foundation to apply a bright, wet-looking hot-pink lipstick.

I drop my backpack on the floor, and she's startled by the clunk. "Where are you going?"

"Oh!" she says. "You're here. Good! I need your help!"

"Okay," I say wearily, and let my body sink down onto the one corner of the bed not covered in makeup.

"I need to take, like, a really good profile picture."

"For what?"

"Don't laugh," she says. "I got a one-month free trial on OtherFishInTheSea.com."

I feel my brow wrinkle in confusion. "What is that?"

"A dating website!"

"Hattie." My voice reminds me of my dad's when he would catch her coming home late during her freshman year. "You're due in eight weeks."

She balances herself on my bedside table as she stands. "Exactly. Which is why I've gotta get to steppin'." She pats her belly. "Little baby ZoeRae is gonna need a man figure in her life."

"ZoeRae?" I ask. Because there is so much she's said that makes my brain hurt that I can only pick it apart one piece at a time.

"Yeah. You like it?"

I shake my head and laugh, because I have no other option. "No. Not even a little bit," I tell her. "In fact, I don't even think I can bring myself to call her that. It sounds like a country singer gone bad."

She growls a little. "You know, I read online that parents oughta keep the baby name to themselves because friends and relatives have too many opinions and can be plain old hurtful."

I inhale deeply through my nostrils. "Maybe we can talk about the name later, okay? I don't mean to be rude, I swear. So what's all this about a dating website?"

She perks up again. "Yes! I need you to take my picture. The member guide said selfies are discouraged and that you should ask a trusted friend for help with your profile picture."

I look down at the little cheer shorts she's squeezed herself into and the shiny red top that is a remnant from Hattie's former party-girl life. "So do you want to finish getting dressed?" I ask.

She giggles. "I'm already dressed," she explains. "The picture's gotta be from boobs up. Remember, like how Auntie Luanne used to only take pictures? Boobs and up!

It's not like I'm going to be pregnant forever."

"Yeah, but shouldn't these guys at least know you're pregnant right now?"

She puts the compact down. "I can see why you'd think that, but I feel like guys would make a bigger deal of it than it is."

I nod despite myself. "All right. Okay. Let's do this. It's already dark, so we might have to take them inside."

It takes a while and we have to fudge with the lighting some, but eventually we come up with one or two good pictures. I put a frozen pizza in the oven and we turn on a made-for-TV movie about a cheerleader with a crazy mom who decides she wants to kill the girl who is in direct competition with her daughter for captain of the cheer squad.

I help Hattie compose her profile for the dating website. I am fully aware of how foolish all of this is and know that I'm encouraging my sister's behavior. Nothing good will come of this, I know.

But sometimes it's easier to play along.

THIRTY-EIGHT

It's not that Mardi Gras here is as crazy as it is in a place like New Orleans, but the town of Eulogy is definitively livelier than normal. The days leading up to Fat Tuesday are peppered with mini parades through downtown and raucous parties on the beach and at bars, and Boucher's is no different.

In fact, last night, Freddie and Adam were in picking up some to-go. At first, I thought about hiding and getting Ruth to cover for me, but I knew I had to suck it up or things would never get back to normal.

"Hey," I said to Freddie. "I saw your name come up in the order queue. Let me see if it's ready."

He nodded silently without ever making eye contact, which pretty much describes all of our interactions since breaking up.

When I returned from the kitchen with their bag, only Adam waited at the counter. "He, uh, went outside to get the car started."

I took his cash and made change. "I get it."

He stuffed the receipt and money into his pocket after dropping a few singles in my tip jar. "I miss seeing you around, by the way," he whispered. "Am I allowed to say that? Or is that, like, crossing enemy lines?"

I tried to smile, but I couldn't. "There are no lines, but it's complicated."

He shrugged. "Doesn't have to be."

I watched as the two of them pulled away in Agnes's car and the din of the restaurant chased them down the street.

During this time every year, Eulogy turns into her summer self. It's a quick and well-earned reprieve from winter, but it never seems to last long enough. Schools are always closed the Monday and Tuesday before Ash Wednesday. Even if they were open, I can't imagine many people would go.

This Fat Tuesday is one of those rainy days where there's no real downpour, but a constant drizzle. After school, Tommy has me downtown handing out flyers with drink specials during one of the big parades. The floats are amazing and ornate, but still nothing compared to what you'd see in NOLA.

Since we're a smaller town, it's pretty much revamped versions of the same floats every year, but I love it. None of it all is quite as impressive as I remember it being when I was a kid, but it feels like home. The good parts of home.

I've braided my recently dyed hair into two long French braids, and my neck is heavy with beads as I walk up and down the sidewalks, waving at familiar faces and passing out flyers.

As the tail end of the parade is rounding the corner, a girl's voice shouts my name. "Ramona!"

I spin on my heel, searching for the source.

"Ramona! Over here!"

And then I see her. The sight of her knocks the wind out of me, and my first reaction is to run the other way.

Grace. She's across the street with her mom, dad, and brother.

I stand there for a moment as a slow-moving float blocks my field of vision. Beads are flying past my head and brass music is blaring in my ears.

I see her again. Just a glimpse.

The moment there's a break in the parade, she runs across the street to me. Her mom waves, and I do, too. Though my head isn't fully aware of my body.

She crashes into me almost, and the crowd around us pushes us close together. She grips my shoulders, and all I see every time I blink is the image of her outside her house when I dropped her off before Freddie and I drove back home to Eulogy.

"Hi!" she shouts over the street noise, her fingers trailing down my arms. "Hey! How are you?"

I take a step back. "Good," I yell back, and then flash her my fist of flyers. "Just working. Are you visiting?" I ask. Even though, yes, of course she is.

"Yeah, my parents wanted to make a quick trip. It's sort of our last family vacation for a little while. I leave for freshman camp at Oklahoma State a few weeks after I graduate, so I won't be back with them this summer."

I nod, not at all surprised. "Good," I tell her. "I'm so happy for you."

"When is your shift over?" she asks, motioning to my flyers.

I pull my phone out of my pocket and check the time. "Two hours."

"You wanna come by after?"

I hesitate. I'm not interested in—I don't know what she has in mind. But I do know I'm not interested in being the grand finale in her last Mississippi Mardi Gras.

"Just to catch up," she says.

"Oh." I nod. "Yeah. Okay."

"Cool. We rented the same place we did over the summer. Text me when you're on your way?"

"Yeah," I say.

We both stand there for a minute, waiting for the other to either leave or speak first. "I wanted to text you." She shakes her head. "But I chickened out every time. When I saw you here, I decided it was fate. Anyway, I'll see you in a little while."

I don't know if I believe in fate, but seeing Grace again is definitely something. I watch as she looks both ways before running back across the street. She turns into a ghost under the Fat Tuesday drizzle.

Grace's vacation house isn't as huge and pristine as I remember, especially in comparison to Adam's house. On this dark February night, the siding is stained with mud and the rosebushes are wilting and brown.

I sit with Grace on the couch. I expect her to sit at the opposite end, but instead she sits on the middle cushion right next to me. My mouth is dry, and I feel like this might be some kind of trap or like a staged intervention, even though I know it's not. I can feel my body responding to her in a familiar way. Yeah, I definitely still like girls.

Hanging out in the living room is definitely new territory for us. Most of my summer with Grace was spent holed up in her room or sneaking around the dark house while the rest of her family slept soundly in their beds. But tonight Grace's mom is in the kitchen doing dishes while her dad and brother watch college basketball upstairs.

"Can I get you anything to drink?" asks Grace.

I smile, knowing her mom would be proud to know she asked. "No, thanks."

Her mom pops her head in the room. "You girls okay in there?"

Grace sighs. "Yes, Mom."

"So dark in here," says Grace's mom, and reaches for the lamp. "Did you offer Ramona anything to drink?"

I grin. "Yes, ma'am, she did."

Grace eyes her mother pointedly.

"Okay, okay," she says, and ducks back into the kitchen.

Grace waits for the sink to turn back on, and then she leans toward me, pressing her lips against mine.

At first my heart races. I close my eyes and kiss her back, picking up where we left off—sort of. Wanting someone is a hard habit to break. But then I realize what's happening, and the sound of her mother doing dishes reminds me of where we are. And Freddie. And the way Grace broke my heart without even looking back.

"Whoa, whoa, whoa," I whisper, pulling as far back as I can.

Grace looks up, searching my face. She presses both hands to her cheeks. "I was a real shithead to you," she blurts.

"Your mom's in the next room," I whisper sharply. And how could she somehow think that a kiss could fix all the damage between us? "It wasn't completely your fault," I add.

She throws a hand back. "That doesn't matter. I . . . I thought that if I could show you I wasn't scared anymore . . ."

I can hear the panic in her voice, and I wonder how many times she's run over this scene in her head, because me sitting here with her? This is something I didn't ever expect to experience again.

I shake my head and am careful to whisper, "Grace, we don't need to make a thing of this. Especially with your mom right there and the rest of your family around." I use my most soothing voice. "It's over. I don't hold anything against you."

"You don't need to whisper." She inhales deeply and then exhales. "I came out. I told my mom first. The day after Thanksgiving. We were Black Friday shopping, actually. My dad didn't find out until a couple weeks ago."

I clap a hand over my mouth. "Oh my God. Are you serious?" This is, without a doubt, the last thing I expected her to say, and I somehow feel guilty. Like I rushed her into something she wasn't ready for. "I didn't mean to—I never meant to push you into anything you weren't ready to do." I think back to my own Thanksgiving, when Freddie kissed me in his backyard.

She grins. "If I waited to be ready, I might not have ever done it, you know? It was a . . . shock, at first. And it's been harder with my dad. But it feels good." She lifts her eyes to the ceiling, pointing upstairs with her gaze. "My brother said he knew all along. Mom said she thought something was up, but wasn't—"

"Do they know? About us?"

She tilts her head to the side. "Some. They know some." She laughs. "Hence my mom barging in with the lights." She smiles. "It's like they knew how to handle boys. No sleepovers. No closed doors. Lights on. But, well, this is complicated. And there were my friends, too. Some were okay." Her gaze drifts for a moment. "Some weren't."

"I'm sorry," I tell her. "What happened? How?" But the truth that makes me feel a little gross inside is that I wish she'd just come out when we were together. It's hard not to imagine how different things might be right now.

"I broke up with Andrew after we . . . after that weekend. With your friend. What was his name? Frankie?"

My cheeks burn with heat. "Freddie."

She nods. "He was nice. Nicer than I deserved."

"I know what you mean," I mutter.

She nods but doesn't ask me to explain.

"So you ended it with Andrew?"

"I think that was the hardest part. I tried not to tell him why, but he kept pressing and pressing. And finally I did. I told him I liked girls. And . . . I don't know, there was something so sad about watching him realize that this wasn't a fixable thing. It wasn't something we could solve."

Her words are salt on an open wound. All I can think of is Freddie and how he wanted to desperately to power through and fix whatever was broken with us. With me. My chin begins to quiver, but I hold back the tears. I can't bring myself to speak, so I nod, encouraging her to continue.

"I don't regret what happened between us," says Grace, "but I hate the way I hurt you. And I'm so sorry for that. I always will be."

I want to tell her we're even, because she ruined our love and I ruined Freddie's and mine, so somehow the universe's heartbreak scale is even. "Thank you," I finally say. "But I'm glad to hear you're happy. Or at least you seem like you are."

Her eyes are bright. "I am." She loops a strand of hair behind her ear, which makes me feel nostalgic. Fondly remembering something that once was, but knowing it never will be again. "What about you?" she asks. "You gotta tell me you're getting out of here."

I shrug. "Hattie needs me. She's on bed rest, and things are only going to get worse when the baby comes."

"Ro, it's not like you're the dad or anything."

A laugh sputters from my mouth. "I know that."

She's quiet for a moment before she clears her throat.

"You shouldn't pay for her mistakes."

Her mother steps into the door frame. "You girls okay? Can I get you anything before I head up?"

"No thanks, Mom," Grace says in an amused voice.

Her mother turns to me. "So good to see you, Ramona. And that hair!" She shakes her head. "You and your hair are like some kind of a fixture here in this sweet little town!"

I force my mouth into a smile as I pull one of my two braids over my shoulder.

"Nice to see you, too, ma'am."

I wait for a moment until I hear her mother's footsteps overhead. "I'm not paying for her mistakes," I finally say. "She's family. She's my sister, and she needs me."

She lets out an exhausted sigh. "You let yourself die on that cross, Ramona. But the only thing keeping you in this town is fear of the unknown."

Silence sinks slowly between us. There was so much I loved about Grace, but I am so irritated at how she's walked back into my life and has decided that she suddenly knows how to live it better than I do.

"I know what it's like to be scared," she says, her voice low. "Life will always be scary, but you can decide not to live in fear."

I can't listen to her lecture me about fear. "I should go." I stand. "I have an early morning."

Grace follows me to the door. "I didn't mean for us to end on that note."

I turn with my hand on the doorknob. "I know. I'm glad we ran into each other."

"Me too," says Grace. "You changed me. You inspired me to step out and be the real me. You pushed me to become that person, and . . ." She takes a deep breath. "It's not like coming out fixed everything for me. In fact, it made a lot of things more complicated. But I'll always be grateful to you, Ramona." She leans in and gently kisses my cheek.

My anger softens at her touch. "I'm really glad you saw me at the parade," I tell her.

"Yeah?" Her lips twist into an uneven smile. "Me too."

As I ride my bike home, all of Eulogy is still awake and buzzing with life. I want so badly to feel all the joy around me, but I can't.

MARCH

THIRTY-NINE

Freddie wasn't in school today. I try not to keep tabs on him, but I'm thankful for his absence. It's been two weeks since Fat Tuesday, and every day at school has been torturous. For once, I don't feel like I want to contort myself into a ball and hide away in my locker.

Everyone moves past me at lightning speeds to vacate the school in time for spring break, but I take my time getting to the bike rack. All that's waiting for me this spring break is more work and a few trips to the baby store with Hattie.

"Ramona!" calls a voice behind me. "Ramona!"

I backtrack to find the source and don't have to go far. "Oh, hey," I say. "Allyster, right?"

"You remembered." His voice is neither surprised nor bitter, but factual. His hair is gelled into a hard spiky shell, and today he is wearing long denim shorts and a black T-shirt that says: *The Dark Side Made Me Do It.* "So listen," he says. "You missed the deadline for senior page first drafts. I need some pictures of you and whatever you want your page to say."

"Here's the deal: someone bought me that page as, like, a gift, and I'm not really interested, ya know? So take the money as a donation and we can call it good. Cool?"

His face is unmoving. "What? Like, you think it's uncool or something?" He pulls his backpack straps tight against his shoulders like a pair of suspenders. "I guess you can tell your grandkids you were too cool when they ask why you don't have a senior page in your yearbook, right? You can do what you want," he says in exasperation. "I mean, we were really striving for a hundred percent participation this year, but I'm not going to chase you all over town trying to get this from you. You have until the end of April to get it to me, but you've already missed the proofreading window, so it better be clean."

"Thanks," I tell him. "If I decide to go for it, I'll be in touch."

"Whatever," he says. "Have a good spring break."

After my paper route on Monday morning, my limbs are aching. Not because I'm sore, but my muscles miss the swimming. My arms and legs want nothing more than to spend an hour in the pool, slicing through water.

I lie in bed for a little while as Hattie snores on the other side of the wall. Watching the clock, I think back to when I would go swimming with Agnes and Freddie. If they even decided to go today, they should be gone by now.

Springing out of my bed, I tear through my room

searching for my swimsuit and goggles. I check my wallet for the guest pass Agnes gave me and hope she hasn't removed me from her YMCA account as swiftly as I've removed myself from their lives.

What little winter we had has melted away, and on the bike ride to the pool, I even begin to break a sweat. It's a reminder that summer is coming and I've once again survived another winter. Except that this summer is different.

There are no hiccups when I hand over my guest pass, but just in case, I find myself jogging to the locker rooms. As I'm headed down the hallway to the pool, the permanently damp carpet squishes against my toes.

"I was wondering where you'd gone off to," says Prudence Whitmire the moment I round the corner.

I gasp and freeze. "You caught me off guard."

Unlike every other time I've seen her, she's soaking wet and panting. She's not shy about adjusting the back of her swimsuit and letting the material snap against her dimpled rear. I can't help but smile, even though the mere sight of her makes me anxious about the future.

"Just been busy," I add. I should tell her that I appreciate her offer, but I can't take her up on it.

She tsks. "I bet you've softened up. Lost all that great momentum you'd been building."

I shrug. "I do this for fun."

She shakes her head. "Well, the way I see it, how you move in the pool is more fierce than fun."

I force myself not to smile, but inside I'm glowing. "It was good seeing you," I say, cutting our interaction short.

I search for an empty lap lane and end up with the one closest to the water aerobics class. The pool is so much busier at this time of day, and spring break is definitely not helping. Extra lifeguards occupy all the chairs that are normally empty, and there's even one monitoring the constantly replenishing line of kids waiting for the diving board.

After using my bathing suit to clean out my goggles and pulling my hair into a braid, I position myself on the blocks. I stretch back deep like a cat with my fingers clinging to the front of the block before diving in.

The chlorinated water washes over me as I propel my body forward like a machine. If it wouldn't cause my lungs to fill with water, I would sigh.

I can have this. I can still have good things.

I let myself have fun and switch strokes as I please, not bothering to focus too much on form. Only speed. When I finally resurface, Prudence is sitting on my diving block in a matching red Windbreaker suit with *Coach Pru* embroidered above her heart. Her fingers are clenched around a stopwatch, and she jots down a time on a piece of scratch paper.

"You on spring break?" she asks.

"Yes, ma'am." My arms are crossed over the lip of the pool and my heart is thudding in my chest.

"This is a pool buoy. Keep it in your gym bag and bring it to the pool to train with next time." She reaches down between her legs and throws a small foam float into the water. "Meet me here tomorrow morning. Same time. We'll run a few drills. You got athletic shoes? Bring those too."

I open my mouth to protest—mainly 'cause I'm in the habit of fighting back—but she stops me when she adds, "Just for fun."

That night after work, Hattie is waiting for me on the porch with bright eyes and flushed cheeks.

"Hey, what's going on?"

"Come sit down," she says.

"What'd you do?" I ask, knowing better than to not be suspicious.

"I went on a date."

"Okay?"

"It was someone from the website. Remember?"

"How could I forget?" I ask.

"Well, when they picked me up, it turned out—it was Tyler. Actually, the profile belonged to this guy we went to high school with, Chad, but when he figured out who I was, he started asking around, because he'd heard me and Tyler were having a baby. And well, when Tyler heard . . ."

"Oh God," I moan. "You can't be serious."

"He's different, Ramona. He really is. He got a job at that video game store on Lamar, and he says that there might be a management position opening up soon. And he just wants what's best for me and the baby."

"Well," I say defiantly, "he should know that's not him."

"Don't be like that," she says. "Come on. I know Tyler isn't perfect, okay? And I know we're not smart and all like you and Freddie and Ruthie, but I gotta give my baby girl every chance at a real family."

"You have a family." I press my hand to her belly. It's one of the few times I've actually touched it. "She has a family."

Hattie reaches up and gathers my hair before pulling it over my shoulder. "I know that. Of course I know that. But what if she could have it all? What if she could have a great grandpa and a badass aunt and a sort of flaky grandma and a mom *and* a dad?" She pulls my hand back to her belly. "Her little foot has been kicking out all day."

I wait for a moment, but nothing.

Suddenly, I yelp. There's a ripple of movement under my sister's shirt. "Holy shit!"

My sister laughs. "I lie around all day and wait for her to kick. She's stingy with her love. Just like her auntie Ramona."

"I'm not stingy," I retort.

"You're like a cat," says Hattie. "Territorial, too." She pulls herself up, using the railing. "You coming in?"

"Not yet. Just give me a few minutes."

She leaves me there on the porch, and I wonder what the logistics of all this means. Is Tyler moving back in? Will they get an apartment? But most of all I wonder what all this means for me. I should feel free, shouldn't I? Hattie has made her choice.

Part of me feels a little sad. Replaced, even. I imagine

what life would look like if I stayed here in this trailer with Dad. I can't think of him alone. I'm scared that somehow he might wilt away without Hattie or me here. But if I stay, I might just wilt away, too.

APRIL

FORTY

Coach Pru makes a schedule for me. After spring break, we start meeting after school before I go to work. I've made it totally clear that I have no immediate plans for college or anything like that, but I like pushing my body further when I'm in the pool, and she likes having someone to push. So I guess we're sort of both fulfilling a need for each other.

She likes that I ride my bike for the paper route, but she wants me to start running and lifting, too. Since the thing that I like most about swimming is, well, swimming, I compromise and run twice a week after my route and lift with her at the Y every Tuesday and Thursday after I swim. She has me concentrating on my turns between laps and my dives. She says that's where most swimmers lose the most time. She drills me on technique and has me doing all kinds of things like counting strokes and swimming with tennis balls in my fists. It's hard, grueling work, but nothing has ever made me feel so in control of my own life.

Tyler and Hattie start attending parenting classes, and

even though he's still technically living back home with his mom, he crashes at our place at least four nights a week. He's still an idiot, but he's trying. Like, the other day he voluntarily did the dishes. For no reason. I thought I was having an out-of-body experience.

Seeing Freddie is less and less horrible. We don't really talk, but there's none of that awkward eye contact anymore. Instead, we wave and move on.

I ran into him outside the school library the other day. Like, literally, he was reading something on his phone, my head was somewhere else, and our bodies collided.

"Hi," I blurted. It wasn't like I could get away without saying something after a head-on collision like that.

He paused for a beat, his forehead creasing. "Hey."

I felt words piling up in my chest and in my throat, like I was about to vomit all my feelings everywhere. Homesickness racked my bones, and all I wanted was to be able to joke around like we used to, and maybe kiss him, too. Mostly, I missed being his friend. But I couldn't make myself regret a single minute of our relationship, because I didn't. Not even a little bit. "How are you doing?" I finally asked.

He slid his phone into his backpack and shoved his fists into his pockets and nodded. "Good. Good. I signed up for freshman weekend at LSU. Swim team tryouts are this summer. I haven't decided if I'm going to give it another go. I'm pretty out of shape."

"You should do it," I told him. "You'll regret it if you don't."

He smiled, but it was nothing like the toothy gap smile I love. "I gotta go to class."

"Right. Better keep those grades up, so they don't take away that acceptance letter." *What a dumb thing to say.*

He nodded again. "It was good to see you."

"You too," I whispered. But he was already halfway down the hall. I wondered what would happen if I caught up to him and just forced him to be with me. As his friend or his girlfriend. Or however he would have me. But I hurt him. When I was hurting the most, I turned around and cut off the person who'd been there for me more than anyone.

One night at the end of our shift, Ruth and I pile into the booth nearest the kitchen to refill all the salt and pepper shakers, hot sauce, and ketchup.

"Hey," says Ruthie. "Do you need all your graduation tickets?"

I shrug. "Probably not. How many do we get?"

"Something like ten."

"Uh, yeah." I laugh. "I just need two. Maybe three."

She glances up at me. "You need three," she tells me. "Have you even seen your mom since Hattie's shower?"

I shake my head. "She's called a few times and texted us both, but I don't know. I mean, I'm not even mad at her, really. She'll always be this way. I think I've come to terms with that. But that doesn't mean I can't be selective about how often and when I see her."

Ruthie sticks a funnel into a hot sauce bottle and

carefully begins to pour. "I wish I could choose when I have to see my family." She sighs heavily. "My mom won't shut up about prom. Saul didn't go to his, and it's like I'm somehow depriving her if I don't give her this. She keeps saying it's a young woman's rite of passage. I don't even think she cares if I actually go. She just wants the picture to put on her mantelpiece."

"Oh God. I haven't even thought about prom. I've never been to a dance."

"I haven't been to one since freshman year," she says.

And something about this makes me wonder if we'll someday regret not going. "So you don't want to go to prom?" I ask.

She shrugs. "I think I'd want to if she wasn't breathing down my neck. Like, I guess it is a sort of big deal, ya know?"

Saul slides into the booth beside me and lays a big, fat, wet kiss on my cheek. "What's a big deal?"

"Prom," says Ruthie. "Mom won't back off about it and you're not around to distract her."

He lays his server apron down on the table and begins to count out his tips. "Think of this as the final gauntlet." Looking up for a moment, he adds, "And maybe you should go, Ruthie. You might even have fun."

She scoffs.

I can't help but think that maybe *we* should go. There have been so many things over the last few years that Ruthie and I never did. Things that felt totally hetero and outside of what two gay girls in a small town should get to do, and school dances are definitely number one on that list. We always joke about Vermont, but maybe we don't have to wait until we're old ladies with fifty cats, making maple syrup.

I lean across the table. "Ruthie, go with me. Be my date to prom."

She shakes her head even as I'm still talking. "No way."

I grab her hand, forcing her to look at me. "What? We're already rejects, right? Why not give these people a real thrill?"

Saul holds a fluttering hand to his chest. "Nothing would excite me more."

Ruthie turns to her brother, and he reaches for her other hand, so that she's stretched across the table holding both of our hands. "Ruthie, you'll have fun and give Mom what she wants on pure technicality, which is basically the exact opposite of what she wants. It's perfect."

I feel myself smiling, because with Saul's insistence, she can only say yes. Using my pointer fingers, I draw a heart in the air around my face. "Ruth, will you be my super-platonic gay date to prom?"

She shakes her head again, but her lips say, "Fine. Yes, I'll go with you, but only because two small-town lesbos at prom completely undermines the hetero bullshit that is our high school's prom."

I grin. "Or just a yes would have been good."

FORTY-ONE

Hattie informs me that because I did the asking, it's my responsibility to buy our tickets to prom. So by the time I've made that dent in my cash supply, I can't bring myself to buy anything more than a thrift-store dress. I'm not the only girl in Eulogy to have this idea, though, so by the time I make my selection a few days before prom, my options are a mauve mother-of-the-bride dress and a short bright-yellow dress with huge velvet sleeves and black velvet polka dots to match.

Yellow it is.

Carefully, Hattie and I detach the sleeves, which actually have tulle inside of them to keep them pouffy, and we are left with a not-so-horrible yellow polka-dot strapless dress with a very pointy sweetheart neckline. The skirt falls into layers of ruffles, none of which we can spare, because I need every bit of length I can get.

"You really should have let me touch up your roots," Hattie says as she curls my hair.

She had me pull a chair into the bathroom from the

kitchen and face it so that my back would be to the mirror. *For the big reveal*, she said.

"I don't like that I can't see what you're doing." I fiddle with the evil-eye charm hanging from my wrist. I'm even wearing the black plastic spider ring from Thanksgiving.

"This is what they'd do if you went to a salon anyway. Trust me, okay? Have I ever led your hair astray in the past?"

It's true. Without Hattie I might have a mullet, and I love the way the freshly warm hair feels against my back every time she releases it from the curling iron. "What are we even supposed to do at prom?"

"Whatever you want," she says. "Dance. Eat. Make fun of people."

My phone buzzes then, but it's not a text or a call. Instead it's an alert from the National Weather Service issuing a severe thunderstorm warning. "Great." I hold up the screen for her to see. "I don't think it will matter much what you do to my hair at this point."

"Text Saul and tell him to put the top on the Jeep."

Since I don't have a license and Ruth doesn't have a car, Saul has volunteered himself as our ride. I shoot off a quick message as Hattie puts the finishing touches on my hair.

"Okay," she finally says, and rests the curling iron on the side of the sink. "Close your eyes and stand up." She kicks the chair into the hallway. "You can look."

When I turn around and open my eyes, it's not that I see some kind of transformation. No, I look very much like myself. I have to duck a little to get the full picture since our mirror is so short, but my watery blue hair has been meticulously curled into loose waves that make me look like the kind of mermaid that might sing you to your untimely end. The yellow-and-black polka-dot dress doesn't hurt my eyes as badly as it did at the thrift store, but maybe that's just the crappy lighting in our bathroom. It almost looks like something you might find in the mall. Still, it's not quite cool enough to be vintage.

I nod. "I love it. You're sure the shoes are okay?"

We both glance down at the pointy red flats Mom got me two years ago for Christmas. Having size-twelve feet has always resulted in limited footwear options.

"I mean, I wouldn't say they match," says Hattie. "But that makes it more Ramona."

"Don't you ever wonder what we might look like if we'd grown up with money?" I ask. "Or if I weren't tall?" I shake my head with my hands on my hips. "I don't know. It makes me think."

Rain begins to splatter against the bathroom window.

"Yeah," she says. "I guess. But then aren't those all the things that make us who we are?" She sits down on the chair in the hallway and holds her belly. "Sorry. Just can't stand up like that for too long. It's not like you wouldn't be Ramona if you weren't poor or tall, ya know? But I feel like dealing with the consequences of those things have been what makes you, well, you."

I nod. And I guess she's right there. Maybe it's not all the little labels that make us who we are. Maybe it's about how all those labels interact with the world around us. It's not that I'm gay. It's that I'm gay in Eulogy, Mississippi. It's not that I'm tall. It's that I'm too tall for the trailer I live in. It's not that I'm poor. It's that I'm too poor to do and have everything I want. Life is a series of conflicts, and maybe the only resolution is accepting that not all problems are meant to be solved.

When Saul pulls up, I run outside with my army jacket draped over my head. Ruth sits in the back in an icy-blue floor-length halter dress with her hair half pulled up and curled into ringlets.

"You look great," I tell her. "Superhot."

"Yeah, she does," says Saul.

"Thanks," Ruth says. "Mom and I actually agreed on the dress." She leans forward. "That's before I told her you were my super platonic gay date."

"She'll live," says Saul as he reaches over my lap and into his glove box to retrieve two corsages, which happen to match each of our dresses. "I knew neither of y'all lesbians would think to buy these."

"You asshole," Ruth says as he slips hers over her wrist, "why'd you have to go and make tonight special?"

"My two babies are off to prom," he says. "It's already special. And hey, I didn't even go to my prom. You're making my gay dreams come true right now."

"Well, I'm glad someone's dreams are coming true tonight," says Ruth.

"Hey now!" I slide the elastic band over my wrist. "FYI, I am a very dreamy date."

The rain softens just barely as we pull up to the Eulogy

Civic Center. I hold my jacket out so that Ruth can duck underneath as we both run inside.

"Y'all, get into some good trouble for me," calls Saul.

Inside, Ruthie and I pose for pictures, and when I feel people staring—including her boyfriend from freshman year—I take her hand to give them something worth remembering.

The halls of the civic center are strewn with white streamers and paper lanterns. With the lights dimmed, I can actually forget that we're in the same place where town elections and the annual craft show are held.

We first stop at the punch bowl, where we run into Adam, who is with a shorter Latino girl whose black curly hair is twisted into an intricate updo. Adam wears a fitted black suit with a black shirt and a skinny red tie to match his date's A-line-cut tea-length dress.

"Well, well, well," says Ruth, "Adam's got a date."

The girl, who I've never seen, blushes even though she doesn't look the least bit amused by her date, who is chugging punch.

Adam glances around before saying, "Ruth, Ramona, this is my"—he coughs into his shoulder—"cousin, Sophia."

I try not to laugh at how obviously he's embarrassed by this. The good news is no one has to know this is his cousin, and the even better news is that Sophia is pretty hot. "It's great to meet you, Sophia. I haven't seen you at school before. Do you live around here?"

"Hell no," she says. "I live outside Hattiesburg. My mom made me come down here for this."

Adam groans into his fist. "Can you at least pretend to be cool with me for one night?"

Ruth and I laugh, and after a minute Sophia does, too.

"Well, I guess we're gonna check things out," I tell them.

"Cool," says Adam. "Just leave me here with her then."

I grab Ruth's hand, but before we leave, I ask, "Do you know if Freddie—"

"Your guess is as good as mine," Adam tells me. "He's been all weird and brooding lately. Like an angsty vampire."

What if he shows up? Or what if he doesn't? Or even worse: What if he brings a date? I don't know if I could handle seeing him with someone else right now.

I nod and pull Ruth behind me to the dance floor. "Hey, Sophia," she calls over her shoulder. "Save me a dance?"

Rather than shy away, Sophia says, "If you think you can handle this."

I squeeze Ruth's hand as we slip into the crowd. "Oh my God! Who are you? I bow down, Queen Sexpot!"

"I know! I know!" Her voice is giddy. "But it might be cool to know someone in Hattiesburg."

"Ruth!" I pull her to me in a huge hug. "You didn't tell me you got into Southern Miss!"

Her eyes water, which is as close as I've ever seen her come to crying. "It's all happening so fast. Everything's going to change."

I hold her hands in mine. "Yeah, it is," I admit. "But we can still be the same."

She nods, and then a slow grin spreads across her face. "She was really hot."

"Yeah, she was. Come on!" I yell at her over the music. "Let's dance." I've never really been the kind of person who dances, but the music reminds me of dancing with Freddie in Jackson Square and how our bodies melted into each other and how perfect that moment was.

I suddenly miss him so much. I miss parking my bike in his driveway every morning and swimming with him and eating all his different breakfast concoctions and making out in car washes and broom closets.

We don't dance in the same way Freddie and I did, with our skin pressed together, but the sight of us is still enough to make a few heads turn. I watch intently as a couple of faculty members whisper back and forth and point at us. I dance so that Ruth's back is facing them, and I wonder if they're going to tell us we can't be here or that we can't dance together. It's the first time I've felt in danger of being told I don't belong simply because I'm being myself. It's a feeling I want to forget, but one I know I will always remember. But then the librarian, Mrs. Treviño, steps into the conversation, and the other teachers quickly disperse. I heave a sigh of relief.

After a few songs, we sort of slip into the background like everyone else and we're no one's spectacle. I can't stop myself from glancing around every once in a while, searching for Freddie. But I can't imagine he'd have a date or that he'd come here by himself. Yet this is just the type of thing

Agnes would force him to attend.

The pounding dance music slows into a quieter song and the crowd thins out. Ruthie's eyes are wide and round, and the smile on her face is nothing short of thrilling. This is not the night she was expecting. "We can sit down," she says as she catches her breath.

I pull her to me. "It's not prom without a slow dance, right? This one's mine. Next one is Sophia."

Even with her heels, she's shorter than me, but she can still hook her chin over my shoulder.

This is new for me—the slow dance. I'm not sure where to put my hands or who's leading whom, so I wrap my arms around her in a hug. I hold her tight and think about all the ways Ruth has been there for me, and how she's always expected more from me than anyone else. I wish I could be the person she thinks I'm capable of becoming. I don't even bother wondering what she would say if I told her about Coach Pru.

It doesn't make me sad to think of Ruthie leaving and becoming some big fancy doctor, because I know that as long as me, Saul, and Hattie are here she'll always come back to see us. But still, there's something about tonight that feels like the end of a good song.

The two of us sway against each other under the twinkling lights strung up by the prom committee, when all of a sudden loud sirens drown out the music.

For a moment, everyone is still and none of us quite know if this is real. And then Mrs. Treviño is on the mic. "Okay, people. Those are the tornado sirens. I need everyone to vacate the banquet hall and head out into the corridor. Please find a seat on the floor and do so in an orderly but swift fashion."

FORTY-TWO

The pilgrimage to the corridor is swift, but in no way orderly. There is screaming and shouting and pushing.

I feel my body beginning to panic.

This isn't the first time I've heard the sirens go off, but I've never been in an actual tornado. And I guess that's why this doesn't feel real. I know what hurricanes look like. And flooding. But a tornado sort of feels like a myth to me.

Ruth pulls me by my arm and grabs my jacket from the table where we left our cups of punch.

"Adam!" I shout, and reach for him and Sophia behind us. The good thing about being so tall is the sight advantage.

As the four of us are huddling down together on the floor in this windowless hallway, Freddie rushes in, soaking wet.

My heart nearly stops. I stand immediately and run to him.

He's in a tux and his pants are a little too short, but he's holding his cell phone and his keys and he's panting.

"You're here," I say, like he somehow owes me an explanation for his presence.

He shakes the water out of his hair. "It's bad out there."

I want to hug him or take his hand, but instead I say, "Come sit down with us."

Ruthie scoots over and the three of us cram in with the rest of the senior class and whatever chaperones volunteered to be here, while Adam and Sophia sit across from us.

"My gram made me come," says Freddie.

Ruthie peers over my shoulder. "We didn't see you inside. Ramona was looking all over the place."

I give her a sideways glance, and she shrugs.

"I was in the car," Freddie quietly admits. "I was just going to chill for a while, and then go back home. You remember Lydia?" he asks. "My friend from Viv's party? She was going to drive down, but the weather was bad up there, too."

My whole body is racked with guilt as I think of him out in the car by himself when he could have been in here with all of us. The only reason he was out there instead of in here is me. "I'm sorry," I blurt.

"You didn't make me come," he says.

"I know. I just—"

The sirens outside kick up again, and the lights begin to flicker. It's nothing like a police ambulance. These sirens are more obnoxious than that, and they have to be, because tornadoes can hit at any time, even in the middle of the night.

"We're all quite safe in this hallway," says Mrs. Treviño over a few shrieks. "This is a stable building that has survived much worse."

A stable building. Oh God. Oh Christ. The trailer. Feverishly, I dig through the pockets of my jacket for my cell phone, but there are no bars next to the tiny battery in the corner of the screen.

"Hattie," I say. I turn to Freddie and then Ruthie. "Hattie's in the trailer. She's by herself. I've got to get to her."

I begin to stand, but Freddie pulls me back. "Ramona, wait it out. You can't go anywhere right now. I promise as soon as it's clear, I'll drive you wherever you want to go."

And then the lights go out entirely. The hallway is lit by the blue light of cell phones. Some students are laughing and making jokes, but I hear a few quiet sobs.

Panic claws at my chest. I wish I could see outside, but the whole purpose of having us here in this hallway is that there are no windows. I pull my knees in to my chest and duck my head in between my legs, not really caring much that I'm in a dress.

Freddie traces patterns into the bare skin of my back, just like he did when Hattie was in the hospital.

Every time I close my eyes, all I can imagine is going home to a slab of concrete and a missing sister. I was so stupid to think I could ever protect her. That I could ever create a real, lasting life for us in that dilapidated trailer.

Above and all around us, the walls and ceiling begin to shake like a freight train is running through the hallway. Ruthie curls into a ball under my jacket at my side, and I grip her hand tightly. Freddie takes off his jacket and holds it over all three of us. I hold on to his leg with my free hand. Dust and drywall falls around us. There's screaming and crying. It echoes until I can't tell which howling is louder: the people or the storm.

Wherever Mrs. Treviño has gone, she's not bothering to comfort us anymore. In the face of Mother Nature, there is no sympathy. She doesn't care if you're poor or straight or gay or a guy or a girl. She only cares if you are in her path.

I can't tell how long we're sitting there for. It could be two minutes or it could be thirty. But eventually the world stops shaking and everyone slowly quiets. As if we're all playing dead, waiting for the storm to move on to her next victims.

"Are you okay?" Freddie asks. "Are you both okay?"

I nod as he drapes his jacket over my shoulders. I shine my cell phone light on Adam and Sophia. "Are you guys all right?"

They both nod, but I can see they're both in about as much shock as everyone else.

"I need to go," I say. "I need to leave."

"Is everyone all right?" Mrs. Treviño calls. A bright flashlight flicks on at the end of the hallway. "We've got to do a head count before anyone can leave."

And that causes an immediate uproar from everyone, including me.

"The louder you are," she shouts, "the more difficult this will be and the longer it will take."

On the other side of the hallway, I hear someone say,

"My dad says everything south of the tracks is wiped."

My heart plummets into my stomach. I pull my cell phone out again. "I don't have any bars. Does anyone have any bars?"

"I've got nothing," says Freddie.

"Me neither," confirms Ruthie. "Oh, wait. Hang on. Here's something from Saul. It says to call him."

She tries over and over, but nothing.

I wait in agony for I don't know how long until finally my phone is struck with several notifications at once. I read them all in rapid succession. "Holy shit. Holy shit." I stand and run past the chaperone at the end of the hallway. Freddie and Ruthie are close behind.

"Ramona!" calls Freddie. "Slow down! You don't have a way to get anywhere without me."

"You three!" shouts someone behind us, but no one has time to chase us down as we bolt through the exit.

"We gotta go," I shout as I frantically search the parking lot for Agnes's Cadillac. I turn to them both. "Hattie's having the baby early. I need to get to the hospital. She's having an emergency C-section."

FORTY-THREE

In the dark of night, it's difficult to see any damage outside, but somehow, I can sense it.

Freddie clicks Agnes's key chain, and I follow the flashing headlights to the last row of the parking lot, where the three of us find a downed tree resting on the hood of the Cadillac.

"Shit," says Freddie.

I turn to him. "We can move it."

And we do. The tree isn't all that big. It leaves a dent in the hood, but after some grunting we're able to roll it off onto the grass in front of the car.

We all pile in. The streets are eerily quiet except for a few police cars and ambulances speeding down the roads with their lights all lit up and sirens singing.

I can't think about what my home might look like at this exact moment. I can only be thankful that Hattie is at the hospital and Dad was at work. The car ride is silent except for the pounding of my frantic heart. Hattie's going to have a C-section, which we already knew, but this is earlier than expected. I don't know much about childbirth, but it seems routine enough. It happens every day without consequence. And yet, if there's a way for this night to go even more to hell, Hattie might find a way to make it happen.

According to Dad's texts, the doctor says the procedure is more high risk than normal because of Hattie's condition. Not to mention that the storm that rolled through Eulogy is about to roll through Gulfport. The power could go out or the whole building could just be destroyed if a tornado really hits. I tell myself that hospitals are prepared for these types of things and that even if the power goes out, they'll have generators. But still, all I can imagine at this moment is my sister bleeding out in the middle of a power outage.

Ruth is in the backseat on the phone with Saul. "Are you okay? Are Mom and Dad? What about Reggie?"

After a moment of silence, she nods. "We're on our way now." Pause. "Yeah, okay, good. We'll see you there."

She hangs up. "Everyone's okay. They lost a few windows at the apartment. Reggie was out on the rig this weekend, and the storm missed them."

"Saul hasn't driven by the trailer park, has he?" I ask, even though the thought of an answer terrifies me.

Ruthie shakes her head. "Not that I know of."

I close my eyes and lean my head against the headrest until Freddie says, "We're here." He pulls up to the carport. "We'll meet you inside."

The hospital is alive with energy as injuries from the

storm trickle in. The elevators are taking too long, so I opt to run the four flights up to the maternity ward. I remind myself to thank Coach Pru for the extra training.

The maternity ward is a serene oasis compared to what's happening downstairs. Dad sits in the waiting room by himself, chewing the quick of his nails.

"Where is she?" I pant.

He stands and pulls me into a suffocating hug. "You're okay."

Just then the double swinging doors leading to the rest of the ward open as Tyler pushes through them. His skin is so pale it's almost translucent, and his eyes are wide and full of terror. "It's about to happen," he says. "Can you make sure to let my mom know? She should be here soon."

"But where is Hattie?" I ask. "I need to get, like, scrubs or whatever."

The elevator doors open and Saul, Ruthie, and Freddie all tumble out.

Tyler turns to me, and in a quieter voice says, "She can only have one person in the operating room with her."

"I know," I say. And then I realize. "Oh."

"Yeah," he says.

My dad's hand is on my back.

I feel it in my lips first, the trembling. I hate myself for crying so much this year, but my entire stupid life has upended itself. This life I've created is a messy room and only I know where everything is hidden and tucked away, but now it's like someone's come in and tidied up and suddenly nothing is as it should be.

"You have to be brave for her," I tell him.

Tyler nods, and I know he's an asshat jerk, but something in my voice resonates with him. I can see it. Then he runs back through the double doors.

I sit down in between my dad and Freddie. Ruthie argues with the vending machine, trying to shake her chips loose before she pokes around the nurse's desk a little bit and starts asking about summer internships.

My entire life is an unknown. It's an ocean without a floor. A pool without an end.

Freddie knocks the toe of his dress shoe against mine. "It's going to be okay," he whispers.

I nod.

I feel betrayed. Sure, I'm not the one who got Hattie pregnant, but I'm the one who's been there to pick up the pieces every step of the way, and if anyone is going to be in that operating room with her, it should be me.

When Tyler's mom arrives, my dad does all the talking. Mrs. Porter is a stout little woman with deep smile lines. I wonder what she did to end up with a kid like Tyler.

From what I know about Tyler and his mom, I understand that being here for the birth of her illegitimate grandchild goes against everything she believes in, but I can still sense the eagerness in her voice that tells me she is going to be a wonderful grandmother. Her presence alone eases my nerves.

"Have you called Mom?" I suddenly blurt.

My dad turns to me and guiltily shakes his head.

I shoot off a quick text to her. **The baby is coming! Hattie's**

in labor and delivery right now!

She responds within seconds. **I get off at midnight, but will try to be there sooner. Are y'all okay?**

I respond to let her know I'm okay. We're all okay. And then we wait.

Sara Belle Leroux is born at 11:53 p.m. at six pounds, three ounces. Her hair is blacker than night, and she hasn't opened her eyes wide enough for me to see what color they are yet.

I am in love. Hattie fought for Sara to have her last name, since Tyler wanted to name her after his great-aunt Sara. And Belle? Well, Hattie's daughter's name had to have a little bit of flair.

Freddie, Ruth, and Saul all peek in on Hattie, but she's still so doped up on drugs.

"I want what she's having," says Saul.

Ruth shakes her head. "We better get going."

After they head off for the elevators, Freddie motions with his head in their direction. "Me too," he says. "Gram said we had a little damage on the roof, and I told her I'd climb up there as soon as the sun comes up."

"You let me know if she needs any shingles replaced," my dad tells him. "You and me can jump up there on my day off and knock it out. No need to call anyone if it's minor." Dad holds out his hand for Freddie, and the two shake firmly. "I appreciate you getting Ramona here."

"Of course," Freddie says. "Congratulations, Hattie. Tyler, you too."

Tyler waves, but doesn't look up from Sara.

Hattie giggles wildly, on the verge of tears. "I'm wearing diapers and so is she."

Freddie's cheeks turn a deep red.

"It's a pad, not a diaper," I tell her.

"And oh my God! These socks are great. Why don't more people talk about how great hospital socks are?"

"I'll, uh, walk you out," I tell Freddie, not bothering to hide my smile.

The walk to the elevators is quiet, but not in a bad way, I don't think.

While we wait for the elevator, Freddie hugs me, pulling me to him with our arms wrapped tight around each other. I feel the weight of everything unsaid between us. But after everything tonight, I don't even know where to begin.

I hold Sara for as long as I can before the nurse shoos us all away. Tyler's mom is bubbling with constant tears, and I think even Dad's eyes might have watered.

Once Mom gets here she seems stunned the whole time, dabbing her eyes nonstop. For once, she doesn't make it about herself, and the only reason I can think of is that she's under Sara's spell, too. Either way, we are all completely smitten, and for those few moments in Hattie's hospital room, it's easy to believe that this sweet little baby is the answer to all of the world's troubles.

Mom sits in the rocking chair with a pillow on her lap for extra support as she holds Sara for the first time. "She looks just like the two of you girls." She turns to my dad. "And she's got Hattie's nose. Doesn't she have Hattie's nose?"

He nods. "And Tyler's ears."

"Guess I don't have to waste money on that paternity test," he says in true Tyler fashion.

But his mom is quick to smack him in the back of the head.

"Sorry," he mumbles.

While the doctor is checking in on Hattie and Sara, I wait in the hallway with my mom while Dad and Mrs. Porter run down to the cafeteria for coffee.

"Hey, honey," says Mom, "thanks for messaging me. I'm . . . I'm glad to be here tonight."

I nod. "Hattie wanted you here."

My mom will never be perfect. She'll never be the mom I want her to be, but she'll always be the mom I've got. We'll never have a perfect relationship, and she might not ever fully understand me, but sometimes you gotta work with what you have.

"I wanted you here, too," I tell her.

She turns so that I can't see her face, but I can hear the tears in her voice. "You look real nice in your prom outfit. Did you and Freddie go together?"

"Ruth was my date. The girl in the blue dress."

She nods, facing me. "She's real pretty. I hope you girls had fun."

It might be a small first step or maybe the most acceptance I'll ever get from her. I don't know. I guess we'll have to see.

"I didn't mean to embarrass you girls at the baby shower," she adds. "I was upset about not being a part of it. But I understand why I wasn't."

I don't say I'm sorry or that I understand why she got drunk, because neither of those things are true. "I'm just glad you're here now," I tell her.

"Me too," she says. "Me too."

After another hour or so, we decide to let Hattie and Sara rest and get better acquainted with each other. I hate to leave my sister at the hospital by herself, but she's not alone. Tyler is staying, too. Besides, how bad can he screw things up with all those nurses around?

FORTY-FOUR

Dad and I drive home, and I sit in the middle seat right beside him as if Hattie were in the truck with us. I know that whatever waits for us is all we have left. My stomach clenches into a fist, and I say a silent prayer that my chocolate box under my bed is intact.

Police officers are set up outside the trailer park, admitting emergency officials and residents only. We are instructed that no matter the state of our home, we must gather necessities and take a Red Cross voucher for a place to stay for the night, as the area has not yet been deemed safe.

There is no electricity in the trailer park, so Dad turns on his brights, lighting the road ahead as our neighbors roam through rubble in their nightgowns.

Some houses are completely untouched, while others look like they've been shredded in a blender. Emergency crews are slowly working their way through the trailer park as they set up huge generator-powered lights to illuminate the damage.

When we finally make it to our house, it's too dark to see at first. Then my dad positions the truck with the headlights showcasing our home.

He gasps, and I hold a shaking hand to my lips.

It's not the worst we've seen, but the roof has been peeled back like a can of tuna, and the half of the trailer containing my dad's little closet of a room and the living room has collapsed.

I know it was a shitty little place to call home, but that's what it was: home. My heart breaks piece by piece as I realize that now we have no place to call ours.

"Okay, let's gather what we can into the back of the truck. Maybe we can get a room at the hotel, so we don't need to stay in the shelter." He says it in a determined yet downtrodden way that reminds me this is not the first time my father has been in this position. "Watch your step," he adds. "Make sure the ground below you feels steady."

As I walk up the steps to our crumbling home, my dad is called across the street to help cut down a tree that's leaning on someone's house. He tells me to go on and collect as much stuff as I can.

Using the huge industrial-strength flashlight my dad keeps in the back of his truck, I begin to fill laundry baskets, backpacks, trash bags, and whatever else can be filled with my and Hattie's belongings. I'm careful to separate all of Sara's diapers and clothing that can be salvaged, and I say a quiet prayer to whoever is listening for sparing the crib, which hasn't even been delivered yet.

Lots of our stuff is soaked, but it can be washed, and most

of Sara's stuff from the shower is still in Agnes's garage. I find one of my boots in the tub and the other in my closet. The mattress was torn off my bed and must be in someone's yard somewhere, but tucked away in the far corner of my room under the frame and box spring is my chocolate box, containing every family photo and my meager life savings.

I clutch the box to my chest. It's not even the money that I'm most concerned about. But the family photos, the notes, and all those childhood games of MASH. Those are things I can never replace no matter how many hours I work.

I search for my Wheaties box with Missy Franklin's head on Michael Phelps's body, but it's destroyed. Pieces of it are scattered everywhere. I can't believe that this is the thing that sends me over the edge, but I begin to cry. I sob and sob. No one rushes to my side, because everyone is crying. I can hear it all around me. So it's just me, crying in my room with no roof because my stupid Wheaties box has been destroyed.

My goggles are gone, too, and the only swimsuit I can find is definitely not suitable for workouts.

I inhale through my nose and exhale through my mouth. I do it over and over again, reminding myself that I am alive. No one I love was injured, and I have a niece. I will survive, because I have survived.

I'm unable to reach my dad's room, but he had a laundry basket full of dirty clothes in the bathroom and a few work shirts that he'd hung to dry in the hallway.

With the help of my dad, we pile what's left of our lives

into the back of the truck. I don't know how we're going to break this to Hattie and explain to her that the stability she'd counted on is no more and that there is no home to bring Sara back to.

With only a few hours until dawn, I text Charlie to let him know I won't be able to run my paper route in the morning since my bike is currently missing. We head to the hotel where my dad works, and while I wait in the car, he speaks with his manager, who agrees to let us stay for a few nights to avoid whatever temporary housing situation the Red Cross is organizing.

FORTY-FIVE

After parking our car underground, where all the maintenance and catering vans park and where our belongings will be safe from the elements, we take the service elevator to the fourth floor, where we've been given a room with two queen beds.

The entire hotel is lush in black-and-white textured wallpaper with splashes of red orchids in extravagant vases, and if I were here under any other circumstances, I might take the time to appreciate it all. But instead I kick off my shoes as my dad pulls the blackout curtains tight against the rising sun, and we both pass out in the clothes we are wearing.

As I drift off to sleep, I wonder what it must be like for my dad to finally spend the night in the beautiful hotel he's spent all these years cooking in and maintaining.

I wake a few hours later to find my dad snoring lightly. My entire body screams like I've been in a car crash as I push the blankets back and walk to the window. Bracing myself for the harsh sunlight, I open the curtains a sliver.

Once my eyes adjust, I'm greeted by a wet world, with branches and debris strewn everywhere, with lawn chairs and umbrellas littering the pool. There's not much real damage here, but there are a few ancient trees that have been turned into nothing more than snapped twigs by the previous night's storm.

If this had been a hurricane, she'd have a name, but instead we'll just call her the storm. Or maybe she'll be known as the Eulogy Prom Night Tornado, like some kind of horror movie. Last night will be remembered as many things for all of us, but for me, the first thing it will always be is the night I became an aunt.

In the bathroom, I find the box of toiletries I gathered from our trailer. It's full of random things I'd never use on a daily basis.

I sit down at the vanity to sort through it and hopefully find some deodorant and a toothbrush when I come across the scissors Hattie always used to trim my hair. Heavy and sharp with an orange handle, they were technically kitchen scissors meant to be used to trim the fat and gristle off meat, but we'd found a better use for them.

My long dark-blond roots melt into a grayish blue. I reach for my brush to comb through a few knots that sit like speed bumps in my otherwise limp hair. But then I put it down and reach for the scissors. It's been a while since Hattie's colored my hair, and I can almost imagine myself without the blue hair. I can almost see what I must have looked like before.

I do it without thinking at first. And then once I've snipped one piece, I can't stop. I don't want to.

I try not to cut recklessly and instead concentrate on cutting the blue out of my hair as I snip close to the scalp. My roots have grown out by an inch and a half or two, so I keep cutting until all the blue is on the floor and free from my head.

Every time I hear the sharp sound of scissors snipping, I'm reminded of the thousands of hours Hattie and I spent maintaining my hair and keeping it that perfect shade of blue. I remember the night I broke things off with Freddie and I came home with my hair in tangles, and the only person who could loosen each knot was my sister.

I love Hattie. I will love her forever. But with every snip, I need her a little less, and somehow that allows me to love her a little more. Last night, when she chose Tyler to join her in the operating room, I felt betrayed and lost.

I don't know if Tyler will be there for her when she and Sara need him most. I don't know if he will provide for them or if he's even emotionally capable of being the father that Sara deserves. I don't know if Hattie's making a mistake or not, but whatever it is, it's a decision that Hattie must make on her own.

I'm her sister. I will always be here to pick up the pieces, but it's time I make some mistakes of my own.

MAY

FORTY-SIX

We stayed in the hotel for a few nights before my dad struck a deal with one of the local extended-stay hotels. I kicked in some of my money for the first two weeks until he got his paycheck, but he refused any other help, so I pitch in with things like groceries and other stuff he doesn't so easily notice.

Hattie, Sara, and Tyler moved in with his mom. Tyler's mom didn't let him off the hook, though. She made him promise to ask for more hours at work and pitch in for utilities and groceries. At first Dad was hesitant for Hattie to move out, but Mrs. Porter showed up to the hospital the morning after the storm in a lavender T-shirt that said *I'm the Grandma in Charge Here*, allaying any of our doubts.

Once things have settled a little, I walk to Hall of Fame, the sporting-goods store downtown, one day after school.

Inside, I peruse the rack of women's swimsuits. Coach Pru says that swimsuits made for actual swimmers are cut longer and that I should pick up one or two. I take a black one, a red one, and a blue one to try on.

After the clerk lets me into the fitting room stall, I slip on the blue one and am shocked to find that it fits. Now, if I were even half an inch taller, I might be in trouble, but it actually fits.

I step closer to the mirror and study the subtle pattern. The suit almost glistens, and the diamond design looks like the sun reflecting off the water, and I sort of like the idea of how this suit could be my own personal camouflage.

I check the tag and groan loudly.

"You okay in there?" the clerk asks over the sports radio broadcast.

"Fine," I answer.

What Coach Pru failed to mention was that a suit like this is . . . an investment. I sit down on the bench.

I remember finding my chocolate box intact and what a relief that was. But what if it had been gone? What if my life savings had been torn to pieces and strewn across the entire trailer park? What good would it do me then?

I stand with my hands on my hips, examining myself in the dusty mirror. Aside from my dingy white socks, I look like a fierce competitor. Maybe this is more money than Ramona from last month would have ever spent on a swimsuit, but it is an investment. In myself.

I'll never forget coming home with my first paycheck and my dad telling me to spend it on something foolish. As I walk to the register with my new swimsuit in hand, I grab a swimming cap and a fancy new pair of goggles. I think I'm ready to spend my little bit of savings on something completely foolish: the future.

Maybe I'm high on my recent purchase or maybe I'm an idiot, but as I'm walking out the door, I spot a bright-red bike in the window of Al's Bikes across the street. *USED!* the sign says. *WHAT A DEAL!*

I flip through my cash and do some quick math on how much more I'll make this month if I can pick up my route again.

As I'm walking through the door of Al's, the bell rings overhead. I tell myself the bike will pay for itself in two weeks. And I'm really freaking tired of walking.

FORTY-SEVEN

With only three weeks of school to go, I've been running around doing things I'd never imagine actually happening to me, like picking up my graduation robe and cleaning out my locker.

Freddie, Adam, Ruthie, and I meet in the courtyard for lunch and to trade notes for various finals.

Freddie and I haven't talked much since the hospital. It's like that night was a safe zone, and nothing we said or did would count against us. And now I see him at lunch or in the hall. I'll wave and he'll smile back. But that night didn't change things. Maybe if my life were a movie, the tornado would have driven us back to each other, but that wasn't how it happened.

The intercom crackles for a moment, before the school secretary says, "Attention, students: yearbooks have arrived. They will be available in the yearbook room and at the front office."

There are a few distant cheers. The school was only

slightly damaged and ended up closing for two days following the tornado. The entire trailer park was condemned, like it should have been years ago.

"It doesn't even matter what we get on these finals," says Ruthie. "We've all already been accepted to colleges."

"Almost," I say. "I still have to mail in my final transcript."

"Come on, Ramona! Hop to it." She nudges me in the ribs. "You're totally in, though. I mean, you're basically on the swim team already."

Freddie smiles but looks away quickly. I want to ask him if he decided to do the open tryouts at LSU, but I don't want to put him on the spot.

When I told Ruth about Coach Pru's offer and that I had decided to take her up on it, she cried. She cried actual human tears. And seeing Ruth cry made me cry. So the two of us sat there outside Boucher's on our lunch break, hugging and crying.

I made the decision last week after swimming in my new suit for the first time. I did some weight lifting with Coach Pru as she sat there reading a copy of *Sports Illustrated*.

"I should charge you for this," she said.

I laughed. "Couldn't afford you anyway."

She glanced up over the edge of her magazine, huffing out a laugh. A moment later, she stood and said, "I'm heading out early. That's not an excuse to slack off."

I groaned, knowing I'd finish my reps regardless.

Afterward, I jumped into the pool to cool off. I let my body sink down to the bottom of the deep end. As I sat there, testing my lung capacity, I realized wherever I can find water, I can find home. I am home.

We all leave lunch early to line up for yearbooks. I didn't shell out money for my own, but I wait with my friends still. After the bell rings, and we part ways with Freddie and Adam, Ruthie and I head to class.

"You mind if I look at that?" I ask as we take our seats, motioning to her yearbook.

She shrugs. "Sure."

As Mr. Galvez goes over our Spanish final review, I flip to the back of the yearbook and search for the page bearing my name.

I tracked down Allyster a few days after we got settled into the extended-stay hotel. I was super late on the deadline, but he was surprisingly sympathetic. I may have guilted him with the whole losing-my-house-and-most-of-my-belongings-in-a-tornado thing.

Everyone's senior page has one photo. Usually it's a picture taken on the beach or in a field. The picture on my senior page is half a strip of black-and-white photo-booth pictures of Freddie and me from our day in New Orleans. It was an old photo booth—the kind that still uses chemicals. We took so many that day despite the line of couples waiting behind us.

In the first photo, he and I are still getting situated, not quite prepared for the first flash of the bulb. In the second photo, Freddie is holding me tight and we're both laughing hysterically. You can even see his orange freckles splattered against his cheeks.

Next to the photos is a single quote.

You know that place between sleep and awake, that place where you still remember dreaming? That's where I'll always love you. That's where I'll be waiting.
—*J. M. Barrie,* PETER PAN

After school, I wait at the bike rack next to my new red Schwinn.

I wait for Freddie. For a second, I worry that he won't come out this way or that he's going to avoid me, but his bike is chained up right next to mine.

He's walking with Adam across the courtyard when Freddie turns to him and says something. Adam nods and waves good-bye. I can see Freddie's finger holding his place in the back of the yearbook.

From across the courtyard, his eyes meet mine, and he walks directly to me.

My heart is thrashing against my rib cage. "I never said thank you for the senior page."

He nods slowly. "I saw it."

I take a deep breath. "It's been—a lot has happened this year," I say. I wish everything about this moment was perfect. I wish it was like that stupid movie we watched before school started. If we lived inside that movie, everything between us would be fixed with a kiss.

He laughs halfheartedly. "Yeah, not the year I expected.

Definitely didn't keep my promise to swear off girls."

I grimace as I remember the two of us, driving back to Eulogy, completely heartbroken. "I'm sorry for ending things the way I did," I say. "I didn't know what else to do."

He holds his jaw with one hand, thinking. "I was really mad at you. I still kind of am. I felt like we built this really amazing thing together—this connection that I'd never had with anyone else before—and then suddenly you decided it was over. It just—if we built it together, it didn't seem fair that we couldn't at least decide to end it together."

I shake my head. "You were right." I take a step closer to him. "You have every right to be mad. I'm mad at myself, too."

"So what do we do now?"

"I was thinking that maybe when you're done being mad you could forgive me?"

"Forgiving you isn't the hard part." He twists the ball of his foot into the dirt before looking up at me again. "I've got to trust that you won't just cut me out of your life again without warning. And I think that's going to take a little while."

"That's fair," I tell him.

He half smiles. "So what does all this mean for us?"

I let out a deep sigh. "Listen," I say, "our lives are about to change in really big ways. Neither of us has had much luck with long distance."

He chuckles. "You're right on that one."

"But I think we can promise each other one day at a

time. I think that's fair . . . if that's what you want."

"I don't want to hold you back from anything," he tells me. "I already tried that with Viv."

"And I don't want to hold you back either, but I also know that I love you, and I think you still love me too."

He takes my hand, tracing circles in my palm. "I've tried to stop," he says. "But no luck."

He pulls me in for a kiss.

With my eyes closed, I almost feel like I'm standing on the beach in the dark. In the pitch-black night. The only clue to where I am is the lapping of the ocean. In this moment, Freddie is my anchor. And the rest? It's unknown. A great and beautiful question mark.

JUNE

FORTY-EIGHT

The first Sunday of June has always been my favorite day of the year. It's the Blessing of the Fleet, the day all the little towns peppering the Gulf Coast bid farewell to the shrimping boats and wish them well as they head out for the season.

Boucher's has a little tent set up where they're serving corn on the cob and po'boys and frozen daiquiris. But I'm not working today. Tuesday was my last day at the restaurant, and this morning I rode my last paper route. I'm spending the next two weeks soaking up my town and my people before I head off to a new town and maybe even some new people.

Ruthie, Saul, and Hattie are all working the tent. This is Hattie's first week back at work, which is why I'm wearing Sara Belle on my chest in one of those baby backpack contraption things. Tyler is around here somewhere, and so is his mom. I wave to my dad, who's having a beer with a few of his friends who still make their living out on the boats. He was able to get us a two-bedroom apartment at a complex that was running a special for people affected by the tornado. The second bedroom is full of both my and Hattie's things, and it all sits waiting for either one of us should we ever need to come back home.

I wave to Adam, who is in a tent across the way with Pam and Cindy, handing out coupons for the car wash. He gave Ruth Sophia's phone number so she'd have at least one friend to start with in Hattiesburg. He also wore absolutely nothing under his robes at graduation last week. The plan was for him to streak, but he chickened out at the last minute. Unfortunately for him it turned out to be a very windy day.

The Mississippi sun is relentless as it throbs above us. I tug down on Sara Belle's white boat hat and hope I slathered her in enough baby sunscreen. She's fair-skinned like her dad. I don't know what the future holds for my niece, but I do know that I have yet to see her in the same outfit twice, and I think that's a good sign.

We duck around behind the tent, and Hattie meets me there.

She hands me a few bottles to put in the baby bag I'm carrying on my shoulder. "Pumped and dumped a little bit ago, so this should hold her over." She takes Sara's hat off and kisses her forehead. "How's Mommy's little cinnamon roll?"

I bounce a little to stop her from fussing. "Mom is supposed to come by after work," I say.

"Yeah." She shrugs. "She said as much the other night."

Becoming a grandmother didn't magically transform

our mother, but I have noticed an effort that was never there before. She will always say the wrong thing and wear clothes that are too young for her, but part of being family is accepting one another's flaws with the knowledge that sometimes people never change, and you have to decide what and who you can live with or without.

Hattie runs her fingers through my hair. "I still can't believe you had the balls to cut your hair without me."

My hair is mostly ashy blond now. Some people in town don't even recognize me.

"Oh well. I'll fix you up real good when I start hair school in September."

My phone buzzes and I glance down to see a message from Freddie. "Hey, I gotta run," I say. "I'll have my phone on me if anything comes up."

My big sister stands up on her tiptoes and kisses my cheek.

I meet Freddie, Agnes, and Bart out near the docks, and the moment Agnes sees Sara, she melts. "Oh, my sweet girl!" she calls.

I give them all quick hugs hello.

"Ramona Blue," says Agnes. "I can't believe you're leaving so soon."

I sigh. "It doesn't feel real." The swim team at Delgado Community College does an on-campus training camp for a month in the middle of the summer, and then I'll come home for a few weeks before the fall semester starts.

The last few weeks have been spent filling out financial aid forms and finalizing class schedules. I haven't quite figured out how I will afford a four-year university or if I even want to go to one, but it seems that I can cover the cost of community college tuition and board with mostly grants and a few loans.

The idea of loans terrifies me, but Coach Pru said it was the only way to cover the gap in tuition until "the government gets their shit together and figures out how to handle the dadgum student loan crisis."

Once the fall semester starts, I can apply for some jobs. I'm hoping for a change of pace with something like a clothing store or even on campus at the bookstore. Maybe something where I'm not always sweating or smelling like crawfish and oysters.

Agnes pries Sara Belle from me and shoves the baby bag onto Bart. "Y'all go have some fun while two old farts talk gibberish to this little meatball."

"Okay," I say reluctantly. "Her milk is in the bag. It's fresh and if she needs an extra set—"

"We'll be right here." Agnes tries to hold back a grin as she points to a shaded picnic bench. "And we'll be sure to call if anything comes up."

I nod and watch as they situate themselves at the table.

Freddie tugs on my hand and whispers against my hair, "I miss you already."

I whip around and give him a quick peck on the cheek.

I'm still trying to figure what I want to call myself. Gay? Bi? Queer? Pansexual? I'm not sure, but I'm going to figure it out as I go along.

Freddie doesn't leave until the middle of August. I'll

have a few weeks with him after swim camp, but for once, it feels nice to be the one leaving. "You better keep up with your morning workout if you don't want your ass handed to you when I get back from camp."

All around us the festival is alive with music and food, and I can't help but feel proud of my little town. Boats of all sizes line the dock, waiting for their blessing.

I lead Freddie to the other end of the docks, where Father Bell from St. Margaret's is about to give his blessings. Father Bell, a young, tall white guy who is way too cute to be a priest, wears a short-sleeved black shirt with black slacks and his priest collar. He and Reverend Don from Eulogy Baptist take turns giving the blessing every other year.

The crowd thickens, and once Father Bell approaches the mic, a soft quiet rolls through the festival so that the only sounds left are the soft waves of the ocean and the squawking cry of seagulls.

Several altar boys and girls stand on either side of him carrying crucifixes and one of those gold-vase-looking things holding holy water. He opens a small leather book to a page he's already bookmarked and begins to read. "Most gracious Lord, who numbered among your apostles the fishermen Peter, Andrew, James, and John, we pray you to consecrate this boat to righteous work in your name. Guide the captain at her helm. So prosper her voyages that an honest living may be made. Watch over her passengers and crew and bring them to a safe return. And the blessing of God Almighty, the Father, the Son, and the Holy Spirit be upon this vessel and all who come aboard, this day and forever. Amen."

I close my eyes and let my head rest against Freddie's shoulder. I've heard the words of this blessing enough times to know it by heart. But today is different. Today this blessing is mine, and I pray it over myself. I tattoo it to my heart. I am the fleet. I am the vessel. I am the captain.

I stand here with my Wendy Darling as I prepare to do what Peter never could. Freddie takes my hand and pulls it to his lips as he kisses each of my knuckles. We sway back and forth until our rhythm is one with the ocean.

May my voyage be prosperous and my return safe.

ACKNOWLEDGMENTS

Writing books never gets any easier, but the more time I spend in publishing, the more people I have to catch me when I fall, which is fairly often.

I took way too long to write this book. I begged for numerous extensions and had countless breakdowns and panic attacks. That must sound awful, I know, but it wasn't nearly as bad as it could have been, and that's because I have the endless joy of working with my incomparable editor, Alessandra Balzer. I am thankful to you for your insight and compassion, and for investing in me as an author and a human being. Oh, and I couldn't forget an extra thank-you for all the pictures of Joey Ramone and Johnny Cash—the cats, obviously.

Magically, there is a woman who is always two steps ahead of me, laying the groundwork, and two steps behind me, covering my tracks. That would be Molly Jaffa, my agent and friend. Molly, I don't think I'll ever run out of ways to thank you or things to thank you for, but thank you for always being there for me in every way and soothing my most illogical worries with your perfect logic. And thank you to John and Donut, too. You're all a package deal now, anyway.

I am additionally grateful for all the support I've received from everyone at Folio Literary Management, all the foreign agents and agencies I've worked with over the years, and all my foreign publishers, who have been so kind to me and my work. I am also deeply thankful to my film agent, Dana Spector.

I am lucky to have found a wonderful home for my books thus far in Balzer + Bray/HarperCollins. Caroline Sun, I am forever impressed by you and must constantly remind myself that I do indeed have as many hours in a day as you do. Aurora Parlagreco, I am obsessed with this cover and cannot thank you and Daniel Stolle enough for all the effort you have put into every detail. I also owe much thanks to Kelsey Murphy, Booki Vivat, Margot Wood, Elena Yip, Suman Seewat, Maggie Searcy, Patty Rosati, Molly Motch, Gina Rizzo, Heather Doss, Jordan Brown, Kristin Daly Rens, Viana Siniscalchi, Bess Braswell, Elizabeth Ward, Sabrina Abballe, Audrey Diestelkamp, Tyler Breitfeller, Nellie Kurtzman, everyone at Harper360, the team at HCC, Andrea Pappenheimer, Kerry Moynagh, Kathy Faber, Jenny Sheridan, Donna Bray, Kate Jackson, and Suzanne Murphy. I'm sure I'm forgetting someone, but every Harper event always feels like a homecoming, and that's thanks to each and every single one of you who have had a hand in my books, even in ways I am unaware of.

Several writers who I admire greatly worked with me

on this book and helped me make it everything it has become. Thank you so much to Natalie C. Parker, Bethany Hagen, and Jessica Taylor. Tessa Gratton and Justina Ireland, thank you so much for your sensitivity reads and for just being badass women in general. Dhonielle Clayton, thank you for reading a scene for me at the last minute and for answering all of my nagging questions about it. To all of you women: thank you for taking the time to talk with me about how our work is part of a bigger conversation and for never steering clear of conversations about sex, gender, race, and politics.

I also have a completely unorganized list of friends and loved ones I would like to thank, so in no specific order at all: Jeramey Kraatz, Jenny Martin, Caron Ervin, Corey Whaley, Adam Silvera, Jason Reynolds, Brendan Kiely, Katie Cotugno, Robin Talley, Dahlia Adler, Tristina Wright, Hannah Moskowitz, Amy Spalding, Gretchen McNeil, Zoraida Cordova, Kate Hart, Sarah Enni, Amy Tintera, Michelle Krys, Cindy Pon, Sarah Henning, Renée Ahdieh, Jennifer Mathieu, Kristin Rae, Robin Murphy, Domino Perez, Leigh Bardugo, Katherine Locke, Sona Charaipotra, Emery Lord, Sarah Combs, Stephanie Appell, Jen Bigheart, Becky Albertalli, Ilene Gregorio, Amy Plum, Anna Carey, Samantha Mabry, Brenna Yovanoff, Tara Hudson, Myra McEntire, Rae Carson, Rachel Caine, Ashley Meredith, the Trevino family, the Pearce-Trevino family, the Murphy family, John Stickney, Mary Hinson, Rose Brock, Hayley Harris, Laura Rahimi Barnes, and Ashley Lindemann. Whether it was a drink, a slice of pie, an email, a hug, a tweet, a writing retreat, or just a shared glance across a room, each of you has been in some way instrumental to me finishing this damn book. Thank you.

I am so glad to live in Texas, where everything is bigger—including the shared passion of librarians and booksellers. I am so grateful for all of you, but especially Kristin Trevino at Irving Public Library, Cathy and Valerie at Blue Willow, and all the wonderful folks at BookPeople.

I would be nowhere without the gracious support of bloggers and reviewers who take time out of their busy lives to share the joy of books with others. A very special thanks to Ginger at G Reads Books, Jen at Pop Goes the Reader, and Kate at Ex Libris Kate.

Ian, thank you for understanding when I'm up writing late enough to see you wake up for work in the morning. Thank you for all the work you do with your students. It inspires me daily. I couldn't ask for a better partner. I love you forever.

Hillary Rodham Clinton, you are my shero. You have been since I was in second grade. Thank you for always inspiring me to do the most good. I am forever and proudly nasty.

Like I said earlier, I took a really long time to write this book, so this one is for everyone who's decided to take the long way home. Take your time. We can wait. I love you.